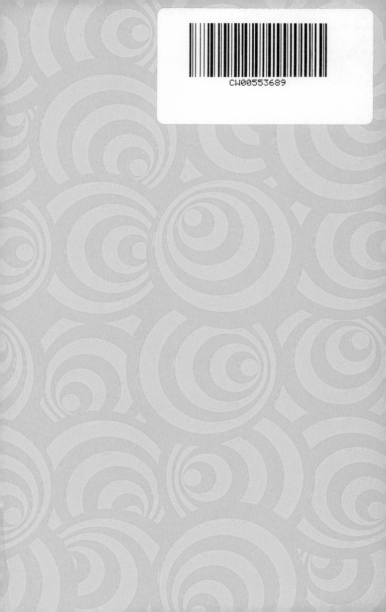

CW00553689

TALES OF HEROES, GODS & MONSTERS

INDIAN

MYTHS & LEGENDS

FLAME TREE PUBLISHING
6 Melbray Mews, Fulham,
London SW6 3NS, United Kingdom
www.flametreepublishing.com

First published and copyright © 2022
Flame Tree Publishing Ltd

22 24 26 25 23
1 3 5 7 9 10 8 6 4 2

ISBN: 978-1-80417-327-5

Cover and pattern art was created by Flame Tree Studio, with elements courtesy of
Shutterstock.com and the following: chasiki, PremiumStock, svekloid.
Inside ornaments courtesy Shutterstock.com/Transia Design.

Judith John (Glossary) is a writer and editor specializing in literature and history. A
former secondary school English Language and Literature teacher, she has subsequently
worked as an editor on major educational projects, including *English A: Literature* for
the Pearson International Baccalaureate series. Judith's major research interests include
Romantic and Gothic literature, and Renaissance drama.

Contributors, authors, editors and sources for this book include:
Donald Alexander Mackenzie, K.E. Sullivan and Epiphanius Wilson.

A copy of the CIP data for this book is available
from the British Library.

Designed and created in the UK | Printed and bound in China

TALES OF HEROES, GODS & MONSTERS

INDIAN

MYTHS & LEGENDS

Reading List & Glossary of Terms
with a New Introduction by
DR. RAJ BALKARAN

CONTENTS

CONTENTS

TALES OF HEROES, GODS & MONSTERS

INDIAN

MYTHS & LEGENDS

SERIES FOREWORD

Stretching back to the oral traditions of thousands of years ago, tales of heroes and disaster, creation and conquest have been told by many different civilizations in many different ways. Their impact sits deep within our culture even though the detail in the tales themselves are a loose mix of historical record, transformed narrative and the distortions of hundreds of storytellers.

Today the language of mythology lives with us: our mood is jovial, our countenance is saturnine, we are narcissistic and our modern life is hermetically sealed from others. The nuances of myths and legends form part of our daily routines and help us navigate the world around us, with its half truths and biased reported facts.

The nature of a myth is that its story is already known by most of those who hear it, or read it. Every generation brings a new emphasis, but the fundamentals remain the same: a desire to understand and describe the events and relationships of the world. Many of the great stories are archetypes that help us find our own place, equipping us with tools for self-understanding, both individually and as part of a broader culture.

For Western societies it is Greek mythology that speaks to us most clearly. It greatly influenced the mythological heritage of the ancient Roman civilization and is the lens through which we still see the Celts, the Norse and many of the other great peoples and religions. The Greeks themselves learned much from their neighbours, the Egyptians, an older culture that became weak with age and incestuous leadership.

It is important to understand that what we perceive now as mythology had its own origins in perceptions of the divine and the rituals of the sacred. The earliest civilizations, in the crucible of the Middle East, in the Sumer of the third millennium BCE, are the source to which many of the mythic archetypes can be traced. As humankind collected together in cities for the first time, developed writing and industrial scale agriculture, started to irrigate the rivers and attempted to control rather than be at the mercy of its environment, humanity began to write down its tentative explanations of natural events, of floods and plagues, of disease.

Early stories tell of Gods (or god-like animals in the case of tribal societies such as African, Native American or Aboriginal cultures) who are crafty and use their wits to survive, and it is reasonable to suggest that these were the first rulers of the gathering peoples of the earth, later elevated to god-like status with the distance of time. Such tales became more political as cities vied with each other for supremacy, creating new Gods, new hierarchies for their pantheons. The older Gods took on primordial roles and became the preserve of creation and destruction, leaving the new gods to deal with more current, everyday affairs. Empires rose and fell, with Babylon assuming the mantle from Sumeria in the 1800s BCE, then in turn to be swept away by the Assyrians of the 1200s BC; then the Assyrians and the Egyptians were subjugated by the Greeks, the Greeks by the Romans and so on, leading to the spread and assimilation of common themes, ideas and stories throughout the world.

The survival of history is dependent on the telling of good tales, but each one must have the 'feeling' of truth, otherwise it will be ignored. Around the firesides, or embedded in a book or a computer, the myths and legends of the past are still the living materials of retold myth, not restricted to an exploration of origins. Now we have devices and global communications that give us unparalleled access to a diversity of traditions. We can find out about Native American, Indian, Chinese and tribal African mythology in a way that was denied to our ancestors, we can find connections, match the archaeology, religion and the mythologies of the world to build a comprehensive image of the human experience that is endlessly fascinating.

The stories in this book provide an introduction to the themes and concerns of the myths and legends of their respective cultures, with a short introduction to provide a linguistic, geographic and political context. This is where the myths have arrived today, but undoubtedly over the next millennia, they will transform again whilst retaining their essential truths and signs.

Jake Jackson
General Editor

TALES OF HEROES, GODS & MONSTERS

INDIAN

MYTHS & LEGENDS

INTRODUCTION
& FURTHER READING

A NEW INTRODUCTION TO
INDIAN MYTHS & LEGENDS

MYTHOLOGICAL STORYTELLING

Storytelling is no ordinary thing. It is how we make meaning. Beyond referring to works of fiction, storytelling is the medium of everything, from news stories to life stories. Creating a narrative is how we make sense of our experience, and the great stories that stand the test of time invariably make sense of the human experience itself. Stories that explore the machinations of the human journey – those that tell the tale of origins, of ideals, of the ultimate, the supreme, the divine – are what we call mythology. In effect, mythology is a space in which cultures encode, disseminate and perpetuate key ideas, beliefs, values and customs. The stories which endure are preserved by virtue of their ongoing relevance. In other words, we continue to tell the stories that tell us who we are, where we come from and what matters to us.

Beyond outer sociocultural concerns, myth provides fodder for inner psychospiritual reflection. Moreover, mythological stories make sense of what it means to be human. They address the large questions of life on which we must all reflect: Where do we come from? Where are we headed? What is the meaning of life? What is right? What is true? The mythological tales of ancient India answer such queries in a most insightful, profound and vivid manner.

INDIAN MYTHOLOGY

Beyond the historical and geographical borders of the modern nation-state, India refers to a civilization that belongs to what is technically known as South Asia or the Indian subcontinent. Like the way in which Egyptian mythology transcends the modern nation-state, or that of Persia reaches far beyond the national state of Iran, this volume explores and celebrates the richness, scope and timelessness of Indian myths. Capped by the Himalayas to the north and bounded by the Bay of Bengal and the Arabian Sea to the south, India was known to Western civilization in ancient times as the land beyond the Indus river, which runs through modern-day Pakistan. The Indic subcontinent has served as fertile soil for humanistic thought, boasting some of the world's most intriguing philosophical and spiritual ideas. Undoubtedly the Indic soil is replete with stories.

Ancient Indian tales are most compelling, vivid and laden with insight into the human experience. They are indeed meant to be told – uttered aloud – but they are also telling in an adjectival sense, i.e. revealing, compelling and significant. Told and retold in manifold vernacular and regional styles, ancient Indian stories are the bedrock of Indian culture; they articulate, encapsulate and perpetuate insights and values core to Indic thought and practice. Indian myth sheds light not only on Indic thought, it illumines all things human. But in order to appreciate their universality, we must first appreciate their particularity, that is, we must acquaint ourselves with the overarching sociocultural contexts from which they hail. The ecosystem of ideas known to us as 'India' might be fruitfully understood as a tapestry comprised of strands of thought spawned from different historical horizons. While in its present state one cannot remove a strand from the tapestry without the whole fabric unravelling, one can come to appreciate its beauty better by tracing each of its individual threads.

THE VEDIC WORLD

A semi-nomadic and pastoral people who called themselves the Aryans (the noble ones) migrated from Central Asia into the Indian subcontinent in waves beginning *c.* 1750 BCE. These people produced the world's oldest surviving religious texts known as the Vedas. The notion of 'text' here is very different in the ancient Indian context, as the Vedas were never written down but rather preserved in memory and passed down orally. The oldest of these is the *Rg Veda*, composed in the northwest of the Indic subcontinent by 1500 BCE. The *Rg Veda* is a collection of 1,028 hymns to different deities, organized into ten books. These hymns consist of cosmological myths, rites and hymns to specific deities – in particular Indra, Agni and Soma. Indra is the heroic, thunder-wielding leader of the Vedic pantheon of gods, praised for slaying the drought demon Vṛtra. Agni is the fire god whose praises befit Vedic religion, which was centred around fire sacrifice for the sake of procuring blessings from the gods. Fire was not only a deity in his own right, but also the means by which the Aryans communicated with the gods through ritual and sacred fire. Finally, Soma is the god of a sacred potion that induces altered states and was used in ancient Vedic ritual.

As with other Indo-European mythic traditions, Vedic myth eulogizes anthropomorphized forces of nature such as Dyaus, the sky father; Prthivi, the earth mother; Surya, the sun; Ushas, the dawn; Vayu, the wind and Apas, the waters. Rivers also feature, especially the Indus. Vedic myth presents a foundationally polytheistic world-view – not dissimilar to that of Ancient Greece – that is presided over by a number of deities. In addition to the aforementioned supernatural entities, other notable deities include the Ashwin Twins who are divine healers; Vac, the goddess of divine sound; Rudra, the god of storms and lightning; Aditi, the mother of the gods; Brihaspati, the priest of the gods; and Yama, the god of death. Each deity is praised as supreme within his or her respective hymn. By worshipping these deities, those in the ancient Vedic world strove to survive and thrive in the world by attaining heaven upon earth in *this* life – the Indic notion of reincarnation does not arise until the next major epoch of Hindu history.

ALONG THE INDUS RIVER

The Indic subcontinent was far from vacant during the time of the Aryan migration. There was in fact a rich, thriving, highly advanced civilization along the banks of the Indus river. The

Indus Valley Civilization was contemporaneous with ancient Mesopotamia and Ancient Egypt, reaching its zenith *c.* 2000 BCE, though lesser known as it was discovered only in 1829. The total population of this great civilization may have reached upward of five million residents and it occupied a region of 1,500 kilometres (930 miles). The civilization declined between *c.* 1900–1500 BCE, the time period in which Aryan migration into the region began to occur. The people indigenous to the Indus Valley Civilization (and the Indic subcontinent since ancient times) are known as Dravidian peoples; they would, without question, have influenced the development of Vedic cultures as so many other indigenous traditions had done throughout the millennia. The reason we present the narrative through the lens of the Sanskritic, Aryan traditions to the exclusion of Dravidian tradition is because nothing but archeological evidence remains of the Indus Valley Civilization. The markings left behind by this lost people are yet to be deciphered and whether or not they represent literature of any kind is not clear. Nevertheless, the compelling figurines excavated from the Indus Valley Civilization inspire speculative storytelling about this ancient Indic civilization.

INDIAN PHILOSOPHY

The second major strand in the Indian tapestry traces the origins of some of the most pervasive and influential spiritual teachings known across the world: the wisdom of the Upanishads. Composed *c.* 700 BCE, the Upanishads are philosophical texts that advocate the human pursuit of ultimate truth. They posit a world-view radically different from that of the Aryans – one that has been adopted by throughout the entire Indic world. It is in these discourses that we see the doctrine of rebirth first expressed. According to the Upanishadic world-view, humans live countless lives upon the earth, in various forms, propelled by the spiritual principle known as *karma*.

Karma is a metaphysical principle that parallels the physical law of motion, as it posits that for every action there is an equal and opposite reaction. By virtue of this principle, we are destined to reap the experiences we have sown through our previous actions and lives. Interestingly, the Sanskrit word *karma* actually means 'action'. So, while we are free to act and create new karma, we are simultaneously destined to experience karma that is scheduled to ripen in our current life as well. We are reborn into the world again and again to work out our karmas, i.e. pay off debts to others, reap rewards and satisfy our desires. However, when we engage in activities and relationships without awareness, we become enmeshed and amass more karmic residue; this in turn incurs more subsequent lifetimes that have to be worked out. The fundamental problem to be overcome in Classical Indian philosophy is thus human bondage to the material world. The Upanishads prescribe the way towards achieving liberation from the cyclical world of incessant rebirth.

HUMAN PERFECTION

Classical Hindu philosophy posits a multilayered model of the human person. It claims that our physical bodies are only one such layer. This is the body that we see in the mirror, the one that modern medicine manipulates for the sake of health. Yet this, according to Indian philosophy, is only part of the picture. Beyond the gross physical body lies a subtle body in which an individual's karmas are stored from life to life. When you are born, the story goes, you already possess skills, aptitudes, proclivities and affinities that result from activities undertaken in previous lifetimes. As a result, we sometimes possess tastes and interests radically different from those of our cultural condition in this life. This Classical philosophy accordingly attributes such discrepancies to cultural conditioning amassed from previous lives. For instance, have you ever experienced love (or hate) at first sight? Or felt an inexplicable comfort in the presence of seemingly unfamiliar persons, places, things or activities? Karmic theory asserts that such phenomena can exist in your life because of the constitution of your subtle body bubbling up to influence your gross body.

However, neither your gross nor subtle bodies represent who you really are. Rather they are masks that you wear from one life to the next; garments to be enjoyed and discarded over millennia. Beyond your gross and subtle bodies lies your true, eternal Self, i.e. your soul. Your supreme Self is the witness within you who watches on as your conditioned self goes through the various experiences that are necessary to cease the process of reincarnation. Your life learning is the process whereby your mundane self inches ever closer to witnessing the wisdom and truth innate to your soul. Your soul is pure existence, awareness and bliss, ultimately dwelling beyond the sway of time. It is the ultimate goal of every human being to realize and experience their identity as the supreme Self, whereby they disidentify with their conditioned self and attain freedom from the cycle of rebirth.

THE PATH TO PERFECTION

In order to pursue self-realization, according to the Upanishads, one must be committed to self-denial and world abnegation. This is the path of the Indian ascetic who renounces society. It is in many ways structurally opposed to the Aryan world-view, predicated upon stringent social and ritual actions for the sake of prospering in life and attaining heaven. Classical Hindu philosophy emerges from ancient Indian traditions of renunciation that advocate the cessation of ritual and departure from society to pursue truth with a spiritual teacher, typically in a forest setting. Human perfection was the undertaking of the rigorous few with the courage and commitment to renounce the world, along with the fortitude and strength of character to subdue their mundane appetites and desires. These were men who renounced social standing, income, sexual activity and children in ardent pursuit of supreme truth. This strand of the Indian tapestry was therefore sharply critical of the Aryan way of life. It rebuked social and ritual engagement, perceiving them as anchors to the transitory mundane world and therefore fetters to the pursuit of truth.

From this rejection of the Aryan world derived the Jain and Buddhist traditions. The founders of these traditions rejected the Vedic priesthood and, more generally, Sanskrit, the sacred language of ancient India. However, in time, the Vedic tradition was able to fold these wisdom teachings back into its canon of beliefs through the codification and adoption of the Upanishads. The Vedic texts and the Upanishads are considered the most sacred strata of Hindu texts; they are known as *śruti*, that which was unauthored and revealed to inspired seers. It is worth remarking that while the term 'Vedic' technically refers to the historically Aryan strand of the Indian tapestry, it also is a word that means holy or pious overall to this day. As such, one might refer to a Vedic lifestyle, which would typically include a vegetarian diet. Similarly, the term used today for the astrological traditions of ancient India is Vedic astrology. Overall, the teachings of the Upanishads represent the lifeblood of Indic thought; they are integral to the tapestry that is the Indian mythos. In order to integrate new thought fully, however, tradition must once again take a turn towards the worldly.

INDIA'S GREAT EPIC

The great literary critic Northrop Frye observed that one cannot properly understand European literature without knowledge of the Bible; the same can be said of Indian narrative and the *Mahābhārata*, India's great epic. At a sprawling 80,000 verses divided over 18 books, the *Mahābhārata* is 15 times the length of the Bible (New and Old Testaments combined) and seven times the length of the *Iliad* and the *Odyssey* combined. This gargantuan epic poem was composed over several centuries between *c.* 300 BCE to 300 CE and is crucial to the foundation of Hinduism. Tales from the *Mahābhārata* underlie much Indic culture; they have been heard, told, performed and dramatized en masse. In the words of A.K. Ramanujan, '[n]o Indian hears the *Mahābhārata* for the first time'.

The central premise of the great epic has to do with a fratricidal war over the rightful successor to the royal throne. The primary heroes are the five Pandavas, fathered by five gods of heaven. With the help of Krishna, their divine cousin, they are able to wage a cataclysmic war against their cousins the Kauravas, and to regain their rightful rule. As is to be expected with so immense a work, the *Mahābhārata* houses far more material than the central story of the dynastic struggle itself. More than three-quarters of the material it contains consists of legends, treatises, folk tales and expositions of theology and philosophy. The epic strives to incorporate a variety of voices from the margins of Brahmanical society, including women, tribal peoples and the lower castes. Both in its primary narrative and within its didactic material, the *Mahābhārata* wrestles with the nature of righteousness (*dharma*), a subtle and slippery principle which at times evades even the most sagacious of its mythic characters.

THE PURSUIT OF RIGHTEOUSNESS

India's great epic presents many a moral quandary, and purposefully so. It is replete with complex characters and situations where one must choose the lesser of two evils; this is not a black and white world. The epic brings into conversation various religious beliefs as well as the ethical and spiritual philosophies of its day. Most significantly, it seeks to reconcile the world-affirming ethos of Aryan religion with the diametrically opposed, world-denying ethos of the Upanishads. As an epic tale about the rightful succession of royal power, it is very much concerned with affairs of the mundane world. However, the *Mahābhārata* equally reveres the lofty spiritual philosophy of the traditions of renunciation.

So how does one reconcile the presence of these two, seemingly antithetical, principles within the work?

This dilemma is rendered all the more complicated in the Indic context by virtue of Indian philosophy's attribution of supreme ethical status to the idea of nonviolence. Violence inflicted upon other beings incurs karma which one must reap in subsequent lifetimes; adherence to nonviolence (along with other values such as truthfulness and chastity) thus constitutes the path towards freedom from the karmic field of this world. While this is well and good for the Indian renouncer, what of Indian kings – required to wield violent force for the sake of the protection of society? Many myths from the *Mahābhārata* involve exiled kings dwelling in the forest; here they engage in conversation with ascetics, which symbolizes the internal conversation within the Indic tradition between Aryan and Upanishadic values. The most famous portion of the *Mahābhārata* is the 700-verse *Bhagavad Gita*, which circulates independently as a sacred text. In this work the Pandava hero Arjuna is overwhelmed with despondency at the outset of the great war; he is morally anguished and distraught at having to kill his own kinsmen. He slumps down in his chariot, beside himself, and asks his cousin-charioteer Krishna for guidance.

Krishna reveals himself as a divine incarnation and answers all of Arjuna's philosophical questions throughout the work. He ultimately advocates a fascinating reconciliation between the sociopolitical need for violence and the spiritual need for nonviolence. He posits that one can engage in one's worldly duty and not incur *karma* if one does so in the spirit of detachment. In essence, then, we are called to be soldiers with our hands and feet, but sages with our heads and heart.

In so doing we engage the world without becoming enmeshed within it – and thus need not renounce the world to progress towards human perfection.

INDIA'S OTHER EPIC

Equally well-known and as beloved as the *Mahābhārata* is India's second epic, the *Rāmāyana*. The name of this epic means the 'goings' – i.e. adventures – of Rāma. More humans have known the story of the royal hero Rāma throughout human history than even the Old Testament story of Moses. His exploits, known throughout South and Southeast Asia, are enshrined in countless retellings and dramatic adaptations. The composition of the earliest forms of the story of Rāma – that in Sanskrit is attributed to the great Sage Vālmīki – was roughly contemporaneous with that of the *Mahābhārata*. It consists of 24,000 verses divided across seven books. While the Vālmīki *Rāmāyana* makes no mention of karmic theory, it evidences acute awareness of the philosophy of the *Bhagavad Gita* as dramatized in the character of Rāma.

A noble prince, Rāma was one of the four sons born to Daśaratha by three wives. Rāma, the eldest son, was heir to the throne, but on the day of his would-be coronation his stepmother Kaikeyī plots to have Rāma exiled and her own son Bharata enthroned in his place. Rāma is lauded because of the completely stoic, selfless manner in which he gladly renounces his throne and accepts forest exile. (Again we have an example of the duty of the warrior complemented by the mindset of a sage.) Rāma's wife Sita insists on accompanying him into forest exile, along with Rāma's devoted little brother

Lakṣmaṇa. The three of them have a great many adventures in the forest, including encountering the monkey people; foremost of the latter is Hanuman, who pledges to serve Rāma. While in the forest Sita is abducted by the demon-king Ravana and a colossal war is waged to retrieve her.

However, due to petty gossiping by the citizens of Ayodhya regarding Sita's fidelity while held captive by Ravana, Rāma has her sent away to a forest hermitage. Here, unknown to Rāma, she gives birth to twins. Sita finds herself in none other than Valmiki's ashram; he composes the story of Rāma in Sanskrit verses and teaches it to Sita's (and Rāma's) sons as he helps Sita to bring them up. The twins become travelling bards and one day end up at Rāma's court, where they perform the *Rāmāyaṇa*. Rāma, recognizing their tale as his own, thus discovers the existence of his sons. While Rāma is lauded by tradition as the ideal ruler, husband and man, his treatment of Sita (among other things) has called his ethical purity into question. The mythmakers of the *Rāmāyaṇa* may have intended here to preserve the tension of the righteous ruler, whose personal wishes are eclipsed by those of his people. There perhaps also exists a hint of how unsatisfying worldly life is, even under righteous rule.

INDIA'S TALES OF OLD

From *c.* 300 CE onwards a class of texts arose known as the *Purāṇas*, literally meaning 'old' or 'ancient'. The *Purāṇas* are a massive and dynamic corpus of text featuring the popular lore of India. There are 18 major *Purāṇas* and a number of minor ones, and they contain a great deal of varied content – from cosmologies to tales of gods and kings, from ritual content to medicine and laudation of specific pilgrimage sites. One of the innovations of the *Purāṇas* (also present in the *Mahābhārata*, but not nearly as developed) are the vast and complex units of time associated with Indian myth. These include the theory of four degenerating world ages. According to traditional reckoning, humanity is about 5,000 years into the final age of existence, but it will last altogether for 4,320,000 years. So, suffice it to say, the idea of a looming apocalypse is incongruent with Indian myth. Moreover, the notion of an 'end of days' so pivotal for Abrahamic mythology is itself entirely foreign to Indian mythology; the latter believes the universe to pass through infinite cycles of creation, preservation, destruction and creation anew. This process is understood to be without beginning or end; it is truly infinite.

It ought to be noted that the bulk of the mythological stories contained in the *Purāṇas* were probably orally preserved long before the appearance of their textual form, and were most certainly performed throughout their composition and reception histories. In truth, texts in Indic tradition are more comparable to scripts than to novels, insofar as they were never intended to be engaged with separately from a qualified teacher or performance culture. The textual traditions of ancient India are very much the residue of embodied experience. In this strata of Indian myth we see the veneration of Hinduism's popular gods, such as Vishnu and Shiva, who are still widely worshipped today.

Shiva the Mountain Man

Few mythic characters are more compelling than the great god Shiva. He is a creature of paradox – both wild and controlled, dangerous and benevolent, an ascetic and a family man. He dwells in the mountains surrounded by the beasts and spends aeons in cosmic meditation, seated and clothed in animal skins. He represents the wilderness, the margins of society and the yogic quest for truth. He is often depicted in Hindu iconography as deep in trance, with matted locks adorned by the crescent moon. He, without question, is a god of tremendous power. Shiva's deeds include neutralizing the poisons emitted from the cosmic oceans by lodging them in his throat, and also offering his own head as a landing pad for the descending Ganges river. Shiva is an aboriginal Indic deity who was eventually folded into Vedic culture, and a myth surrounds the means by which he finally achieves a share of the Vedic sacrifice. Upon assimilation into the Vedic milieu, Shiva is associated with the Vedic storm god Rudra, the howler.

There exists also the tragic tale of his wife Sati. Sati's father, the arrogant aristocrat Daksha, greatly disapproved of his daughter's marriage to Shiva, whom he considered uncivilized. As an expression of disapproval, Daksha commissioned a great Vedic sacrifice and invited everyone but his own daughter and son-in-law Shiva, intending to snub the newly married couple. Enraged by her father, Sati burst onto the scene and immolated herself in the sacrificial fires. From his rage Shiva then manifested a dreadful warrior, Virabhadra, after whom the yogic posture warrior pose is actually named (see *The Stories Behind the Poses*, page 36), who destroys Daksha's sacrifice. Shiva then grieves bitterly for the loss of his beloved. Finally he is convinced to let her corpse go so that it may be scattered across India to bless the land with the power of the Goddess. Sati is then reborn as Shiva's current consort, Parvati.

Shiva the Family Man

Perhaps the central paradox of Shiva's personage lies in the fact that he is both a chaste, ascetic recluse and the devoted lover and consort of the mountain goddess Parvati. The couple's amorous escapades are well known throughout the heavens and are even at times leverage for the creation of supernatural beings. Parvati possesses a supernatural quality of patience as she waits for Shiva's return after his aeon-long departures to engage in his cosmic meditations. On one such occasion Parvati, who was lonely, decided to procreate of her own accord. She did so by crafting a son from the skin of her arm; she adored the boy and raised him in Shiva's absence. This son is none other than the elephant-headed Ganesha, lord of wisdom and auspicious beginnings.

Yet other Shiva myths tell of a second son, the strong and swift Skanda, general of the army of the gods. Beyond being an ever docile and patient partner, there are times when Parvati is so provoked by Shiva that she manifests as the intensely wrathful Kali to teach Shiva a lesson. Despite their ups and downs, however, Shiva and Parvati are in essence two peas in a cosmic pod: deeply in love, two halves of a whole.

Vishnu the Compassionate

Vishnu, too, has an enormous following within the Indic world and is encapsulated within a vibrant mythology known to his devotees. While Shiva is known for assuming the cosmogonic function of destroying the universe at the end of the age (so that a new universe may be created), it is Vishnu's role to tend to the universe for as long as it exists; he is venerated as the great preserver. To this end, Vishnu assumes incarnation within the world to accomplish this very task. Popular myths of Vishnu include his incarnation as a fish to protect Manu and his family from the great flood, and another occasion when he took on the form of a great tortoise to assist in the churning of the cosmic oceans in search for the elixir of life.

The most famous and influential of Vishnu's incarnations are as the semi-divine human heroes of both the Sanskrit epics. It is said that Vishnu incarnates as Rāma, the hero of the *Rāmāyaṇa*, and as Krishna, the hero of the *Mahābhārata*. Krishna has a vibrant following and mythology of his own – not only as the great strategist and wisdom teacher in the *Mahābhārata* but also as the playful, mischievous youth of the *Bhagavata Purana*. Vishnu's consort is Lakshmi, the goddess of prosperity born from the churning of oceans, in search of the elixir of everlasting life.

THE INDIAN OCEAN OF MYTH

The body of writing that follows sketches out the overarching stands within the tapestry of Indian mythology, with the aim of supporting your tracing and appreciation of its intricacies. These threads work as a whole in the life of tradition; by the time of the popular Purāṇic myths, we see traces of the Vedic, Upaniṣadic and Epic ideas being intricately interwoven. From cosmogonies to the exploits of kings to animal fables, Indian myth is laden with profound insight into both ancient India and the aspects of the human experience more broadly. You are advised to compartmentalize and engage with each myth on its own terms, for Indian mythology does not do the work of cohesive world-building.

Perhaps the metaphor of an ocean is more apt. You can discern certain patterns in certain places, but the ocean itself is beyond your ability to grasp. Indian myth celebrates perspectival thinking, like gems which glitter precisely because you view them from different vantage points. Indian myth holds space for paradox, preserving the very tensions by which we live and breathe as human beings. This is why its stories remain eternally relevant; encoding philosophy and spiritual truths in their very plots and characterizations, imparting life wisdom all the while.

Dr. Raj Balkaran
rajbalkaran.com
Founder, School of Indian Wisdom
Instructor, Oxford Centre for Hindu Studies

FURTHER READING

Balkaran, Raj, *The Stories Behind the Poses* (Leaping Hare Press, 2022)

Balkaran, Raj, *The Mother's Majesty* (SUNY, 2023).

Bailey, Greg, *The Mythology of Brahmā* (Oxford University Press, 1983)

Bailey, Greg, *The Gaṇeśa Purāṇa* (Harrassowitz, 1995)

Goldman, Robert P., *The Rāmāyaṇa of Vākmīki* (Princeton University Press, 2022)

Doniger, Wendy, *Asceticism and Eroticism in the Mythology of Śiva* (Oxford University Press, 1973)

Doniger, Wendy, *Hindu Myths* (Penguin 1975)

Doniger, Wendy, *The Rig Veda* (Penguin, 2005)

Doniger, Wendy, *Winged Stallions and Wicked Mares* (Speaking Tiger Books, 2021)

Kinsley, David, *The Sword and the Flute* (University of California Press, 1975)

Olivelle, Patrick, *Upanishads* (Oxford University Press, 1996)

Olivelle, Patrick, *The Pañcatantra* (Oxford University Press, 1997)

Smith, John, *The Mahabharata* (Penguin, 2009)

A NOTE ON SPELLINGS

The texts that follow often do not include diacritics, due to the mix of source material and the transliteration practices at the time. As such, there is some variation in accents and spellings for works and names such as the *Rāmāyaṇa*, the *Mahābhārata* and others.

Dr. Raj Balkaran is a prolific scholar of Indian mythology and seasoned online educator. He teaches online at the Oxford Centre for Hindu Studies and at his own School of Indian Wisdom where he delivers original courses applying Indian wisdom teachings to modern life. Beyond teaching, speaking and research, Dr. Balkaran runs a thriving one-on-one spiritual counsel practice and serves as McMaster University's Chaplain of Indian Spirituality. He also hosts the New Books in Indian Religions podcast. See rajbalkaran.com for more information.

TALES OF
THE RAMAYANA

The **Ramayana** is an epic poem of about 50,000 lines, which was originally composed by the hermit Valmiki, probably in the third century BCE. Many versions of this great work exist across India where Rama, the seventh incarnation of Vishnu, and hero of the poem, was worshipped. The *Ramayana* was originally divided into seven books, each of which celebrated a part of Rama's life. Rama was the greatest human hero of Hindu mythology, the son of a king and the avatar of Vishnu. He was the model of every good man, for he was brave, chivalrous and virtuous. He had but one wife and his name has become synonymous with loyalty and fidelity in many parts of the Indian nation.

It is believed that this epic poem is cleansing – even a reading of the *Ramayana* will remove the sins of the reader, for the text itself is regarded as charismatic. Many events befell Rama in his earthly form, and he left behind two sons. The following tales represent some of the most fascinating and profound occurrences in the life of Rama, whose name, even today, is in many parts of the Hindu community the word for 'God'.

THE BIRTH OF RAMA

Once, long, long ago, in the great city of Ayodhya there lived a king. Ayodhya was a prosperous city, one where its citizens were happy, pure of heart and well educated in the teachings of both man and god. Its king was also a good man and happy in almost every respect, for he had many wise counsellors and sages in his family and he had been blessed with a lovely daughter, Santa. This king was called Dasharatha, and he married his sweet daughter to the great sage Rishyasringa, who became a member of his inner circle, advising him on all matters with great wisdom and foresight. Two fine priests – Vashishtha and Vamadeva – were also part of his family, and they were known to all as the most saintly of men.

But Dasharatha had one hole in his glittering life; he longed for a son to carry on his line, a son who would one day be king. For many years he made offerings to the great powers, but to no avail, until such time as he made the most supreme sacrifice, that of a horse. His three wives were overjoyed by the prospect of having a son and when, after one year, the horse returned from the sacrifice, Rishyasringa and Vashishtha prepared the ceremony. With the greatest of respect and joy Rishyasringa was able to announce to Dasharatha that he would father four sons, and they would carry his name into the future.

When any sacrifice is made by man, all of the deities come together to take their portion of what has been offered, and so it was on this occasion that they had assembled to take from the sacrificial horse. There was, however, a dissenter among their ranks, one who was greedy and oppressive, and who caused in his colleagues such dissension that they came forward to Brahma with a request that he be destroyed. The evil rakshasa was called Ravana, and at an early age he had been granted immunity from death by yakshas, rakshasas or gods. His immunity had led him to become selfish and arrogant, and he took great pleasure in flaunting his exemption from the normal fates. Brahma spoke wisely to the gathered deities.

"Ravana is indeed evil," he said quietly, "and he had great foresight in requesting immunity from death by his equals. But," and here Brahma paused. "But," he went on, "he was not wise enough to seek immunity from death by humans – and it is in this way that he must be slain."

The deities were relieved to find that Ravana was not invincible, and as they celebrated amongst themselves, they were quietened by a profound presence who entered their midst. It was the great God Vishnu himself, and he appeared in flowing yellow robes, his eyes sparkling. He carried with him mace, and discus and conch, and he appeared on the back of Garuda, the divine bird attendant of Narayana. The deities fell at his feet, and they begged him to be born as Dasharatha's four sons in order to destroy the deceitful Ravana.

And so it was that Vishnu threw himself into Dasharatha's fire and taking the form of a sacred tiger, spoke to the anxious father-to-be, pronouncing himself the ambassador of God himself. He presented Dasharatha with spiritual food, which he was to share with his wives – two portions to Sumitra, one to Kaikeyi, and one to Kaushalya. And soon, four strong, healthy babies were born to Dasharatha's wives and they were named by Vashishtha, the divine priest. They were Rama, born to Kaushalya, Bharata, born to Kaikeyi, and Lakshman and Satrughna born to Sumitra.

RAMA AND VISHVAMITRA

Dasharatha's four sons grew into robust and healthy young men. They were brave and above all good, and they were revered for their looks and good sense. The greatness of Vishnu was spread amongst them, and each glowed with great worth. The young men travelled in pairs – Satrughna devoting himself to his brother Bharata, and Lakshman dedicating himself to Rama. Rama was very much the favoured son, favourite of both Dasharatha and the people. He was a noble youth, well-versed in arts, sciences and physical applications alike; his spirituality was evident in all he did. By the age of sixteen, Rama was more accomplished than any man on earth, inspiring greatness in all who came into contact with him.

There lived, at this time, a rishi by the name of Vishvamitra who had become a brahma-rishi, an excellent status which had been accorded to him by the gods themselves. He lived in Siddhashrama, but his life there was far from easy. He was a religious man, and took enormous strength from his daily prayers and sacrifices. Each day his sacrificial fires and prayers were interrupted by two wily and evil rakshasas, Maricha and Suvahu, who received their orders from Ravana himself. Knowing that Rama was the incarnation of Vishnu,

Vishvamitra approached Dasharatha and begged him to send Rama to rid him of these evil spirits.

Now Dasharatha was against the idea of sending his favourite son to what would surely be a dangerous and perhaps fatal mission, but he knew as well that a great brahma-rishi must be respected. And so it was that Rama and Lakshman travelled to Vishvamitra for ten days, in order to stand by the sacrificial fire. The young men were dressed in the finest of clothes, glittering with jewels and fine cloths. They were adorned with carefully wrought arms, and they glowed with pride and valour. All who witnessed their passing was touched by the glory, and a ray of light entered each of their lives.

They arrived at Siddhashrama in a cloud of radiance, and as the sacrifice began, Rama wounded Maricha and Suvahu, until they fled in dismay. The other evil spirits were banished, and the little hermitage was once again in peace, cleansed of the evil of Ravana.

RAMA AND THE BOW OF JANAKA

Rama was greeted with great acclaim after he rid Vishvamitra's hermitage of the evil spirits, and his taste of heroism whetted in him a great appetite for further adventure. He begged Vishvamitra to present him with further tasks, and he was rewarded by the hallowed priest's plans to visit Janaka, the Raja of Mithila.

Janaka was owner of a splendid bow, one which no man was able to string. He had come by this bow through his ancestor, Devarata, who had received it personally from the gods, who had themselves been presented the bow by Shiva. The bow was now worshipped by all who had seen it, for gods, rakshasas and even the finest warriors had been unable to bend its mighty back.

Janaka was planning a marvellous sacrifice, and it was for Mithila that the three men would depart, in order to take part in the festivities, and to see the great bow in person. As they travelled along the Ganges, they were followed by all the birds and animals who inhabited Siddhashrama, and by the monkey protectors who had been presented to the two brothers upon their birth. They arrived in Mithila in a burst of splendid colour and radiance, and Janaka knew at once that the company he was about to keep was godly in every way. He bowed deeply to the men, and set them carefully among the other men of nobility.

The following day, Janaka brought the men to the bow, and explained to them its great significance.

He said to Rama, "I have a daughter, Sita, who is not the product of man, or of animal, but who burst from a furrow of the earth itself as I ploughed and hallowed my field. She is a woman of supreme beauty and godliness, and she will be presented to any man or god who can bend the bow."

Rama and his brother bent their heads respectfully, and Rama nodded towards the bow. A chariot pulled by four thousand men moved the bow forward, and he quietly reached towards it. The case sprung open at his touch, and as he strung it, it snapped into two pieces with a bolt of fire. There was a crack so loud that all the men in the room, bar Rama, Vishvamitra, Janaka and Lakshman, fell to the ground, clutching their ears and writhing. And there was silence – a quiet brought on by fear and reverence. The spectators struggled to their knees and bowed to the great Rama, and a jubilant Janaka shouted his blessing and ordered the wedding preparations to begin. Messengers were sent at once to the household of Dasharatha, and upon his arrival, the festivities began.

Sita was presented to Rama, and Urmila, the second daughter of Janaka was promised to Lakshman. Mandavya and Srutakirti, who were daughters of Kushadhwaja, were presented to Bharata and Satrughna. All around the world erupted in a fusion of light and colour – fragrant blossoms were cast down from the heavens upon the radiant brothers and their brides, and a symphony of angelic music wove its way around them. There was happiness like none ever known, and the four young men cast down their heads with deep gratitude. They returned home, in a shower of glory, to Ayodhya, where they would serve their proud and honoured father, Dasharatha.

KAIKEYI AND THE HEIR APPARENT

After many years of happiness at Ayodhya, Dasharatha decided that the time had come to appoint an heir apparent. Rama was still the most favoured of the brothers, a fine man of sterling integrity and wisdom.

He was known across the land for his unbending sense of justice, and he was friend to any man who was good. His brothers had no envy for their honourable brother for he was so kind and serene that he invited their good intentions and they wished him nothing but good fortune.

Rama was the obvious choice for heir, and Dasharatha took steps to prepare for his ascendance. He drew together all of his counsellors and kings, and he advised them of his plans. He explained how his years had been kind and bounteous, but that they weighed down on him now, and he felt the need to rest. He proposed that his son Rama become heir apparent.

The uproar astonished the elderly king. There was happiness and celebration at his proposal, and at once the air grew clear and the skies shone with celestial light. Bemused, he turned to the esteemed parliament of men and he said, "Why, why do you wish him to be your ruler?"

"By reason of his many virtues, for indeed he towers among men as Sakra among the gods. He speaks the truth and he is a mighty and even bowman. He is ever busied with the welfare of the people, and not given to detraction where he finds one blemish among many virtues. He is skilled in music and his eyes are fair to look upon. Neither his pleasure nor his anger is in vain; he is easily approached, and self-controlled, and goes not forth to war or the protection of a city or province without victorious return. He is beloved of all. Indeed, the Earth desires him for her lord." And once again the cheers rose and the preparations began.

The finest victuals were ordered – honey and butter, rices and milk and curds. There were golds, silvers and gems of great gleaming weight, and elephants and bulls and tigers ordered. Fine cloths and skins were draped around the palace, and everyone hummed with incessant, bustling excitement. And above it all was Rama, serene and calm, as cool as the winter waters of the Ganges, as pure of heart as the autumn moon. And just before the time when he would stand forward in his father's shoes, he was brought before the great Dasharatha, who greeted his kneeling form with warmth and lifted him up upon the seat of kings. He said to him then:

"Though you are virtuous by nature, I would advise you out of love and for your good: Practise yet greater gentleness and restraint of sense; avoid all lust and anger; maintain your arsenal and treasury; personally and by means of others make yourself well acquainted with the affairs of state; administer justice freely to all, that the people may rejoice. Gird yourself, my son, and undertake your task."

Rama, for all his wisdom, found great solace in his father's words, and as the town around him buzzed with the activity of thousands of men preparing for the holy fast, he sat calmly, in worship and in gratitude.

Now throughout this time, all of Dasharatha's household celebrated the choice of Rama for heir apparent – his mother, Kaushalya, and his wife, Sita, were honoured, and his aunts, too, revelled in their relation to this fine young man. There was no room for envy in their hearts, until, that is, the deceitful old nurse, Manthara, took it upon herself to stir up the seeds of discontent. And this she did by the subtle but constant pressures she applied to her mistress, Kaikeyi, the mother of Bharata.

Kaikeyi was by nature a fair woman, easy natured and gentle. It took many months of persuasion before a hole was pierced in her goodness, and the beginnings of evil allowed to enter. It was a misfortune for Rama to become king, said Manthara, for Bharata would be cast out and Kaikeyi would be the subordinate of

Kaushalya. Kaikeyi dismissed such nonsense and carried on with her daily work. Several days later, Manthara was back. Bharata would be sent away, she said. Did that not worry his mother? But Kaikeyi was calm. She said, "Why grieve at Rama's fortune? He is well fitted to be king; and if the kingdom be his, it will also be Bharata's for Rama ever regards his brothers as himself."

Manthara did not give up. She twisted her sword a little deeper and was rewarded by hitting at Kaikeyi's pride. "Don't you know, Kaikeyi," she said, "that Rama's mother will seek revenge upon you. Yours will be a sorry lot when Rama rules the earth."

Kaikeyi's rage burst from within her and she stalked around her chambers.

"Why he will have to be deported at once," she said furiously. "But how can I do it? How can I install Bharata as heir?"

The treacherous Manthara was again at her side, needling the pain and fury that she had inspired in her gentle mistress.

"You have two unused gifts from Dasharatha," she reminded her. "Have you forgotten that fateful day when you found him near dead on the battlefield? What did he promise you then, my mistress?" she asked her. "Why he has made you his favourite of wives and he has done everything in his power to keep you happy. This is what you must do." And the evil witch leaned forward and whispered in Kaikeyi's ear. Her eyes widened, and their glitter dimmed. She bowed her head and she left the room.

Kaikeyi cast off her jewels and fine clothes, and pulled down her hair. She dressed herself in sacks and she laid down on the floor of the anger chamber where she cried with such vigour that Dasharatha could not fail to hear her sobs. Finding her there, stripped of her finery, he laid beside her and spoke gently to his favourite wife.

"What has happened. What is it?" he whispered. "If you are ill, there are many doctors who can cure what ails you. If someone has wronged you, we can right that wrong. Indeed, whatever you want, my dear Kaikeyi, I will ensure you have. Your desire is mine. You know that I can refuse you nothing."

Kaikeyi sat up and brushed away her tears. "You know," she said, "that you promised me that day long ago, when I carried you from the battlefield and administered your wounds, when I saved you from the jaws of death, you know, dear husband, that you promised me two gifts, two boons. You told me then that I could have my desire and until this day I have asked you for nothing."

Dasharatha roared with approval. "Of course, dear wife," he said. "Whatever you wish, it shall be yours. This I swear on Rama himself."

"I wish," she said softly, "I wish, as Heaven and Earth and Day and Night are my witness, I wish that Bharata become heir and that Rama is cast out, clad only in deer-skins, to lead the life of a hermit in the forests of Dandaka, and that he remain there for fourteen years."

Kaikeyi knew that in fourteen years her own son, who was good and true, could bind himself to the affections of the people and that Rama, upon his return, could not shift him from a well-regarded throne. Her plan was about to unfold and she shivered with anticipation. As expected, her husband let out a mighty roar and sank down to his knees once again. He begged Kaikeyi to change her mind, and he pleaded with her to allow his son to stay with him, but she refused to relent.

And so it was that Rama was summoned to the weeping Dasharatha, and as he travelled, the crowds rose to greet him, feeling their lives changed in some small way by the benefit of his smile, his wave, his celestial presence. And bolstered by the adoration, and glowing with the supreme eloquence of his righteousness, he entered his father's chamber with unwitting happiness and calm. His father's distress wiped the smile from his lips, and the clouds filled the autumn sky.

"What is it father," he asked, sensing deep grief and misfortune. But his father could only mutter, "Rama, Rama, I have wronged you."

Rama turned to Kaikeyi, "Mother, mother," he asked, "what ill has overcome my father?"

And Kaikeyi uttered with pride and something approaching glee, "Nothing, Rama, but your imminent downfall. He cannot frame the words that will cause you distress and unhappiness, but you must do as he asks. You must help him to fulfil his promise to me. You see, Rama, long ago he promised me two gifts. If you swear to me now that you will do as he wishes, I will tell you all."

Rama spluttered with indignation. "Of course, dear Mother. Anything for my father. I would walk in fire. I would drink poison, or blood, for him. Tell me now, so that I may more quickly set about easing his poor soul."

Kaikeyi related to him the story of her gifts from Dasharatha, and told him of her father's decision that he should be sent away to dwell as a hermit in Dandaka forest for fourteen years. Bharata, she said, would be installed as heir at once.

Rama smiled warmly and with such sincerity that Kaikeyi was stung with shame. "Of course," he said serenely, "I am only sad for my father, who is suffering so. Send at once for Bharata while I go to the forest. Allow me some time to comfort my mother, and Sita, and I shall do as you wish."

He saluted Kaikeyi, and he left at once. His mother was grieved by her son's fate, but she lifted her head high and she swore to him that she would follow him. "My darling," she said, "I shall follow you to the forest even as a cow follows her young. I cannot bear to wait here for your return and I will come with you."

Lakshman was greatly angered by the decision, and he vowed to fight for his brother who had been so wronged. But Rama calmed them both, and he spoke wisely and confidently.

"Gentle brother, I must obey the order of my father. I will never suffer degradation if I honour the words of my father." Rama paused and turned to Kaushalya. "Mother," he said, taking her hands, "Kaikeyi has ensnared the king, but if you leave him while I am gone he will surely die. You must remain and serve him. Spend your time in prayer, honouring the gods and the Brahmans and your virtue will be preserved."

Sita greeted his news with dignity. "I too will go forth into the forest with my husband," she said. "A wife shares in her husband's fate and I shall go before you, treading upon thorns and prickly grass, and I shall be happy there as in my own father's house, thinking only of your service."

And Rama granted Sita her desire, and he said to her, "Oh, my fair wife, since you do not fear the forest, you shall follow me and share my righteousness. Make haste, for we go at once."

RAMA'S EXILE

Lakshman could not bear to remain in his father's home without Rama and he too decided to leave with Rama and Sita for the forest, shunning the wealth and entrapments of his lifestyle to take a part of Rama's righteousness. There was hysteria in the household as the three prepared to leave, and a noble Brahman named Sumantra threw himself on the mercy of Kaikeyi to give in, begging her to allow Rama to remain. But Kaikeyi's will had turned her heart to stone and she refused all requests for clemency. Dasharatha sat dully, numbed by grief and shame at his wife's ill will. He motioned to send all his own wealth, and that of his city, with Rama into the forest, but Kaikeyi stood firm and insisted that Dasharatha stick to his vows and send Rama into the forest as a beggar.

As their new clothes of bark were set out for them, Sita collapsed and wept – fearing for her future and loathe to give up the easiness of her life, to which she had been both born and bred. The loyal subjects of Dasharatha begged him to allow Rama's wife to take the throne in his stead – there is no one, they said, who did not love Rama, and they would honour his wife as deeply as they honoured him. Yet again, Kaikeyi resisted all suggestions.

But then Dasharatha stood tall and he spoke firmly, drawing strength from his conviction. Sita shall not go without her jewels, and her robes, he commanded. So Sita's worldly goods were returned to her, and she shone like the sun in a summer sky, flanked by the bark-clad brothers whose goodness caused them to shine with even greater glory than Sita in her finery.

They climbed up onto their chariot and set off for the forest, the citizens of Ayodhya falling in front of the carriage with despair.

And then Dasharatha turned to his wife Kaikeyi, and with all of his kingly disdain he cursed her, and cast her from his bed and his home.

"Take me to Kaushalya," he said majestically. "Take me swiftly for it is only there that I will find peace."

At the same time, Lakshman, Sita and Rama had made their way from the city and had reached the shores of the blessed Ganges, a river as clear as the breath of the god, and inhabited by gods and angels alike. They were greeted there by Guha, the king of Nishadha, who fed their horses and made them comfortable for the night. Rama and his brother requested a paste of grain and water and they formed their hair into the customary locks of the forest hermits. The following night they slept by a great tree on the far bank of the Ganges, and the two brothers spoke quietly to one another, pledging to protect and care for the other, and for Sita. Rama expressed his great grief at leaving his father, and his concern for Ayodhya. He begged Lakshman to return in order to care for Kaushalya, but Lakshman gently rebuked him.

"Oh Rama," he said softly, "I can no more live without you than a fish can taken out of water – without you I do not wish to see my father, nor Sumitra, nor Heaven itself." The two men slept silently, comforted by their love and devotion for one another. There was only one way to get through the years ahead, and that was as a united twosome.

The following day they reached the hermitage of Bharadwaja, where the great rishi told them of a wonderful place on the mountain of Chitrakuta, a place which teemed with trees, and peacocks and elephants, where there were rivers and caves and springs and many fruits and roots on which to feed. It was a place befitting their stature, he said, and they would be safe there. And so the following morning they set off, crossing the Jamna by raft and arriving at Shyama. There they prayed and set about building a house of wood, next to the hermitage of Valmiki.

A deer was slain by Lakshman, and a ritual sacrifice was offered to the divinities. And then they settled in together and allowed the happiness of their new life to enter their souls, banishing their grief for what they had left behind.

BHARATA IS KING

Dasharatha was a broken man, and it was not long before his grief stripped him of his life. He died in the arms of Kaushalya, bewildered by his fate and recalling an incident which had occurred once in the forest, when as a youth he had accidentally slain a hermit with an errant arrow. Dasharatha had been spared punishment by a kind rishi, but he had been warned then that he would one day meet his death grieving for his son. That memory now clung to his mind, suffocating it until he gave in to his untimely death.

Ayodhya was in mourning for the loss of their finest son Rama, and the death of their king was a blow they could scarcely fathom. There was no rain and the earth dried up; an arid curse lay over the land and the dead Dasharatha's people could not even find the energy to go about their daily toil without the wisdom and leadership of the great and wise king. An envoy was half-heartedly sent for Bharata, with a message that he must return at once, but the people cared little about his arrival, and he was not told about the fate of his father and his brother Rama.

On the seventh day, Bharata, son of Kaikeyi, arrived at Ayodhya at sunrise, the first rays of morning failing to light the dark silence that the city had become. He entered his father's palace, and finding no one awake, entered the bed chamber, which he too found empty. And then Kaikeyi appeared, glowing with vanity and pride at her new position.

"Your father is gone," she said crisply, caring little about the man who had once been her great love. Her son had taken her place in her affections, and she lusted now for the power that he was in the position to accord her.

Bharata wept silently for his father, and then, lifting a weary head, asked quietly, "Where is Rama, I am happy for him. Was he present to perform the death-bed rites? Where is he, mother? I am his servant. I take refuge at his feet. Please inform him that I am here. I wish to know my father's last words."

"Blessed are they that see Rama and the strong-armed Lakshman returning here with Sita," said Kaikeyi. "That is what he said."

Bharata looked at her for a moment and paused. "Where, may I ask, are Lakshman, Rama and Sita," he asked then, his face losing colour.

"Rama has taken Sita and Lakshman and they have been exiled to Dandaka forest," she said nobly, and then spilling over with the excitement of her conquest, she poured out the whole story to her son, explaining the wishes granted her by Dasharatha and the wonderful honours which would now be his.

"You are a murderer," cried Bharata and leapt to his feet, casting his mother to one side. "I loved Rama. I loved my father. It is for their sake alone that I call you mother, that I do not renounce you now. I do not want the kingdom. I want Rama – and I intend to bring him back from the forest! At once!"

Taking only the days necessary to prepare the funeral rites and to mourn his dead father, Bharata prepared to set out to find his brother. His tears were shared for his father and for his dear brother and he resolved to find him as soon as he could. He refused the throne which was offered to him by the ministers and preparing his chariots, he rode quickly towards the forest, following in the footsteps of Rama and the others. He reached him quickly, and was shocked and dismayed to find that Rama had adorned himself in the dress of a hermit – shaggy locks framed his pale face, and he wore the skin of a black deer upon his shoulders. But that pale face was serene, and he gently wiped away his brother's tears.

"Bharata," he said, "I cannot return. I have been commanded by both my father and my mother to live in the forest for fourteen years. That I must do. You must rule, as our father would have wished."

Bharata thought for a moment. "If it was our father's will for me to have the kingdom in your place, then I have the right to bestow it upon you."

Rama smiled kindly then, and shook his head. "The kingdom is yours, Bharata. Rule it wisely. For these fourteen years I shall live here as a hermit."

Bharata took his brother's sandals and it was agreed that in fourteen years he would be joined by Rama, and that the sandals would be restored to him then – with the government and kingship of Ayodhya herself.

And Rama, Sita and Lakshman waved their farewells to Bharata and his men, and then they turned to leave themselves, no longer content in a house that had been trampled by feet of the outside world. They drew themselves deeper into Dandaka, where the cool darkness of the forest beckoned.

THE GOLDEN DEER

For ten years Rama, Sita and Lakshman wandered through the forests of Dandaka, resting and living for spells with hermits and other men of wisdom along their path. They befriended a vulture, Jatayu, who claimed to have been a friend of Dasharatha, and he pledged to guard Sita, and to offer Rama and Lakshman his help. They settled finally at Panchavati, by the river Godaveri, where lush blossoms hung over the rippling waters and the air was filled with the verdant scent of greenery. Sita, Rama and Lakshman lived happily there, in the green, fecund woodland, and lived virtually as gods, and undisturbed, until one day they were set upon by an evil rakshasi, sister of Ravana called Surpanakha. There ensued a terrible battle when this ugly sister sought to seduce Rama and Lakshman chased her away, cutting off her ears and nose in the process.

Surpanakha fled deep into the forest, angered and bleeding and she stumbled upon her brother Khara who flew into such a rage at his sister's plight that he set out for Rama's clearing, taking fourteen thousand rakshasas with him – each of which was great, courageous and more horrible in appearance that any rakshasa before him.

Rama had been warned of their coming by Jatayu and was prepared, sending Lakshman and Sita to a secret cave and fighting the rakshasas alone, slaying each of the fourteen thousand evil spirits until at last he stood face to face with Khara. Their battle was fierce and bloody, but Rama stood his ground. At last Khara was consumed by a fiery arrow. And there was silence.

Now far from this scene Ravana was brought news of his sister's maiming and his brother's death.

He was filled with such a rage that he plotted to destroy Rama by secreting away Sita. Ravana sought the advice of his most horrible accomplice, Maricha, who counselled him. Ravana was insistent that he could slay Rama single-handedly, and he ignored Maricha's advice to avoid meddling with Rama who could, if angered, quite easily destroy Ravana's city of Lanka.

Ravana's plan was put into action and the unwilling Maricha took on the form of a golden deer, with horn-like jewels and ears like two rich blue lotus flowers.

He entered the forest clearing, where he flitted between the trees, golden hide glinting. As expected, Sita looked up and cried out with delight. She called to Rama and to Lakshman and she begged them to catch the deer for her pleasure. Rama, too, suspecting nothing, was enchanted by the deer's beauty, and set out to catch her. He began to give chase.

Lakshman stayed behind, suspicious about the extraordinary beauty of the deer, where he kept watch over Sita. There was silence until, from the darkness of the woods, came the cry, "Sita, Lakshman."

The words were spoken in Rama's own voice, but they came from the body of the golden deer who had been hit by Rama's arrow. As the deer died he took on the shape of Maricha once again and in a last attempt to lure Lakshman from the forest clearing, he called out as Rama himself. And then he was dead.

Rama moved swiftly, realizing the ruse, but the cry had worked its magic. Lakshman was sent out into the forest by Sita, who feared for Rama's safety, and as that brave one made his way back to Panchavati, Sita was left alone.

RAMA AND SITA

Alone in the clearing of Panchavati, Sita paced restlessly, concern for her husband and his brother growing ever greater as the moments passed. And then she was startled by a movement in the trees. Into the clearing came a wandering yogi, and Sita smiled her welcome. She would not be alone after all.

She offered the yogi food and water, and told him her identity. She kindly asked for information in return and was startled when he called himself Ravana, and asked her to renounce Rama and become his wife. Ravana gazed at the lovely Sita and a deep jealousy and anger filled his soul. He determined to have her and he cared little now for his revenge of Rama.

Now Sita was enraged by the slight afforded her husband, the great Rama, by this insolent Ravana and she lashed out at him:

"I am the servant of Rama alone, lion among men, immovable as any mountain, as vast as the great ocean, radiant as Indra. Would you draw the teeth from a lion's mouth? Or swim in the sea with a heavy stone about your neck? You are as likely to seek the sun or moon as you are me, for Rama is little like you – he is as different as is the lion from the jackal, the elephant from the cat, the ocean from the tiny stream and gold from silver." She stopped, fear causing her to tremble.

Ravana roared into the empty clearing, and taking his own shape once again, grabbed the lovely Sita by the hair and made to rise into the air with her. His cry woke the great vulture Jatayu, who had been sleeping in a nearby tree. He rose in outrage and warned the evil spirit of the wrath of Rama, who would certainly let no spirit live who had harmed his most prized possession. But Ravana sprang upon the poor great bird and after a heroic battle, cut away his wings, so that he fell down near death.

Ravana swept Sita into his carriage and rose into the sky. As she left the clearing, Sita cried out to the flowers, and the forest, begging them to pass on her fate to Rama and Lakshman upon their return. And then she cast down her veil and her jewels as a token for her husband.

Ravana returned her to his palace and begged her to become his wife. Her face crumpled in bitter pain and she refused to speak. And as he persisted, she turned to him then and prophesied his certain death at the hands of Rama. And she spoke no more.

Rama returned from the chase of the golden deer with an overwhelming sense of trepidation, and as he met with his brother, far from the clearing, his fears were confirmed.

Rama and Lakshman raced towards the hermitage, but Sita had gone. There they found the weapons which had cut down the brave Jatayu, and the dying bird, who raised himself just enough to recount the events of the previous hours. And then, released of his burden, the soul of the great Jatayu rose above the clearing, leaving his body to sag to the ground below.

And so it was that Rama set out with Lakshman to search for Sita, travelling across the country but hearing little news and having no idea where Ravana kept his palace. He met with Sugriva, a king who had been robbed of his wife and his kingdom by his cruel brother Vali, and with the help of Hanuman, chief of the monkeys they continued their search.

Sugriva and Rama formed an alliance and it was agreed that Sugriva would be restored to his throne with the help of Rama. In return Sugriva would put at his disposal the monkey host, to find the poor Sita, already four months lost.

Rama's signet ring was put in Hanuman's possession, to show to Sita as a sign when he found her, but the monkey chief returned with his host, ashamed and saddened that they had been unable to find the beautiful princess. But then, as hope began to fade, there was news. On the coasts of the sea, where the monkeys sat deep in dejection, was a cave in which an old and very wise vulture made his home. He was Sampati, and he was brother to Jatayu. When he heard of his brother's fate he offered to the host his gift of foresight. Ravana, he announced, was with Sita in Lanka.

Hanuman was chosen for the task of retrieving Sita, and he swelled with pride at the prospect of his task. He sprang easily across the thousands of leagues, and across the sea – carelessly knocking down any foe who stood in his path. And so it was that he arrived on the walls of Lanka, and made his way towards the palace. The moon sat high in the sky, and the occupants of the golden city went about their nightly activities.

Making himself invisible, he entered the private apartments of Ravana, who lay sleeping with his many wives around him. But there was no sign of Sita. Hanuman roamed the city, increasingly anxious for the safety of Rama's wife, but she was not to be found. A deep desolation overtook him and he realized the enormity of his task. If he was unable to find the beautiful Sita then Lakshman and Rama would surely die of grief. And Bharata and Satrughna would die too. And the shame that would be brought on Sugriva, and the monkey host – it was too great to contemplate. Hanuman gritted his teeth, and in monkey fashion swung over the palace walls and into the wood.

The wood was cool and shining with gold and gems. In its midst was a marble palace, guarded by the ugliest of rakshasis. In the palace lay the form of a woman, scantily clad in rags and thinner than any living woman.

Hanuman watched as Ravana raised himself and approached the woman, who must surely be Sita. And he watched as the woman scorned him, and ignored his advances. The glitter in her eye betrayed her identity and Hanuman leapt up and down with glee. As Ravana left, the movement of the monkey caught Sita's eye and she looked at him with distrust. Probably Ravana in disguise, she thought tiredly, used to his tricks. But Hanuman whispered to her, and spoke reams of prayers for Rama, extolling his virtues. Sita was bemused and intrigued. She leant forward to hear more. Hanuman leapt down and spoke to Sita of Rama, presenting her with his ring as a token of his continual concern for his dear wife. Sita knew then that Hanuman was friend, not foe, and she poured out stories of Rama, begging Hanuman to return at once to Rama in order that she could be rescued.

Hanuman took with him a jewel from her hair, and departed. His high spirits caused him to frolic on the way, and he could not resist destroying a few of the trees around the palace. His activities drew attention, and he fought at the rakshasas who leapt up to meet him. He wounded or slayed all who approached him until at last he was caught by the enraged Ravana, who promised him instant death.

What could be worse for a monkey, he pronounced, than having his tail set fire? And so it was ordered that Hanuman's tail should be set alight, in order that he should burn to certain death. Now Sita still had powers of her own, and she prayed then, in Rama's name, that the fire should not burn Hanuman, but rage on at the end of his tail, leaving him unscathed. And so it was that Hanuman was able to leap away across Lanka, touching his tail here and there, in order to burn most of that glittering city to the ground. And then, dousing his tail in the wide, curving ocean, he flew across the sea to Rama.

Rama greeted Hanuman which caused the monkey to squirm with delight. He recounted all that had happened in the forest of Lanka, and he told what he had done with his burning tail. The monkey host leapt and cheered for Hanuman for he had brought them great glory with his bravery, and his craftiness.

Sugriva issued orders that all the monkey host should march to the south, in order to lay siege to Lanka. They reached the shores of the sea at Mahendra, and there they made camp. Rama joined them, and the plan to release Sita was formed.

RAMA'S BRIDGE

Vibhishana was brother to Ravana, and on the day that Rama set his camp on the shores of the sea, he was pacing around the palace at Lanka. He spoke angrily to his brother, pointing out that if a monkey could lay waste to half the city, what chance did they have against Rama and his monkey host? There could be nothing but death for all.

"From the day that Sita came," said Vibhishana, "there have been evil omens – the fire is ever obscured by smoke, serpents are found in kitchens, the milk of kine runs dry, wild beasts howl about the palace. Do restore Sita, lest we all suffer for your sin."

But Ravana dismissed his brother and said that Sita would be his. Vibhishana begged his brother to see reason, but Ravana had become blind in his obsession with Sita and he would not allow anything to stand in his path. Vibhishana rose then, and heading over the sea with his four advisers, he said to Ravana, "The fey refuse advice, as a man on the brink of death refuses medicine."

And so it was that Vibhishana flew across the sea to Rama's camp and announced himself as an ally to the great Rama. A deal was struck.

The ocean was a formidable obstacle to the rescue of Sita, and Rama laid himself flat on the ground, begging the turbulent waters to open for him, in order that they could cross. After many days, if Rama had received no response, he would dry up the sea, and lay Varuna's home bare. Mighty storms erupted and across the world people trembled with fear. At last the ocean himself rose up and spoke to Rama, his head a mass of jewels pinning the great rivers Ganges and Sindhu to its peak. He spoke gently, his power simmering beneath a gentle exterior.

"Great Rama," he said, "you know that every element has its own qualities. Mine is this – to be fathomless and hard to cross. Neither for love nor fear can I stay the waters from their endless movement. But you can pass over me by way of a bridge, and I will suffer it and hold it firm."

And so Rama was calmed, and plans were made to build a bridge. With the permission of the ocean, Rama dried up the waters of the north, causing the sea there to become a desert. Then he sent a shaft which caused that dry earth to bloom with woods and vines and flowers. The ocean presented to Rama and his men a fine monkey named Nala, Vishvakarma's son, and the monkey set in force a plan to build a bridge like none other. The host of monkeys began to follow his orders, and bit by bit, timber and rocks were thrust on to the sea until a mighty bridge was formed across its girth. And the monkey host and Rama passed over, in order that the siege of Lanka would begin.

The siege of Lanka was a story which took many years to resolve, and it involved the near deaths of Rama and each of his men. Garuda himself came down to heal their wounds, and the men fought on until, finally, Ravana was slain by Rama – with the Brahma weapon given to him by Agastya. Only this weapon had the force to take the life of the evil spirit, and the wind lay on the wings of this weapon, the sun and fire in its head, and in its mass the weight of Meru and Mandara. Rama held a mighty bow and the arrow was sent forth, where it met its mark on the breast of Ravana. The lord of the rakshasas was slain, and all of the gods poured bouquets of blossoms, rainbows of happiness upon Rama and his men. Rama's greatest achievement – the reason for Vishnu ever having taken human form – had been accomplished. Rama ordered Sita to be brought to him at once.

SITA'S SECOND TRIAL

Rama knew that Sita would not be accepted by his people, for she had lived in another man's house and they had no reason to believe that she was not stained by his touch. Rama greeted her coldly, and told her that he had no choice but to renounce her, as he must renounce everything that had been in contact with the greatest of evils. Sita, begged and pleaded – insisting upon her dedication to her glorious husband, and her continual and undying devotion.

"Oh king," wept Sita, throwing herself at Rama's feet, "why did you not renounce me when Hanuman came? I could have given up my life at that time, and you need not have laboured to find me, nor laid a burden on your friends. You are angry – like a common man you are seeing nothing in me but womanhood. I am the daughter of Janaka, Rama, and I am also daughter of the earth. I was born of earth and you do not know my true self."

She turned then to Lakshman, and she said bravely, "Build me a funeral pyre, for there is my only refuge. I will not live with an undeserved brand."

And the fire was prepared.

The gods threw themselves upon the mercy of Rama, praying that he should relent. And an elderly Brahma came forward and spoke words that fell on the ears of the gods and all around them like jewels: "Sita is Lakshmi and you are Vishnu and Krishna. No stain has touched Sita, and although she was tempted in every way, she did not even consider Ravana in her innermost heart. She is spotless." The fire roared up in approval, and added, "Take her back."

And so Sita was returned to Rama's side, where he pledged his undying love for her. He explained then that this test had been for her own safety – that their followers would now respect her once again for she had been proved pure. Together they set out for Ayodhya, and home.

It had been fourteen long years since Rama had left Ayodhya, but the memory of him and his goodness had remained etched in the hearts of every citizen. When they arrived through the gates of the city, they were greeted with uproarious cheers, and celebrations like none other were begun across the land. Bharata bowed to Sita and threw himself at Rama's feet. The kingdom was restored to Rama, and Bharata cried:

"Let the world behold you today, installed, like the radiant sun at midday. No one but you can bear the heavy burden of our empire. Sleep and rise to the sound of music and the tinkle of women's anklets. May you rule the people as long as the sun endures, and as far as the earth extends."

"So it shall be," said Rama.

Rama reigned happily in Ayodhya for ten thousand years, and then the day came when Sita conceived a child. Delighted by her news, he begged her to allow him to honour her with any wish, and she expressed a wish to visit the hermitages by the Ganges. Her wish was instantly granted and preparations were made for her travel. Lakshman was to accompany her, but before he left, he took counsel with his brother, the great Rama.

"I am concerned," said Rama, "that we know the feelings of our ministers and our people. We must call a conference to ensure that all is well in the kingdom."

And so a conference was duly called and all of the counsellors and friends of Rama pledged their love for him, and their devotion. There was, however, one unhappiness which stained the otherwise perfect fabric of his rule.

"The people murmur that you have taken back Sita, although she was touched by Ravana and dwelt for many years in Lanka. For all that, they say, you still acknowledge her. That is the talk." Rama's finest officer uttered these words and as he heard them, Rama's heart was chilled through and through. He sent for Lakshman and pronounced Sita's sorry fate.

"I am crushed by these slanders," said Rama, "for Sita was pronounced unstained by gods and fire and wind. But the censure of the people has pierced and this ill-fame can only bring me great disgrace. Take Sita tomorrow and leave her there, brother, and remove yourself now before I can change my mind."

And so Sita and Lakshman travelled to the Ganges, armed with gifts for the hermits. When they arrived, Lakshman explained Rama's wish. Sita fell into a deep faint from which it took many minutes to recover. When she did, she spoke of her desolation, and her fear at being able to survive in the forest. She could not live there, she feared, and yet she would do so because her master had decreed it. She was faithful. She was unstained. She was prepared to prove it.

THE SONS OF RAMA

The world about Rama was changing, and he was advised by the gods and by his counsellors that the age of Kali had begun. He continued to undertake acts of great kindness and goodness and his fine name sat comfortably on the tongues of subjects across the kingdom. But Rama was lonely. He longed for his great love Sita, and he longed for the day when she would be declared cleansed of all unrighteousness.

And that day came at last, when Rama prepared a horse sacrifice, and invited the hermit Valmiki to the ceremony. He was accompanied by two young boys, Kusha and Lava, and Rama was overjoyed to discover that these were the sons born of Sita, and that she was well and still living with the hermit Valmiki.

INDIAN MYTHS & LEGENDS

His two sons were born in his likeness, with voices as pure as a bird's. They were humble and kind, and when he offered them money for their performance to the people of the kingdom, they refused, saying that they had no need of money in the forest.

Sita was sent for, and Valmiki returned to his hermitage to fetch her. Sita followed Valmiki into a waiting assembly, where the hermit made a pronouncement: "Oh Rama, Sita is pure and she did follow the path of righteousness but you renounced her because of the censure of your people. Do you now permit her to give testimony of her purity? These twin children are your sons, Rama, and I swear before you that if any sin can be found in Sita I will forgo the fruit of all austerities I have practised for many thousand years."

And so Sita said quietly, "I have never loved nor thought of anyone but Rama, even in my innermost heart. This is true. May the goddess of the earth be my protection. I pray now for Vasundhara to receive me."

And the earth then thrust under the lovely Sita a throne so beautiful that each in the assembly gasped with pleasure. But the earth curled that throne around Sita and drew her back again into itself, home once again and part of the beginning and end of all things.

Rama screamed with despair and fought against the anger that threatened to engulf him. Rama carried on ruling then, for some time, but his heart was no longer in his country. Lakshman travelled to a hermitage and was eventually returned to Indra as part of Vishnu. Bharata no longer wished the kingdom, although Rama begged him to take it back, and eventually it was decreed that Kusha and

70

Lava should rule the kingdom as two cities. But Ayodhya, as it once was, was no longer a kingdom to be ruled, for when Rama left he was followed by all of his people.

Rama joined together with his brothers then, and with the blessing and prayers of the gods and the entire population of his kingdom, he returned to Heaven as Vishnu, in his own form, with his brothers. All of the gods knelt down before him and they rejoiced.

And Brahma appointed places in the heavens for all who had come after Rama, and the animals were given their godly form. Each reached his heavenly state, and in Heaven, all was once again at peace.

On earth it was decreed that the *Ramayana* should be told far and wide. And to this day, it is.

THE SAGA OF THE MAHABHARATA

The *Mahabharata* is one of the most magnificent epic poems of all time, and the longest in any language. The name *Mahabharata* probably applies to the Bharatas, who were descendants of King Bharata, the brother of Rama. The poem is unique in Indian literature, for it is driven mainly by the interplay of real people, rather than gods and demons, and it uses a plethora of very lively, dramatic and exciting personalities to present its message. Many believe that the entire philosophy of India is implicit in its romance, and its message is acted out in the great war waged between two ancient families – the Pandavas and the Kauravas.

Our narrative begins with the romantic stories centred around the names of the legendary ancestors of the Kauravas and the Pandavas. The sympathies of the Brahmanic compilers are with the latter, who are symbolized as 'a vast tree formed of religion and virtue', while their opponents are 'a great tree formed of passion'. The father of the great King Bharata was Dushyanta of the lunar race, the descendant of Atri, the Deva-rishi, and of Soma, the moon; his mother was beautiful Shakuntala, the hermit maiden, and daughter of a nymph from the celestial regions.

The poem was finally edited by Krishna Dvaipayana, or Vyasa the Compiler, but since this character is, too, mythical, it is doubtful that his contribution is authentic. There have

been many interpretations and many hands turning the text
and indeed the pages of the *Mahabharata* over the centuries
– and they have served not to clutter but to make clear the
extraordinary vividness of the characterization, and the
reasons this has become the Indian national saga.

DUSHYANTA AND SHAKUNTALA

One day King Dushyanta, that tiger among men, left his
stately palace to go hunting with a great host and many
horses and elephants. He entered a deep jungle and there
killed numerous wild animals; his arrows wounded tigers
at a distance; he felled those that came near with his great
sword. Lions fled from before him, wild elephants stampeded
in terror, deer sought to escape hastily, and birds rose in the
air uttering cries of distress.

The king, attended by a single follower, pursued a deer
across a desert plain, and entered a beautiful forest which
delighted his heart, for it was deep and shady, and was cooled
by soft winds; sweet-throated birds sang in the branches, and
all round about there were blossoming trees and blushing
flowers; he heard the soft notes of the kokila, and beheld
many a green bower carpeted with grass and canopied by
many-coloured creepers.

Dushyanta, abandoning the chase, wandered on until he
came to a delightful and secluded hermitage, where he saw
the sacred fire of that austere and high-souled Brahman, the
saintly Kanva. It was a scene of peace and beauty. Blossoms
from the trees covered the ground; tall were the trunks, and

the branches were far-sweeping. A silvery stream went past, breaking on the banks in milk-white foam; it was the sacred River Malini, studded with green islands, loved by water fowl, and abounding with fish.

Then the king was taken with desire to visit the holy sage, Kanva, he who is without darkness. So he relieved himself of his royal insignia and entered the sacred grove alone. Bees were humming; birds trilled their many melodies; he heard the low chanting voices of Brahmans among the trees – those holy men who can take captive all human hearts....

When he reached the home of Kanva, he found that it was empty, and called out: "Who is here?" and the forest echoed his voice.

Then a beautiful black-eyed virgin came towards him, clad in a robe of bark. She reverenced the king and said: "What do you seek? I am your servant."

Dushyanta replied to the maiden of faultless form and gentle voice: "I have come to honour the wise and blessed Kanva. Tell me, fair and amiable one, where he has gone?"

The maiden answered: "My illustrious father is gathering herbs, but if you will wait he will return before long."

Dushyanta was entranced by the beauty and sweet smiles of the gentle girl, and his heart was moved towards her. So he spoke, saying: "Who are you, fairest one? Where do you come from and why do you wander alone in the woods? Beautiful maiden, you have taken captive my heart."

The bright-eyed one answered: "I am the daughter of the holy and high-souled Kanva, the ever-wise and ever-constant."

"But," said the king, "Kanva is chaste and austere and has always been celibate. He cannot have broken his rigid vow.

How could it be that you were born the daughter of such a one?"

Then the maiden, who was named Shakuntala, because of the birds (shakunta) who had nursed her, revealed to the king the secret of her birth. Her real father was Vishwamitra, the holy sage who had been a Kshatriya and was made a Brahman in reward for his austerities. It came to pass that Indra became alarmed at his growing power, and he feared that the mighty sage of blazing energy would, by reason of his penances, cast down even him, the king of the gods, from his heavenly seat. So Indra commanded Menaka, the beautiful Apsara, to disturb the holy meditations of the sage, for he had already achieved such power that he created a second world and many stars. The nymph called on the wind god and on the god of love, and they went with her towards Vishwamitra.

Menaka danced before the brooding sage; then the wind god snatched away her moon-white garments, and the love god shot his arrows at Vishwamitra, whereupon that saintly man was stricken with love for the nymph of peerless beauty, and he wooed her and won her as his bride. So was he diverted from his austerities. In time Menaka became the mother of a girl babe, whom she cast away on the river bank.

Now the forest was full of lions and tigers, but vultures gathered round the infant and protected her from harm. Then Kanva found and took pity on the child; he said: "She will be mine own daughter."

Shakuntala said: "I was that child who was abandoned by the nymph, and now you know how Kanva came to be my father."

The king said: "Blessed are your words, princess. You are of royal birth. Be my bride, beautiful maid, and you will have garlands of gold and golden earrings and white pearls and rich robes; my kingdom also will be yours, timid one."

Then Shakuntala promised to be the king's bride, on condition that he would choose her son as the heir to his throne.

"As you desire, so let it be," said Dushyanta. And the fair one became his bride.

When Dushyanta went away he promised Shakuntala that he would send a mighty host to escort her to his palace.

When Kanva returned, the maiden did not leave her hiding place to greet him; but he searched out and found her, and he read her heart. "You have not broken the law," he said.

"Dushyanta, my husband, is noble and true, and a son will be born to me who will achieve great renown."

SHAKUNTALA'S APPEAL

In time fair Shakuntala became the mother of a handsome boy, and the wheel mark was on his hands. He grew to be strong and brave, and when just six years old he sported with young lions, for he was suckled by a lioness; he rode on the backs of lions and tigers and wild boars in the midst of the forest. He was called All-tamer, because he tamed everything.

Now when Kanva perceived that the boy was of unequalled prowess, he spoke to Shakuntala and said: "The time has come when he must be anointed as heir to the throne." So he ordered his disciples to escort mother and son to the city of Gajasahvaya, where Dushyanta had his royal palace.

So it came that Shakuntala once again stood before the king, and she said to him: "I have brought to your son, Dushyanta. Fulfil the promise you made, and let him be anointed as your heir."

Dushyanta had no pleasure in her words, and answered: "I have no memory of you. Who are you and where did you come from, wicked hermit woman? I never took you for my wife, nor care I whether you are to linger here or to depart speedily."

Stunned by his cold answer, the sorrowing Shakuntala stood there like a log.... Soon her eyes became red as copper and her lips trembled; she cast burning glances at the monarch. For a time she was silent; then she exclaimed: "King without shame, well do you know who I am. Why will you deny knowledge of me as if you were but an inferior person? Your heart is a witness against you. Be not a robber of your own affections.... The gods behold everything: nothing is hidden from them; they will not bless one who degrades himself by speaking falsely regarding himself. Spurn not the mother of your son; spurn not your faithful wife. A true wife bears a son; she is the first of friends and the source of salvation; she enables her husband to perform religious acts, her sweet speeches bring him joy; she is a solace and a comforter in sickness and in sorrow; she is a companion in this world and the next. If a husband dies, a wife follows soon afterwards; if she is gone before, she waits for her husband in heaven. She is the mother of the son who performs the funeral rite to secure everlasting bliss for his father, rescuing him from the hell called Put. Therefore a man should reverence the mother of his son, and look upon his son as if he saw his own self in a mirror, rejoicing as if he had found heaven…. Why, king, do you spurn your own child? Even the ants will protect their eggs; strangers far from home take the children of others on their knees to be made happy, but you have no compassion for this child, although he is your son, your own image…. What sin did I commit in my former state that I should have been deserted by my parents and now by you!… If I must go, take your son to your bosom."

Dushyanta said: "It has been well said that all women are liars. Who will believe you? I know nothing regarding you or your son…. Go away wicked woman, for you are without shame."

Shakuntala replied, speaking boldly and without fear: "King, you can perceive the shortcomings of others, although they may be as small as mustard seeds; you are blind to your own sins, although they may be big as Vilwa fruit. As the swine loves dirt even in a flower garden, so do the wicked perceive evil in all that the good relate. Honest men refrain from speaking ill of others: the wicked rejoice in scandal. Truth is the chief of all virtues. Truth is God himself. Do not break your vow of truth: let truth be ever a part of you. But if you would rather be false, I must go, for such a one as you should be avoided…. Yet know now, Dushyanta, that when you are gone, my son will be king of this world, which is surrounded by the four seas and adorned by the monarch of mountains."

Shakuntala then turned from the king, but a voice out of heaven spoke softly down the wind, saying: "Shakuntala has uttered what is true. Therefore, Dushyanta, cherish your son, and by command of the gods, let his name be Bharata ('the cherished')."

When the king heard these words, he spoke to his counsellors and said: "The celestial messenger has spoken.... Had I welcomed this my son by pledge of Shakuntala alone, men would suspect the truth of her words and doubt his royal birth."

Then Dushyanta embraced his son and kissed him, and he honoured Shakuntala as his chief rani; he said to her, soothingly: "I have concealed our union from all men; and for the sake of your own good name I hesitated to acknowledge you. Forgive my harsh words, as I forgive yours. You spoke passionately because you love me, great-eyed and fair one, whom I love also."

The son of Shakuntala was then anointed as heir to the throne, and he was named Bharata.

When Dushyanta died, Bharata became king. Great was his fame, as befitted a descendant of Chandra. He was a mighty warrior, and none could withstand him in battle; he made great conquests, and extended his kingdom all over Hindustan, which was called Bharatavarsha.

King Bharata was the father of King Hastin, who built the great city of Hastinapur; King Hastin the father of King Kuru, and King Kuru the father of King Shantanu.

KING SHANTANU AND THE GODDESS BRIDE

It is said of the King Shantanu that he was pious and just and all-powerful, as was proper for the great grandson of King Bharata. His first wife was the goddess Ganga of the Ganges river. She was divinely beautiful. Before she assumed human form for a time, the eight Vasus (the attendants of

Indra) came to her. It happened that when the Brahman Vasishtha was engaged in his holy meditations the Vasus flew between him and the sun, whereupon the angered sage cursed them, saying: "Be born among men!" They could not escape this fate, so great was the Rishi's power over celestial beings. So they hastened to Ganga, and she consented to become their human mother, promising that she would cast them one by one into the Ganges soon after birth, so that they might return to their celestial state. For this service Ganga made each of the Vasus promise to confer an eighth part of his power on her son, who, according to her wishes, should remain among men for many years, but would never marry or have any offspring.

Soon a day came when King Shantanu walked beside the Ganges. Suddenly a maiden of surpassing beauty appeared before him. She was Ganga in human form. Her celestial garments had the splendour of lotus blooms; she was adorned with rare ornaments, and her teeth were as radiant as pearls. The king was silenced by her charms, and gazed at her.... In time he perceived that the maiden looked at him with love-lorn eyes, as if she sought to look at him forever, and he spoke to her, saying: "Fair one, are you one of the Danavas, or are you of the race of Gandharvas, or are you of the Apsaras; are you one of the Yakshas or Nagas, or are you of human kind? Be my bride."

The goddess answered that she would marry the king, but said she must leave him at once if he spoke harshly to her at any time, or attempted to stop her doing as she willed. Shantanu consented to her terms, and Ganga became his bride.

In time the goddess gave birth to a son, but soon afterwards she cast him into the Ganges, saying: "This for your welfare."

The king was stricken with horror, but he spoke not a word to his beautiful bride in case she should leave him.

So were seven babies, one after another, destroyed by their mother in this way. When the eighth was born, the goddess sought to drown him, too; but the king's pent-up wrath finally broke, and he reprimanded his heartless wife. Thus his marriage vow was broken, and Ganga was given power to leave him. But before she went she revealed to the king who she was, and also why she had cast the Vasus, her children, into the Ganges. Then she suddenly vanished from before his eyes, taking the last baby with her.

THE STORY OF SATYAVATI

One day the fair goddess briefly returned to Shantanu. She brought with her a fair and noble son, who was endowed with the virtues of the Vasus. Then she departed never to come again. The heart of king Shantanu was moved towards the child, who became a handsome and powerful youth, and was named Satanava.

When Shantanu had grown old, he sought to marry a young and beautiful bride whom he loved. For one day as he walked beside the Jumna river he was attracted by a sweet and alluring perfume, which drew him through the trees until he beheld a maiden of celestial beauty with luminous black eyes. The king spoke to her and said: "Who are you, and whose daughter, timid one? What are you doing here?"

The maiden blessed Shantanu and said: "I am the daughter of a fisherman, and I ferry passengers across the river in my boat."

Now, the name of this fair maiden was Satyavati. Like Shakuntala, she was of miraculous origin, and had been adopted by her reputed father. It happened that a fish once carried away in its stomach two unborn babies, a girl and a boy, whose father was a great king. This fish was caught by a fisherman, who opened it and found the children. He sent the boy to the king and kept the girl, who was reared as his own daughter. She grew to be beautiful, but a fishy odour ever clung to her.

One day, as she ferried pilgrims across the Jumna, the high and pious Brahman Parashara entered her boat. He was moved by the maiden's great beauty. He desired that she should become the mother of his son, and promised that ever afterwards an alluring perfume would emanate from her body. He then caused a cloud to fall on the boat, and it vanished from sight.

When the fisher girl became the mother of a son, he grew suddenly before her eyes, and in a brief space was a man. His name was Vyasa; he wished his mother farewell, and rushed to the depths of a forest to spend his days in holy meditation. Before he left he said to Satyavati: "If ever you have need of me, think of me, and I will come to your aid."

When this wonder had been accomplished, Satyavati became a virgin again through the power of the great sage Parashara, and a delicious odour lingered about her ever afterwards.

On this maiden King Shantanu gazed with love. Then he sought the fisherman, and said he desired the maiden to be his bride. But the man refused to give his daughter to the king in marriage until he promised that her son should be chosen as heir to the throne. Shantanu could not consent to disinherit

Satanava, son of Ganga, and went away with a heavy heart.

Greatly the king sorrowed in his heart because of his love for the dark-eyed maiden, and eventually Satanava was told of his secret love. So the noble son of Ganga went to search for the beautiful daughter of the fisherman, and he found her. After he told the fisherman of his mission, the fisherman said to him: "If Satyavati bears sons, they will not inherit the kingdom, for the king already has a son, and he will succeed him."

So Satanava made a vow renouncing his claim to the throne, and said: "If you will give your daughter to my father to be his queen, I, who am his heir, will never accept the throne, nor marry a wife, or be the father of children. If, then, Satyavati will become the mother of a son, he will surely be chosen as king." After he said this, the gods and Apsaras (the mist fairies) caused flowers to fall out of heaven on to the prince's head, and a voice came down the wind, saying: "This one is Bhishma."

From that day on, the son of Ganga was called Bhishma, which signifies the 'Terrible', for the vow that he had taken was terrible indeed.

Then Satyavati was given in marriage to the king, and she bore him two sons, who were named Chitrangada and Vichitra-virya.

In time Shantanu sank under the burden of his years, and his soul departed from his body. Bhishma was left to care of the queen-mother, Satyavati, and the two princes.

When the days of mourning went past, Bhishma renounced the throne in accordance with his vow, and Chitrangada was proclaimed king. This youth was a haughty ruler, and his reign was brief. He waged war against the Gandharai of the hills for three years, and was slain in battle by their king. Then Bhishma placed Vichitra-virya on the throne, and, as he was but a boy, Bhishma ruled as regent for some years.

MARRIAGE BY CAPTURE

Many years later the time came for the young king to marry, and Bhishma set out to find wives for him. It so happened that the King of Kasi (Benares) had three fair daughters whose swayamvara was being proclaimed. When Bhishma was told of this he immediately climbed aboard his chariot and drove from Hastinapur to Kasi to discover if the girls were worthy of the monarch of Bharatavarsha. He found that they had great beauty, which pleased him.

The great city was thronged with kings who had gathered from far and near to woo the maidens, but Bhishma would not wait until the day of the swayamvara. He immediately seized the king's fair daughters and placed them in his chariot. Then he challenged the assembled kings and sons of kings in a voice like thunder, saying: "The sages have decreed that a king may give his daughter with many gifts to one he has invited when she has chosen him. Others may barter their daughters, and some may give them in exchange for gold. But maidens may also be taken captive. They may be married by consent, or forced to consent, or be obtained by sanction of their fathers. Some are given wives as reward for performing sacrifices, a form approved by the sages. Kings ever favour the swayamvara, and obtain wives according to its rules. But learned men have declared that the wife who is to be most highly esteemed is she who is taken captive after battle with the royal guests who attend a swayamvara. Hear and know, then, mighty kings, I will carry off these fair daughters of the king of Kasi, and I challenge all who are here to overcome me or else be overcome themselves by me in battle."

The royal guests who were there accepted the challenge, and Bhishma fought against them with great fury. Bows were bent and ten thousand arrows were discharged against him, but he broke their flight with innumerable darts from his own mighty bow. Strong and brave was he indeed; there was no one who could overcome him; he fought and conquered all, until not one king was left to contend against him.

So Bhishma, the terrible son of the ocean-going Ganga, took the three fair daughters of the King of Kasi captive; and he drove away with them in his chariot towards Hastinapur.

When he reached the royal palace he presented the maidens to Queen Satyavati, who was very pleased. In return she gave many costly gifts to Bhishma. She decided that the captives should become the wives of her son, King Vichitra-virya.

Before the wedding ceremony was held, the eldest maiden, whose name was Amba, pleaded with the queen to be set free, saying: "I have been betrothed already by my father to the King of Sanva. Oh, send me to him now, for I cannot marry a second time."

Her prayer was granted, and Bhishma sent her with an escort to the King of Sanva. Then the fair Amba told him how she had been taken captive; but the king exclaimed, with anger: "You have already dwelt in the house of a strange man, and I cannot take you for my wife."

The maiden wept bitterly, and she knelt before the monarch and said: "No man has wronged me, mighty king. Bhishma has taken a terrible vow of celibacy which he cannot break. If you will not have me for your wife, I pray you to take me as your concubine, so that I may live safely in your palace."

But the king spurned the beautiful maiden, and his servants drove her from the palace and out of the city. So was she compelled to seek refuge in the lonely forest, and there she practised great austerities in order to secure power to slay Bhishma, who had wronged her. In the end she threw herself on a pyre, so that she might attain her desire in the next life.

Her two sisters, Amvika and Amvalika, became the wives of Vitchitra-virya, who loved them well; but his days were brief, and he wasted away with sickness until eventually he died. No children were born to the king, and his two widows mourned for him.

The heart of Queen Satyavati was stricken with grief because her two sons were dead, and there was no heir left to the throne of King Bharata.

ORIGIN OF DHRITARASHTRA, PANDU, AND VIDURA

Now it was the custom in those days that a kinsman should become the father of children to succeed the dead king. So Queen Satyavati spoke to Bhishma, saying: "Take the widows of my son and raise up sons who will be as sons of the king."

But Bhishma said: "That I cannot do, as have I not vowed never to be the father of any children."

In her despair Satyavati then thought of her son Vyasa, and he immediately appeared before her and consented to do what she wished.

Now Vyasa was a mighty sage, but, because of his austerities in his lonely jungle dwelling, he had grown gaunt and ugly so that women shrank from him; he was fearsome to look at.

Amvika closed her eyes with horror when she saw the sage, and she had a son who was born blind: he was named Dhritarashtra. Amvalika turned pale with fear: she had a son who was named Pandu, 'the pale one'.

Satyavati wished that Vyasa should be the father of a son who had no defect; but Amvika sent her handmaiden to him, and she bore a son who was called Vidura. As it happened, Dharma, god of justice, was put under the spell of a Rishi at this time, to be born among men, and he chose Vidura to be his human incarnation.

The three children were reared by Bhishma, who was regent over the kingdom, but nevertheless subject to Queen Satyavati. He taught them the laws and trained them as warriors. When the time came to select a king, Dhritarashtra was passed over because that he was blind, and Vidura because of his humble birth, and Pandu, 'the pale one', was set upon the throne.

THE BIRTH OF KARNA

King Pandu became a mighty monarch, and was renowned as a warrior and a just ruler of his kingdom. He married two wives: Pritha, who was chief rani, and Madri, whom he loved best.

Now Pritha was of celestial origin, for her mother was a nymph; her father was a holy Brahman, and her brother, Vasudeva, was the father of Krishna. As a baby she had been adopted by the King of Shurasena, whose kingdom was among the Vindhya mountains. She was of pious heart, and ever showed reverence towards holy men. Once the great Rishi Durvasas came to the palace, and she ministered to him faithfully by serving food at any hour he desired, and by kindling the sacred fire in the sacrificial chamber. After his stay of a full year, Durvasas, in reward for her services, imparted to Pritha a powerful charm, by virtue of which she could compel the love of a celestial being. One day she had a vision of Surya, god of the sun; she muttered the charm, and received him when he came near in the attire of a king, wearing the celestial earrings. In secret she became in time the mother of his son, Karna, who was equipped at birth with celestial earrings and an invulnerable coat of mail, which had power to grow as the wearer increased in stature. The child had the eyes of a lion and the shoulders of a bull.

In her maidenly shame Pritha resolved to conceal her newborn babe. So she wrapped him in soft sheets and, laying his head on a pillow, placed him in a wicker basket which she had smeared over with wax. Then, weeping bitterly, she set the basket afloat on the river, saying: "My babe, be you protected by all who are on land, and in the water, and in the sky, and in the celestial regions! May all who see you love you! May Varuna, god of the waters, shield you from harm. May your father, the sun, give you warmth!... I shall know you in days to come, wherever you may be, by your

coat of golden mail…. She who will find you and adopt you
will be surely blessed…. Oh my son, she who will cherish
you will behold you in youthful prime like to a maned lion
in Himalayan forests."

The basket drifted down the River Aswa until it was no
longer seen by that lotus-eyed damsel, and after some time it
reached the Jumna; the Jumna gave it to the Ganges, and by
that great and holy river it was carried to the country of Anga….
The child, lying in soft slumber, was kept alive because of the
virtues possessed by the celestial armour and the earrings.

Now there was a woman of Anga whose name was Radha,
and she had peerless beauty. Her husband was Shatananda,
the charioteer. Both husband and wife had long wished for a
son of their own. One day, however, their wish was granted.
It happened that Radha went down to the river bank, and
she saw the basket drifting on the waves. She brought it
ashore; and when it was uncovered, she gazed with wonder
at a sleeping babe who was as fair as the morning sun. Her
heart was immediately filled with happiness, and she cried
out: "The gods have heard me at last, and they have sent me
a son." So she adopted the babe and cherished him. And the
years went past, and Karna grew up and became a powerful
youth and a mighty bowman.

KING PANDU'S DOOM

Pritha, who was beautiful to behold, chose King Pandu
at her swayamvara. Trembling with love, she placed the
flower garland on his shoulders.

Madri came from the country of Madra, and was black-eyed and dusky-complexioned. She had been purchased by Bhishma for the king with gold, jewels, elephants and horses, as was the marriage custom among her people.

The glories of King Bharata's reign were revived by Pandu, who achieved great conquests and extended his territory. He loved well to go hunting, and eventually he retired to the Himalaya mountains with his two wives to hunt deer. There, as fate had decreed, he met with dire misfortune. One day he shot arrows at two deer; but as he discovered to his sorrow, they were a holy Brahman and his wife in animal form. The sage was mortally wounded, and before he died he assumed his human form. He cursed Pandu, and foretold that he would die in the arms of one of his wives.

The king was stricken with fear; he immediately took vows of celibacy, and gave all his possessions to Brahmans; then he went away to live in a solitary place with his two wives.

Some have told that Pandu never had children of his own, and that the gods were the fathers of his wives' great sons. Pritha was mother of Yudhishthira, son of Dharma, god of justice, and of Bhima, son of Vayu, the wind god, and also of Arjuna, son of mighty Indra, monarch of heaven. Madri received from Pritha the charm which Durvasas had given her, and she became the mother of Nakula and Sahadeva. These five princes were known as the Pandava brothers.

King Pandu was followed by his doom. One day he met with Madri, his favourite wife; they wandered together in a forest, and when he clasped her in his arms he immediately fell dead as the Brahman had foretold.

His sons, the Pandava brothers, built his funeral pyre, so that his soul might pass to heaven. Both Pritha and Madri wished to be burned with him, and they debated together which of them should follow her lord to the region of the dead.

Pritha said: "I must go with my lord. I was his first wife and chief rani. Madri, yield me his body and raise our children together. Let me achieve what must be achieved."

Madri said: "I should be the chosen one. I was King Pandu's favourite wife, and he died because he loved me. If I survived you I would not be able to raise our children as you can. Do not refuse your sanction to this which is dear to my heart."

So they could not agree; but the Brahmans, who heard them, said that Madri must be burned with King Pandu, having been his favourite wife. And so it came to pass that Madri laid herself on the pyre, and she passed in flames with her beloved lord, that bull among men.

THE RIVAL PRINCES

Meanwhile **King Pandu's blind brother**, Dhritarashtra, had ascended the throne to reign over the kingdom of Bharatavarsha, with Bhishma as his regent, until the elder of the young princes should come of age.

Dhritarashtra had married Gandharai, daughter of the King of Gandhara. When she was betrothed she went to the king with eyes blindfolded, and ever afterwards she so appeared in his presence. She became the mother of a hundred sons, the eldest of whom was Duryodhana. These were the princes who were named the Kauravas.

The widowed Pritha returned to Hastinapur with her three sons and the two sons of Madri also. When she told Dhritarashtra that Pandu, his brother, had died, he wept and mourned. The blind king gave his protection to the five princes who were Pandu's heirs.

So the Pandavas and Kauravas were raised together in the royal palace at Hastinapur. Favour was not shown to one cousin more than another. The young princes were trained to throw the stone and to cast the noose, and they engaged lustily in wrestling bouts and practised boxing. As they grew up they shared work with the king's men; they marked the young calves, and every three years they counted and branded the cattle. Yet, despite all that could be done, the two families lived at enmity. Of all the young men Bhima, of the Pandavas, was the most powerful, and Duryodhana, the leader of the Kauravas, was jealous of him. Bhima was always the victor in sports and contests. The Kauravas could not endure his triumphs, and they plotted among themselves to accomplish his death.

It happened that the young men had gone to live in a royal palace on the banks of the Ganges. One day as they feasted together, Duryodhana put poison in Bhima's food. Shortly afterwards he fainted and seemed to be dead. Then Duryodhana bound him hand and foot and cast him into the Ganges; his body was swallowed by the waters.

But it was not fated that Bhima should perish. As his body sank down, the fierce snakes, which are called Nagas, attacked him; but their poison counteracted the poison he had already swallowed, so that he regained consciousness. Then, bursting his bonds, he scattered the reptiles before him, and they fled in terror.

Bhima found that he had sunk down to the city of serpents in the underworld. Vasuki, king of the Nagas, having heard of his prowess, hastened towards the young warrior, whom he greatly desired to behold.

Bhima was welcomed by Aryaka, the great grandfather of Pritha, who was a dweller in the underworld. He was loved by Vasuki, who, for Aryaka's sake, offered great gifts to the fearless Bhima. But Aryaka chose rather that the boy should be given a draught of strength which contained the virtues of a thousand Nagas. This great favour was granted by the king of serpents, and Bhima was permitted to drain the bowl eight times. He immediately fell into a deep sleep, which lasted for eight days. Then he awoke, and he returned again to his mother, who was mourning for him all the while. So it happened that Bhima triumphed over Duryodhana, forever afterwards he possessed the strength of a mighty giant. He told his brothers all that had happened to him, but they counselled him not to reveal his secret to the Kauravas, his cousins.

THE PRINCES LEARN TO SHOOT

Bhishma was royal grandfather to the houses of Pandava and Kauravas, and he was eager for the princes of these royal houses to have a teacher who could train them in the dignified and royal use of arms. He had put out a search for such a teacher when it happened that the boys themselves were playing ball in the forests outside Hastinapura, when their ball rolled away from them and fell into a well. Although they struggled, and used all of their inventiveness, all efforts to reach it failed, and the ball was lost to them.

The boys sat glumly by the well, gazing with frustration at its walls when suddenly there was a movement from the corner of their eyes. There, thin and dark, sat a Brahman who seemed to be resting after his daily worship.

The boys eagerly surrounded him and begged him to recover their ball.

The Brahman smiled at their boyish jinks and teased them, for what offspring of a royal house could not shoot well enough to retrieve a ball? He promised to do so himself, for the price of a dinner. And then the Brahman threw his ring into the well and promised to bring that up too – using only a few blades of grass.

The boys surrounded the Brahman, intrigued. "Why that's magic," said one of the boys. "We could make you rich for life if you could do as you say."

The Brahman was true to his word and selecting a piece of grass he threw it as if it were a sword, deep into the heart of the well and there it pierced the ball straight through. He immediately threw another blade, which pierced the first, and then another, which pierced the second, until soon he had a chain of grass with which to draw up the ball.

The boys had by now lost interest in their ball, but their fascination with the Brahman was growing by the moment.

"The ring," they chorused. "Show us how you can get the ring."

And so it was that Drona, which was the name of that Brahman, took up his bow, which had been lying by his side, and choosing an arrow, and then carefully fitting it to the bow, he shot it into the well. Within seconds it had returned, bearing with it the ring. He handed it to the boys who whooped and hollered with glee.

They surrounded Drona again, begging him to allow them to help him, to offer him some gift. Drona grew silent and then with great effort he spoke, carefully choosing his words.

"There is something you can do," he said quietly. "You can tell Bhishma your guardian that Drona is here."

The boys trooped home again and recounted their adventure to Bhishma. Their guardian was at once struck by the good fortune of this visit for he did indeed know of Drona and he would, it seemed, be the perfect teacher for these unruly boys. Bhishma had known Drona as the son of the great sage Gharadwaja, whose ashrama in the mountains had been a centre of higher learning. Many illustrious students had attended as scholars, and most of these had befriended Drona who had been, even then, gifted with divine weapons and the knowledge of how to use them.

Drona had fallen upon hard times when he had pledged his allegiance to Drupada, now king of the Panchalas. Drupada and Drona had been fast friends as scholars, but as regent, Drupada scorned their ancient friendship and set the poor Brahman in the position of a beggar. Hurt by his friend's actions, Drona had left to pursue his studies, and his first task was to find the best pupils to which he could apply his knowledge.

Bhishma did not ask what purpose Drona had for these good pupils, and it was with warmth and genuine delight that he welcomed Drona to his household.

"String your bow, Drona," he said, "and you may make the princes of my house accomplished in the use of arms. What we have is yours. Our house is at your disposal."

The first morning of instruction found Drona lying the boys flat on their backs. He asked them then to promise that when they became skilled in the use of arms they would carry out for him a purpose that he had borne in mind. Ever eager, Arjuna, the third of the Pandavas, jumped up and promised that whatever that purpose might be, he was prepared to accomplish it. Drona drew Arjuna to him and the two men embraced. From that time there would be a special closeness between teacher and student.

The princes came from all the neighbouring kingdoms to learn of Drona and all the Kauravas and the Pandavas and the sons of the great nobles were his pupils. There was, among them, a shy and wild-looking boy called Karna who was by reputation the son of a royal charioteer. Arjuna and Karna became rivals, each seeking to outdo the other with his skill and accuracy.

At this time, Arjuna was becoming well versed in the vocabulary of arms. One night while eating, the lantern blew out and he realized that he could still continue to eat in the darkness. It set his mind on to the thought that it would certainly be possible to shoot in darkness, for it surely was habit as much as putting food to one's mouth. Drona applauded Arjuna's crafty mind and declared him to have no equal.

Another of those who travelled to Drona to become a pupil was a low-caste prince known as Ekalavya. Drona refused to take him on because of his caste, and Ekalavya retired to the forest where he made an image of Drona from the earth, which he worshipped and revered as the man himself. He practised often in the forest and soon became so fine a shot that his activities were drawn to the attention of Drona and his pupils.

Drona sought him out and when Ekalavya saw him coming, he fell to the ground. "Please, Drona," he cried, "I am your pupil, struggling here in the woods to learn the skills of military science."

Drona looked down on the boy. "If you are," he said, "give me my fee."

Ekalavya leapt to his feet. "Master, just name your fee and you shall have it. There is nothing I would not do for you." His face was broken by a wide smile.

"If you mean it," said Drona coolly, "cut off your thumb."

Ekalavya allowed no reaction to cross his proud face and he did as his master bid at once. He laid the thumb of his left hand at the feet of Drona and held up his head.

Drona turned with Arjuna and left, and as Ekalavya bent to collect his bow he realized that he could no longer hold it. His lightness of touch was gone.

And so it was by these means, and others like them that Drona ensured the supremacy of the royal princes, who had, now, no rivals in the use of arms. Each had a speciality and they were all capable of fighting with resourcefulness, strength and perseverance.

THE PRINCES' TRIAL

Drona's pupils had now come to the end of their education, and Drona applied to Dhritarashtra the king to hold a tournament in which they could exhibit their skill.

Preparations began at once for the great event, and a hall was built for the queens and their ladies.

When the day arrived, the king took his place, surrounded by his ministers and minions, and by Bhishma and the early tutors of the princes. And then Gandharai, the mother of Duryodhana, and Pritha, the mother of the Pandavas, entered the area, beautifully dressed and bejewelled as befitted their stature. Last came Drona, who entered the lists dressed in white, as pure as the heart of Vishnu. Beside him walked his son, Ashvathaman, who held himself with great pride and authority.

In came the princes to a procession, led by Yudhishthira, and there began the most incredible display of expertise seen by any one of the noble spectators of that tournament. Arrow after arrow flew, never missing its mark. Horses pulled chariots and there was much vaulting and careering, but never did the princes lose control or exhibit anything other than the greatest of skill and precision. The princes fought together, and exhibited alone. Their mastery left none in any doubt that he was witnessing the finest example of marksmanship in the land. And then entered Arjuna, and Pritha gave a sigh of delight. Her son was even superior to his splendid cousins and he shot arrows that became water, and then fire, and then mountains, and then an arrow that made them all disappear. He fought with sword, and mace, and then pole and on the breast of his chariot. He met every mark with perfect precision. Here was a champion, and the audience hardly dared expel breath at this show of proficiency.

But the respectful silence that had fallen over the crowd was disturbed by a rustling in the corner. And then a great noise was heard in the direction of the gate. Into the centre of the ring came none other than Karna, grown to manhood and splendid in his arms. Far from the prying eyes of her neighbours, Pritha swooned and shivered with fear. Karna was none other than the son she had given up long ago, the son of the sun itself. He shone as brightly as any summer ray, his good looks matched by his eagerness to fight. He was tall and strong, and his presence caused the crowd to gasp with admiration.

Karna walked towards Arjuna and spoke quietly. "Oh prince," he said, "I have a wish that we should engage in single combat."

Arjuna could hardly hold back the spittle that multiplied on his tongue. He spluttered and then whispered angrily to Karna, "The day will come when I will kill you."

"That is yes, then?" shouted Karna. "Today I will strike off your head before our master himself."

The two men stood facing one another, antipathy growing between them like the strongest of armour. They moved into position for single combat, but just as they did so there was a cry from the master of ceremonies. Quietly he made his way across the field and drew the warriors to one side. Until Karna could show noble lineage, he was not by law able to fight with the sons of kings. Princes could not fight with men of inferior birth.

Karna's fury was tangible, but just as he turned to the master he was rewarded by a cry from Duryodhana, who was eager to see Arjuna defeated. "I'll install him as king of Anga!" he shouted. "And Arjuna can fight him on the morrow."

Priests appeared at once, and a throne was brought for Karna, who beamed when he saw his old father Shatananda, the ancient charioteer.

He embraced his son, pride at his position as king causing him to weep with joy. There was some sniggering amongst the crowd, for how could a king have such a lowly father? But before anyone could speak, Duryodhana leapt forward once again, having pledged eternal support and friendship to Karna.

"We do not know the lineage of all heroes," he shouted to the crowd. "Who asks for the source of a river?" And to the cheers of the gathering, he wrapped his arms around Karna's shoulders and helped his aged father to a seat.

The princes and Karna left together. Pritha stared quietly at her sons – princes and now a king. She said nothing and watched them leave, undefeated and grand in every sense. Pritha looked then to the sun…and smiled.

DRONA'S WAR

The **Pandavas and Kauravas** had become accomplished warriors, and now it was time for their teacher, Drona to claim his reward. He said to his pupils, "Go fight Drupada, King of the Panchalas; wound him in battle and bring him to me."

The cousins were jealous of each other and could not agree to wage war together. So the Kauravas, led by Duryodhana, were first to attack Drupada; they rode in their chariots and invaded the hostile capital. The warriors of Panchala arose to fight; their shouting was like the roaring of lions, and their arrows were showered as thickly as rain dropping from the clouds. The Kauravas were defeated, and they left in disorder, uttering cries of despair.

The Pandavas then rushed against the enemies of Drona. Arjuna swept forward in his chariot, and he destroyed horses and cars and warriors. Bhima struck down elephants big as mountains, and many horses and charioteers also, and he covered the ground with rivers of blood.

Drupada endeavoured to turn the tide of battle; surrounded by his mightiest men, he opposed Arjuna. But the strong Pandava overcame him, and after fierce fighting, Arjuna seized Drupada. The remnant of the Panchalas forces then broke and fled, and the Pandavas began to lay waste the capital. Arjuna, however, cried to Bhima: "Remember that Drupada is the kinsman of the Kauravas; therefore cease slaying his warriors."

Drupada was led before Drona, who said: "At last I have conquered your kingdom, and your life is in my hands. Is it your desire now to revive our friendship?" Drona smiled and continued: "Brahmans are full of forgiveness; therefore have no fear for your life. I have not forgotten that we were children together. So once again I ask for your friendship, and I grant you half of the kingdom; the other half will be mine, and if it pleases you we will be friends."

"You are indeed noble and great. I thank you, and desire to be your friend." Drupada replied.

So Drona took possession of half of the kingdom. Drupada went to rule the southern Panchalas; he was convinced that he could not defeat Drona, and he resolved to discover means whereby he might obtain a son who could overcome his Brahman enemy.

Thereafter the Pandavas waged war against neighbouring kings, and they extended the territory over which the blind king held sway.

FIRST EXILE OF THE PANDAVAS

The Kauravas were rendered more jealous than ever by the successes achieved by the Pandavas, and also because the people favoured them. Duryodhana wanted to become heir to the throne, but the elder prince of the conquering Pandavas could not be set aside. In the end Yudhishthira was chosen by the blind king, and he became Yuva-rajah, 'Little Rajah', supplanting Bhishma, who had been regent during the minority. Yudhishthira, accordingly, ruled over the kingdom, and he was honoured and loved by the people; for although he was not a mighty warrior like Arjuna, or powerful like Bhima, he had great wisdom, and he was ever just and merciful, and a lover of truth.

Duryodhana remonstrated with his blind father, and he spoke to him, saying: "Why, my father, have you so favoured the Pandavas and forgotten your own sons? You were Pandu's elder brother, and should have reigned before him. Now the children of your younger brother are to succeed you. The kingdom is your own by right of birth, and your sons are your heirs. Why, then, have you lowered us in the eyes of your subjects?"

Dhritarashtra replied: "Duryodhana, my son, you know that Pandu, my brother, was the mightiest ruler in the world. Could I, who am blind, have set him aside? His sons have great wisdom and worth, and are loved by the people. How, then, could I pass them over? Yudhishthira has greater accomplishments for governing than you possess, my son. How could I turn against him and banish him from my council?"

Duryodhana said: "I do not acknowledge Yudhishthira's superiority as a ruler of men. And this I know full well, I could

combat against any number of Yudhishthiras on the battlefield....
If, my father, you will set me aside and deny me my right to a
share of government in the kingdom, I will take my own life and
end my sorrow."

To this Dhritarashtra responded: "Be patient, my son. If you
wish, I will divide the kingdom between you and Yudhishthira,
so that no jealousy may exist between you both."

Duryodhana was pleased to hear these words, and he said:
"I agree and will accept your offer. Let the Pandavas take their
own land and rule over it, and I and my brothers will remain at
Hastinapur with you. If the Kauravas and Pandavas continue to
live here together, there will be conflicts and bloodshed."

Dhritarashtra replied: "Neither Bhishma, the head of our
family, nor Vidura, my brother, nor Drona, your teacher, will
consent to the Pandavas being sent away."

To which Duryodhana said: "Do not consult them; they
are beneath you. Command the Pandavas to go to the city
of Varanavartha and live there; when they have gone no one
will speak to you regarding this matter."

Dhritarashtra listened to his son and followed his counsel.
He commanded Yudhishthira to go with his brothers to the
city of Varanavartha, rich in jewels and gold, to live there
until he recalled them. So the Pandava brothers said farewell
to Dhritarashtra and left Hastinapur, taking with them their
mother, the widowed queen Pritha, and went towards the
city of Varanavartha. The people of Hastinapur mourned
for them.

Before they departed, Vidura spoke to them in secret,
telling them to be aware of the perils of fire. He repeated
a verse to Yudhishthira and said: "Put your trust in the

man who will recite these words to you; he will be your deliverer."

Now Duryodhana had plotted with Shakuni, the brother of Queen Gandharai, to destroy his kinsmen. Then their ally, Kanika the Brahman, said in secret to Dhritarashtra: "When your enemy is in your power, destroy him by whatever means is at your disposal, in secret or openly. Show him no mercy, nor give him your protection. If your son, or brother, or kinsman, or your father even, should become your enemy, do not hesitate to slay if it gives you prosperity. Let him be overcome either by spells, or by curses, or by deception, or by payment of money. Do not forget your enemy."

The maharajah lent a willing ear thereafter to the counsel of his son, whom he secretly favoured most.

Before the Pandavas had left Hastinapur, Duryodhana sent his secret agent, Purochana, to build a roomy new dwelling for them in Varanavartha. This was accomplished quickly, and it became known as the 'house of lac'. It was built of combustible material: hemp and resin were packed in the walls and between the floors, and it was plastered over with mortar mixed with pitch and clarified butter.

Purochana welcomed the Pandavas when they arrived at their new home. But Yudhishthira smelt the mortar, and he closely examined the whole house before saying to Bhima: "The enemy has built this house for us. It is full of hemp and straw, resin and bamboo, and the mortar is mixed with pitch and clarified butter."

In due time a stranger visited the Pandavas, and he repeated the secret verse which Vidura had told to Yudhishthira. He said: "I will construct for you a secret passage underground which will lead to a place of safety should you have to escape from this house when the doors are locked and it is set on fire." So the man set to work in secret, and before long the underground passage was ready. Then Bhima resolved to deal with Purochana in the very manner that he had undertaken to deal with the princes.

One evening Pritha gave a feast in the new dwelling to all the poor people in Varanavartha. When the guests had left, a poor Bhil woman and her five sons remained behind. They had drunken heavily and were unable to rise up. They slept on the floor.

Meanwhile, a great windstorm had arisen, and the night was dark. So Bhima decided that the time had come to accomplish his mission. He went outside and secured the doors of Purochana's house, which stood beside that of the Pandavas; then he set it on fire. Soon the flames spread towards the new mansion and it burned fiercely and quickly. Pritha and her sons fled through the underground passage and took refuge in the jungle. In the morning the people discovered the blackened remains of Purochana's body and the bodies of his servants among the embers of his house. In the ruins of the Pandavas' mansion they found that a woman and five men had perished, and they lamented, believing that Pritha and her sons were dead. There was great sorrow in Hastinapur when the news reached there. Bhishma and Vidura wept, and blind Dhritarashtra was moved to tears also. But Duryodhana secretly rejoiced, believing that his enemies had all been destroyed.

BHIMA AND THE FAIR DEMON

The Pandavas, having escaped through the subterranean passage, travelled southwards and entered the forest, which was full of reptiles and wild animals and with ferocious man-eating Asuras and gigantic Rakshasas. Weary and sore, they were overcome with tiredness and fear. So the mighty Bhima lifted up all the others and hastened on through the darkness: he took his mother on his back, and Madri's sons on his shoulders, and Yudhishthira and Arjuna under his arms.

He went swifter than the wind, breaking down trees by his breast and furrowing the ground that he stamped on. After some time the Pandavas found a place to rest in safety; and they all lay down to sleep under a great and beautiful Banyan tree, except mighty Bhima who kept watch over them.

Now in the forest there lived a ferocious Rakshasa named Hidimva. He was terrible to behold; his eyes were red, and he was red-haired and red-bearded; his mouth was large, with long, sharp-pointed teeth, which gleamed in darkness; his ears were shaped like arrows; his neck was as broad as a tree, his belly was large, and his legs were long.

The monster was exceedingly hungry on that fateful night. Scenting human flesh in the forest, he yawned and scratched his grizzly beard, and spoke to his sister, saying: "I smell excellent food, and my mouth waters; tonight I will devour warm flesh and drink hot, frothy blood. Hurry now and bring the sleeping men to me; we will eat them together, and afterwards dance merrily in the wood."

So the Rakshasa woman went towards the place where the Pandavas slept. When she saw Bhima, the long-armed one, clad in royal garments and wearing his jewels, she immediately fell in love with him, and said to herself: "This man with the shoulders of a lion and eyes like lotus blooms is worthy to be my husband. I will not slay him for my evil brother."

She transformed herself into a beautiful woman; her face became as fair as the full moon; on her head was a garland of flowers, her hair hung in ringlets; and she wore rich ornaments of gold with many gems.

Timidly she approached Bhima and said: "Oh bull among men, who are you and where did you come from? Who are these fair ones sleeping there? Know that this forest is the abode of the wicked chief of the Rakshasas. He is my brother, and he has sent me here to kill you all for food, but I want to save you. Be my husband. I will take you to a secret place among the mountains, for I can speed through the air at will."

Bhima said: "I cannot leave my mother and my brothers to become food for a Rakshasa."

The woman said: "Let me help you. Awaken your mother and your brothers and I will rescue you all from my fierce brother."

To which Bhima replied: "I will not wake them, because I do not fear a Rakshasa. You can go as it pleases you, and I care not if you send your brother to me."

Meantime the Rakshasa chief had grown impatient. He came down from his tree and went after his sister, with gaping mouth and head thrown back.

The Rakshasa woman said to Bhima: "He comes here in anger. Wake up your family, and I will carry you all through the air to escape him."

"Look at my arms," said Bhima. "They are as strong as the trunks of elephants; my legs are like iron maces, and my chest is powerful and broad. I will slay this man-eater, your brother."

The Rakshasa chief heard Bhima's boast, and he fumed with rage when he saw his sister in her beautiful human form. He said to her: "I will slay you and those whom you would help against me." Then he rushed at her, but Bhima cried: "You will not kill a woman while I am near. I challenge you to single combat now. Tonight your sister will see you slain by me as an elephant is slain by a lion."

The Rakshasa replied: "Boast not until you are the victor. I will kill you first of all, then your friends, and last of all my treacherous sister."

Having said this, he rushed towards Bhima, who nimbly seized the monster's outstretched arms and, wrestling violently, cast him on the ground. Then as a lion drags off his prey, Bhima dragged the struggling Rakshasa into the depths of the forest, so that his yells should not wake his sleeping family. There they fought together like furious bull elephants, tearing down branches and overthrowing trees.

Eventually the clamour woke the Pandavas, and they gazed with wonder at the beautiful woman who kept watch in Bhima's place.

Pritha said to her: "Oh celestial being, who are you? If you are the goddess of woods or an Apsara, tell me why you linger here?"

The fair demon said: "I am the sister of the chief of the Rakshasas, and I was sent here to slay you all; but when I saw your mighty son the love god wounded me, and I chose him for my husband. Then my brother followed angrily, and your son is fighting with him. They are filling the forest with their shouting."

All the brothers rushed to Bhima's aid, and they saw the two wrestlers struggling in a cloud of dust, and they appeared like two high cliffs shrouded in mist.

Arjuna cried out: "Bhima, I am here to help you. Let me slay the monster."

Bhima answered: "Fear not, but look on. The Rakshasa will not escape from my hands."

"Do not keep him alive too long," Said Arjuna. "We must act quickly. The dawn is near, and Rakshasas become stronger at daybreak; they exercise their powers of deception during the two twilights. Do not play with him, therefore, but kill him quickly."

At these words Bhima became as strong as Vayu, his father, when he is angered. Raising the Rakshasa aloft, he whirled him round and round, crying: "In vain have you gorged on unholy food. I will rid the forest of you. No longer will you devour human beings."

Then, dashing the monster to the ground, Bhima seized him by the hair and by the waist, laid him over a knee, and broke his back. The Rakshasa was slain.

Day was breaking, and Pritha and her sons immediately turned away to leave the forest. The Rakshasa woman followed them, and Bhima cried to her: "Be gone! Or I will send you after your brother."

Yudhishthira then spoke to Bhima, saying: "It is unseemly to slay a woman. Besides, she is the sister of that Rakshasa, and even although she became angry, what harm can she do us?"

Kneeling at Pritha's feet, the demon wailed: "Oh illustrious and blessed lady, you know the sufferings women endure when the love god wounds them. Have pity on me now, and command your son to take me for his bride. If he continues to scorn me, I will kill myself. Let me be your slave, and I will carry you all wherever you desire and protect you from perils."

Pritha heard her with compassion, and persuaded Bhima to take her for his bride. So the two were married by Yudhishthira; then the Rakshasa took Bhima on her back and sped through the air to a lonely place among the mountains which is sacred to the gods. They lived together beside silvery streams and lakes sparkling with lotus blooms; they wandered through woods of blossoming trees where birds sang sweetly, and by celestial sea-beaches covered with pearls and nuggets of gold. The demon bride had assumed celestial beauty, and often played sweet music. She made Bhima happy.

In time the woman became the mother of a mighty son; his eyes were fiercely bright, his ears were like arrows, and his mouth was large; he had copper-brown lips and long, sharp teeth. He grew to be a youth an hour after he was born. His mother named him Ghatotkacha.

Bhima then returned to his mother and his brothers with his demon bride and her son. They lived together for a time in the forest; then the Rakshasa bade all the Pandavas farewell and left with Ghatotkacha, who promised to come to the Pandavas' aid whenever they called on him.

THE KING OF THE ASURAS

One day thereafter Vyasa appeared before the Pandavas and told them to go to the city of Ekachakra and to live there for a time in the house of a Brahman. Then he vanished from sight, promising to come again.

So the Pandavas went to Ekachakra and lived with a Brahman who had a wife and a daughter and an infant son. Disguised as holy men, the brothers begged for food. Every evening they brought home what they had obtained, and Pritha divided it into two portions; one half she gave to wolf-bellied Bhima, and the rest she kept for his brothers and herself.

Now the city of Ekachakra was protected against every enemy by a forest-dwelling Rakshasa named Vaka, who was king of the Asuras. Each day the people had to supply him with food, which consisted of a cartload of rice, two bullocks, and the man who carried the meal to him.

One morning a great wailing broke out in the Brahman's house because the holy man had been chosen to supply the demon's feast. He was too poor to purchase a slave, so he said he would deliver himself to Vaka. "Although I reach Heaven," he cried, "I will have no joy, because my family will perish when I am gone." His wife and his daughter pleaded to take his place, and the three wept together. Then the little boy plucked a long spear of grass, and with glowing eyes he spoke sweetly and said: "Do not weep, Father; do not weep, Mother; do not weep, Sister. With this spear I will slay the demon who devours human beings."

Pritha was deeply moved by the grief of the Brahman family, and she said: "Sorrow not. I will send my son Bhima to slay the Asura king."

The Brahman answered her, saying: "That cannot be. Your sons are Brahmans and are under my protection. If I go, I will be obeying the king; if I send your son, I will be guilty of his death. The gods hate the man who causes a guest to be slain, or permits a Brahman to perish."

To this Pritha said: "Bhima is strong and mighty. A demon cannot do him any harm. He will kill this bloodthirsty Rakshasa and return again safely. But, Brahman, you must not reveal to anyone who has performed this mighty deed, so that the people do not trouble my son and try to obtain the secret of his power."

So Bhima collected the rice and drove the bullocks towards the forest. When he got near to the appointed place, he began to eat the food himself, and called the Rakshasa's name over and over again. Vaka heard and came through the trees towards him. Red were his eyes, and his hair and his beard were red also; his ears were pointed like arrows; he had a mouth like a cave, and his forehead was puckered in three lines. He was terrible to look at; his body was huge, indeed.

The Rakshasa saw Bhima eating his meal, and approached angrily, biting his lower lip. "Fool," he cried, "would you devour my food before my very eyes?"

Bhima smiled, and continued eating with his face averted. The demon struck him, but the hero only glanced round as if someone had touched his shoulder, and he went on eating as before.

Raging furiously, the Rakshasa tore up a tree, and Bhima rose leisurely and waited until it was flung at him. When that was done, he caught the trunk and hurled it back. Many trees were uprooted and flung by one at the other. Then Vaka attacked, but the Pandava overthrew him and dragged him round and round until the demon gasped with fatigue. The earth shook;

trees were splintered into pieces. Then Bhima began to strike the monster with his iron fists, and he broke Vaka's back across his knee. Terrible were the loud screams of the Rakshasa while Bhima was bending him double. He died howling.

All the other Asuras were terror-stricken, and, bellowing horribly, they rushed towards Bhima and bowed before him. Bhima made them take vows never to eat human flesh again or to oppress the people of the city. They promised to do so, and he allowed them to depart.

Afterwards Pritha's son dragged the monster's body to the main gate of Ekachakra. He entered the city secretly and hurried to the Brahman's house, and he told Yudhishthira all that had taken place.

When the people of the city discovered that the Asura king was dead, they rejoiced, and hurried towards the house of the Brahman. But the holy man was evasive, saying that his deliverer was a certain high-souled Brahman who had offered to supply food to the demon. The people established a festival in honour of Brahmans.

DRUPADA'S CHILDREN

The Pandavas remained in the city of Ekachakra. One day they were visited by a saintly man who told them the story of the miraculous births of Drupada's son and daughter from sacrificial fire.

When Drupada had lost half of his kingdom, he made pilgrimages to holy places. He promised great rewards to superior Brahmans, so that he might have offspring, ever desiring revenge against Drona. He offered the austere Upayája a million cows if he would procure a son for him, and that sage sent him to his brother Yája. Now Yája was reluctant to help the king; but eventually he consented to perform the sacrificial rite, and prevailed upon Upayája to help him.

So the rite was performed, and when the vital moment came, the Brahmans called for the queen to partake in it. But Drupada's wife was not prepared, and she asked them all to wait a little while. But the Brahmans could not delay the consummation of the sacrificial rite. Before the queen came, a son sprang from the flames: he was clad in full armour, and carried a sword and bow, and a crown gleamed brightly on his head. A voice out of the heavens said: "This prince has come to destroy Drona and to increase the fame of the Panchalas".

Next a daughter rose from the ashes on the altar. She was exceedingly beautiful, with long curling locks and lotus eyes. A sweet odour clung to her body. A voice out of heaven said: "This dusky girl will become the chief of all women. Many Kshatriyas must die because of her, and the Kauravas will suffer from her. She will accomplish the decrees of the gods."

The son was named Dhrishtadyumna and the daughter Draupadi.

THE BRIDE OF THE PANDAVAS

Having heard the story of the birth of Draupadi, Pritha made up her mind to go to Panchala. Before they went away, the saintly man said that Draupadi had been destined to become a Pandava queen.

The princes were silent when their guest had gone and Pritha mourned for her sons who had been cast out. She smiled brightly at them and said, "Perhaps it is time to depart from Ekachakra – I for one am glad to renew our wanderings."

The spirits of the princes were lifted at once, and the following day they set off, thanking their gentle host for all his many kindnesses. Pritha and her sons wandered from the banks of the Ganges and went northwards on the road to Kampilya, the capital of Drupada. They soon fell in with a great number of people all going the same way. Yudhishthira spoke to a troop of Brahmans, and he asked them where they were going. They answered saying that Drupada of Panchala was observing a great festival, and that all the princes of the land were heading to the swayamvara of his daughter, the beautiful Draupadi.

So the Pandavas went towards Panchala with the troop of Brahmans. When they reached the city they took up home in the humble dwelling of a potter, still disguised as Brahmans, and they went out and begged food from the people. In their hearts the brothers secretly wished to win the fair bride whose fame had spread.

Alone in his castle, Drupada perused the swayamvara that he was about to hold and he wondered aloud at the choice of suitors. He had held for many years a secret wish that Arjuna should wed Draupadi, a wish that he had kept close to his breast over the last years. Arjuna's mastery of the bow at the tournament was fresh in his memory as he formed the instrument that would be required to shoot an arrow through a ring suspended at great height. It would not be easy to win his princess. In fact, thought Drupada, there was likely only one man who could do it.

THE SAGA OF THE MAHABHARATA

The day of the swayamvara dawned bright and clear and the crowds poured in from adjoining kingdoms and lands. Duryodhana came with his dear friend Karna, and the Pandavas arrived in disguise, taking the form of Brahmans once again.

As the festivities began, the lovely Draupadi entered the arena, her stunning robes and jewellery matched only by her shimmering beauty. She held in her hands a wreath and she stood quietly while her twin brother Dhrishtadyumna stepped forward, his booming voice carrying across the crowds, "Today you are assembled here for one purpose. He who can use this bow" – he gestured down and then up – "to shoot five arrows through that ring, having birth, good looks and breeding, shall take today my sister for his bride."

A cheer went up among the crowd and the first name on the list was called forward. Many men reached for that sturdy bow, but none was able even to string it. Karna, sensing the embarrassment of his peers, stood and moved toward the weapon, his head held high, his good looks glowing in the morning sunlight. But as Draupadi caught sight of Karna, her lips curled and she called out with great disdain, "I will not be married to the son of a charioteer."

Karna managed a smile and shrugging his shoulders, returned to the crowd. There appeared, then, a movement from its masses, and the gathering parted to let through the strong but bedraggled form of a Brahman. Some of the Brahmans in the crowd cheered aloud as a symbol of sovereignty. Others shook their heads at what was bound to be a disgrace for Brahmans altogether.

Arjuna walked forward in his Brahman disguise and he lifted the bow with ease. Stopping to say a quiet prayer he walked slowly round the weapon until as quick as a flash he drew it up and sent five arrows flying straight through the ring. The cheering was uproarious. Brahman's across the crowd waved their scarves and flowers were sent flying from each direction. The other Pandavas kept down their heads, fearing that Arjuna's victory would draw attention to them all. So far no one had noticed that the Brahman was none other than Arjuna, and Draupadi brought forward a white robe and garland of marriage, which she placed eagerly about his neck.

"I take you as my lord," she said happily.

Suddenly a roar went up from the crowds, and coming towards them were the other suitors, angered that a Brahman should steal what they thought was rightfully theirs. A great fight broke out and Arjuna and his brother Bhima stood firmly against the masses, proving themselves once again to be excellent fighters. Bhima tore out a tree by its roots and used it to fend off the crowds, a trick he had learned at the hand of Drona. The crowd gasped once again in delight. It was not often that they were treated to such a display.

In the royal gallery, a prince by the name of Krishna stood up.

"Look," he shouted, pointing out Arjuna and Bhima to his brother, "I would swear as my name is Krishna that those are the Pandavas." He watched silently and said no more, waiting for his moment.

On the field the fighting continued until, finally, after much bloodshed, Arjuna was able to extract himself with his brothers and his new bride and return to the home of the potter. As they entered they addressed their mother, saying: "We have won a great gift today."

Pritha replied: "Then share the gift between you, as brothers should."

Yudhishthira was shocked to hear his mother's words, and said: "What have you said, mother? The gift is the Princess Draupadi whom Arjuna won at the swayamvara."

"Alas! What have I said?" said Pritha, "But the fatal words have been spoken; you must work out how they can be obeyed without wronging one another."

Each one of the Pandavas secretly yearned to have Draupadi for his bride, but the brothers agreed it should be Drupada's decision as to which of them his daughter should be given. Meanwhile Pritha greeted the princess warmly and welcomed her to the family, allowing her the honour of serving the food for them on that first night.

Back at the palace, King Drupada felt troubled after his daughter had been led away to the potter's house, so he sent his valiant son to watch her. To his joy Dhrishtadyumna discovered that the Brahmans were really the Pandava brothers. He returned to the king and related all that had happened. In the morning, Drupada sent two chariots to the potter's house with a messenger bidding the Pandavas to come to the palace for the nuptial feast.

The Pandava guests were made welcome, and the king and his son and all his counsellors sat down to feast with them. And after revealing to the king that they were in fact the Pandava princes, King Drupada glowed with joy and satisfaction. He asked the brothers to remain at the palace, and entertained them for many days.

After some time, the king spoke with Yudhishthira, saying: "You are the elder brother. Is it your desire that Arjuna be given Draupadi for his bride."

Yudhishthira replied: "I would like to speak with Vyasa, the great Rishi, regarding this matter."

So Vyasa was brought before the king, who spoke to him regarding Draupadi. The Rishi said: "The gods have already declared that she will become the wife of all the five Pandava brothers." Then Vyasa told that Draupadi was the reincarnation of a pious woman who once prayed to the god Shiva for a husband: five times she prayed, and the god rewarded her with the promise of five husbands in her next existence. Vyasa also revealed that the Pandava brothers were five incarnations of Indra, and therefore were but as one.

Drupada gave consent for his daughter to become the bride of all the brothers, so on five successive days she was led round the holy fire by each of the five Pandava princes. He gave many great gifts to his sons-in-law – much gold and many jewels, numerous horses and chariots and elephants, and also a hundred female servants clad in many-coloured robes.

But, when Duryodhana learned that the Pandava brothers were still alive, and had formed a powerful alliance with Drupada, he was furious. A great council was held, at which it was agreed that the Pandava princes should be invited to return to Hastinapur so that the kingdom might be divided between them and the sons of Dhritarashtra. Vidura was sent to Panchala to speak with Drupada and his sons-in-law regarding this matter.

RETURN TO HASTINAPUR

And so the Pandava brothers returned to Hastinapur with Vidura. They took with them their mother, Queen Pritha, and their wife, Draupadi, and the people welcomed them home. There was much rejoicing and many banquets.

Dhritarashtra spoke at length to Yudhishthira and his brothers and said: "I will now divide the kingdom between you and my sons. Your share will be the southwestern country of Khandava-prastha." So the Pandava princes bade farewell to all their kinsmen and to wise Drona, and they went towards their own country.

On the banks of the Jumna they built a strong fort, and in time they made a great clearance in the forest. When they had gathered together the people who were subject to them, they erected a great and wonderful city called Indra-prastha. High walls, which resembled the Mandara mountains, were built round about, and these were surrounded by a deep moat as wide as the sea.

In time the fame of King Yudhishthira went far and wide. He ruled with wisdom and with power, and he had great piety. Forest robbers were pursued constantly and put to death, and wrongdoers were always brought to justice.

The brothers lived happily together. In accordance with the advice of a Rishi, they made a pact that when one of them was sitting beside Draupadi, none of the others should enter, and that if one of them should be guilty of intrusion, he must go into exile for twelve years.

As it chanced, Yudhishthira was sitting with Draupadi one day when a Brahman, whose cattle had been carried off, rushed to Arjuna and asked him to pursue the band of robbers. The weapons of the prince were in the king's palace, and to obtain them Arjuna entered the room in which Yudhishthira and Draupadi sat, therefore breaking the pact. He hurried after the robbers and recovered the stolen cattle, which he brought back to the Brahman.

On his return to the palace, Arjuna said to his brother that he must go into exile for twelve years to make amends for his offence. Yudhishthira, however, prevailed upon him not to go. But Arjuna replied that he had pledged his oath to fulfil the terms of the pact. "I cannot waver from truth," he said; "truth is my weapon." So after he said goodbye to Pritha and Draupadi and his four brothers, he left the city of Indra-prastha. A band of Brahmans went with him.

ARJUNA'S EXILE

Arjuna wandered through the jungle, and he visited many holy places. One day he went to Hurdwar, where the Ganges flows on the plain, and he bathed in the holy waters. There he met Ulúpí, the beautiful daughter of Vasuka, king of the Nagas. She fell in love with him, and she led him to her father's palace, where he stayed for a time. She also gave him the power to render himself invisible in water. A child was born to them, and he was named Iravat.

Afterwards Arjuna went southwards until he came to the Mahendra mountain. He was received there by Parasu Rama, the Brahman hero, who gave him gifts of powerful weapons, and taught him the secret of using them.

So he wandered from holy place to holy place until he reached Manipur. Now the king of that place had a beautiful daughter whose name was Chitrángadá. Arjuna loved her, and sought her for his bride. The king said: "I have no other child, and if I give her to you, her son must remain here to become my heir, for the god Shiva has decreed that the kings of this realm can have each but one child." Arjuna married the maiden, and he lived in Manipur for three years. A son was born, and he was named Chitrangada. Afterwards Arjuna set out on his wanderings once more.

Travelling westward, he passed through many strange lands, eventually reaching the city of Prabhása on the southern sea, the capital of his kinsman Krishna, king of the Yádhavas.

Krishna welcomed Arjuna, and took the Pandava hero to live in his palace. Then he gave a great feast on the holy mountain of Raivataka, which lasted for two days. Arjuna looked with love at Krishna's fair sister, Subhadra, a girl of sweet smiles, and desired her for a bride.

Now it was the wish of Krishna'a brother, Balarama, that Subhadra should be given to Duryodhana, whom she would have chosen had a swayamvara been held. So Krishna advised Arjuna to carry her away by force, in accordance with the advice of the sages, who had said: "Men applaud the princes who win brides by abducting them."

When the feast was over, Arjuna drove his chariot from the holy mountain towards Dwaraka until he came close to Subhadra. Nimbly he leapt down and took her by the hand and lifted her into his chariot; then he drove quickly towards the city of Indra-prastha.

Balarama was furious and wanted to pursue Arjuna. He spoke to Krishna, saying: "You are calm, and I can see that Arjuna has done this with your knowledge. You should not have given our sister to him without my consent. But let the deed be on his own head. I will pursue him and kill him and his brothers, one and all."

Krishna replied: "Arjuna is our kinsman and of noble birth, and is a worthy husband for Subhadra. If you pursue him and bring back our sister, no one else will marry her now because that she has been in the house of another. It is better if we send messengers after Arjuna and ask him to return here, so that the marriage may be held according to our rites."

Balarama said: "So be it, seeing that you are obviously pleased with this matter."

And so it came to pass that messengers followed Arjuna and asked him to return with Subhadra to Dwaraka. A great feast was held, and they were married. Arjuna lived there for many months, until the time of his exile came to an end.

THE TRIUMPH OF THE PANDAVAS

When Arjuna returned to Indra-prastha with Subhadra, he was received with great rejoicing by his brothers, and Subhadra was welcomed by Draupadi. The two women grew to love one another, and were both very dear to Pritha. In time, Draupadi became the mother of five sons to her five husbands. Subhadra had one son only, whose name was Abhimanyu, and in the years that followed was an illustrious warrior.

As time went on, the Pandavas grew more and more powerful. They waged great wars, until many kings owed them allegiance; and eventually Yudhishthira decided that the time had come to hold his great Rajasuya sacrifice to celebrate the supremacy of his power over all.

Krishna came to Indra-prastha at this time and said: "There is now just one king who must be overcome before the Imperial sacrifice can be performed: his name is Jarasandha, monarch of Magadha. He has already conquered a great number of kings, slaughtering our dear kinsmen."

This king was of great valour and matchless strength. His body was invulnerable against weapons; not even the gods could wound him. He was also of miraculous birth – he was born of two mothers who had eaten a charmed mango which fell into the lap of his father. Also he had not come to life after birth until he was united by a Rakshasa woman, named Jara, the goddess of the household. So the child was called Jarasandha, meaning 'united by Jara'.

Krishna said to Yudhishthira: "This monarch of Magadha cannot be defeated in battle even by gods or by demons. But he may be overcome in a conflict, fighting with bare arms. Now I am 'Policy', Bhima is 'Strength', and Arjuna is 'Protector'. Together we will surely accomplish the death of Jarasandha."

So Yudhishthira agreed to let Krishna help them. Krishna, Arjuna, and Bhima disguised themselves as Brahmans and went towards the city of Mathura, Jarasandha's capital. When they arrived there they boldly entered the palace of the mighty king. They stood before him decked with flowers, and the king greeted them warmly.

Arjuna and Bhima were silent, but Krishna spoke to Jarasandha, saying: "These two men are observing vows, and will not open their mouths until midnight; after then they will speak."

The king provided for his guests in the sacrificial chamber, and after midnight he visited them. Discovering that they were warriors, he asked them: "Tell me honestly who you are, and why you have come here."

Krishna said: "We are decked with flowers to achieve prosperity, and we have entered the home of our enemy to fulfil the vows of Kshatriyas."

Jarasandha responded: "I have never done you an injury. Why, therefore, do you regard me as your enemy?"

Then Krishna revealed himself, and said: "You have slaughtered our kinsmen because you imagine there lives no man who is as powerful as you. For your sins you are doomed to go to Yama's kingdom to be tortured. But you can go instead to the Heaven of Indra by dying the death of a Kshatriya in battle with your peers. Now, we challenge you to combat. Set free the kings who are in your dungeons, or die at our hands!"

The king refused to set his captives free. Instead he agreed to meet one of them in battle, eventually choosing Bhima. It was agreed that they should fight without weapons, and the two got ready for the fray. Jarasandha fought so fiercely that the combat lasted for thirteen days. In the end the king was slain – his back broken over Bhima's knee.

Krishna went boldly into the palace and set free all the kings who were in captivity. And one by one they took vows to attend the Imperial sacrifice. Then Krishna met with Sahadeva, son of Jarasandha, and installed him as King of Magadha.

When Yudhishthira learned that Jarasandha had been slain, he sent his four brothers with great armies to collect tribute from every king in the world. Some welcomed them; others had to be conquered in battle. But when they had sworn allegiance to Yudhishthira, they joined the Pandava force and assisted in achieving further victories. A whole year went past before the brothers returned to Indra-prastha.

Krishna came from Dwaraka to help Yudhishthira at the ceremony, and he brought with him much wealth and a mighty army.

Stately pavilions were erected for the kings who came to attend the great sacrifice: their turrets were high, and they were swan-white and flecked with radiant gold. Silver and gold adorned the walls of the rooms, which were richly perfumed and carpeted and furnished to befit the royal guests.

The kings came to Indra-prastha in all their splendour and greeted mighty Yudhishthira. Those who were friends brought gifts, and those who had been subdued in battle brought tribute. White-haired and blind old Dhritarashtra came, and with him were Kripa and Bhishma and Vidura. Proud Duryodhana and his brothers also came, professing friendship, and Karna came with bow and spear and mace. Drona and his son, and their enemies Drupada and his son, were there also, and Balarama, Krishna's brother, and their father Vasudeva. And among many others were jealous Sishupala, King of Chedi, and his son, and both wore bright golden armour. Many Brahmans also assembled at Indra-prastha, and Krishna honoured them and washed their feet.

Now there were deep and smouldering jealousies among the assembled kings, and when the time came to honour him who was regarded as the greatest among them by presenting the Arghya, their passions were set ablaze. First Bhishma spoke and said that the honour should be given to Krishna, who was the noblest and greatest among them all. "Krishna," he said, "is the origin of all things; the universe came into being for him alone. He is the incarnation of the Creator, the everlasting one, who is beyond man's comprehension."

When the Arghya was given to Krishna, Sishupala, the King of Chedi, was angered and said: "It does not become you, Yudhishthira, to honour an uncrowned chieftain. Gathered around you are ruling kings of the highest fame. If the honour is due to age, then Vasudeva can claim it before his son; if it is due to the foremost king, then Drupada should be honoured; if it is due to wisdom, Drona is the most worthy; if it is due to holiness, Vyasa is the greatest. Drona's son has more knowledge than Krishna, Duryodhana is peerless among younger men, Kripa is the worthiest priest, and Karna the greatest archer. For what reason should homage be paid to Krishna, who is neither the holiest priest, the wisest teacher, the greatest warrior, nor the foremost chieftain? To the shame of this assembly does it honour the murderer of his own king, this cowherd of low birth." Sishupala hated Krishna because he had kidnapped the beautiful Rukmini, who had been betrothed to him, the mighty King of Chedi.

Krishna then spoke, his voice clam but his eyes bright. To the kings he said: "The evil-tongued Sishupala is descended from a daughter of our race, and in my heart, I have never sought to work ill against a kinsman. But once, when I went eastward, he sacked my sea-swept Dwaraka and laid low its temple; once he broke faith with a king and cast him into prison; once he seized the consort of a king by force; and once he disguised himself as the husband of a chaste princess and deceived her. I have suffered because of his sins, but have sought vengeance because he was of our own race. He has even come after my consort Rukmini, and is worthy of death."

As he spoke, the faces of many kings grew red with shame and anger, but Sishupala laughed aloud and said: "I seek no mercy from Krishna, nor do I fear him."

Then Krishna thought of his discus, and immediately it was in his hand. In anger he shouted: "Hear me, lords of earth! I have promised the mother of Sishupala to pardon a hundred sins committed by her son. And I have fulfilled my vow. But now the number is more than full, and I will slay him before your eyes." Krishna flung the discus, and it struck Sishupala on the neck, so that his head was severed from his body. Then the assembled kings saw a great wonder, for the passion-cleansed soul of Sishupala flowed from his body, beautiful as the sun in heaven, and went towards Krishna. Its eyes were like lotus blooms, and its form like a flame; and it adored Krishna and entered into his body.

The kings all looked on, silent and amazed, while thunder bellowed out of heaven, and lightning flashed, and rain poured down in torrents. Some grew angry, and laid hands on their weapons to avenge the death of Sishupala; others rejoiced that he had been slain; the Brahmans chanted the praises of Krishna.

Yudhishthira commanded his brothers to perform the funeral rites, so the body of Sishupala was burned and then his son was proclaimed King of Chedi.

Afterwards the great sacrifice was performed in peace. Krishna, who had maintained the supremacy of Yudhishthira by slaying a dangerous and jealous rival, looked on benignly.

Holy water was sprinkled by the Brahmans, and all the monarchs bowed and honoured Yudhishthira, saying: "You have extended the fame of your mighty father, Pandu, and you have become even greater than he was. With this sacrifice you have graced your high station and fulfilled all our hopes. Now, emperor over all, permit us to return to our own homes, and bestow your blessing upon us." So one by one they left, and the four Pandavas accompanied the greatest of them to the confines of their kingdoms. Krishna was the last to bid farewell.

Yudhishthira said to him: "To you I owe all things. Because you were here, I was able to perform the great sacrifice."

Krishna replied: "Monarch of all! Rule over your people with a father's wisdom and care. Be to them like rain which nourishes the parched fields; be a shade in hot sunshine; be a cloudless heaven bending over all. Be ever free from pride and passion; ever rule with power and justice and holiness." Then he was gone, and Yudhishthira turned homeward with tear-dimmed eyes.

Meanwhile, Duryodhana had witnessed the triumph of the Pandavas, and his heart burned with jealous rage. He envied the splendour of the palaces at Indra-prastha; he envied the glory achieved by Yudhishthira. He well knew that he could not overcome the Pandavas in open conflict, so he plotted with his brothers to accomplish their fall by artifice and by wrong.

THE GREAT GAMBLING MATCH

Shakuni, **Prince of Gandhara**, and brother of Dhritarashtra's queen, was renowned for his skill as a gambler. He always enjoyed good fortune because he played with loaded dice. Duryodhana plotted with him, determined to conquer the Pandavas, and Shakuni said: "Yudhishthira loves the dice, although he does not know how to play. Ask him to throw dice with me, because there is no gambler who is my equal. I will put him to shame. I will win his kingdom from him."

Duryodhana was pleased at this proposal, and he went to his blind father and asked him to invite the Pandavas to Hastinapur for a friendly gambling match, despite the warnings of the royal counsellors. "If the gods are merciful, my sons will cause no dispute," said Dhritarashtra, "No evil can happen so long as I am near, and Bhishma and Drona are near also. Therefore, let the Pandavas be invited here as my son wishes."

So Vidura, who feared trouble, was sent to Indra-prastha to say: "The maharajah is about to hold a great festival at Hastinapur, and he wishes that Yudhishthira and his brothers, their mother Pritha and their joint wife Draupadi, should be present. A great gambling match will be played."

These words saddened Yudhishthira, who well knew that dice-throwing was often the cause of bitter disputes. Besides, he was unwilling to play Prince Shakuni, that desperate and terrible gambler.... But he could not refuse Dhritarashtra's invitation, or, like a true Kshatriya, disdain a challenge either to fight or to play with his peers.

So it came to pass that the Pandava brothers, with Pritha and Draupadi, travelled to Hastinapur in all their splendour.

Dhritarashtra welcomed them in the presence of Bhishma, Drona, Duryodhana and Karna; then they were received by Queen Gandharai, and the wives of the Kaurava princes. All the daughters-in-law of the blind maharajah became sad because they were jealous of Draupadi's beauty.

The Pandava lords and ladies went to the dwelling which had been prepared for them, and there they were visited in turn by the lords and ladies of Hastinapur.

The following day, Yudhishthira and his brothers went together to the gambling match, which was held in a gorgeous pavilion, roofed with arching crystal and decorated with gold and lapis lazuli: it had a hundred doors and a thousand great columns, and it was richly carpeted. All the princes and great chieftains and warriors of the kingdom were gathered there. And Prince Shakuni of Gandharai was there also with his false dice.

Once the great company were seated, Shakuni invited Yudhishthira to play. Yudhishthira said: "I will play if my opponent will promise to throw fairly, without trickery and deceit. Deceitful gambling is sinful, and unworthy a Kshatriya; there is no prowess in it. Wise men do not applaud a player who wins by foul means."

To this Shakuni replied: "A skilled gambler always plays to beat his opponent. Such is the practise in all contests; a man plays or fights to achieve victory.... But if you are in dread of me, Yudhishthira, and afraid that you will lose, perhaps it better if you did not play at all."

"Having been challenged, I cannot withdraw," said Yudhishthira. "I do not fear to fight or to play with any man.... But first tell me who is to lay stakes equally with me."

Then Duryodhana spoke, saying: "I will supply jewels and gold and any stakes of equal value to what you can set down. It is for me that Shakuni, my uncle, is to throw the dice."

Yudhishthira replied: "This is a strange challenge. One man is to throw the dice and another is to lay the stakes. Such is contrary to all practice. If, however, you are determined to play in this fashion, let the game begin."

The king of Indra-prastha knew then that the match would not be played fairly. But nevertheless he sat down to throw dice with Shakuni. At the first throw Yudhishthira lost; indeed, he lost at every throw on that fateful day. He gambled away all his money and all his jewels, his jewelled chariot with golden bells, and all his cattle; still he played on, and he lost his thousand war elephants, his slaves and beautiful slave girls, and the remainder of his goods; and next, he staked and lost the whole kingdom of the Pandavas, except for the lands which he had gifted to the Brahmans. Still he did not quit, despite the advice offered him by the chieftains who were there. One by one he staked and lost his brothers; he even staked himself and lost.

Shakuni then said to Yudhishthira: "You have done wrong in staking your own self, for now you have become a slave; but if you will stake Draupadi now and win, all that you have lost will be restored to you."

Yudhishthira replied: "So be it. I will stake Draupadi."

At these words the whole company was stricken with horror. Vidura fainted, and the faces of Bhishma and Drona grew pale; many groaned; but Duryodhana and his brothers openly rejoiced. So Shakuni threw the dice, and Yudhishthira lost this the last throw. Draupadi had been won by Duryodhana.

Then all the onlookers gazed at one another, silent and wide-eyed. Karna and Duhsasana and other young princes laughed aloud. Duryodhana rose proudly and spoke to Vidura, saying: "Now go to Draupadi and ask her to come here to sweep the chambers with the other helpers."

Vidura angrily replied: "Your words are wicked, Duryodhana. You cannot command a lady of royal birth to become a household slave. Besides, she is not your slave, because Yudhishthira staked his own freedom before he staked Draupadi. You can win nothing from a slave who had no power to stake the princess."

Duryodhana cursed Vidura, and asked one of his servants to bring Draupadi to him. But Vidura continued: "Today Duryodhana is deprived of his reason. Dishonesty is one of the doors to hell. By practising dishonesty Duryodhana will accomplish the ruin of the Kauravas."

The beautiful Draupadi was sitting peacefully outside the palace on the banks of the Ganges when suddenly, as a jackal stealthily enters the den of a lion, the servant sent by Duryodhana arrived and stood before her. He said to her: "Oh Queen, the mighty son of Pandu has played and lost; he has lost all, even his reason, and he has staked you, and you have been won by Duryodhana. And now Duryodhana sends me to say that you are to become his slave, and must obey him like the other female slaves. So come with me."

Draupadi was astonished by words, and in her anguish, she cried: "Have I heard you right? Has my husband, the king, staked and lost me in his madness? Did he stake and loose anything else besides?"

The man replied: "Yudhishthira has lost all his riches and his kingdom; he staked his brothers and lost them one by one;

he staked himself and lost; and then he staked you and lost also. Therefore, come with me."

To this Draupadi angrily replied: "If my lord staked himself and became a slave, he could not wager me, because a slave owns neither his own life nor the life of another. Say this to my husband, and to Duryodhana say: 'Draupadi has not been won'."

The man returned to the assembly and repeated the words which Draupadi had said, but Yudhishthira bowed his head and was silent.

Duryodhana was angered by the defiant answer of the proud queen, and he said to his brother Duhsasana: "The sons of Pandu are our slaves, and your heart is without fear for them. Go to the palace and ask the princess, my humble servant, to come here quickly."

Red-eyed and proud Duhsasana hurried to the palace. He entered the inner chambers and stood before Draupadi, who was dressed in a single robe, while her hair hung loosely.

The evil-hearted Kaurava said: "Oh princess of Panchala with fair lotus eyes, you have been staked and lost fairly at the game of hazard. Hurry, therefore, and stand before your lord Duryodhana, for you are now his bright-eyed slave."

Draupadi trembled with fear. She covered her eyes with her hands before the hated Duhsasana; her cheeks turned pale and her heart sickened. Then suddenly she leapt up and tried to escape to an inner room.

But the evil-hearted prince seized her by the hair. He no longer feared the sons of Pandu, and the beautiful princess quivered and shook. Crouching on her knees, she cried angrily, tears streaming from her lotus eyes: "Be gone! Oh shameless prince. Can a modest woman appear before strangers in loose attire?"

The stern and cruel Duhsasana replied: "Even you were naked now, you must follow me. Have you not become a slave, fairly staked and fairly won? From now on you will serve among the other slaves."

Trembling and faint, Draupadi was dragged through the streets by Duhsasana. When she stood before the elders and the chieftains in the pavilion she cried: "Forgive me for coming here in this unseemly plight...." Bhishma, Drona and the other elders who were there hung their heads in shame.

To Duhsasana Draupadi said angrily: "Stop your wickedness! Defile me no longer with unclean hands." Weeping, she cried: "Hear and help me, elders. You have wives and children of your own. Will you permit this wrong to be continued. Answer me now."

But no man said a word.

Draupadi wept and said: "Why this silence?... Will no man among you protect a sinless woman?... Lost is the fame of the Kauravas, the ancient glory of Bharata, and the prowess of the Kshatriyas!... Why will the sons of Pandu not protect their outraged queen?... And has Bhishma lost his virtue and Drona his power?... Will Yudhishthira no longer defend one who is wronged?... Why are you all silent while this deed of shame is done before you?"

Draupadi glanced round the sons of Pandu one by one, and their hearts thirsted for vengeance. Bhishma's face was dark, Drona clenched his teeth, and Vidura, white and angry, gazed at Duhsasana with amazement while he tore off Draupadi's veil and addressed her with foul words. When she looked towards the

Kaurava brothers, Duhsasana said: "Ha! On whom dare you to look now, slave?"

Shakuni and Kama laughed to hear Draupadi called a slave, and they cried out: "Well said, well said!"

Duhsasana tried to strip the princess naked before the assembly; but Draupadi, in her distress, prayed aloud to Krishna, invoking him as the creator of all and the soul of the universe, and begged him to help her. Krishna heard her, and multiplied her garments so that Duhsasana was unable to accomplish his wicked purpose.

Karna spoke to Draupadi and said: "It is not your fault, princess, that you have fallen so low. A woman's fate is controlled by her husband; Yudhishthira has gambled you away. You were his, and must accept your fate. From now on, you will be the slave of the Kaurava princes. You must obey them and please them with your beauty…. You should now seek for yourself a husband who will love you too well to stake you at dice and suffer you to be put to shame…. Be assured that no one will blame a humble servant, as you now are, who looks lovingly at great and noble warriors. Remember that Yudhishthira is no longer your husband; he has become a slave, and a slave can have no wife…. Ah, sweet Princess of Panchala, those whom you chose at your swayamvara have gambled and lost you; they have lost their kingdom and also their power."

At these words Bhima's chest heaved with anger and shame. Red-eyed he scowled at Karna; he seemed to be the image of flaming Wrath. To Yudhishthira he spoke grimly, saying: "If you had not staked our freedom and our queen, elder brother, this son of a charioteer would not have taunted us in this manner." Yudhishthira bowed his head in shame, not saying a word.

Arjuna reprimanded Bhima for his bitter words; but Pritha's mighty son, the slayer of Asuras, said: "If I am not permitted to punish the tormentor of Draupadi, bring me a fire so that I may thrust my hands into it."

A deep uproar rose from the assembly, and the elders applauded the wronged lady and censured Duhsasana.

Bhima clenched his hands and, with quivering lips, cried out: "Hear my terrible words, Oh Kshatriyas…. May I never reach Heaven if I do not seize Duhsasana in battle and, tearing open his breast, drink his very life blood!…" He continued: "If Yudhishthira will allow me, I will slay the wretched sons of Dhritarashtra without weapons, as a lion slays small animals."

Bhishma, Vidura and Drona begged Bhima to refrain, whilst Duryodhana gloried in his hour of triumph. He taunted Yudhishthira saying: "You are the spokesman for your brothers, and they owe you obedience. Speak and say, have you lost your kingdom and your brothers and your own self? Have you even lost the beautiful Draupadi? And has she, your wedded wife, become our humble servant?"

Yudhishthira heard him with downcast eyes, but his lips did not move…. Then Karna laughed; but Bhishma, pious and old, wept in silence.

Then Duryodhana looked at Draupadi, and, baring his knee, invited her to sit on it. Bhima gnashed his teeth – unable to restrain his pent-up anger. With eyes flashing like lightning, and in a voice like thunder he cried out: "Hear my vow! May I never reach Heaven or meet my ancestors if, for these sinful deeds, I do not break Duryodhana in battle, and drink the blood of Duhsasana!"

Meanwhile, Dhritarashtra was sitting in his palace, knowing nothing of what was happening. The Brahmans were peacefully chanting their evening mantras, when a jackal howled in the sacrificial chamber. Asses brayed in response, and ravens answered their cries from all sides. Dhritarashtra shook with terror when he heard these dreadful omens, and when Vidura had told him all that had taken place, he said: "The sinful Duryodhana has brought shame upon the head of King Drupada's sweet daughter, and so has courted death and destruction. May the prayers of a sorrowful old man remove the wrath of Heaven which these dark omens have revealed."

The blind maharajah was led to Draupadi, and in front of all the elders and princes he spoke to her, kindly and gently, saying: "Noble queen and virtuous daughter, wife of Yudhishthira, and purest of all women, you are very dear to my heart. My sons have wronged you today. Please forgive them now, and let the wrath of Heaven be averted. Whatever you ask of me will be yours."

Draupadi replied: "Oh mighty maharajah, you are merciful. I ask you to set free my lord and husband Yudhishthira. Having been a prince, it is not seemly that he should be called a slave."

"Your wish is granted," said Dhritarashtra. "Ask a second favour and blessing, fair one. You deserve more than one."

So Draupadi said: "Let Arjuna and Bhima and their younger brothers also be set free and allowed to leave now with their horses and their chariots and their weapons."

Dhritarashtra replied: "So be it, princess. Ask yet another favour and blessing and it will be granted." But to this Draupadi said: "I seek no other favour: I am a Kshatriya by birth, and do not crave for gifts without end. You have freed my husbands from slavery: they will regain their fortunes by their own mighty deeds."

Then the Pandava brothers departed from Hastinapur with Pritha and Draupadi, and returned to the city of Indra-prastha.

The Kauravas were furious. Duryodhana approached his royal father and said: "You have permitted the Pandava princes to go in anger; now they will get ready to wage war against us to regain their kingdom and their wealth; when they return they will kill us all. Allow us, therefore, to throw dice with them once again. We will stake our liberty, and will agree that the side which loses shall go into exile for twelve years, and into hiding for a year thereafter. By this arrangement a bloody war may be averted."

Dhritarashtra granted his son's wish and recalled the Pandavas. So it came to pass that Yudhishthira sat down once again to play with Shakuni, and once again Shakuni brought out the loaded dice. Before long the game ended, and Yudhishthira had lost.

Duhsasana danced with joy and cried out: "Now the empire of Duryodhana is established."

But Bhima replied: "Do not be too happy, Duhsasana. Hear and remember my words: May I never reach Heaven until I drink your blood!"

The Pandava princes then cast off their royal garments and dressed themselves in deerskins like humble beggars. Yudhishthira said farewell to Dhritarashtra and Bhishma and Kripa and Vidura, one by one, and he even said farewell to the Kaurava brothers. Vidura said to him: "Your mother, the royal Pritha, is too old to wander with you through forest and jungle. Let her remain here until the years of your exile have passed away." Yudhishthira agreed and asked for his blessing. Vidura blessed each one of the Pandava princes, saying: "Be saintly in exile, subdue your passions, learn truth in your sorrow, and return in happiness. May these eyes be blessed by seeing you in Hastinapur once again."

Pritha wept over Draupadi and blessed her. But before the Princess of Panchala left the city she made a vow, saying: "From this day on my hair will fall over my forehead until Bhima has slain Duhsasana; then Bhima shall tie up my tresses while his hands are still wet with Duhsasana's blood."

The Pandava princes wandered towards the deep forest, and Draupadi followed them.

THE PANDAVAS' SORROW

Yudhishthira lamented his fate to the Brahmans as he wandered towards the forest. "Our kingdom is lost to us," he said, "and our fortune; everything is lost; we go in sorrow, and must live on fruits and roots and the produce of the chase. In the woods are many perils – reptiles and hungry wild animals seeking their prey."

A Brahman advised him to call upon the sun god, so Yudhishthira prayed: "Oh sun, you are the eye of the universe, the soul of all things that are; you are the creator; you are Indra, you are Vishnu, you are Brahma, you are Prajapati, lord of creatures, father of gods and man; you are fire, you are mind; you are lord of all, the eternal Brahma." Then Surya appeared and gave Yudhishthira a copper pot, which was ever to be filled with food for the brothers.

For twelve long years the Pandavas lived in the woods with their wife Draupadi, and Dhaumya, the Brahman. Whatever food they obtained, they set apart a portion for the holy men and ate the rest. They visited holy shrines; they bathed in sacred waters; they performed their devotions. Often they talked with Brahmans and sages, who instructed them in religious works and blessed them, and also promised them that their lost kingdom would be restored in time.

They wandered in sunshine and in shade; they lived in pleasant places, amidst abundant fruits and surrounded by flowers. They also suffered from tempests and heavy rains, when their path would be torn by streams, and Draupadi would faint, and all the brothers would be weary and in despair. Then the mighty Bhima would carry them all on his back and under his arms.

The gods appeared before the brothers during their exile. Dharma, god of wisdom and holiness, asked his son, Yudhishthira many questions which he answered well. Hanuman, son of Vayu, the wind god, came to Bhima. One day the strong Pandava, who was also Vayu's son, was hurrying on his way and went swift as the wind; the earth shook under him and trees fell down, and at one touch of his foot he killed tigers and lions and even great elephants that sought to block his path. Hanuman shrank to the size of an ape, but his tail spread out in such great proportions across Bhima's path, that he was compelled to stop and stand still. He spoke to Bhima and told the tale of Rama and Sita. Suddenly he grew as tall as a mountain and transported his brother, the Pandava, to the garden of Kuvera, King of Yakshas, lord of treasure, who lived on Mount Kailasa in the Himalayas. There Bhima found sweet-scented flowers which gave youth to those who had grown old and turned grief into joy; these he gave to Draupadi.

Krishna came to visit the Pandavas in the forest, and Draupadi said to him: "The evil-hearted Duryodhana dared to claim me for his slave. Shame on the Pandavas who looked on in silence when I was humiliated. Is it not the duty of a husband to protect his wife?... These husbands of mine, who have the prowess of lions, saw me afflicted, but did not lift a hand to save me." Draupadi wept bitter tears from her exquisite coppery eyes, but Krishna comforted her by saying: "You will yet live to see the wives of those men who persecuted you grieving over their fallen husbands as they lie soaked in their blood.... I will help the Pandavas, and you will once again be a queen over kings."

Krishna said to Yudhishthira: "Had I been at Dwaraka when you were called upon to visit Hastinapur, this unfair match would not have taken place, as I would have warned Dhritarashtra. But I was waging a war against demons.... What can I do, now that this disaster is done?... It is not easy to confine the waters after the dam has burst."

After Krishna returned to his kingdom, Draupadi continued to lament her fate. She said to Yudhishthira: "The sinful, evil-hearted Duryodhana has a heart of steel.... Oh king, I lie on the ground, remembering my soft luxurious bed. I, who sit on a grass mat, cannot forget my chairs of ivory. I have seen you in the court of kings; now you are a beggar. I have gazed at you in your silken robes, who are now dressed in rags.... What peace can my heart know now, remembering the things that have been? My heart is full of grief.... Does your anger not rise up, seeing your brothers in distress and me in sorrow? How can you forgive

your cruel enemy? Are you devoid of anger, Yudhishthira?...
A Kshatriya who does not act at the right moment – who
forgives the enemy he should strike down, is the most despised
of all men. The hour has now come for you to seek vengeance;
the present is not a time for forgiveness."

But the wise Yudhishthira replied: "Anger is sinful; it is
the cause of destruction. He who is angry cannot distinguish
between right and wrong. An angry man may commit his own
soul to hell. Wise men control their wrath in order to achieve
prosperity both in this world and in the next. A weak man
cannot control his wrath; but men of wisdom and insight seek
to subdue their passions, knowing that he who is angry cannot
see things in their true perspective. Only ignorant people regard
anger as equivalent to energy.... Because fools commit folly,
should I who seek wisdom do likewise?... If wrongs were not
righted except by chastisement, the whole world would quickly
be destroyed, because anger is destruction; it makes men kill one
another. It is right to be forgiving; a man should forgive every
wrong. He who is forgiving shall attain to eternal bliss; he who
is foolish and cannot forgive is destroyed both in this world and
in the next. Forgiveness is the greatest virtue; it is sacrifice; it is
tradition; it is inspiration. Forgiveness, beautiful one, is holiness;
it is truth; it is Brahma. The wise man who learns how to forgive
attains to Brahma (the highest god). Draupadi, remember the
verses of the sage:

> Let not thy wrath possess thee,
> But worship peace with joy;
> Who yieldeth to temptation
> That great god will destroy.

He who is self-controlled will attain to sovereignty, and the qualities of self-control are forgiveness and gentleness. Let me attain with self-control to everlasting goodness!"

To this Draupadi replied: "I bow down before the Creator and Ordainer of life and the three worlds, because my mind, it seems, has been dimmed. Men are influenced by deeds, as deeds produce consequences; by works they are set free.... Man can never gain prosperity by forgiveness and gentleness; your virtue has not shielded you; you are following a shadow.... Men should not obey their own wills, but the will of the god who has ordained all things.... Like a doll is moved by strings, so are living creatures moved by the lord of all; he plays with them like a child with a toy.... Those who have done wrong are now happy, and I am full of grief and distress. Can I praise your god who allows such inequality? What reward does your god receive when he allows Duryodhana to prosper – he who is full of evil; he who destroys virtue and religion? If a sin does not rebound on the sinner, then a man's might is the greatest force and not your god, and I sorrow for those who are devoid of might."

Shocked, Yudhishthira said: "Your words are the words of an unbeliever! I do not act merely for the sake of reward. I give because it is right to give, and I sacrifice because it is my duty to do so. I follow in the paths of those who have lived wise and holy lives, because of that my heart turns toward goodness. I am no trader in goodness, ever looking for the rewards. The man who doubts virtue will be born among the brutes; he will never achieve everlasting bliss. Do not doubt the ancient religion of your people!

God will reward; he is the giver of fruits for deeds; virtue and vice bear fruits.... The wise are content with little in this world; the fools are not content although they receive a lot, because they will have no joy in the future.... The gods are shrouded in mystery; who can pierce the cloud which covers the doings of the gods? Although you cannot see the fruits of goodness, do not doubt your religion or the gods. Let your scepticism give room to faith. Do not slander the great god, but endeavour to learn how to know him. Do not turn away from the Supreme One who gives eternal life, Draupadi."

Draupadi said: "I do not slander my god, the lord of all, for in my sorrow I simply rave.... But yet I believe that a man should act. Without acts no one can live. He who believes in chance and destiny and is inactive, lives a life of weakness and helplessness which cannot last long. Success comes to he who acts, and success depends on time and circumstance. So a wise Brahman once taught me."

Bhima then spoke, charging Yudhishthira with weakness, and pleading with him to seize the sovereignty from Duryodhana: "You are like froth," he cried. "You are unripe fruit! Oh king, strike down your enemies! Battle is the highest virtue for a Kshatriya."

But Yudhishthira calmly replied: "My heart burns because of our sufferings. But I have given my pledge to remain in exile, and it cannot be violated, Bhima. Virtue is greater than life and prosperity in this world; it is the way to celestial bliss."

Then they were all silent, and they pondered over these things.

ARJUNA'S CELESTIAL GIFTS

Now the Pandavas needed celestial weapons, because these were owned by Drona, Bhishma and Karna. In time, therefore, the holy sage Vyasa appeared before Arjuna and told him to go to Mount Kailasa, the high seat of the gracious god Shiva, and to perform penances there with deep devotion in order to obtain gifts of arms. So Arjuna went on his way, and when he reached the mountain of Shiva he went through great austerities: he raised his arms in the air and, leaning on nothing, stood on his tiptoes; for food he ate withered leaves at first, then he fed on air alone.

The Rishis pleaded with Shiva, fearing disaster from the penances of Arjuna. Then the god assumed the form of a hunter and went towards Indra's warrior son, whom he challenged to single combat. First they fought with weapons; then they wrestled one another fiercely. In the end Arjuna fell to the ground. When that brave Pandava regained consciousness he made a clay image of Shiva, threw himself down in worship, and made an offering of flowers. Soon afterwards he saw his opponent wearing the garland he had given, and he knew that he had wrestled with Shiva himself. Arjuna fell down before him, and the god gave him a celestial weapon named Pasupata. Then a great storm broke out, and the earth shook, and the spirit of the weapon stood beside Arjuna, ready to obey his will.

Next appeared Indra, king of gods, Varuna, god of waters, Yama, king of the dead, and Kuvera, lord of treasures, and they stood on the mountain summit in all their glory; to Arjuna they gave gifts of other celestial weapons.

Afterwards Indra transported his son to his own bright city, the celestial Swarga, where the flowers always bloom and sweet music is forever wafted on fragrant winds. There he saw sea-born Apsaras, the heavenly brides of gods and heroes, and music-loving Gandharvas, who sang songs and danced merrily in their joy. Urvasi, a beautiful Apsara with bright eyes and silken hair, looked with love at Arjuna; but she sought in vain to subdue him, at which she scornfully said: "Kama, god of love, has wounded me with his arrows, yet you scorn me. For this, Arjuna, you will live for a season as a dancer and musician, ignored by women." Arjuna was troubled by this, but Indra told him that this curse would work in his favour. So Arjuna remained in Indra's fair city for five years. He achieved great skill in music, in dance and song. He was also trained to wield the celestial weapons which the gods had given to him.

Now the demons and giants who are named the Daityas and Danavas were the ancient enemies of Indra. They hailed from the lowest division of the underworld beneath the ocean floor, in a place called Patala. And a day came when Arjuna waged war with them. He rode away in Indra's great car, which sailed through the air like a bird, driven by Matali. When he reached the shore of the sea, the waves rose against him like great mountains, and the waters were divided; he saw demon fish and giant tortoises, and vessels laden down with rubies. But he did not pause, as he was without fear. Arjuna was eager for battle, and he blew a mighty blast on his war shell: the Daityas and Danavas heard him and quaked with terror. Then the demons beat their drums and blew their trumpets, and amid the dreadful racket the wallowing sea monsters rose up and leapt over the waves against Indra's great son. But Arjuna chanted mantras; he shot clouds of bright arrows; he fought with his bright celestial weapons, and the furies were thwarted and beaten back. They then sent fire against him and water, and they flung huge rocks; but he fought on until in the end he triumphed, killing all that stood against him.

Afterwards the valiant hero quickly rode towards the city of demons and giants which is named Hiranyapura. The women came out to lure him, calling aloud. He heard them but did not pause. All these evil giant women fled in confusion, terrified by the noise of Indra's celestial car and the driving of Matali, and their earrings and necklaces fell from their bodies like boulders tumbling and thundering down mountain slopes.

When Arjuna entered the city of Hiranyapura he gazed with wonder at the mighty chariots with ten thousand horses, which were stately and proud. And he wrecked the dwellings of the Daityas and Danavas.

Indra praised his warrior son for his valour in overcoming the demons and giants of the ocean, and he gave him a chain of gold, a bright crown, and the war shell which gave a mighty, thunderous blast.

SECOND EXILE OF THE PANDAVAS

During the years that Arjuna lived in Indra's celestial city, Yudhishthira and his three younger brothers, with Draupadi and the priest Dhaumya, stayed for a time in the forest of Kamyaka. Great sages visited them there, one teaching Yudhishthira the skill of throwing dice. Others led the wanderers to sacred waters, in which they were cleansed of their sins, and they achieved great virtues. And the sages told them many tales of men and women who suffered and made self-sacrifices, undergoing long exiles and performing penances so as to learn great wisdom and win favour from the gods.

Thereafter the exiles went northward towards the Himalayas, and eventually in the distance they saw the home of Kuvera, lord of treasure and King of Yakshas. They gazed at palaces of crystal and gold; the high walls were studded with jewels, and the gleaming ramparts and turrets were adorned by dazzling streamers. They saw beautiful gardens of bright flowers, and soft winds came towards them laden with perfume; wonderful were the trees, and they were vocal with the songs of birds.

Kuvera came and spoke words of wisdom to Yudhishthira, counselling him to be patient and long-suffering, and to wait for the right time and place to display his Kshatriya prowess.

The exiles wandered on, and one day they saw the bright car of Indra, and they worshipped Matali, the charioteer. Then Indra arrived with his hosts of Apsaras and Gandharvas, and when they had adored him, the god promised Yudhishthira that he would once again reign in splendour over all men.

Arjuna appeared, and the Pandavas family rejoiced. They all returned together to Kamyaka. There they were visited by Markandeya, the mighty sage, whose life endures through all the world's ages, and he spoke of the mysteries and all that had taken place from the beginning, and revealed to them full knowledge of the Deluge.

Now while the Pandavas were enduring great suffering in the forest, Karna spoke to Duryodhana and prevailed upon him to spy on their misery. So Dhritarashtra's son left, as was the custom every three years, to inspect the cattle and brand the calves. And with him went Karna and many princes and courtiers, and also a thousand ladies of the royal household. However, when they all drew near to the forest, they found that the Gandharvas and Apsaras, who had descended to make merry there, would not permit the royal train to advance. Duryodhana sent messages to the Gandharva king, commanding him to leave; but the celestial spirits did not fear him, and instead came forward to fight. A great war was waged, and the Kauravas were defeated. Karna fled, whilst Duryodhana and many of his courtiers and all the royal ladies were taken prisoners.

It happened that some of Duryodhana's followers who managed to flee soon reached the place where the Pandavas were, and told them how their kinsmen had been overcome. So Arjuna, Bhima and the two younger brothers went to the Gandharvas and fought with them until they were compelled to release the royal prisoners. The proud Duryodhana was humbled by his enemies' actions.

Yudhishthira gave a feast to the Kauravas, and he called Duryodhana his 'brother'. Duryodhana pretended to be pleased, although in his heart he was mortified. After this the sullen and angry Duryodhana resolved to end his life. His friends protested with him, but he said: "I have nothing to live for now. I do not desire friendship, or wealth, or power, or enjoyment. Do not delay my purpose, but leave me now. I will eat no more food, and I will wait here until I die. Return, therefore, to Hastinapur and respect and obey those who are greater than me." Then he purified himself with water, and sat down to wait for the end, dressed in rags and absorbed in silent meditation.

But the Daityas and Danavas did not want their favourite king to end his life in case their power should be weakened, so they sent a strange goddess to the forest, who carried him away in the night. Then the demons promised to help him in the coming struggle against the Pandavas. Duryodhana was comforted by this, and abandoned his vow to die in solitude. So he quickly returned to Hastinapur and resumed his position.

Soon afterwards, when the princes and the elders sat in council with the maharajah, wise old Bhishma praised the Pandava princes for their valour and generosity, and advised Duryodhana to offer them his friendship, so that the kinsmen might ever afterwards live together in peace. Duryodhana did not answer. Instead, smiling bitterly, he rose up and walked out of the council chamber. This made Bhishma angry, and he too left and went to his own house.

Then Duryodhana sought to rival the glory of Yudhishthira by holding an Imperial sacrifice. Duhsasana, with evil heart, sent messengers to Yudhishthira, inviting him to attend with his brothers; but Yudhishthira said: "Although this great sacrifice will reflect honour on all the descendants of King Bharata, and therefore on me and my brothers, I cannot be present because our years of exile have not yet come to an end."

He spoke calmly and with dignity, but Bhima was enraged and exclaimed: "Messengers of Duryodhana, tell your master that when our years of exile are over, Yudhishthira will offer up a mighty sacrifice with weapons and burn the whole family of Dhritarashtra."

Duryodhana received these messages in silence. And when the sacrifice was held, Karna took a vow and said Duryodhana: "I will neither eat venison nor wash my feet until I have slain Arjuna."

Spies rushed to the Pandavas and related all that had taken place at the sacrifice, and also the words which Karna had spoken. When Yudhishthira heard of Karna's terrible vow, it caused him great sorrow, because he knew that a day must come when Arjuna and Karna would meet in deadly conflict.

One day Surya, god of the sun, warned Karna that Indra had resolved to strip him of his celestial armour and earrings. "But," said Surya, "you can demand in exchange a heavenly weapon which has the power to slay gods and demons and mortal men."

So it came that Indra stood before Karna, disguised as a Brahman, and asked for his armour and earrings. Having vowed to give the Brahmans whatever they might ask of him, Karna took off his armour and earrings and gave them to the king of the gods. In exchange he demanded an infallible weapon. Indra granted his request, but smiled and went on his way, knowing that the triumph of the Pandavas was now assured.

One day soon after this Jayadratha, King of Sindhu, passed through the wood when the Pandavas had gone hunting. He watched Draupadi with eyes of love, and, despite her warnings, carried her away in his chariot.

When the Pandavas returned and were told what had taken place, they set out in pursuit of the king of Sindhu, who left his chariot and hid when they came near. Bhima turned to Yudhishthira and said: "Return now with Draupadi and our brothers. Although the king should seek refuge in the underworld, he will not escape my vengeance."

Yudhishthira replied: "Remember, Bhima, that although Jayadratha has committed a grievous sin, he is our kinsman. He is married to the sister of Duryodhana."

To this Draupadi exclaimed: "He is worthy of death. He is the worst of kings and the vilest of men! Have the sages not said that he who carries off the wife of another in times of peace must certainly be put to death?"

When Bhima found Jayadratha, he threw him down and cut off his hair except five locks; then the strong warrior promised to spare the king's life if he would swear allegiance to Yudhishthira and declare himself his slave. So the King of Sindhu had to bow down to Yudhishthira like a humble servant. He then left in shame and returned to his own country.

THE VOICE OF THE WATERS

When the twelfth year of exile was near to an end, the Pandava brothers thought it was time to leave the forest. But before they went a strange and awful adventure threatened them with disaster. One day a stag appeared and carried away the twigs with which a Brahman was accustomed to use to kindle his holy fire. The Brahman begged Yudhishthira to pursue the animal, and the Pandavas endeavoured in vain to kill it or recover the sacred twigs. Weary with the chase, they eventually sat down to rest. They were all thirsty, and one of them climbed a tree to look for signs of water. When it was discovered that a pond was nearby, Yudhishthira sent Nakula towards it. The young man approached the water, and as he bend down he heard a voice which said: "Answer what I shall ask of you before you drink or draw water."

But Nakula's thirst was greater than his fear, so he drank the waters; then he fell dead. Sahadeva followed him, wondering what had delayed his brother. He too gazed greedily at the pool, and he too heard the voice, but did not listen and drank; and he also fell dead.

Arjuna was next to go towards the water. The voice spoke to him, and he answered with anger: "Who are you that would hinder me so? Reveal yourself, and my arrows will speak to you!" Then he drew his bow, and his arrows flew thick and fast like raindrops. But his bravery was for nothing, because when he drank he also fell dead like the others. Bhima followed him, and stooped and drank, unheeding the voice, and he was stricken down just like Arjuna, Nakula and Sahadeva before him.

Eventually wise Yudhishthira approached the pond. He saw his brothers lying dead, and grieved over them. Then, as he neared the water, the voice spoke once again, and he answered it, saying: "Who are you?"

The voice said: "I am a Yaksha. I warned your brothers not to drink this water until they had answered what I should ask them, but they disregarded my warning and I laid them in death. If you will answer my questions you can, however, drink here and not be afraid."

Yudhishthira replied: "Speak and I will answer you."

The voice said: "Who makes the sun rise? Who keeps him company? Who makes the sun go down? In whom is the sun established?"

Yudhishthira responded: "Brahma makes the sun rise; the gods accompany him; Dharma makes the sun set; in truth is the sun established."

The voice then said: "What sleeps with open eyes? What does not move after birth? What is that which has no heart? What is that which swells of itself?"

Yudhishthira answered: "A fish sleeps with open eyes; an egg does not move after birth; a stone has no heart; a river swells of itself."

The Voice went on: "What makes The Way? What is called Water? What is called Food? What is called Poison?"

Yudhishthira retorted: "They that are devout make The Way; space is called Water; the cow is Food; a request is Poison."

The voice said: "Who is spoken of as the unconquered enemy of man? What is spoken of as the enemy's disease? Who is regarded as holy? Who is regarded as unholy?"

Yudhishthira replied: "Man's unconquered enemy is anger, and his disease is greed; he who seeks the good of all is holy; he who is selfishly cold is unholy."

The voice said: "Who are worthy of eternal torment?"

Yudhishthira responded: "He who says to the Brahman whom he has asked to his house, I have nothing to give; he who declares the Vedas to be false; he who is rich and yet gives nothing to the poor."

The voice addressed many such questions to wise Yudhishthira, and he answered each one patiently and with knowledge. Then the Yaksha revealed himself in the form of Dharma, god of wisdom and justice. He was the celestial father of Yudhishthira. To his son he granted two favours; and

Yudhishthira requested that his brothers should be restored to life, and that they should all have the power to remain unrecognized by anyone in the three worlds for the space of a year.

AN END TO THE EXILE

efore the Pandavas left the forest, Yudhishthira invoked the goddess Durga, giver of favours, saying: "Oh slayer of the Buffalo Asura, you are worshipped by the gods, for you are the protector of the three worlds. Chief of all deities, bless us. Grant us victory, and help us in our distress." The goddess heard Yudhishthira, and confirmed the promise of Dharma that the Pandava brothers and Draupadi would remain unrecognized during the last year of their exile.

Then the wanderers concealed their weapons in a tree, and went together towards the city of Virata so that they might hide themselves. According to the terms of their banishment, they would have to spend a further twelve years in the jungle if the Kauravas discovered their whereabouts.

The Pandavas found favour in the eyes of the king. Yudhishthira became his instructor in the art of playing with dice, because he was accustomed to lose heavily. Bhima was made chief cook. Arjuna taught dancing and music to the ladies of the harem. Nakula was given care of horses, and Sahadeva of cattle. The queen was drawn towards Draupadi, who offered to become a servant on condition that she should not have to wash the feet of anyone, or eat food left over after meals; and on these terms she was engaged. The queen feared that Draupadi's great beauty would attract lovers and cause strife; but the forlorn woman said that she was protected by five Gandharvas, and was without fear.

Bhima soon won renown for his matchless strength. At a great festival he overcame a wrestler from a far country who was named Jimúta, and he received many gifts. The king took great pride in him, and often took him to the apartments of the women, where he wrestled with caged tigers and lions and bears, slaying each one at will with a single blow. Indeed, all the brothers were well loved by the monarch because of their loyal services.

It happened that the queen's brother, Kichaka, a mighty warrior and commander of the royal army, was smitten with the beautiful Draupadi, and in time he sought to carry her away. But one night Bhima waited for him when he came stealthily towards Draupadi, and after a long struggle the strong Pandava killed him. Then Bhima broke all this prince's bones and rolled up his body into a ball of flesh.

Kichaka's kinsmen were horrified when they discovered what had happened, and they said: "No man has done this awful deed; the Gandharvas have taken vengeance." In their anger they seized Draupadi, intent on burning her on the pyre with the body of Kichaka; but Bhima disguised himself and went to her rescue. He scattered her tormentors in flight, killing many with a great tree which he had uprooted.

The king was terror-stricken, and spoke to the queen, who in turn asked Draupadi to leave Virata. But the wife of the Pandavas begged to remain in the royal service; and she said that her Gandharva protectors would serve the king in his greatest hour of peril, which, she foretold, was already near to him. So the queen supported her, and Draupadi stayed there.

Soon afterwards the King of Trigartis, hearing that mighty Kichaka was dead, plotted with the Kauravas at Indra-prastha to attack the city of Virata in order to capture the kingdom. Duryodhana agreed to help him, so the King of Trigartis invaded the kingdom from the north, while the Kauravas marched against Virata from the south.

And so it came to pass that on the last day of the thirteenth year of the Pandavas' exile, the first raid took place from the north, and many cattle were carried off. Yudhishthira and Bhima, with Nakula and Sahadeva, offered to help when they heard that the King of Virata had been captured by his enemies. The Pandavas went off to rescue the monarch. They soon defeated the raiders and rescued their prisoner; they also seized the King of Trigartis, and forced him to submit to his rival before he was allowed to return to his own city.

Meanwhile the Kauravas had advanced from the south. Uttar, son of the King of Virata, went against them, with Arjuna as his charioteer. When the young man, however, saw his enemies, he wanted to flee, but his driver forced him to remain in the chariot.

Arjuna recovered his own weapons from the tree in which they were hidden. Then, fully armed, he rode against the Kauravas, who said: "If this is Arjuna, he and his brothers must go into exile for another twelve years."

Bhishma responded: "The thirteenth year of concealment is now ended." The Kauravas, however, persisted that Arjuna had appeared before the full time was spent.

Indra's great son advanced boldly. Suddenly he blew his celestial war shell, and all the Kauravas were stricken with fear. They fainted and lay on the field like they were sleeping. Arjuna refrained from killing them, instead he commanded Uttar to take possession of their royal attire. Then the great archer of the Pandavas returned to the city with the king's son.

Now when the monarch discovered how Arjuna had served him by warding off the attack of the Kauravas, he offered the brave Pandava his daughter, Uttara, for a bride; but Arjuna said: "Let her be given to my son."

It was then that the Pandava brothers revealed to the King of Virata who they were. All those who had assembled in the palace rejoiced and honoured them.

Many great kings came to the marriage of Abhimamju, son of Arjuna and Subhadra. Krishna came with his brother Balarama, and the King Drupada came with his son Dhrishtadyumna.

Now the King of Virata resolved to help Yudhishthira claim back his kingdom from the Kauravas, who continued to protest that their kinsmen had been discovered before the complete term of exile had ended.

Shakuni, the cunning gambler, and the vengeful Karna supported the proud and evil-hearted Duryodhana in refusing to make peace with the Pandava brothers, despite the warnings of the sages who sat around the Maharajah Dhritarashtra.

DURYODHANA'S DEFIANCE

Before the wedding guests departed from Virata, the elders and princes and chieftains assembled in the council chamber. Drupada was there with his son, and Krishna with his brother Balarama and Satyaki his kinsman, and all the Pandava brothers were there also, and many others both valiant and powerful. As bright and numerous as the stars were the gems that glittered on the robes of the mighty warriors.

For a time they spoke kindly greetings one to another, and joked and made merry. Krishna sat pondering in silence, and after some time he rose and said: "Oh kings and princes, may your fame endure forever! You well know that Yudhishthira was deprived of his kingdom by the evil trickster Shakuni. He has endured twelve years of exile, and has served, like his brothers, as a humble servant for a further year in the palace of the King of Virata. After all his suffering Yudhishthira desires peace; his heart is without anger, although he has endured great shame. The heart of Duryodhana, however, still burns with hate and jealous anger; still, as in his youth, he desires to work evil by deceit against the Pandava brothers. Now we must consider what Yudhishthira should do. Should he call many chieftains to his aid and wage war to punish his ancient enemies? Or should he send friendly messengers to Duryodhana, asking him to restore the kingdom which he still continues to possess?"

Balarama then spoke and said: "Kings, you have heard the words of my brother, who loves Yudhishthira. It is true, indeed, that the Kauravas have wronged the Pandavas. Yet I would counsel peace, so that this matter may be arranged between kinsmen. Yudhishthira has brought his sufferings upon his own head. He was unwise to play with cunning Shakuni, and also to continue playing, despite the warnings of the elders and his friends. He has suffered for his mistake. Now let a messenger be sent to Duryodhana, asking him to restore the throne to Yudhishthira. I do not advise war. What has been gambled away cannot be restored in battle."

Next stood Satyaki, the kinsman of Krishna. He said: "Oh Balarama, you have spoken like to a woman! You remind me that weaklings are sometimes born to warriors, like barren saplings sprung from sturdy trees. Timid words come from timid hearts. Proud monarchs do not listen to such weak counsel. Can you justify Duryodhana and blame the pious-hearted and gracious Yudhishthira? If it had happened that Yudhishthira while playing with his brothers had been visited by Duryodhana, who, having thrown the dice, had won, then the contest would have been fair in the eyes of all men. But Duryodhana plotted to ruin his kinsman, and invited him to Hastinapur to play with the evil-hearted Shakuni, who threw loaded dice. But that is ended. Yudhishthira has fulfilled his obligation; his exile is past, and he is entitled to his kingdom. Why, therefore, should he beg for that which is his? A Kshatriya begs of no man; what is refused him he seizes in battle at all times.... Duryodhana still clings to Yudhishthira's kingdom, despite the wise counsel of Bhishma and Drona. Remember Balarama, it is not sinful to kill one's enemies, but it is shameful to beg from them. I now declare my advice to be that we should give the Kauravas an opportunity to restore the throne of Yudhishthira; if they hesitate to do so, then let the Pandavas secure justice on the battlefield."

Then Drupada, King of Panchala, rose to his feet and said: "Monarchs, I fear that Satyaki has spoken truly. The Kauravas are a stubborn people. I think it is useless to ask Duryodhana, whose heart is consumed with greed. It is useless to plead with

Dhritarashtra, who is like clay in the hands of his proud son. Bhishma and Drona have already counselled in vain. Karna thirsts for war, and Duryodhana plots with him and also with false and cunning Shakuni. I think it would be wrong to follow the advice of Balarama. Duryodhana will never give up what he now possesses, nor does he desire peace. If we should send to him an ambassador who will speak mild words, he will think that we are weak, and become more boastful and arrogant than before. My advice is that we should gather together a great army without delay: the kings will side with him who askes first. Meanwhile let us offer peace and friendship to Duryodhana: my family priest will carry our message. If Duryodhana is willing to give up the kingdom of Yudhishthira, there will be peace; if he scorns our friendship, he will find us ready for war."

Krishna again addressed the assembly and said: "Drupada has spoken wisely. The Pandavas would do well to accept his counsel. If Duryodhana will agree to restore the kingdom to Yudhishthira, there will be no strife or bloodshed.... You all know that the Pandavas and Kauravas are my kinsmen; know also that they are equally dear to me.... I will now be gone. When you send out messengers of war, let them enter my kingdom last of all."

After Krishna had returned home, he was visited by Duryodhana and Arjuna, both parties wanting his help in the war. He spoke to the rival kinsmen and said: "I stand before you as in the balance; I have put myself on one side, and all my army is on the other. Choose now between you whether you want me or my forces. I will not fight, but will give my advice in battle."

Duryodhana asked for the army, but Arjuna preferred to have Krishna alone. Krishna promised to be Arjuna's charioteer.

Duryodhana also tried to persuade Balarama to help him, but Krishna's brother said: "I have no heart for this war. You know that you have wronged Yudhishthira, and that you should act justly in this matter. Do your duty, and your renown will be great." Angered by Balamara's words, Duryodhana returned home.

In time Drupada's priest appeared in the city of Hastinapur, and the elders and princes sat with Dhritarashtra to hear his message. The Brahman said: "So speaks the Pandavas – 'Pandu and Dhritarashtra were brothers: why, therefore, should Dhritarashtra's sons possess the whole kingdom, while the sons of Pandu are denied inheritance? Duryodhana has worked evil against his kinsman. He invited them to a gambling match to play with loaded dice, and they lost their possessions and had to go into exile like beggars. Now they have fulfilled the conditions, and are prepared to forget the past if their kingdom is restored to them. If their rightful claim is rejected, then Arjuna will scatter the Kauravas in battle.'"

Bhishma said: "What you have said is well justified, but it is wrong to boast regarding Arjuna. It would be wise of you not to speak of him in such a manner again."

Karna angrily added: "If the Pandavas have suffered, they are themselves to blame. It is fitting that they should plead for peace, because they are without followers. If they can prove their right to possessions, Duryodhana will give them; but he will not be forced by vain threats, or because the Kings of Panchala and Virata support them. Brahman, tell the Pandavas that they have failed to fulfil their obligations, because Arjuna was seen by us before the thirteenth year of banishment was completed. Let them return to the jungle for another term, and then come here and submit to Duryodhana and beg for his favours."

To this Bhishma replied: "You did not boast in this manner, Karna, when Arjuna opposed you at the Virata cattle raid. Remember that Arjuna is still powerful. If war comes, he will trample you into the dust."

Dhritarashtra scolded Karna for his hasty speech, and said to Bhishma: "He is young and unaccustomed to debate; do not be angry with him."

Then the blind old king sent his minister and charioteer, Sanjaya, to the Pandavas to say: "If you desire to have peace, come to me and I will do justice. Except wicked Duryodhana and hasty Karna all who are here are willing to make peace."

When Sanjaya reached the Pandavas, he was astonished to see that they had assembled a mighty army. He greeted the brothers and delivered his message.

Yudhishthira said: "We honour Dhritarashtra, but fear that he has listened to the counsel of his son Duryodhana, who wishes to have us in his power. The maharajah offers us protection, but not the fulfilment of our claims."

Krishna added: "The Pandavas have assembled a mighty army, and cannot reward these soldiers unless they receive their kingdom. It is not too late to make peace. Sanjaya, deliver this message to the Kauravas: 'If you seek peace, you will have peace; if you desire war, then let there be war.'"

Before Sanjaya left, Yudhishthira spoke to him once more, saying: "Tell Duryodhana that we will accept that portion of the kingdom which we ourselves have conquered and settled: he can keep the rest. My desire is for peace."

Many days went past, and the Pandavas waited in vain for an answer to their message. Then Yudhishthira spoke to Krishna, saying: "We have offered to make peace by accepting just a portion of our kingdom, yet the Kauravas remain silent."

Krishna replied: "I will go to Hastinapur and address the maharajah and his counsellors on your behalf."

Yudhishthira responded: "May you secure peace between kinsmen."

Then Draupadi entered and, addressing Krishna, she said: "Yudhishthira is too generous towards the Kauravas in offering to give up part of his kingdom to them. He pleads with them too much, as well, to grant him that which does not belongs to them. If the Kauravas wage war, my father and many other kings will assist the Pandavas.... Oh, can it be forgotten how Duhsasana dragged me by the hair to the Gambling Pavilion, and how I was put to shame before the elders and the princes?..."

She wept bitterly, and Krishna pitied her. "Why do you despair?" he asked with gentle voice. "The time is drawing near when all the Kauravas will be laid low, and their wives will shed tears more bitter than yours that fall now, fair one."

Messengers who arrived at Hastinapur announced the coming of Krishna. Wise Vidura counselled that he should be welcomed in state, so Duryodhana proclaimed a public holiday, and all the people rejoiced, and decorated the streets with streamers and flowers.

Vidura was very pleased, and he said to Duryodhana: "You have done well. But these preparations are in vain if you are unwilling to do justice to the Pandavas."

Duryodhana was irate, and said: "I will give nothing except what they can win in battle. If the success of the Pandavas depends on Krishna, then let us seize Krishna and put him in prison."

Dhritarashtra was horror-stricken, and cried out: "You cannot so treat an ambassador, and especially an ambassador like Krishna."

Bhishma rose up and said: "Oh maharajah, your son desires to work evil and bring ruin and shame on us all. I thinks disaster is now not far off." He then departed to his own house, and Vidura did likewise.

All the Kauravas went forward to meet the royal ambassador except Duryodhana, who scarcely looked at Krishna when he arrived at the palace. Krishna went to the house of Vidura, and there he saw Pritha, who wept and said: "How are my sons, whom I have not seen for fourteen years? How is Draupadi? I have heard about their sufferings in desolate places. Who can understand my own misery, as every day is full of weariness and grief to me?"

Krishna comforted her and said: "Your sons have many allies, and before long they will triumphantly return to their own land."

Afterwards Krishna went to the house of Duryodhana, who sat haughtily in the feasting chamber. Eventually Dhritarashtra's son spoke to his kinsman, who ate nothing. He said: "Why are you unfriendly towards me?"

Krishna replied: "I cannot be your friend until you act justly towards your kinsmen, the Pandavas."

When Krishna went again to the house of Vidura, the aged counsellor said to him: "It would have been better if you had not come here. Duryodhana will take no man's advice. When he speaks he expects all men to agree with him."

Krishna said: "It is my desire to prevent bloodshed. I came to Hastinapur to save the Kauravas from destruction, and I will warn them in the council chamber tomorrow. If they will listen to me, all will be well; if they scorn my advice, then let their blood be on their own heads."

When the princes and the elders sat with Dhritarashtra in the council chamber, Narada and other great Rishis appeared in the heavens and were invited to come down and share in the deliberations. After a few moments Krishna stood, and in a voice like thunder said: "I have come here not to seek war, but to utter words of peace and love. Maharajah, do not let your heart be stained with sin. Your sons have wronged their kinsmen, and a danger threatens all: it approaches now like an angry comet, and I can see kinsmen slaying kinsmen, and many noble lords laid in the dust. All of you here gathered together are already in the clutch of death. Dhritarashtra, man of peace, stretch forward your hand and avert the dreadful calamity which is about to fall on your house. Grant the Pandavas their rightful claim, and your reign will close in unsurpassed glory and in blessed peace…. What if all the Pandavas were killed in battle! Would their fall bring you joy? Are they not your own brother's children?… But you know that the Pandavas are as ready for war as they are eager for peace; and if war comes, it will be polluted with the blood of your sons. Oh gracious maharajah, let the last years of your life be peaceful and pleasant, so that you may indeed be blessed."

Dhritarashtra wept and said: "I would gladly do as you have counselled so wisely, Krishna, but Duryodhana, my vicious son, will not listen to me or obey, nor will he listen to his mother, nor to Vidura, nor to Bhishma."

Next Bhishma spoke, and he addressed Duryodhana, saying: "All would be well if you would follow the advice of Krishna. You are evil-hearted and a wrongdoer; you are the curse of our family; you take pleasure in disobeying your royal father and in scorning the advice of Krishna and Vidura. Soon your father will be stripped of his kingdom because of your actions; your pride will bring death to your kinsmen. Hear and follow my advice; do not bring eternal sorrow to your aged parents."

Duryodhana heard these words in anger, but was silent.

Then Drona addressed him, and said: "I join with Bhishma and Krishna in appealing to you. Those who advise you to make peace are your friends; those who counsel war are your enemies. Do not be too certain of victory; do not tempt the hand of vengeance; leave the night-black road of evil and seek out the road of light and well-doing, Duryodhana."

Next Vidura stood up. He spoke with slow, gentle voice, and said: "You have heard words of wisdom, Duryodhana.... I am deeply saddened. My grief is not for you, but for your old mother and father, who will fall into the hands of your enemies; my grief is for kinsmen and friends who must die in battle, and for those who will afterwards be driven away as beggars, friendless and without a home. The few survivors of war will curse the day of your birth."

Again Bhishma spoke. He praised the courage of the Pandavas, and said: "It is not too late to avoid calamity. The field of battle is still unstained by the blood of thousands; your army has not yet met the arrows of death. Before it is too late, make your peace with your kinsmen, the Pandavas, so that all men may rejoice. Banish evil from your heart forever; rule the whole world with the heirs of Pandu."

The Rishis, too counselled peace like the elders. And all the while Dhritarashtra still wept.

When Duryodhana finally spoke, his eyes burned bright and his brows hung darkly. He said: "Krishna counsels me to be just, yet he hates me and loves the Pandavas. Bishma scowls on me, and Vidura and Drona look coldly on; my father weeps for my sins. Yet what have I done that you all should turn my father's affection from me? If Yudhishthira loved gambling and staked and lost his throne and freedom, am I to blame? If he played a second time after being set free, and became an exile, why should he now call me a robber? Dull is the star of the Pandavas' destiny: their friends are few, and their army is feeble. Shall we, who do not fear Indra even, be threatened by the weak sons of Pandu? No warrior lives who can overcome us. A Kshatriya fears no enemy; he may fall in battle, but he will never give in. So the sages have spoken…. Hear me, my kinsmen! My father gifted Indra-prastha to the Pandavas in a moment of weakness. Never, so long as I and my brother live, will they possess it again. Never again will the kingdom of Maharajah Dhritarashtra be severed in two. It has been united, and so it will remain forever. My words are firm and plain. So tell the Pandavas, Krishna, that they ask in vain for territory. No town or village will they possess again with my consent. I swear by the gods that I will never humble myself in front of the Pandavas."

Krishna responded: "How can you speak in such a manner, Duryodhana? How can you pretend that you never wronged your kinsmen? Be mindful of your evil thoughts and deeds."

Duhsasana whispered to his elder brother: "I fear, if you do not make peace with the Pandavas, the elders will seize you and send you as a prisoner to Yudhishthira. They desire to make you and me and Karna kneel before the Pandavas."

Duryodhana was furious. He rose and left the council chamber. Duhsasana, Karna and Shakuni followed him.

Krishna then turned to Dhritarashtra and said: "You should arrest these four rebellious princes and act freely and justly towards the Pandavas."

The weak old maharajah was stricken with grief, and he sent Vidura for his elder son. Shakuni, Karna and Duhsasana waited outside for Duryodhana, and they plotted to seize Krishna so that the power of the Pandavas might be weakened. But to Krishna came knowledge of their thoughts, and he informed the elders.

Once again the maharajah summoned Duryodhana before him, and Krishna said: "Ah! You of little understanding, is it your desire to take me captive? Know now that I am not alone here; all the gods and holy beings are with me."

Having uttered these words, Krishna suddenly revealed himself in divine splendour. His body was transformed into a tongue of flame; gods and divine beings appeared around him; fire flowed out from his mouth and eyes and ears; sparks broke from his skin, which became as radiant as the sun.... All the kings closed their eyes; they trembled when an earthquake shook the palace. But Duryodhana remained defiant.

Krishna, having resumed his human form, then said farewell to the maharajah, who lamented the doings of Duryodhana. The divine one spoke and said: "Dhritarashtra, you I forgive freely; but a father is often cursed by the people because of the wicked doings of his own son."

Before Krishna left the city he met Karna and spoke to him, saying: "Come with me, and the Pandavas will regard you as their elder brother, and you will become the king."

Karna responded: "Although Duryodhana is the future king, he rules according to my counsel…. I know, without doubt, that a great battle is coming which will cover the earth with blood. Terrible are the omens. Calamity awaits the Kauravas…. Yet I cannot desert those who have given me their friendship. Besides, if I went with you now, men would regard me as Arjuna's inferior. Arjuna and I must meet in battle, and fate will decide who is greater. I know I shall fall in this war, but I must fight for my friends…. Oh mighty one, may we meet again on earth. If not, may we meet in heaven."

Then Krishna and Karna embraced one another, and each went his own way.

Vidura spoke to Pritha, mother of the Pandavas, and said: "My desire is always for peace, but although I cry myself hoarse, Duryodhana will not listen to my words. Dhritarashtra is old, yet he does not work for peace; he is intoxicated with pride for his sons. When Krishna returns to the Pandavas, war will certainly break out; the sin of the Kauravas will cause much bloodshed. I cannot sleep, thinking of approaching disaster."

Pritha sighed and wept. "To hell with wealth!" she said, "That it should cause kinsmen to slaughter one another. War should be waged between enemies, not friends. If the Pandavas do not fight, they will suffer poverty; if they go to war and win, the destruction of kinsmen will not bring triumph. My heart is full of sorrow. And it is Karna who supports Duryodhana in his foolishness; he has again become powerful."

Pritha regretted the mistakes of her girlhood which caused Karna to be, and she went out to look for him. She found her son bathing in sacred waters, and she said to him: "You are my own son, and your father is Surya. I hid you at birth, and Radha, who found you, is not your mother. It is not right that you should plot in ignorance with Duryodhana against your own brothers. Let the Kauravas see the friendship of you and Arjuna. If you two were side by side you would conquer the world. My eldest son, you should be with your brothers now. Be no longer known as one of lowly birth."

A voice spoke from the sun, saying: "What Pritha has said is truth. Oh tiger among men, great good will be accomplished if you will obey her command."

Karna remained steadfast, because his heart was full of honour. He said to Pritha, his mother: "It is too late to command my obedience now. Why did you abandon me at birth? If I am a Kshatriya, I have been deprived of my rank. No enemy could have done me a greater injury than you have done. You have never been a mother to me, nor do your sons know I am their brother. How can I now desert the Kauravas, who trust me to wage this war. I am their boat on which to cross a stormy sea.... I will speak without deceit to you. For the sake of Duryodhana I will fight your sons. I cannot forget his kindness; I cannot forget my own honour. Your command cannot be obeyed by me. Yet your solicitation to me will not be fruitless. I have the power to kill Yudhishthira, and Bhima, and Nakula, and Sahadeva, but I promise they shall not fall by my hand. I will fight with Arjuna alone. If I slay Arjuna, I will achieve great fame; if I am slain by him, I will be covered with glory."

Pritha responded: "You have pledged the lives of four of your brothers. You must remembered this in the perils of battle. I bless you."

Karna said: "So be it," and then they parted, the mother going one way and the son another.

After this the Pandavas and Kauravas gathered together their mighty armies and marched to the field of battle.

THE EPIC BATTLE OF EIGHTEEN DAYS

Soon after Krishna had returned from Hastinapur, Duryodhana sent a challenge to the Pandavas. His messenger spoke, saying: "You have vowed to wage war against us. The time has come for you to fulfil your vow. Your kingdom was seized by me, your wife Draupadi was put to shame, and you were all made exiles. Why have you not yet sought to be avenged in battle? Where is drowsy Bhima, who boasted that he would drink the blood of Duhsasana? Duhsasana is weary with waiting for him. Where is arrogant Arjuna, who has Drona to meet? When mountains are blown about like dust, and men hold back the wind with their hands, Arjuna will take captive the mighty Drona…. Of what account was the mace of Bhima and the bow of Arjuna on the day when your kingdom was taken from you, and you were banished like vagabonds?… Krishna's help will be of no use when you meet us in battle."

Krishna answered the messenger, saying: "Vainly do you boast of prowess, but before long your fate will be made known to you. I will consume your army like fire consumes withered grass. You will not escape me, because I will drive Arjuna's chariot. And let Duhsasana know that the Bhima's vow will be fulfilled before long."

Arjuna then added: "Tell Duryodhana, it is unseemly for warriors to boast like women.... It is well that Duhsasana comes to battle."

When the messenger repeated these words to Duryodhana, Karna said: "Stop this chatter! Let the drums of war be sounded."

So at dawn on the following day the armies of the Kauravas and the Pandavas were assembled for battle on the wide plain of Kuru-Kshetra. Bhishma had been chosen to lead Duryodhana's army, and Karna, who had quarrelled with him, vowed not to fight so long as the older warrior remained alive. "Should he fall, however," Karna said, "I will attack Arjuna."

The army of the Pandavas was commanded by Dhrishtadyumna, son of Drupada, and brother of Draupadi. Among the young heroes were Arjuna's two sons, the noble Abhimanyu, whose mother was Krishna's beautiful sister Subhadra, and brave Iravat, whose mother was Ulupi, the serpent nymph, daughter of the king of the Nagas. Bhima's Rakshasa son, the terrible Ghatotkacha, who had the power to change his shape and create illusions, had also rushed to assist his kinsmen. Krishna drove the chariot of Arjuna, who carried his celestial bow, named Gandiva, the gift of the god Agni; and his standard was the image of Hanuman, the chief ape god, who was the son of Vayu, the wind god. But the army of Duryodhana was much larger than the army of Yudhishthira.

Drona led the right wing of the Kaurava forces, which was strengthened by Shakuni, the gambler, and his Gandharai lancers. The left wing was led by Duhsasana, who was followed by Kamboja cavalry and fierce Sakas and Yavanas mounted on fast horses. The peoples of the north were there and the peoples of the south, and also of the east. Blind old Dhritarashtra was in the rear, and with him was Sanjaya, his charioteer, who told him all that took place, having been gifted with divine vision by Vyasa.

Yet before the conflict began, Yudhishthira walked unarmed towards the Kauravas, at which his kinsmen laughed, thinking he was terror-stricken. But Pandu's noble son first spoke to Bhishma and asked permission to fight against him. Bhishma gave consent. Then he addressed Drona in similar terms, and Drona also gave consent. And before he returned to his place, Yudhishthira called out to the Kaurava army: "Whoever desires to help our cause, let him follow me." When he had said this, Yuyutsu, the half-brother of Duryodhana, called out: "If you will elevate me, I will serve you well." Yudhishthira replied: "Be my brother." Then Yuyutsu followed Yudhishthira with all his men, and no man tried to hold him back.

As the armies were getting ready for battle, Arjuna urged Krishna to drive his chariot to the open space on which the struggle would take place. Indra's mighty son surveyed the hosts, and when he saw his kinsmen, young and old, and his friends and all the elders and princes on either side ready to attack one another, his heart was touched, and he trembled with pity and sorrow. He spoke to Krishna, saying: "I do not seek victory, or kingdom, or any joy on earth. Those for whose sake we might wish for power are gathered against us in battle. What joy can come to us if we commit the crime of slaying our own kinsmen?" Then he dropped his celestial bow and sat down on the bench of his chariot with a heart full of grief.

Krishna admonished Arjuna, saying: "You are a Kshatriya, and it is your duty to fight, no matter what may happen to you or to others. He who has wisdom does not sorrow for the living or for the dead. As one casts off old clothing and puts on new, so the soul casts off this body and enters the new body. Nothing exists that is not of the soul."

After long instruction, Krishna revealed himself to Arjuna in his celestial splendour and power and said: "Let your heart and your understanding be fixed in me, and you shall dwell in me from now on. I will deliver you from all your sins.... I am the same to all creatures; there is none hateful to me – none dear. Those who worship me are in me and I am in them. Those who hate me are consigned to evil births: they are deluded birth after birth."

Arjuna listened to Krishna's counsel, and prepared for the fray. The war shell bellowed loudly, and the drums of battle were sounded. The Kauravas got ready to attack with horsemen, footmen, charioteers, and elephants of war. The Pandavas were gathered to meet them. And the air was filled with the shouting of men, the roaring of elephants, the blasts of trumpets, and the beating of drums: the rattling of chariots was like thunder rolling in heaven. The gods and Gandharvas assembled in the clouds and saw the hosts which had gathered for mutual slaughter.

As both armies waited for sunrise, a tempest rose up and the dawn was darkened by dust clouds, so that men could scarcely see one another. Evil were the omens. Blood dropped like rain out of heaven, while jackals howled impatiently, and kites and vultures screamed hungrily for human flesh. The earth shook, peals of thunder were heard, although there were no clouds, and angry lightning broke the horrid gloom; flaming thunderbolts struck the rising sun and broke in fragments....

The undaunted warriors never faltered, despite these signs and warnings. Shouting defiance, they mingled in conflict, eager for victory, and strongly armed. Swords were wielded and ponderous maces, javelins were hurled, and numerous darts too; countless arrows whistled in flight.

When the wind fell and the air cleared, the battle rose in fury. Bhishma achieved mighty deeds. Duryodhana led his men against Bhima's, and they fought with courage. Yudhishthira fought with Salya, King of Madra; Dhrishtadyumna, son of Drupada, went against Drona, who had once captured half of the Panchala kingdom with the help of the Pandavas. Drupada was opposed to Jayadratha, the King of Sindhu, who had attempted to carry off Draupadi, and was compelled to acknowledge himself as the slave of Yudhishthira. Many single combats were fought with uncertain result.

All day the armies battled with growing enthusiasm. As evening was coming on, Abhimanyu, son of Arjuna, perceived that the advantage lay with the Kauravas, mainly because of Bhishma's prowess. So he hurried towards that mighty warrior, and cut down the flag of his chariot. Bhishma said he had never seen such a youthful hero who could perform greater deeds. Then he advanced to attack the Pandava army. Victoriously he went, cutting a blood-red path through the stricken legions; no one could resist him for long. The heart of Arjuna was filled with shame, and he rode against

Bhishma, whose advance was stopped. The two heroes fought desperately until dusk. Then Bhishma withdrew; but Arjuna followed him, and pierced the heart of the Kaurava host, achieving great slaughter. The truce was sounded, and the first day's battle came to an end.

Yudhishthira was despondent because the fortunes of war seemed to be against him; in the darkness he went to Krishna, who told him to lift his spirits, and Yudhishthira was comforted.

On the morning of the second day Bhishma once again attacked the Pandava forces, shattering their ranks; but Arjuna drove him back. Seeing this, Duryodhana lamented to Bhishma that he had quarrelled with Karna. The old warrior answered: "I am a Kshatriya and must fight even against my beloved kinsman." Then he rode against Arjuna once more, and the two warriors fought fiercely and wounded one another.

Drupada's son waged a long battle with Drona, and Bhima performed mighty deeds. He leapt on the back of an elephant and killed the son of the King of Maghadha; and with a single blow of his mace he killed the king and his elephant, too.

Towards evening a furious battle was being fought by Abhimanyu, son of Arjuna, and Lakshmana, son of Duryodhana. The young Pandava was about to achieve victory, when Duryodhana came to his son's aid with many kings. Shouts were raised: "Abhimanyu is in peril; he will be overcome by force of numbers!" Arjuna heard these words, and rode to the rescue. Then the Kauravas cried out in terror: "Arjuna! Arjuna!" and scattered in flight. That evening Bhishma spoke to Drona and said: "I think the gods are against us."

On the third day the army of the Pandavas advanced in crescent formation and drove back the Kaurava army. Many were slain, and rivers of blood stained the earth; horses writhed in agony, and the air was filled with the shrieking and moaning of wounded men. Terrible were the omens, for headless men rose up and fought against one another; then the people feared that all who fought in that dreadful battle would be slain.

When he saw the fallen standard, and the heaps of murdered elephants, horses and men, Duryodhana said to Bhishma: "You should give your place to Karna. I think you are swayed by Arjuna and the Pandavas."

Bhishma replied: "Your struggle is in vain, foolish Duryodhana. No one can wipe away the stain of your sins; cunning is of no avail against a righteous cause. You shall perish because of your mistakes…. I have no fear of battle, and I will lead the Kauravas until I triumph or fall."

Then angry Bhishma urged his charioteer to attack the enemy; and he drove back all who opposed him, even Arjuna. The fighting became general, nor did it end until night obscured the plain.

Bhima was the hero of the fourth day of battle. He swept against the Kauravas like a whirlwind; darts were thrown and arrows shot at the strong Pandava but all were in vain. He wounded both Duryodhana and Salya, King of Sindhu. Then fourteen of Duryodhana's brothers rushed to attack him. Like the lion who licks his lips when he sees his prey coming close, Bhima awaited them. Brief and terrible was the conflict, and before six princes fled in terror, eight were slaughtered by the mighty Pandava.

Another day dawned, and Arjuna and Bhima advanced in triumph until they were met and held back by Drona. Once again the sons of Duryodhana and Arjuna sought out one another. Their blows were swift and mighty, and for a time all men watched them in wonder. Eventually Lakshmana was grievously wounded, and was carried from the field by his kinsmen. Abhimanyu returned in triumph to Yudhishthira. On that same day the ten great sons of Satyaki, Krishna's kinsman were killed.

Another day dawned, and it was a day of peril for Bhima. Confident of victory, he pressed too far into the midst of the Kaurava forces, and was surrounded by overwhelming numbers. Drupada saw this threat and rushed to help him, but neither could retreat. Then Arjuna's fearless son, the slayer of Lakshmana, with twelve brave chieftains shattered the Kaurava hosts and rescued Bhima and Drupada from the surging warriors who thirsted for their blood.

The seventh day was the day of Bhishma. No one could withstand him in his battle fury. The Pandavas cowered before him, nor could Bhima or Arjuna drive him back. Before night fell, the standard of Yudhishthira was cut down, and the Kauravas rejoiced, believing that they would achieve a great victory.

On the day that followed, however, the tide of battle turned. As Bhishma advanced, his charioteer was slain, and the horses took flight in terror. Then confusion fell on the Kaurava army. For a time the Pandavas made resistless advance amidst mighty slaughter. Then the six Gandharai princes advanced to beat back the forces of Yudhishthira. Riding on milk-white horses, they swept like sea birds across the ocean. They had vowed to kill Iravat, son of Arjuna and the Naga princess. The gallant youth did not fear them and fought triumphantly, stirred with the joy of battle; he killed five of the princes, but the sixth, the eldest prince, struck down Arjuna's son, taking his life. When Arjuna was told that his son had fallen he was stricken with grief. Then with tear-dimmed eyes he raced towards his enemies, thirsting for vengeance; he broke through the Kaurava ranks, and Bhima, who followed him, killed more of Duryodhana's brothers.

Bhima's terrible son, the Rakshasa Ghatotkacha, also sought vengeance after Iravat fell. Roaring like the sea, he assumed an awesome shape, and advanced with flaming spears like the Destroyer at the end of Time, followed by other Rakshasas. Warriors fled from his path, until Duryodhana went against him with many elephants; but Ghatotkacha scattered the elephant host. Duryodhana fought like a lion and killed four Rakshasas, whereupon Bhima's son, raging furiously, his eyes red as fire, charged at Duryodhana; but that mighty Kaurava shot arrows like angry snakes, and he wounded his enemy. An elephant was brought in front of Duryodhana's chariot for protection. Ghatotkacha cut down the great animal with a flaming dart. Next Bhishma pressed forward with a division to shield Dhritarashtra's son, and the Rakshasa fought fiercely; he wounded Kripa, and with an arrow severed the string of Bhishma's bow. Then the Panchalas rushed to help Bhima's son, and the Kauravas were scattered in flight.

Duryodhana was stricken with sorrow, and went to the snow-white tent of Bhishma that night and said: "Forgive my harsh words, mighty chieftain. The Pandavas are brave in battle, but they are unable to resist you. If, however, you love them too much to overcome them, let Karna take your place, so that he may lead the army against our enemies."

Bhishma replied: "Duryodhana, your struggle is of no avail. The just cause must win; they who fight for the right are doubly armed. Besides, Krishna is with the Pandavas: he drives Arjuna's chariot, and not even the gods could strike them down. You are confronted by utter ruin! I will fight as I have fought until the end, which is not far off."

The next day Bhishma was like a fire which burns up a dry and withering forest. In his chariot he advanced triumphantly, wreaking havoc and carnage as he went.

Yudhishthira was in despair, and when night fell he spoke to Krishna, who said: "Bhishma has vowed that he will not kill one who had been born a woman, knowing that the righteous would defame him if he murdered a female. Therefore let Sikhandin be sent against him with Arjuna."

Arjuna responded: "No! I cannot fight behind another, or achieve the fall of Bhishma by foul means. I loved him as a child; I sat on his knee and called him 'Father'. I would rather perish than slay the saintly hero."

Krishna replied: "It is fated that Bhishma will fall tomorrow, a victim of wrong. As he has fought against those whom he loves, so must you, Arjuna, fight against him. He has shown you how Kshatriyas must always wage war, whether their enemies are hated or loved."

And so on the tenth day of battle, Arjuna left for battle with Sikhandin, who had been born a woman and made a male by a Yaksha.

Once again Duryodhana tried to persuade Bhishma to give his place to Karna, and Bhishma answered him in anger: "Today will I overcome the Pandavas or perish on the battlefield."

Then the ancient hero advanced and challenged Arjuna. A terrible conflict ensued, lasting for many hours; all the warriors on either side stopped fighting and watched. In time Sikhandin rushed forward like a foaming wave, and when Bhishma saw him his arms fell, because he could not fight against one who had been born a woman. Then the arrows of Arjuna pierced Bhishma's body, and the old hero fell from his chariot and lay dying…. The sun went down, and darkness swept over the plain.

There was misery on the blood-drenched plain that night. Arjuna wept like a son weeps for a father, and he carried water to Bhishma. Yudhishthira cursed the day the war began. Duryodhana and his brothers also came to the dying chieftain. Friends and enemies grieved together over the fallen hero.

Bhishma spoke to Duryodhana, saying: "Hear the counsel of your dying kinsman; his voice speaks as from the dead. If your heart of stone can be moved, you will bring this slaughter of kinsmen by kinsmen to an end now. Restore to Yudhishthira his kingdom and make your peace with him, and let Pandavas and Kauravas be friends and comrades together."

But he spoke in vain, as his words stirred Duryodhana's heart to hate the Pandavas with a deeper hatred than before.

Karna came to the battlefield, and Bhishma said to him: "We have been proud rivals; always jealous of one another, and ever in conflict. My voice fails, yet I must tell you that Arjuna is not greater than you are on the battlefield. Nor is he of higher birth, because you are the son of Pritha and the sun god Surya. As Arjuna is your own brother, it would be good for you to bring this trouble to an end."

But again Bhishma spoke in vain. Karna hated his brother and thirsted for his life.

A guard was set around Bhishma, who lay supported by a pillow of arrows, waiting for the hour of his death. But he was not to die until after the great war was over.

The Kauravas held a war council, and they chose Drona to be their leader. The battle standard of the Brahman was a water jar and a golden altar on a deerskin. He vowed to Duryodhana that he would take Yudhishthira prisoner.

On the first day of Drona's command, and the eleventh day of the great war, Abhimanyu was leading in the fight. He dragged a chieftain by the hair out of his chariot, and would have taken him prisoner, but Jayadratha, the king who had endeavoured to abduct Draupadi, intervened, and broke his sword on the young man's shield. Jayadratha fled, and Salya, King of Madra, attacked Arjuna's noble son. But Bhima dashed forward and engaged him in fierce combat. Both were mighty wielders of the mace; they were like two tigers, like two great elephants; they were like eagles tearing one another with blood-red claws. The sound of their blows was like the echoing thunder, and each stood as firm as a cliff which is struck in vain by fiery lightning.... After a long time both staggered and fell, but Bhima immediately sprang up to strike the final blow. Before he could accomplish his fierce desire, however, Salya was rescued by his followers and carried to safety.... Afterwards the battle raged with more fury than ever, until night fell and all the living and the dead were hidden from sight.

Drona sought to fulfil his vow on the second day of his command, and he prompted Susarman, the king who had invaded Virata when the Pandavas were servants there, to send a challenge to Arjuna for single combat. Susarman selected a place away from the main battlefield. Arjuna fought for many hours, until at last he put the boastful king and his followers to flight; then he taunted them for their cowardice. Meanwhile Drona had attacked Yudhishthira, who, when confronted by certain death, leapt on the back of a horse and escaped from the battlefield. But it was no shame for a Kshatriya to flee a Brahman.

Duryodhana went against Bhima: he was wounded after a brief combat, and retreated from the field. Many warriors then pressed against Bhima, but Arjuna had returned after fighting Susarman, and drove furiously against the Kauravas; he swept over the blood-red plain in triumph. Karna watched his rival with jealous rage and entered the fray. The fire burned in his eyes, and he attacked Arjuna, resolved to conquer or die. The fight raged for hours, and when night fell the two great warriors reluctantly withdrew from the field.

The next day Drona arranged his army like a spider's web, and once again Susarman challenged Arjuna, in order to draw him away from the battle-front. It was the day of Abhimanyu's triumph and the day of his death. Yudhishthira sent Arjuna's son to break the web of enemies, and he rode his chariot against elephants and horses with conquering fury. Duryodhana attacked the youthful hero with a band of warriors, but fell wounded by Abhimanyu, who also killed the warriors. Salya next dashed against Arjuna's son, but before long he was carried from the field grievously wounded. Then Duhsasana came forward, frowning and fierce.

Abhimanyu cried out: "Evil prince, who plotted with Shakuni to win the kingdom of Yudhishthira and put Draupadi to shame,

I welcome you, as I have waited a long time for you. Now you will receive proper punishment for your sins."

As he spoke, the fearless youth flung a dart, and Duhsasana fell stunned and bleeding, but was rescued from death by his followers.

Lakshmana, son of Duryodhana, rode proudly against Arjuna's son, and fought bravely and well; but he was cut down, and died on the battlefield.

Then the evil Jayadratha, who had vowed to be Yudhishthira's slave in the forest, stealthily advanced with six warriors to fight the lordly youth. The seven men surged forwards, and Abhimanyu stood alone. His charioteer was killed and his chariot was shattered; he leapt to the ground and fought on, slaying one by one…. Noticing his peril, the Pandavas tried to rescue Arjuna's son; but Jayadratha held them back, and Karna helped him. Eventually Abhimanyu was wounded on the forehead, blood streamed into his eyes and blinded him, and he stumbled. Before he could recover, the son of Duhsasana leapt forward and dashed out his brains with a mace. So died the gallant youth, pure as he was at birth. He died like a forest lion surrounded by hunters; he sank like the red sun at evening; he perished like a tempest whose strength is spent; Abhimanyu was lost.

So that day's battle ended, and Abhimanyu slumbered in the soft starlight, lifeless and cold.

When Arjuna was told that his son was gone, the mighty warrior lay on the ground and silently wept. After some time he leapt up and cried: "May the curse of a father and the vengeance of a warrior smite the murderers of my boy!… May I never reach heaven if I do not slay Jayadratha tomorrow…." A spy hurried to the Kauravas' camp and told of Arjuna's vow. Jayadratha trembled with fear.

Early the next morning Arjuna said to Krishna: "Drive swiftly, as this will be a day of great slaughter." He wanted to find Jayadratha; with him went Bhima and Satyaki. Many warriors engaged them in battle, as the Kauravas hoped that the sun should go down before Arjuna could fulfil his terrible vow.

Mounted on an elephant, Duhsasana opposed Arjuna; but he took flight when the rattling chariot drew near. Drona blocked the way; but Arjuna refused combat, saying: "You are like a father to me…. Let me find my son's killer…." He passed on. Then Duryodhana came up and engaged him. Karna fought with Bhima, and Bhurisrava attacked Satyaki. Long waged the bitter conflicts, and after a while Krishna saw that his kinsman was about to be slain. He called to Arjuna, who cast a celestial weapon at Bhurisrava, which cut off both his arms; then Satyaki killed him. Afterwards many warriors confronted Arjuna, and many fell. But the day wore on and evening drew near, and he could not find Jayadratha. Eventually Arjuna urged Krishna to drive furiously onward, and not to stop not until he found his son's killer. The chariot sped like a whirlwind, until at last Arjuna saw the evil-hearted Jayadratha; he was guarded by Karna and five great warriors, and at that time the sun had begun to set.

Karna leapt forward and engaged Arjuna; but Krishna used his divine power to cause a dark cloud to obscure the sun. Everyone believed that night had fallen. Karna immediately withdrew; but Arjuna drove on, and as the sun shot out its last ray of dazzling light, he pounced on Jayadratha like a falcon swoops down on its prey. The struggle was brief, and before daylight faded completely, Arjuna overthrew the slayer of his son and cut off his head. Bhima uttered a roar of triumph when he saw Jayadratha's head held high, and the Kauravas despaired because their wicked plan had been thwarted.

Night fell, but the fighting was renewed. In the darkness and confusion men killed their kinsmen, fathers cut down their sons, and brothers fought against brothers. Yudhishthira sent men with torches to light up the blood-red plain, and the battle was waged for many hours. Swords were splintered and spears were lost, and warriors threw great boulders and chariot wheels against one another. All men were maddened with the thirst for blood, and the night was filled with horrors.

At last Arjuna called for a truce, and it was agreed that the warriors should sleep on the battlefield. So all lay down, the charioteer in his chariot, the rider on his horse, and the driver of the elephant on his elephant's back....

Duryodhana scolded Drona for not slaying the Pandavas in their sleep.... "Let Karna," he said, "lead the army to victory."

But Drona replied: "You are reaping the red harvest of your sins.... But know now that tomorrow either Arjuna will fall or I will be slain by him."

When the bright moon rose in the heavens the conflict was renewed. Many fell on that awful night. Ghatotkacha, the Rakshasa son of Bhima, was leading the fray, and he slaughtered numerous Kaurava warriors. At last Karna went against him, and then the air was filled with blazing arrows. Each struck the other with powerful weapons, and for a time the conflict hung in the balance. Ghatotkacha created illusions, but Karna kept his senses in that great fight, even after his horses had been slain; he leapt to the ground, then flung a celestial dart, the gift of Indra, and Ghatotkacha, uttering terrible cries, fell down and breathed his last breath. The Kauravas shouted with gladness, and the Pandavas wept.

Before the night was ended, Drona killed his ancient enemy Drupada, King of Southern Panchala, and he also cut down the King of Virata.

Before dawn broke, Dhrishtadyumna, son of Drupada, went out in search of Drona, the slayer of his beloved father. But Bhima said to him: "You are too young to strike down as great a warrior as Drona. I will fight with him until he is wearied, then you can approach and be avenged."

Bhima struggled with the sage, his teacher, for many hours; then Dhrishtadyumna engaged him, but neither could prevail over Drupada's killer. Eventually the Pandava warriors falsely shouted: "Aswatthaman, son of Drona, is slain." When Drona heard this he fainted in his chariot, and vengeful Dhrishtadyumna rushed forward and cut off his head. Then the son of Drupada threw the head of Drona towards Duryodhana, saying: "Here is the head of your mighty warrior; I will cut off the heads of each Kaurava prince!"

The fall of Drona was like the sinking of heaven's sun; it was like the drying up of the ocean; the Kauravas fled in fear.

When Aswatthaman returned that evening and found that his father had been slain he was grief-stricken. Night fell while he wept, and he vowed to kill Dhrishtadyumna and all his family.

Karna was next chosen to be the leader of the Kaurava army, and Duryodhana praised him and said: "You alone can stem the tide of our disasters. Arjuna has been spared by Bhishma and by Drona because they loved him. But the arm of Karna is strengthened by hatred of the proud Pandava archer."

When morning broke over the plain, the first battle of Karna began, and it continued all day long. Countless warriors were slain; blood ran in streams, and the dead and mangled bodies of men and elephants and horses were strewn in confusion. The air was darkened with arrows and darts, and it rang with the shouts of the fighters and the moans of the wounded, the bellowing of trumpets, and the clamour of drums.

At last evening came and the carnage ended.... Duryodhana summoned his war council and said: "This is the sixteenth day of the war, and many of our strongest heroes have fallen. Bhishma and Drona are gone, and many of my brothers are now dead."

Karna then said: "Tomorrow will be the great day of the war. I have vowed to kill Arjuna or fall by his hand."

Duryodhana was cheered by Karna's words, and all the Kauravas were once again hopeful of victory.

In the morning Karna rode out in his chariot. He chose Salya, King of Madra, as his driver whose skill was so great that even Krishna was not his superior.

Arjuna was again engaged in combat with Susarman when Karna attacked the Pandava army. So the son of Surya went against Yudhishthira and cast him on the ground, saying: "If you were Arjuna I would kill you."

Bhima then attacked Karna, and they fought fiercely for a time, until Arjuna, having overcome Susarman, returned to fight with Karna.

Duhsasana, who put Draupadi to shame, came up to help Karna, and Bhima attacked him. Bhima had always hoped to meet this evil-hearted son of the blind maharajah, so that he might fulfil his vow. He swung his mace and struck so mighty a blow that the advancing chariot was shattered. Duhsasana fell heavily on the ground and broke his back. Then Bhima seized him and, whirling his body up in the air, cried out: "Oh Kauravas, come those who dare and rescue Karna's helper."

No one dared to approach, and Bhima cast down Duhsasana's body, cut off his head, and drank his blood as he had vowed to do. Many Kaurava warriors fled, and they cried out: "This is not a man, because he drinks human blood!"

All men watched the deadly combat which was waged between the mighty heroes Arjuna and Karna. They began by shooting arrows one at another, while Krishna and Salya skilfully guided the chariots. Arjuna's arrows fell on Karna like summer rain; Karna's arrows were like stinging snakes, and they drank blood. Eventually Arjuna's celestial bow Gandiva was struck and the bowstring severed.... Arjuna said: "Pause, Karna. According to the rules of battle, you cannot attack a disabled enemy." But Karna did not listen. He showered countless arrows, until his proud rival was grievously wounded.

When Arjuna had restrung his bow, he rose up like a stricken and angry tiger held at bay, and cast a screen of arrows against his enemy. But Karna did not fear him, nor could Arjuna take him down. The fight hung in the balance.... Then suddenly a wheel of Karna's chariot sank in the soft ground, and Salya could not get the horses to advance.

Karna cried out: "Pause now, Arjuna, do not wage unequal war. It is not manly to attack a helpless enemy."

Arjuna paused; but Krishna spoke quickly, saying: "Oh Karna, you speak the truth; but was it manly to shoot arrows at Arjuna whilst he was restringing his bow? Was it manly to scoff at Draupadi when she was put to shame before elders and princes in the gambling hall? Was it manly of you and six warriors to surround Abhimanyu in order to murder him without compassion?"

When Arjuna heard his son's name, his heart burned with consuming fury. He drew his bow and shot a crescent-bladed arrow at Karna, whose head was immediately struck off. So fell in that dreadful battle a brother by a brother's hand.

The Kauravas fled in terror when Karna was killed, and Kripa said to Duryodhana: "Now that our greatest warriors are dead, it would be wise to ask for peace."

Duryodhana replied: "After the wrongs I have done the Pandavas, how can I ask or expect mercy at their hands? Let the war go on till the end comes."

Salya was then chosen as the new leader of the Kaurava army, which had greatly shrunken in numbers, and on the morning of the eighteenth day of the war the battle was waged with fury. But the Pandavas were irresistible, and when Duryodhana saw that they were sweeping all before them, he secretly fled, carrying his mace. He had the power to hide under water for as long as he wished, thanks to a mighty charm which had been given to him by the demons; so he plunged into a lake and lay hidden below the waters.

Salya was slain by Yudhishthira, and he fell like a thunder-splintered rock. Sahadeva overthrew Shakuni, the gambler, who had played against Yudhishthira with loaded dice, and Bhima cut down all Duryodhana's brothers who had survived until that last fateful day. Of all the Kaurava heroes the only ones left alive were Aswa-thaman, son of Drona, Kripa, Kritavarman and the hidden Duryodhana.

Finally Bhima discovered where Duryodhana was hidden. Yudhishthira went to the lakeside and urged him to come out and fight.

Duryodhana cried: "Take my kingdom now and have pleasure in it. Go and leave me, as I must retire to the jungle and engage in meditation."

Yudhishthira replied: "I cannot accept anything from you except what is won in battle."

So Duryodhana said: "If you promise to fight one by one, I will come out of the water and kill you all."

Yudhishthira said: "Come out, and the battle will be fought as you wish. Now you have spoken like a true Kshatriya."

Still Duryodhana hung back, and Bhima shouted: "If you do not come out of the lake at once, I will plunge in and drag you to the shore."

Then Duryodhana came forward, and the Pandavas laughed at the sight of him, as he was covered with mud, and water streamed down from his clothing.

Duryodhana responded: "Soon your high spirits will be turned to grief."

Now, all during the time of the Pandava exile, Duryodhana had practised with the mace, so that he became the equal of Bhima. But he had no one to support him there. The other survivors remained in hiding. Then Balarama appeared, and he caused the fight to be waged in the middle of the blood-red plain; he was Duryodhana's supporter.

The warriors fought like two fierce bulls, and hit one another with heavy blows, until their faces were reddened with blood.

Once Duryodhana almost achieved victory; he struck Bhima on the head so hard that everyone thought the Pandava hero had received his death blow. Bhima staggered but recovered himself, and soon afterwards he struck Duryodhana a foul blow to the knee, which smashed the bone so that he fell to the ground. He danced around Duryodhana for a while then, kicking his enemy's head, cried out: "Draupadi is avenged." The vow of Bhima was at last fulfilled.

Yudhishthira was angry; he struck Bhima on the face and said: "You will cause all men to speak ill of us."

Then Arjuna led Bhima away, and Yudhishthira knelt beside Duryodhana and said: "You are still our ruler, and if you order me to kill Bhima, your command will be obeyed. You are now very close to death, and I despair for the Kaurava wives and children, who will curse us because you have been laid low."

Balarama added: "Bhima has broken the laws of combat, because he struck Duryodhana below the waist."

But Krishna responded, saying: "My brother, did Duryodhana not wrong the Pandavas with foul play at dice? And did Bhima not, when he saw Draupadi put to shame, vow to break the knee of Duryodhana?"

Balarama replied: "So you approve of this?... Can I forget that Bhima kicked the head of our wounded kinsman?"

Krishna held off the vengeful hand of Balarama, and persuaded him to take vows not to fight against the Pandavas.

When night fell, the dying Duryodhana was visited on the battlefield by Aswatthaman, son of Drona, and Kripa and Kritavarman. He gave Aswatthaman permission to attack the

Pandavas while they slept…. Then Drona's son went out in
the darkness to satisfy his hunger for vengeance because his
father had been slain…. The pale stars looked down on the
dead and the dying as Aswatthaman crossed the battlefield
and went stealthily towards the tents of his enemies with
Kripa and Kritavarman.

At the gate of the Pandava camp an awful figure rose up
against the conspirators. Aswatthaman was not afraid, and
he fought with his adversary until he realised that he was
the god Shiva, the Blue-throated Destroyer. Then Drona's
son drew back, and he kindled a fire to worship the all-
powerful deity. Then, having nothing else to sacrifice,
he cast his own body on the flames. By this supremely
religious act Shiva was appeased; he accepted Drona's son
and entered his body, saying: "Until now, for the sake of
Krishna, I have protected the sons of Draupadi, but now
their hour of doom has come."

Then Aswatthaman rushed into the camp and slaughtered
with the cruel arm of vengeance. He rudely awakened
Dhrishtadyumna, who cried out: "Coward! Would you attack
a naked man?"

Aswatthaman did not answer his father's killer, but took
his life with a single blow…. Through the camp he went,
striking down everyone he met, and shrieks and moans rose
up on every side.

Draupadi was awakened by the noise, and her five
young sons sprang up to protect her. Aswatthaman
murdered each one without pity…. Then he lit a great
fire to discover those who had concealed themselves, and
he completed his ghastly work of slaughter. Meanwhile

Kripa and Kritavarman, with weapons in their hands, kept watch at the gate, and cut down everyone who tried to escape.

Meanwhile, on that night of horror, the Pandava princes slept safely in the camp of the Kauravas, so that they all escaped the sword of Drona's son.

When his job was done, the bloodthirsty Aswatthaman cut off the heads of Draupadi's five sons and carried them to Duryodhana, who rejoiced, believing that they were the heads of Yudhishthira and his brothers. But when he saw that the avenger of night had killed the children of Draupadi instead, he cried out: "What horror have you committed? You have murdered innocent children, who, had they lived, would have perpetuated our name and our fame. My heart burns with anger against the fathers and not their harmless sons."

Duryodhana groaned heavily: his heart was oppressed with grief, and, bowing his head down, he died in despair.

Aswatthaman, Kripa and Kritavarman quickly fled, fearing the wrath of the Pandavas.

THE AFTERMATH OF WAR

When the Pandava brothers were told that their camp had been raided in darkness by the bloodthirsty Aswatthaman, Yudhishthira exclaimed: "After all our suffering, now the greatest sorrow of all has fallen. Draupadi mourns the death of her brother and her five sons, and I fear she will die of grief!"

Draupadi came to her husbands and, weeping bitterly, said: "For thirteen cruel years you have endured shame and exile so that your children might prosper. But now that they are all slain, can you desire to have power and kingdom?"

Krishna said: "Oh daughter of a king, is your grief as great as is Pritha's and Gandharai's, and as great as those who mourn the loss or their husbands on the battlefield? You have less cause than others to wail now."

Draupadi was somewhat soothed, but she turned to Bhima and said: "If you will not bring to me the head of Aswatthaman, I will never look at your face again."

Yudhishthira replied: "Aswatthaman is a Brahman, and Vishnu, the greatest of the gods, will punish him if he has done wrong. If we kill him now, Draupadi, your sons and your brother and your father would not be restored to you."

Draupadi said: "So be it. But Aswatthaman has a great jewel which gleams in darkness. Let it be taken from him, because it is as dear to him as his life."

Then Arjuna went in pursuit of Aswatthaman and found him, and returned with the jewel.

Blind old Dhritarashtra then came to the battlefield, mourning the death of his hundred sons. And with the weeping maharajah were Queen Gandharai and the wives of the Kaurava princes, who cried and sobbed. Wives wept for their husbands, their children wailed beside them, and mothers moaned for their sons. The anguish of tender-hearted women was bitter, and the air was filled with wailing on that blood-red plain of Kuru-kshetra.

When Queen Gandharai saw the Pandavas she cried out: "The smell of Duryodhana is on you all."

Dhritarashtra plotted in his weak mind to crush Bhima, the slayer of Duryodhana. When he embraced Yudhishthira he said: "Where is Bhima?" and they placed in front of him an image of the strong Pandava. Dhritarashtra put forward his arms, and he crushed the image in his embrace and fell back fainting. Then he wailed: "Bhima was as a son to me. Although I have killed him, the dead cannot return."

The maharajah was pleased when he was told that Bhima still lived; and he embraced his son's slayer tenderly and with forgiveness, saying: "I have no children now except the sons of Pandu, my brother."

Pritha was delighted to see her five sons, and she embraced them one by one. Then she went towards Draupadi, who fainted in her arms. They wept together for the dead.

The bodies of the dead kings and princes were collected together. Each was wrapped in perfumed linen and laid on a funeral pyre and burned. The first pyre which was kindled was that of Duryodhana. The Pandavas mourned for their kinsmen. Then they bathed in the holy Ganges, and took up water and sprinkled it in the name of each dead hero. Yudhishthira poured out the oblation for Karna, his brother, and he gave great gifts to his widows and his children. Afterwards all the remaining bodies were burned on the battlefield.

Yudhishthira was proclaimed king in the city of Hastinapur, and he wore the great jewel in his crown. A great sacrifice was offered up, and Dhaumya, the family priest of the Pandavas, poured the Homa offering to the gods on the sacred fire. Yudhishthira and Draupadi were anointed with holy water.

THE ATONEMENT

In the days that followed, Yudhishthira mourned over the carnage of the great war; he could not be comforted. Eventually Vyasa, the sage, appeared and advised that he should perform the horse sacrifice to atone for his sins.

So a search was made for a moon-white horse with a yellow tail and one black ear, and when it was found a plate of gold, inscribed with the name of Yudhishthira, was tied to its forehead. The horse was then let loose, and was allowed to wander wherever it wished. A great army, led by Arjuna, followed the horse.

Now it was the custom in those days that when the sacred horse entered a kingdom, that kingdom was proclaimed to be subject to the king who performed the ceremony. And if any ruler detained the horse, he was compelled to fight with the army that followed the wandering animal. Should he be overcome in battle, the opposing king immediately joined forces with those of the conqueror, and followed the horse from kingdom to kingdom. For a whole year the animal was allowed to wander.

The horse was let loose on the night of full moon.

Arjuna met with many adventures. He fought against a king and the son of a king, who had a thousand wives in the country of Malwa, and defeated them. But Agni, who had married a daughter of the king, came to rescue his family. He fought against Arjuna with fire, but Arjuna shot celestial arrows which produced water. Then the god made peace, and the king who had detained the horse went away with Arjuna. After that the horse came to a rock which was the wife of a

Rishi who had been transformed because of her wickedness. "So will you stay," her husband had said, "until Yudhishthira performs the Aswa-medha ceremony." The horse was unable to leave the rock. Then Arjuna touched the rock, which immediately became a woman, and the horse was set free.

In time the horse entered the land of Amazons, and the queen detained it, and came out with her women warriors to fight against Arjuna, who, however, made peace with them and went on his way. Next the holy animal reached a strange country where men, women, horses, cows and goats grew on mighty trees like fruit, and came to maturity and died each day. The king fought against Arjuna, but was defeated. Then all the army fled to the islands of the sea, for they were Daityas, and Arjuna plundered their homes and took their treasure.

Once the horse entered a pond, and was cursed by the goddess Parvati, and it became a mare; it entered another pond and became a lion, owing to a Brahman's spell.

In the kingdom of Manipura the horse was seized, and soldiers armed with fire weapons were ready to fight against the Pandavas and their allies. But when the king, whose name was Babhru-váhana, discovered that the horse bore the name of Yudhishthira, he said: "Arjuna is my father;" and he went forward and bowed, and put his head under the foot of the Pandava hero. But Arjuna spurned him, saying: "If I were your father, you would have no fear of me."

Then the king challenged Arjuna to battle, and was victorious on that day. He took all the great men prisoners, and he severed Arjuna's head from his body with a crescent-bladed arrow. The king's mother, Chitrangada, was stricken with grief, as was Ulupi, the daughter of Vasuka, the king of serpents, who had borne a son to Arjuna. But Ulupi remembered that her father possessed a magic jewel which had power to restore a dead man to life, and she sent the king of Manipura to get it from the underworld. But the Nagas refused to give up the jewel, so Arjuna's mighty son fought against them with arrows which were transformed into peacocks; and the peacocks devoured the serpents. Then the Naga king delivered up the magic jewel, and the king returned with it. He touched the body of Arjuna with the jewel, and the hero came back to life, and all his wounds were healed. When he left Manipura city the king, his son, accompanied him.

So from kingdom to kingdom the horse wandered while the army followed, until a year had gone by. Then it returned to Hastinapur.

In the meantime, Yudhishthira had lived a life of purity and self-restraint. Each night he lay on the ground, and always slept within the city. Beside him lay Draupadi, and a naked sword was always between them.

When the horse came back the people rejoiced: they came to welcome the army with gifts of fine clothing, jewels and flowers. Money was scattered in the streets, and the poor were made happy. Yudhishthira embraced Arjuna, kissed him and wept tears of joy. He welcomed Arjuna's son, Babhru-váhana, King of Manipura, and also the other kings who had followed the sacred horse.

Twelve days after Arjuna's return, and on the day when the full moon marked the close of the winter season, the people assembled in great crowds from far and near to share Yudhishthira's generous hospitality and witness the

Aswa-medha ceremony, which was held on a green and level portion of consecrated ground. Stately pavilions, glittering with jewels and gold, had been erected for the royal guests, and there were humbler places for the Brahmans. Maharajah Dhritarashtra and King Yudhishthira sat on gold thrones, and the other kings had thrones of sandalwood and gold. The royal ladies were brought together in their appointed places. Wise Vyasa was there, and he directed the ceremony. And Krishna, the holy one, was there too.

When all the guests were assembled, Yudhishthira and Draupadi bathed together in the sacred waters of the Ganges. Then a portion of ground was measured out, and Yudhishthira ploughed it with a golden plough. Draupadi followed him, and sowed the seeds of every kind in the kingdom, while all the women and the Brahmans chanted holy mantras. Then a golden altar was built with four broad layers of golden bricks, and stakes of sacred wood from the forest and from Himalaya, and it was canopied and winged with gold-brocaded silk.

Then eight pits were dug for Homa of milk and butter to be made ready for the sacrificial fire. Then portions of every kind of vegetable and curative herb which grew in the kingdom were wrapped and placed in the Homa pits.

On the ground there were numerous sacrificial stakes, to which countless animals were tied – bulls, buffaloes and horses, wild beasts from the forests and mountains and caves, birds of every kind, fishes from rivers and lakes, and even insects.

The priests offered up animals in sacrifice to each celestial power, and the feasting was watched by sacred beings. The

Gandharvas sang, and the Apsaras, whom the Gandharvas wooed, danced like sunbeams on the grass. Messengers of the gods were also gathered there, and Vyasa and his disciples chanted mantras to celestial music. The people lifted up their voices at the sound of the rain drum and the blast of the rain trumpet. The glory of Yudhishthira's fame was bright.

When all the kings, royal ladies and sages took their places to be blessed by the horse sacrifice, Yudhishthira sat on his throne, and in his hand he held the horn of a stag.

Vyasa sent many kings and their wives to draw water from the holy Ganges. Many musicians went with them beating drums and blowing trumpets and playing sweet instruments, and girls danced in front. And all the kings and their wives were given splendid clothing by Yudhishthira, and also jewelled necklaces. The Brahmans were given gold and jewels, as well as elephants, horses and cattle.

Yudhishthira then sat naked in his throne, and each one who had drawn holy water poured some over his head; pouring what remained over the head of the sacred white horse.

Nákula held the horse's head, and said: "The horse speaks."

Those who were near him asked in loud voices: "What does the horse say?"

Nákula replied: "So speaks the horse – 'In other such ceremonies the horse that is sacrificed goes to Swarga, but I shall rise far above Swarga, because Krishna is here'."

Then Dhaumya, having washed the horse, gave Bhima a sword to strike off the head at a single blow. But before this was done, Dhaumya pressed an ear of the holy animal, and milk flowed out. Then he said to Bhima: "The horse is pure; the gods will certainly accept the sacrifice. Strike now, strong one."

Bhima raised the sword and severed the head, which immediately ascended to heaven and vanished from view. The assembled crowd was filled with joy and wonder.

Krishna, along with other kings and sages, then cut open the horse's body, from which a bright light shone out. They found that the animal was pure, and Krishna said to Yudhishthira: "This, your sacrifice, is acceptable to Vishnu."

Draupadi was made Queen of the Sacrifice, and mantras were chanted, and she was adored and given rich offerings, because of her virtue and her wisdom.

The body of the slain horse was divided, and the flesh gave off the smell of camphor. Priests lifted portions in their ladles and placed these on the sacrificial fire, and they made Soma. And King Yudhishthira and all his brothers stood in the sin-cleansing smoke and breathed its fragrance.

As he laid a piece of flesh on the altar fire, Dhaumya cried out: "Oh Indra, accept this flesh which has turned to camphor."

When he had uttered these words, Indra, accompanied by many gods, appeared in front of the people, who bowed with fear and secret joy. Indra took portions of the flesh from Vyasa and gave these to each of the gods. Then he vanished from sight with all his companions.

Vyasa blessed Yudhishthira, and Krishna embraced him and said: "Your fame will last forever."

Yudhishthira responded by saying: "I owe all these blessings to you."

After that Krishna and the kings poured holy water over the heads of Yudhishthira and Draupadi.

All the fragments of the herbs which had been provided for Homa were then ground into powder. And Yudhishthira gave balls of the powder to everyone present, so that they might eat of the sacred herbs and share in the blessings of the Aswa-medha. He ate his own portion last of all. The fragments of the offerings that remained were burnt on the altar.

Then Pritha and all the maidens who were with her enjoyed themselves, while the musicians played sweet music.

Yudhishthira distributed more gifts. To Vyasa he assigned an estate. And to the Brahmans who officiated he gave many animals, pearls and slaves. To the kings he gave war elephants, horses and money, and to the kings' wives gifts of clothing, jewels and gold.

Finally, he wept as he said farewell to Krishna, his friend in peace and in war, who climbed aboard his chariot bound for sea-washed Dwaraka.

A NIGHT OF WONDER

There was prosperity in the kingdom under Yudhishthira's wise and just government; but blind old Dhritarashtra never ceased to mourn the death of Duryodhana, his first-born, and eventually he retired to live in a humble dwelling in the jungle. With him went Queen Gandharai, and Pritha, the mother of the Pandavas, and Vidura, and others who were of great age.

Years went past, and a day came when Yudhishthira and his brothers and their wife Draupadi travelled to the home of their elders. They found them all there except for Vidura, who had gone to a sacred place on the banks of the Ganges to undergo penance and wait for the coming of Yama, god of the dead. Then all the relatives, young and old, went off to find Vidura; but when they found him he was wasted with hunger and old age, nor could he speak to them. They waited beside him until he died, and then they mourned together. This new sorrow awakened their grief, and they spoke of all those who had fallen in the great war. Fathers and mothers mourned for their sons, and wives for their husbands....

While they wept and moaned together, the great sage Vyasa came and said: "I will soothe all your sorrows.... Let each one bathe at sunset in the holy waters of the Ganges, and when night falls your lost ones will return to you once again."

Then they all sat waiting on the river bank until evening arrived. The day passed slowly; it seemed to be as long as a year.

Eventually the sun went down, and they chanted mantras and went into the Ganges. Vyasa bathed beside the old Maharajah Dhritarashtra and Yudhishthira.... Then all came out and stood on the bank.

Suddenly the waters began to heave and foam, and Vyasa muttered holy words and called out the names of the dead one by one.... Soon all the heroes who had been slain appeared one by one. They came in chariots, on horseback and on the backs of elephants. They all uttered triumphant cries; drums were sounded and trumpets were blown; and it seemed as if the armies of the Pandavas and Kauravas were once again assembled for battle. They swept over the river like a mighty tempest.

Many of the onlookers trembled with fear, until they saw Bhishma and Drona, clad in armour, standing overhead in their chariots in splendour and pride; then came Arjuna's son, the noble Abhimanyu, and Bhima's Asura son. Soon Gandharai saw Duryodhana and all his brothers, while Pritha looked with glad eyes at Karna, and Draupadi welcomed her brother Dhrishtadyumna and her five children who had all been killed by vengeful Aswatthaman. All the warriors who had fallen in battle returned again on that night of wonder.

With the army came minstrels who sang of the deeds of the heroes, and beautiful girls who danced in front of them. All strife had ended between kinsmen and rivals; in death there was peace and sweet companionship.

The ghostly warriors crossed the Ganges and were welcomed by those who waited on the bank around Vyasa. It was a night of supreme and heart-stirring happiness.

Fathers and mothers found their sons, widows clung to their husbands, sisters embraced their brothers, and all wept tears of joy. The elders who were living conversed with those who were dead; the burdens of grief and despair fell from all hearts after years of mourning; the past was suddenly forgotten in the rapture of seeing those who had died.

The night passed swiftly as if it had last for an hour. Then when dawn began to break, the dead men returned to their chariots and their horses and their elephants and said their farewells....

Vyasa spoke to the widows and said that those of them who desired to be with their husbands could go with them. Then the Kaurava princesses and other high-born ladies, who never ceased to mourn for their own, kissed the feet of the Maharajah Dhritarashtra and Queen Gandharai and plunged into the Ganges with the departing army.... Vyasa chanted mantras, and all the drowned widows were transported to heaven with their husbands.

THE ASCENT TO HEAVEN

The Pandavas returned to Hastinapur, and after two years had gone past they received more tragic news. One day Narada, the sage, arrived and told Yudhishthira that a great fire had swept through the jungle, and that Dhritarashtra, Gandharai and Pritha, and all who were with them, had perished.

Soon afterwards the Pandavas began to see terrible omens, and realised that another great tragedy was coming, but no man could tell what it was or when it would take place.

Before long it became known that the city of Dwaraka was doomed to be destroyed. A horror in human shape was seen in the night; it was yellow and black, its head was bald and its limbs misshapen, and men said it was Yama, god of the dead.... Visions of headless men fighting in battle were seen at sunset.... The moon was eclipsed, a tempest ravaged the land, and a plague of rats afflicted the city.

Krishna forbade all the people, on pain of death, to drink wine, and commanded them to perform devotions on the seashore....

Then the night was haunted by a black woman with yellow teeth who grinned horribly at house doors. All the inhabitants of the city were stricken with terror.... Evil spirits also came and robbed the jewels of the women and the weapons of the men.... Eventually the chakra of Krishna went up to heaven, and his chariot and horses followed it.... The end of the Yádavas was not far off, and the day came when Apsaras called out of heaven: "Depart from here," and all the people heard them.

When the people gathered on the seashore they held a feast, and being allowed to drink wine for one day, they drank heavily and began to argue. After some time Satyaki killed Kritavarman, who had gone to the Pandava camp with Drona's son on the night of slaughter. Then Kritavarman's friends killed Satyaki and one of Krishna's sons. Krishna put the rebels to death, but he could not stop the tumult and the fighting which ensued; fathers murdered their sons, and sons their fathers, and kinsmen fought fiercely against kinsmen.

Then Krishna and Balarama left the city, and both died in the jungle. From Balarama's mouth emerged a mighty snake, as he was the incarnation of the world serpent.... Krishna was mistaken for a gazelle by a hunter, who shot an arrow which pierced his foot at the only spot where he could be mortally wounded. He then departed to his heaven, which is called Goloka.

Before Krishna had left Dwaraka he sent messengers to Arjuna, who came quickly to find the women wailing for the dead. Then Vasudeva, father of Krishna, died, and Arjuna laid the body of the old man on the pyre, and he was burned with four of his widows, who no longer wanted to live. The bodies of Krishna and Balarama were also cremated.

Arjuna then set off towards Indra-prastha with a remnant of the people; and when they had left Dwaraka, the sea rose up and swallowed the whole city, with those who had refused to leave.

A deep gloom fell on the Pandavas after this, and Vyasa, the sage, appeared before them, and revealed that their time had come to leave this world.

Then Yudhishthira divided the kingdom in half. He made Parikshit, son of Abhimanyu, one King of Hastinapur; and Yuyutsu, the half-brother of Duryodhana, who had joined the Pandava army on the first day of the great war, was made the second King of Hastinapur. He counselled them to live at peace one with another.

Afterwards the Pandavas cast off their royal attire and their jewels and put on the clothing of hermits, and the bright-eyed and faithful Draupadi did likewise. Yudhishthira left first of all, and his brothers walked behind him one by one, and Draupadi went last of all, followed by a hound. They all walked towards the rising sun on the long path which leads to Mount Meru, through forests and over streams and across the burning plains, never to return again.

One by one they fell by the wayside, all except Yudhishthira. Draupadi was the first to sink down, and Bhima cried: "Why has she fallen who has never done wrong?"

Yudhishthira replied: "Her heart was bound up in Arjuna, and she has her reward."

Sahadeva was next to fall, and then Nakula. After some time Yudhishthira heard the voice of Bhima crying in distress: "No! Now the noble Arjuna has fallen. What sin has he committed?"

Yudhishthira explained: "He boasted confidently that he could destroy all his enemies in one day, and because he failed in his vow he has fallen."

The two surviving brothers walked on in silence; but the time came when mighty Bhima sank down. He cried: "Yudhishthira, tell me why I have fallen now."

Yudhishthira said: "Because of your cursing and gluttony and your pride."

Yudhishthira walked on, calm and unmoved, followed by his faithful hound. When he came close to sacred Mount Meru, the world-spine, Indra, king of the gods, came out to welcome him, saying: "Ascend, resolute prince."

Yudhishthira replied: "Oh king of the gods, let my brothers who have fallen by the wayside come with me. I cannot enter heaven without them. Let the fair and gentle princess come too; Draupadi has been a faithful wife, and is worthy of bliss. Hear my prayer, Indra, and have mercy."

Indra said to him: "Your brothers and Draupadi have gone before you."

Then Yudhishthira pleaded that his faithful hound should also enter heaven; but Indra said: "Heaven is no place for those who are followed by hounds. Do you not know that demons rob religious ordinances of their virtues when dogs are nearby?"

To this Yudhishthira replied: "No evil can come from the noble. I cannot have joy if I desert this faithful friend."

Indra said: "You left behind your brothers and Draupadi. Why, therefore, can you not abandon your hound?"

Yudhishthira answered: "I have no power to bring back to life those who have fallen by the wayside: there can be no abandonment of the dead."

As he spoke, the hound was transformed into Dharma, god of justice. He stood by the king's side and said:

"Yudhishthira, you are indeed my son. You would not abandon me, your hound, because I was faithful to you. Your equal cannot be found in heaven."

Then Yudhishthira was transported to the city of eternal bliss, and there he found Duryodhana sat on a throne. All the Kauravas were in heaven too, but the king could not find his brothers or Draupadi.

Indra said: "Yudhishthira, here you will live in eternal bliss. Forget all earthly ties and attain to perfection; your brothers have fallen short, therefore they sank by the wayside."

Yudhishthira said: "I cannot stay here with the Kauravas who have done me wrong. Where my brothers are, is where I should be with our wife Draupadi."

Then a celestial being led Yudhishthira to the home of his brothers and the Princess of Panchala. He entered the forest of the nether regions, where the leaves were like sharp weapons and the path was covered with knives. Darkness hung heavily, and the way was sodden with blood and strewn with foul and mutilated corpses. Shapes of horror flitted round about like shadows; fierce birds of prey feasted on human flesh. The damned were burning in everlasting fires, and the air reeked with foul odours. A boiling river went past, and Yudhishthira saw the place of torture with thorns, and the desert of fiery sand: he gazed mutely at each horror that was unfolded before his eyes.

Gladly would Yudhishthira have turned back, but in the darkness he heard the voices of his brothers and Draupadi calling him to stay a little while to comfort them while they suffered torment.

Yudhishthira said to the celestial being: "Leave me here; I must stay to relieve the sufferings of my brothers and Draupadi." As he spoke the gods appeared, and the scene of horror vanished from before his eyes, for it was an illusion conjured up to test his constancy.

Then Yudhishthira was led to the heavenly Ganges, and having bathed in its sacred waters, he cast off his mortal body and became a celestial.

Then, rejoicing, he entered Swarga, the celestial city of Indra, and was welcomed by Krishna in all his divine glory, and by his brothers and by Draupadi, and all whom he had loved on earth.

Indra spoke and said: "This is the beautiful and immortal one, who sprang from the altar to be your wife, and these bright beings are her five children. Here is Dhritarashtra, who is now the king of the Gandharvas; there is Karna, son of Surya, the peerless archer who was slain by Arjuna. Here comes towards you Abhimanyu, son of Arjuna; he is now the star-bright companion of the lord of night…. Here are Pandu, your father and Pritha, your mother, now united in heaven. See too, Yudhishthira, the wise Bhishma, whose place is with the Vasus round my throne: Drona sits with Dharma, god of wisdom. Here are all the peerless warriors who fell in battle and have won heaven by their courage and their constancy. So may all mortals rise to eternal bliss, casting off their mortal bodies and entering by the shining door of the celestial city, by doing good deeds, by uttering gentle words, and by enduring all suffering with patience. The holy life is prepared for all the sons of men."

So ends the story of the Great War of the Bharatas.

MORE TALES OF THE MAHABHARATA

Embedded in the narrative of the Great Bharata War between the Pandavas and the Kauravas is the tale of King Samvarana and the fairy-like Tapati, a daughter of the sun god, Surya. This charming story was told to Arjuna, the Pandava prince, by a Gandharva whom he had defeated in single combat. Its message tells of how in Indian mythology the folk of the spirit world might woo or be wooed by impressionable mortals.

It is also within the Vana Parva book of the *Mahabharata* that we discover the enchanting love story of Nala, king of the Nishadha kingdom, and Damayanti, the beautiful daughter of King Bhima. Essentially, this is a tale of two lovers who strive to overcome numerous obstacles in their quest to marry and live happily together. In it we find bright examples of masculine morality, purity, loyalty, constancy and love.

SAMVARANA AND TAPATI

Tapati was of all nymphs the most beautiful; she was perfectly symmetrical and exquisitely attired; she had faultless features, and black, large eyes; she was chaste and exceedingly well behaved. For a time the sun god considered that no husband could be found who was worthy of his daughter; and therefore knew no peace of mind, always thinking of the person he should choose.

One day, however, King Samvarana worshipped the sun, and made offerings of flowers and sweet perfumes, and Surya resolved to bestow his daughter upon this ideal man.

It came to pass that Samvarana went hunting deer on the mountains. He rode swiftly in pursuit of a nimble-footed stag, leaving his companions behind, until his horse expired with exhaustion. Then he wandered around alone. In a secluded wood he came across a maiden of exquisite beauty; he gazed at her for a while, thinking she was a goddess or the embodiment of the rays emanating from the sun. Her body was as radiant as fire and as spotless as the crescent moon; she stood motionless like a golden statue. The flowers and the creepers round about partook of her beauty, and seemed to be converted into gold. She was Tapati, daughter of the sun.

The king's eyes were captivated, his heart was wounded by the arrows of the love god Kama; he lost his peace of mind. Eventually he spoke and said: "Who are you, fair one? Maiden of sweet smiles, why do you linger in these lonely woods? I have never seen or heard of one so beautiful as you…. The love god tortures me."

That lotus-eyed maiden made no answer; she vanished from sight like lightning in the clouds.

The king rushed through the forest, mourning for her: he searched in vain; he stood motionless in grief; he fell down on the earth and fainted.

Then, smiling sweetly, the maiden appeared again. In honeyed words she said: "Arise, you tiger among kings. It is not proper that you should lose your reason in this manner."

Samvarana opened his eyes and saw Tapati. Weak with emotion he uttered: "I am burning with love for you, you black-eyed beauty. Oh, accept me. My life is ebbing away.... I have been bitten by Kama, who is like a venomous snake. Have mercy on me.... You of striking and faultless features, you of face like the lotus or the moon, you of voice sweet as that of singing Kinnaras, my life now depends on you. Without you, timid one, I am unable to live. Please do not cast me off; I need you to relieve me from this affliction by giving me your love. At the first sight you have distracted my heart. My mind wanders. Be merciful; I am your obedient slave, your adorer. Accept me.... you of lotus eyes, the flame of desire burns within me. Extinguish that flame by throwing on it the water of your love...."

Tapati replied: "I am not mistress of my own self. I am a maiden ruled by my father. If you love me, demand me of him. My heart has been robbed by you."

Then, revealing her identity, Tapati ascended to heaven, and once again Samvarana fell on the earth and fainted.

The ministers and followers of the king came searching for him, and found him lying forsaken on the ground like a rainbow dropped from the heavens. They sprinkled his face with cool lotus-scented water. When he revived, the monarch sent away all his followers except one minister. For twelve days he constantly worshipped the sun on the mountain top. Then a great Rishi, whom he had sent for, came to him, and the Rishi ascended to the sun. Before long he returned with Tapas, the sun god, having declared that Varanasi would be a worthy husband for his daughter.

For twelve years the king lived with his fairy bride in the

mountain forests, and a regent ruled over the kingdom. But although the monarch enjoyed much bliss living the life of a celestial, the people of the kingdom suffered. For twelve years no rain fell, not even a drop of dew came from the skies, and no corn grew. The people were afflicted with famine; men grew reckless, and deserted their wives and children; the capital became like a city of the dead.

Then a great Rishi brought Varanasi back to his capital with his celestial bride. And after that things became as they were before. Rain fell in abundance and corn was grown. Revived by that foremost of monarchs of virtuous soul, the capital and the country was filled with joy. A son was born to the king, and his name was Kuru.

NALA AND DAMAYANTI

Once upon a time there reigned in Nishadha a great king whose name was Nala. He was skilled in taming horses; he was a peerless archer, and was devoted to truth. Nala commanded a mighty army and he was held above all other kings. He was deeply religious, and was well read in the Vedas, but he was also a passionate lover of dice. Many a high-born lady sang his praises, for he was generous of heart, self-controlled, and the guardian of law.

Now, over the neighbouring state of Vidarbha ruled the mighty King Bhima, the terrible in strength, who was likewise of choicest virtues. He was childless, and he yearned for children. For many years he had been known to perform holy deeds intent on offspring, but without avail.

It chanced, however, that one day a Brahman named Damana came to his court. Bhima welcomed the sage and in return the queen was blessed: she became the mother of one sweet girl, the pearl of maidens, who was named Damayanti, and of three noble sons, Dama, Danta, and the renowned Damana, who all grew great and powerful.

When fair Damayanti had reached the full bloom of her beauty, she was unequalled throughout the world for her brilliance and her grace. A hundred female servants and a hundred virgin handmaidens waited on the beautiful princess, and she shone among them, decked with jewels and rich ornaments, like the goddess of beauty. Never among the gods, or the Yakshas, or among mortal men was a maiden more fair ever heard of or ever seen than Damayanti, who disturbed the souls of the gods.

In the presence of Bhima's sweet daughter, the ladies of Vidarbha took joy in constantly praising Nala, that tiger among kings. Likewise before Nishadha's king, Damayanti was ever extolled because of her beauty. So it happened that, hearing so much of each other's virtues, the silent passion of love was nurtured in both their hearts.

As his love increased, Nala grew impatient and he was known to wander in a grove within his palace garden secretly musing over Damayanti. On one such walk he discovered a flock of beautiful swans with wings all flecked with gold. The king crept forward and seized one, and he marvelled to hear it cry out in human language: "Slay me not, oh gentle king, and to you I will render a service, for I will praise you in the presence of Damayanti so that forever after she shall think of no other mortal man but you."

Immediately Nala set the bird free, and it flew off with its bright companions towards Vidarbha. When they reached the garden of Bhima's palace they settled down at Damayanti's feet, who was lying in the shade with her handmaidens. All the young women gazed in wonder at the swans, admiring their graceful forms and their plumage gleaming with gold, and before long they began to pursue them among the trees. Then suddenly the bird that Damayanti followed spoke to her in human language and said: "Damayanti, listen! The noble king Nala lives in Nishadha. He is as handsome as a god. His equal cannot be found in the world. You are the pearl of women, and he is the pride of men. If you were married to him, then perfect beauty and noble birth would be united. Blessed indeed would be the union of the peerless with the peerless."

Damayanti listened in wonder while the bird spoke, and then she said: "Speak also to Nala in this manner."

The swan answered: "So be it," and it took flight with the others to Nishadha, where it told Nala all that had taken place.

After that day Damayanti ceased to live for herself alone; all her thoughts were given up to Nala. She mostly sat alone in silent reverie; the bloom faded from her cheeks, and she grew dejected and melancholy. She gave up her soul to sorrow, and she secretly sighed, gazing upward and meditating, because love had taken hold of her heart. She also stopped finding pleasure in sleep, or in gentle conversation. In the midst of her broken slumbers she was known to weep and cry out: "Oh, woe is me!"

The handmaidens read her heart, and they went to her father and told that his gentle daughter was pining for the monarch among men. When Bhima heard this, he reflected on what should be done for Damayanti, and he decided that her time for the swayamvara had come. So he summoned all the princes on earth.

Then the whole land resound with the trampling of elephants and horses and the rumbling of chariots, for the stately princes, followed by their armies, swarmed towards the court of Bhima.

Now it happened that at this time two wise sages, Narada and Parvata, ascended Mount Meru to Swarga, the heaven of Indra, and they saluted the Cloud-compeller within his palace. The immortal lord welcomed them, and asked how it fared with the world. Narada said it fared well with the world and with all the mighty kings. Then Indra asked: "Where are all the royal heroes? Why do they not come here as my honoured guests?"

The wise sage answered: "The great kings cannot appear before you because they are hurrying one and all to the swayamvara of Damayanti, the renowned daughter of Bhima, the fairest woman on earth. Oh slayer of drought demons, every king seeks to woo this maid of transcending beauty, because she is the pearl of all the world."

As Narada spoke, the other gods came and listened to his words. Then together they exclaimed with rapture: "We shall also will go there…." In an instant they were hurtling through the air in their chariots towards the city of Vidarbha to mingle with the wooers of Bhima's fair daughter.

Meanwhile Nala had set off with joy, his heart full of love for Damayanti. The gods saw him standing on the surface of the earth with radiance like the sun, and they stopped their course, gazing in mute wonder, for he was as handsome as the god of love. Then, dropping down through the blue air, they hailed the stately hero, saying: "Do as we now ask you, oh most excellent of princes; be the bearer of our message."

Nala adored the gods with folded hands and promised to obey their will, saying humbly: "Who are you that now command my service?"

Indra spoke and said: "We are the guardians of the world. I am Indra, lord of heaven; here is Agni, god of fire; here is Varuna, king of the waters; and there is Yama, lord of the dead. You must inform Damayanti that we have come to woo her and say to her: 'Choose for your husband one of the celestial beings'."

But Nala replied: "I beg you not to send me on this mission. How can I who am enamoured with the maiden, plead the cause of another? In mercy spare me – spare me this unwelcome service."

But the gods would not be moved from their purpose. They reminded Nala he had already promised to do their will, and they therefore urged him to go without delay. Then the lord of Nishadha pleaded: "The palace of Bhima is strongly guarded, and I cannot enter there."

Indra responded: "You will indeed enter." And even as the god spoke, Nala found himself standing in front of Damayanti in her secret bower.

The beautiful maiden was surrounded by her virgin band, and he gazed at her faultless limbs and slender waist and into her entrancing eyes. Her shining beauty excelled even the tender rays of the moon. Nala's love grew deeper and stronger as he looked at the smiling princess; but he curbed his passion, remembering his mission.

All the maidens gazed with wonder and joy at the noble form, and in their hearts they exclaimed: "Oh the splendid one; the strong and mighty hero – who is he?... Is he god, or Yaksha, or Gandharva?" But they spoke not a word, as his beauty made them bashfully silent.

Nala smiled at Damayanti, and first she smiled softly in return; then she exclaimed: "Who are you that has come here like a celestial being to awaken all my love. Tell me, how did you manage to enter the palace unseen, for surely all the chambers are strongly guarded by stern orders of the king?"

The king answered by saying: "Oh fairest one, know now that I am Nala, and that I come here as the messenger of the gods Indra, Agni, Varuna and Yama, and through their power I have entered here, unseen nor stopped, for it is their desire that I should say to you, 'Choose for your husband one of the celestial beings'. This is the purpose of my mission from the great world guardians. Having heard me, you may decide as you will."

Damayanti paid homage to the gods at once. Then she smiled at Nala said: "I am yours already, and whatever I possess is yours also. Oh give me your love in return, Nala. Know that my love was increased by the endearing words of the swan, and it is because of you that the kings are all gathered here now. If you will despise me, I will suffer death for your sake by fire, or by water, or even by the noose."

The king answered: "Will you despise these, the gods, and choose for your husband a mortal who is more lowly than the dust they walk on? Let your heart aspire to them. Remember, too, that the man who incurs the anger of the world's guardians will meet with certain death. Shield me from such a fate, fairest one!... So choose one of the perfect gods, and you shall have robes unsullied by dust, garlands that never fade, and celestial joy without end."

Trembling, and with tear-dimmed eyes, Damayanti said: "I do homage with due humility to all the gods, but I desire you for my husband, you and you only."

But Nala replied: "I am charged with the mission of the celestial beings, and cannot plead for myself now. But afterwards I will come to claim you, and will speak boldly, so remember me in your heart."

The maiden smiled through her tears. "Ah!" she said, "Now I see a way of escape.... When you come to the swayamvara, enter together with the gods, and I will name you as my own, so that no sin may be charged against you."

Then Nala returned to the gods, who eagerly awaited him, and he told them all that the maiden had said, word for word.

When the day of the swayamvara finally arrived, Bhima summoned all the love-sick kings, and they passed through the court of golden columns and under the bright portal arch, and entered the Hall of State like lions on the mountains. The kings were then seated on their thrones, adorned with garlands and with dangling earrings. The arms of some were robust and powerful like the battle mace; those of others were delicate and smooth like a serpent. With flowing hair, shapely noses, and arching eyebrows, the faces of these great lords were as radiant as the stars in heaven.

When Damayanti entered, every eye and every soul was entranced by her dazzling beauty; all these lords of earth gazed at her with unmoving eyes.... The name of each king was proclaimed in turn, and Nala, looking around her, was suddenly stricken with dismay, as she saw that there were five Nalas present who were undistinguishable from another. The four gods who desired to win her had each assumed the likeness of her beloved one.

Whichever of these she gazed at, he seemed to be her king, and in her secret heart she wailed: "How can I recognise Nala among the celestial beings?"

In her distress the trembling maiden folded her hands and prayed to the gods, saying: "When I heard the sweet words of the swans, I pledged my heart to Nala. I urge you by this truth. Oh, reveal my lord! I have never swerved from my faith either by word or by deed. I urge you by this truth. Oh, reveal my lord! The gods have destined that Nala should be my husband. I urge you by this truth. Oh, reveal my lord! The vow that I pledged to Nala is holy, and I must always keep it. I urge you by this truth. Oh, reveal my lord! Oh mighty ones, guardians of the world, now assume your divine forms, so that I may know Nala, the monarch of men."

The gods marvelled at the sad maiden's piteous prayer. They saw that her resolve was firm, that she was constant in truth and in love, and was holy and wise, and that she remained faithful to her lord. So they revealed the tokens of their greatness…. Then Damayanti was able to recognise the four celestial beings because their skins were without moisture and their eyes never winked, there was no dust on their garlands and their feet did not touch the earth.

She also knew Nala because he cast a shadow; there was dust on his clothing, and his garland was beginning to fade; drops of moisture stood on his skin, and his eyelids moved.

Gazing first at the celestial beings and then at him who was her heart's desire, Damayanti named Nala as her lord. She modestly touched the hem of his garment and threw a wreath of bright flowers round his neck, thereby choosing him for her husband.

All the rivals of Nala uttered cries of sorrow, but the gods and the sages exclaimed: "Well done! Well done!" and honoured the lord of Nishadha.

Nala turned to fair Damayanti, and said: "Since you have chosen me for your husband in the presence of the gods, know that I will be a faithful consort who will forever take delight in your words. I am yours, and so long as my life endures I will be yours only."

The happy pair then paid homage to the gods, and these resplendent guardians of the earth joyfully bestowed eight rare gifts upon Nala. Indra gave him the power to walk unhindered by any obstacle wherever he desired; Agni gave him power over fire, and power over the three worlds; Varuna gave him power over water, and power to obtain fresh garlands at will; and Yama gave him the subtle skill of preparing food, and eminence in every virtue. Each of the gods also gave his double blessing to Nala, and afterwards they departed.

All the princes watched in wondered when they saw the maiden's choice confirmed in this manner, and they went away as they came, with joy, and returned to their own kingdoms.

After the wedding, Bhima bade Nala adieu when he set out to return to his native city with the pearl of women whom he had won.

Meanwhile, as the gods were leaving the swayamvara they met Kali, the demon of evil in the midst of the blue air. He was accompanied by the wicked spirit Dwapara. Indra, the slayer of giants, spoke and said: "Where are you going with Dwapara, Kali?"

Kali answered: "We are hurrying to the swayamvara, because it is my desire to obtain Damayanti as my bride."

Smiling, the king of gods said: "The matter is now arranged and ended. The fair Damayanti has chosen Nala for her husband in our presence."

Kali was furious, and he exclaimed: "Since she has preferred a mortal in the presence of the celestial beings, let her choice be her own doom."

But the gods said: "Our consent was freely given because Damayanti has chosen a husband endowed with all the virtues, and equal even to the guardians of the world. If anyone should curse Nala, the curse will recoil fatally, and the curser will be cast into the torments of the dark lake of hell." The bright deities then ascended to the heavens.

Kali turned to Dwapara and declared: "I cannot control my fierce wrath. I will be avenged on Nala – I will enter his body, and he will be bereft of his kingdom and of his bride. You, Dwapara, will enter the dice and assist me."

So a malignant pact was arranged between the demon of evil and his dark ally, and together they went towards Nishadha to haunt the stately palace of Nala, waiting for the fatal moment.

WANDERINGS IN THE FOREST

For twelve bright years Nala and Damayanti lived happily together. The great king ruled his people justly; he offered up every sacrifice to the gods, and he gave sumptuous gifts to holy men. Fair Damayanti became the mother of a beautiful daughter named Indrasena, and of a handsome son named Indrasen. The blessings of life were showered on the blissful pair.

But eventually there came a day when, after performing an unclean act, Nala sipped holy water and went to pray with unwashed feet. The watchful Kali seized this fatal opportunity, and straightway entered the king and possessed his soul. Then that evil demon summoned Pushkara, the brother of Nala, saying: "Come and throw dice with the king. I will give you mine help, so that you will be able to win the whole kingdom for yourself."

At once Pushkara challenged his brother, and the wicked spirit Dwapara entered the dice.

Nala readily agreed to take part in the game of hazard, as he was swayed by evil Kali. Then the two rivals began to play together in the presence of Damayanti.

The great king staked his wealth, and he lost; he staked his golden treasures and he staked his chariots, and still he lost; he staked his rich clothing, and he continued to lose. The passion for dice had possessed Nala like a sudden madness, and in vain his friends tried to restrain him.

Rumours of dire happenings quickly spread throughout the city, and the king's faithful subjects, accompanied by high counsellors of state, assembled at the palace gate to try to persuade him to stop playing. They urged Damayanti to intervene, and the broken-spirited daughter of Bhima approached Nala in anguish and dismay, and cried: "All your subjects have gathered outside because they cannot endure the thought that misfortune should fall on you."

Nala heard her but did not answer because his soul was clouded by evil Kali. Then the wise men said: "It is not he;" and they returned to their homes in sorrow and shame....

So the play went on every day for many weary months, and Nala was always beaten.

In the end, when Damayanti realised that all the treasures were lost, she sent for her faithful charioteer, Varshneya, and said: "Hurry now and yoke Nala's horses, and place my children in the chariot. Then drive quickly to the city of my family and leave them in the care of my father, the King Bhima. When you have done me that service, Varshneya, you may go wherever you choose."

So the charioteer took Indrasena and Indrasen to the city of Vidarbha, and he delivered them safely to Bhima, whom he told of the fall of Nala. Then, with great sadness, he went to the city of Ayodhya, where he was took employment from the renowned King Rituparna.

Nala played on; he continued to throw the dice, until at last he had lost all his possessions. Then Pushkara smiled and spoke to his stricken brother, saying: "Now, throw once more. Where is your stake? Ah, you have nothing left now except Damayanti. Let us throw the dice for her."

At these words Nala's heart was broken. Mute with sorrow, he gazed at his brother.... He rose up and stripped off his rich vestments one by one. Then slowly and in silence he left, naked and alone. Damayanti, wearing just a single garment, followed him. Together they stood at the city gates.

Then Pushkara, who had become king, proclaimed a dreadful decree throughout the city: "Whoever gives food or drink to Nala shall immediately be put to death".

In their terror the people could not help the fallen king, and for three days and three nights he drank only water. His only food was plucked wild fruit and roots from the earth. After that Nala wandered away from Nishadha, an outcast among men, and Damayanti followed behind.

Tortured by hunger, the fallen king eventually saw a flock of birds with gold-flecked wings on the ground and he decided to try to catch one. So he crept forward and flung his only garment over them; but they rose in the air, carrying it away with them. As they went they cried out mockingly in human language and said: "Oh foolish king, we are the dice. We came here on purpose to utterly plunder you, because so long as you had a single garment left our joy was incomplete."

Nala spoke to Damayanti in his anguish, saying: "Oh blameless one, by whose anger have I been driven from my kingdom and rendered unable to find any food? Now listen to me. The roads diverge here before us, and one leads southward past the caves of holy hermits, which are stored with food, towards the kingdom of your father." Nala anxiously pointed out the way and urged Bhima's fair daughter to take refuge in Vidarbha before he entered the great forest.

Weighed down by sadness and with tear-streaked cheeks, Damayanti replied: "Your words cause my heart to break and my limbs to fail me. How can I leave you all alone in the forest when you have lost your kingdom and your riches, and whilst you are thirsty and tortured by hunger? Instead let me comfort you, my husband. Wise physicians have said that a wife is the only healing herb for her husband's sorrow."

Nala replied: "Your words are true. There is indeed no medicine for a stricken man like his wife's love. Please know that I do not wish to part from you."

Weeping, Damayanti replied: "If you would not leave me, why do you make my sorrow heavier by pointing out the way to Vidarbha? You are too noble to abandon me, yet you show me the road southward. If it is right that I should return to my father, come with me and he will welcome you, and we could live happily together in his palace."

Nala responded sadly: "Ah! I can never return in my shame to that city where I have appeared once before in pride and splendour."

Then, comforting Damayanti, Nala wandered on with her through the deep forest, and they made one garment serve them both. They suffered from hunger and thirst, and at last when they came to a lonely hut, they sat down on the hard ground. Damayanti was overcome with weariness, and soon she fell asleep; she lay naked on the bare floor. But there was no rest for Nala; he harrowed at the thought of his lost kingdom and the friends who had deserted him, and of the weary journey he must make in the midst of the great forest. "Ah! Would it be better to die now and end all?" he mused, "Or to desert her whom I love? She is more devoted to me than I deserve. If she were abandoned she would return to Vidarbha. She is unable to endure my suffering and the constant sorrow which must be mine."

He pondered over this for a long time until Kali swayed him to desert his faithful wife. So he severed her garment and used half of it. He turned away from the fair princess as she lay fast asleep. Repenting in his heart, Nala turned and gazed at Damayanti with love and pity. He wept bitterly, saying: "Ah, here you sleep on the bare hard ground. Oh my loved one, you have always awakened with a smile. How will you fare when you discover that your lord has abandoned you in the midst of the perilous forest?... May sun and wind and the spirits of the wood protect you, and may you be shielded forever by your own great virtue!"

Then the distracted king, prompted by Kali again, ran away; but his heart was torn by his love, which drew him back.... So time and again he came and went, like to swing, backward and forward, until in the end the evil spirit conquered him, and he left Damayanti, who moaned fitfully in her sleep; and he plunged into the depths of the forest.

Before long the fair princess awoke, and when she saw that she was all alone she screamed and cried out: "Oh! Where are you, my king, my lord, my sole protector?... I am lost; I am undone. I am helpless and alone in the perilous wood.... Ah, now you are just deceiving me. Do not mock me, my lord. Are you hidden there among the bushes? Oh, speak!... Why do you not answer?... I do not sorrow for myself only. I cannot endure that you should be alone, that you should thirst and be hungered and very weary, and without me to give you comfort...."

So she wailed as she searched through the forest for Nala. At last she said: "Oh, may he who causes Nala to suffer endure even greater agony than he endures, and may he live forever in darkness and misery!"

Suddenly a great serpent rose up and coiled itself round her fair body....

"Oh, my guardian!" she cried, "I am now undone. The serpent has seized me. Why are you not near?... Who will comfort you now in your sorrow, Nala?"

A passing huntsman heard her cries; he broke through the jungle and saw Damayanti in the coils of the serpent.... Nimbly he darted forward and with a single blow struck off the monster's head, and rescued the beautiful lady from her peril. Then he washed her body and gave her food.

"Who are you, fair-eyed one?" he asked. "Why do you wander alone in the perilous wood?"

Damayanti told the huntsman the story of her sorrow. As she spoke, his frail heart was moved by her great beauty, and he uttered amorous words with whining voice.... Perceiving his evil intent, she was roused to fierce anger. Her chastity was her sole defence, and she cursed him so that he immediately fell down dead like a tree that has been struck by lightning.

Freed from the savage huntsman of wild beasts, the lotus-eyed Damayanti wandered on through the deep forest, which resounded everywhere with the sound of crickets. All around her were trees of every form and name, and she saw shady arbours, deep valleys, and wooded hill summits, and lakes and pools, loud resounding waterfalls, and great flowing rivers. The forest was dreary and appalling: it was full of lions and tigers, of countless birds and fierce robbers. She saw buffaloes and wild boars feeding, and the fierce and awesome forms that were also there – serpents and giants and terrible demons.... But, protected by her virtue, she wandered on all alone without fear.

Her sole anxiety was for Nala, and she wept for him, crying: "Ah! Where are you? Remember your vows and your plighted faith. Remember the words of the gold-winged swan.... Am I not your loved one?... Oh, why do you not answer in this dark and perilous forest? The savage beasts are ready to devour me. Why are you not near to save me?... I am weak and dust-stained, and have need of you, my protector.... Whom can I ask for Nala? The tiger is before me, the king of the forest, and I am not afraid. I address him, saying: 'Oh! I am lonely, and wretched, and sorrowful, searching for my exiled husband. If you have seen him, console me; if you have not seen him, devour me, and set me free from this misery.'...But the tiger turns down to the river bank, and I wander onward towards the holy mountain. 'Hear me!' I cry. I am a king's daughter and the consort of a king, the illustrious lord of Nishadha, the pious, the faultless one, who is as courageous as the elephant.... Have you seen my Nala, Oh mighty Mountain?... Ah, why do you not answer me?... Comfort me as if I were your own child.... Shall I ever see him again, and ever hear his honey-sweet voice, like music, saying: 'Daughter of Vidarbha,' while it soothes all my pain with its blessed sound?..."

Having addressed the mountain, Damayanti turned northward and wandered on for three days and three nights. Then she reached a holy grove, and she entered it humbly and without fear. She witnessed the cells of hermits and their bright sacred fires. The holy men were struck with wonder by her beauty, and they made her welcome, saying: "Are you a goddess of the wood, or of the mountain, or of the river?"

Damayanti replied: "I am not a goddess of the wood, or a mountain spirit, or a river nymph, but a mortal woman."

Then she told the holy men the story of her sorrow and her wandering, and they told her: "A time will come soon, a time of beauty, when you will once again see Nala in splendour and ruling over his people."

After they had said these words, all the holy men and their sacred fires vanished. Damayanti wondered if see had seen a vision. Then she went towards another region.

Mourning for Nala, the fair one came to a beautiful asoka tree: its green branches were studded with gleaming fruit, and the songs of birds filled the air. "Oh happy tree," she cried. "Take away all my grief.... Say, have you seen my Nala, my beloved lord? Have you seen my one love, with smooth, bright skin, wandering alone in the forest? Answer me, blessed Asoka, so that I may go in joy. Hear and speak, happy tree...."

So, wailing in her deep anguish, Damayanti moved round the asoka. Then she went towards a lonelier and more fearsome region.... She passed many a river and many mountains, and she saw numerous birds and deer as she wandered on and on, searching for her lost lord.

Eventually she came across a great caravan of merchants. Ponderous elephants and eager camels, prancing horses and rumbling cars came through a river. All the noble animals of the caravan came splashing noisily across the ford. The great crowd of travellers stared with wonder at the maniac-like woman, clad in only half a garment, smeared with dust and pale and sorrowful, her long hair all matted and muddy. Some fled from her in fear. But others took pity and said: "Who are you and what are you seeking in the lonely forest? Are you a goddess of the mountain, or of the forest, or of the plain?... We pray for your protection; be mindful of our welfare so that we may prosper on our journey."

Damayanti told the story of her misfortune and all the travellers gathered around to hear – boys and young men and grey-haired sages. "Oh, have you seen my lord, my Nala?" she cried to them.

The captain of the gang answered her "No"; and she asked him where the caravan was headed, to which he said: "We are going to the realm of Chedi, over which Subahu is king." When the merchants resumed their journey, Damayanti went with them.

They travelled a long distance through the forest, and by evening they had reached the green shore of a beautiful wide lake which sparkled with bright lotus blooms. The camp was pitched in the middle of a deep grove. The men bathed with their wearied animals in the delicious, ice-cool waters.

At midnight all slept.... In the deep silence a herd of wild forest elephants came down to drink from the gurgling stream which flowed near to the camp. When they sensed the tame elephants lying sleeping, they trumpeted aloud and all of a sudden charged and fell on them. Trees and tents were thrown down as they trampled through the camping ground, and the travellers awoke panic-stricken. Some fled through the forest; others stood gasping with wonder, and the elephants killed them. The camp was scattered in the confusion; many animals were gored; men overthrew one another, trying to escape; many shrieked in terror, and a few climbed trees. Voices were heard calling: "It is a fire!" and merchants screamed, "Why fly away so speedily? Save the precious jewels."

Amid the tumult and the slaughter Damayanti awoke, trembling with fear, and she quickly escaped without harm. In the deep forest she came by the few men who had found refuge, and she heard them say one to another: "What deed have we done to bring this misfortune on us? Have we forgotten to adore Manibhadra, the high king of the Yakshas? Before we set off, did we not worshipped the spirits that bring disasters? Was it doomed that all omens should be prove to be false? How has it come that such a disaster has happened to us?"

Others who had been robbed of their family and their wealth, miserably said: "Who was she – that ill-omened, maniac-eyed woman who came with us? In truth she seemed scarcely human. Surely it is because of her evil power that disaster has befallen us. She is a witch, or she is a sorceress, or maybe a demon.... Without doubt she is the cause of all our woes.... We should find her – the evil destroyer! Let us slay the murderess with clods and with stones, with canes and with staves, or else with our fists...."

When the terrified and innocent Damayanti heard these fearsome threats, she fled through the trees, wailing: "My terrible doom haunts me still! Misfortune dogs my footsteps.... I have no memory of any sin of thought or deed – of any wrong done by me to living beings. Perhaps I did sin in my former life, and am now suffering due punishment.... I have lost my husband; my kingdom is lost; I have lost my family; my noble Nala has been taken from me, and I am far removed from my children, and I wander alone in the wood of serpents."

When morning broke, the sorrowful queen met with some holy Brahmans who had escaped the night's disaster, and she went with them towards the city of Chedi.

The people gazed with wonder at Damayanti when she walked through the streets with her dust-smeared body and matted hair. The children danced around her as she wandered like a maniac, so miserable and weary and emaciated.

By chance, as she came near to the royal palace the mother of the king looked out of a window, and saw her and said:

"Hurry, and allow this poor wanderer to enter. Although stricken and half-clothed she has, I think, the beauty of Indra's long-eyed queen. Let her have refuge from those staring men."

Damayanti was then led before the queen mother, who spoke gently, saying: "Although bowed down with grief, you are beautiful. You fear no one. Who are you so well protected by your own chastity?"

Bhima's daughter wept and told all that had happened to her, but did not reveal who she was. Then the queen mother said: "You may live here with me, and our servants shall go in quest of your husband."

Damayanti said: "Oh mother of heroes, if I stay here with you I must not do menial service, nor can I speak with any man except the holy Brahmans who promise to search for my husband."

The royal lady replied: "As you wish, so be it." Then she spoke to Sunanda, her daughter, saying: "This lady will be a handmaiden and a friend to you. She is your own age and a worthy peer. Be happy together."

Princess Sunanda happily led the strange woman to her home. There Damayanti stayed for a time, waiting for her lost husband.

NALA'S EXILE

Soon after Nala had fled into the forest depths, deserting the faithful Damayanti, he witnessed a great fire which blazed furiously. As he came close he heard a voice crying over and over again from the midst of the sacred flames: "Hurry, Nala! Oh, hurry, Nala, and come here!"

Now, Agni had given Nala power over fire, so crying: "Have no fear," he leapt through the flames.... In the space within that blazing circle be saw the king of serpents lying coiled up in a ring with folded hands and unable to move. "I am Karkotaka," the serpent said, "And am suffering this punishment because I deceived the holy sage Narada, who cursed me, saying: 'You will remain here in the midst of the flames until Nala comes to free you from my curse'.... So I lie without the power to move. Oh mighty king, if you will rescue me, I will reward you with my noble friendship, and help you find great happiness. Oh lift me quickly from out of this fiery place, noble king!"

After he had said this, Karkotaka, king of the serpents, shrank to the size of a man's finger, and Nala lifted him up and carried him safely through the flames to a cool and refreshing space. The serpent then said: "Now walk on and count your steps, so that good fortune may be assured to you."

Nala walked nine steps, but before he could take the tenth the serpent bit him, and the king was suddenly transformed into a misshapen dwarf with short arms. Then Karkotaka said: "Know that I have changed your form so that no man may know you. My poison, too, will cause unceasing anguish to the evil one who possesses your soul; he will suffer until he sets you free from your sorrow. So will you be delivered from your enemy, Oh blameless one.... My poison will not harm you, and from now on you will have no need to fear the wild boar, or any enemy, or a Brahman, or the sages. In battle you will always be victorious.... Now, go on your way, and be called 'Vahuka, the charioteer'. Hurry to the city of Ayodhya and enter the service of the royal King Rituparna, the skilful in dice. You will teach him how to tame horses, and he will give you the secret of dice. Then will you again have joy. Do not sorrow, therefore, because your wife and your children will be restored to you, and you will regain your kingdom."

Then the serpent gave Nala a magic robe, saying: "When it is your wish to be as you were, oh king, think of me and put on this garment, and you will immediately resume your usual form." Having said this, the king of serpents vanished from sight.

So Nala went towards the city of Ayodhya, and he stood in the presence of King Rituparna, to whom he said: "My name is Vahuka. I am a tamer of steeds, nor is my equal to be found in the world; and I have exceptional cooking skills."

The king welcomed him and took him into his service, saying: "You shall be master of my own horse, and your reward will be great." He was pleased and gave to Vahuka for comrades Varshneya, who had been in Nala's service, and Jivala too. So the transformed king lived for a long time at Ayodhya, and every evening, sitting alone, he sang a single verse:

> *Where is she all worn but faithful,*
> *weary, thirsty, hungering too?*
> *Thinks she of her foolish husband?...*
> *Does another man her woo?*

His comrades often wondered at his singing. Then one evening Jivala asked Nala: "For whom do you mourn for, Vahuka? I pray you to tell me. Who is the husband of this lady?"

Nala answered him with a sad voice: "Once there was a peerless lady, and she had a husband of weak will. And as they wandered in a forest together, he fled from her without cause, and yet he greatly sorrowed. Every day and night is he consumed by his overwhelming grief, and always brooding, he sings this melancholy song. He is a weary wanderer in the wide world, and his sadness is without end; it is never still.... His wife wanders all forlorn in the forest. She did not deserve such a fate. Thirsty and hungry she wanders alone because her lord abandoned her and fled; wild beasts are around her, seeking to devour; the wood is full of perils.... It may be that she is not now alive...."

Meanwhile King Bhima was searching for his lost daughter and her royal husband. Abundant rewards were offered to Brahmans, who went through every kingdom and every city in pursuit of the missing pair. One day, by chance, a Brahman named Sudeva entered Chedi when a royal holiday was being celebrated, and he saw Damayanti standing beside the Princess Sunanda and the queen mother at the royal palace.

Sudeva saw that her loveliness had been dimmed by sorrow, and as he gazed at her he said to himself: "Ah, the lady with lotus eyes is like the moon, darkly beautiful; her splendour has shrunken like the crescent moon veiled in cloud – she who once before was seen in the full moonlight of her glory. Pining for her lost husband, she is like a dark night when the moon is swallowed; her sorrow has stricken her like a river which has become dry, like a shrunken pool in which lotus blooms shrivel and fade; she is, indeed, like a withered lotus.... Does Nala live now without the bride who so mourns for him?... When, oh when shall Damayanti be restored to her lord?...

The Brahman then approached Damayanti and said: "I am Sudeva. Your royal father and mother and your children are well.... A hundred Brahmans have been sent out throughout the world to search for you, Oh noble lady."

Damayanti heard him and wept.

The Princess Sunanda spoke to her queen mother, saying: "Our handmaiden weeps because the Brahman has spoken to her.... We shall soon know who she is."

Then the queen mother directed the holy man to her chambers and asked him: "Who is she – this mysterious and noble stranger?"

Sudeva answered: "Her name is Damayanti, and her father is King Bhima, lord of Vidarbha. Her husband is Nala.... From birth she has had a dark beauty spot like to a lotus between her fair eyebrows. Although it is covered with dust, I saw it, and so I knew her. This spot was made by Brahma as the sign of his beauty-creating power."

The queen mother urged Sudeva to remove the dust from the beauty spot of Bhima's daughter. When this was done the royal lady and her daughter wept together and embraced the fair Damayanti. Then the queen mother said: "You are my own sister's daughter, beautiful one. Our father is King Sudaman who reigns at Dasarna.... Once I saw you as a child.... Ask of me whatever you desire and it shall be yours."

"I am a banished mother," Damayanti cried with fast-flowing tears. "Allow me, therefore, to return to my children who have been orphaned of mother and father."

The queen mother responded: "So be it."

Damayanti was given an army to guard her on her journey towards her native city, and she was welcomed with great rejoicing by all her family and friends. King Bhima rewarded Sudeva generously.

When Damayanti was embraced by her mother she said: "Now our chief duty is to bring home Nala."

The queen wept, and spoke to her husband, the royal Bhima, saying: "Our daughter still mourns for her lost lord and cannot be comforted."

So Bhima urged the Brahmans to search for Nala, offering huge reward when he should be found. Damayanti addressed these holy men before they departed and said to them: "Wherever you go, speak this message over and over again: 'Where are you, oh gambler, who tore my garment in half? You left your loved one as she lay sleeping in the savage wood. She is awaiting your return: by day and by night she sits alone, consumed by her grief. Oh hear her prayer and have compassion, you noble hero, because she forever weeps for you in the depths of her despair!'"

So the holy men went through every kingdom and every city repeating Damayanti's message over and over again; but when they began to return one by one, each told with sadness that his quest had been in vain.

Then the wise Brahman, Parnada came to Vidarbha, having stayed for a time in the city of Ayodhya. He said to the daughter of Bhima: "I spoke to Rituparna regarding your husband, repeating your message, but he answered not a word. Then his charioteer came to me, a man with short arms and misshapen body. His name is Vahuka, and he is skilled in driving the swift chariot and in preparing food. With melancholy voice he said these words: 'In the excess of her sorrow a noble woman will compose herself and remain constant, and so win heaven by her virtues. She is protected by the breastplate of her chastity, and will suffer no harm. Nor will she give in to anger although she was deserted by her lord, whose robe the birds have taken away, leaving him in distress. She will not be moved to anger against her husband, the sorrow-stricken and famine-wasted, who has been deprived of his kingdom and robbed of happiness.' When I heard the stranger's speech I came speedily here to repeat it to you."

Damayanti immediately went and spoke to her mother privately, because she was sure that Vahuka, the charioteer, was her royal lord. Then she gave her wealth to the Brahman, saying: "You will get more if Nala returns home." The wise Parnada was weary with travel, and he returned to his own village.

Neither Damayanti nor her mother told King Bhima of their discovery or of their immediate purpose. The wife of Nala spoke secretly to Sudeva and said: "Hurry to the city of Ayodhya, and appear before King Rituparna as if you had come by chance, and say to him: 'Once again the daughter of Bhima is to hold her swayamvara. All the kings and all the sons of kings are heading as once before to Vidarbha. Tomorrow at dawn she will choose a new lord for herself, for no one knows whether Nala lives or not.'"

So Sudeva went to Ayodhya and spoke as Damayanti wished, and then said: "If you would win the princess, Rituparna, you must go swiftly, for when the sun rises she will choose a second husband."

Rituparna sent for Vahuka at once and said: "Oh skilled charioteer, I need to hurry to Vidarbha in a single day, because the fair Damayanti holds her swayamvara at dawn tomorrow."

At these words Nala's heart was torn with grief, and he said to himself: "Is this just a plan to deceive me? Or has she whom I wronged grown fickle of heart, she who has been stricken by grief in the depths of despair?"

Then he said to Rituparna: "As you wish, Rituparna. I will drive you in a single day to Vidarbha." He selected four courageous horses which were as swift as the wind. He quickly yoked them, spoke to them soothingly, and then set off with Rituparna and Varshneya at full speed.

The king sat in silent wonder as the chariot went swiftly, and said to himself: "Vahuka has the god-like skill of the charioteer of heaven.... Can he be Nala, who has taken another body? If he is not Nala, he is one who has equal skill. Great men are wandering at times in disguise – gods who are hidden in human form."

Quickly they went. Over hills and rivers and over forests and lakes the chariot glided like a bird through the air.... All of a sudden the king's robe was swept away, and he cried to the charioteer: "Stop for a moment, so that Varshneya may rush back and recover my garment."

Without pausing Nala replied: "Your robe is now five miles behind us, and we cannot wait to recover it." So they went on at full speed. Before long Rituparna saw a lofty fruit tree and he said to Vahuka: "Now, skilful charioteer, you shall witness my ability in numbers. No single mind is accomplished in every kind of knowledge. On two branches of that fruit tree are fifty million leaves and two thousand and ninety-five berries."

Vahuka said: "The leaves and the fruit are invisible to me. But I will tear off a branch and count the berries while Varshneya holds the bridle."

"But," urged the king, "we cannot pause on our journey."

Vahuka said: "You may stay with me, or you can let Varshneya drive you at full speed."

Then the king spoke soothingly, saying: "Oh matchless charioteer! I cannot go on without you to Vidarbha. I trust in you. If you will promise that we will reach the city before night falls, I will do as you wish."

The transformed Nala answered: "I will indeed make haste when I have counted the berries."

So the horses were drawn up, and Nala tore a branch from the tree. Having counted the berries, he found there were the exact number that the king had said, and he exclaimed: "Your power is wonderful indeed, Rituparna! I would gladly know your secret."

Now the king was eager to proceed on his way, and he said: "I know the secret of the dice, and am therefore skilled in numbers."

"Then," said Nala, "if you will tell me your secret, I will give you knowledge of horses."

Rituparna replied: "So be it;" and then and there he taught the charioteer the science of dice.

Now when Nala grew skilful in dice, Kali immediately passed out of his body, and Nishadha's fallen king vomited out the serpent poison and was weakened with the struggle. Released from the venom, Kali resumed his usual form, but he was seen by Nala alone, who sought to curse him.

In his terror, the evil demon folded his hands and said: "Do not injure me and I will give you matchless fame.... Know that Damayanti cursed me in her anger when you deserted her in the forest, and I have endured great agony ever since. Night and day, too, I have been scorched by the poison of the king of serpents.... Now I seek your pity. I come to you that you may be my refuge. I promise, if you will not curse me, that he who from now on does not fail to praise you, will have no fear of me in his heart."

Nala's anger subsided, and he permitted Kali to enter the cloven fruit tree. Then he leapt into the chariot and drove on, and Kali returned to his own place.

The chariot flew on like a bird, and the soul of Nala was elated. But he still retained the form of Vahuka.

In the evening the watchmen on the walls of Vidarbha proclaimed the arrival of Rituparna, and King Bhima gave permission that he should enter by the city gate.

The thunder of the rumbling chariot echoed across the land. Nala's horses, which Varshneya had driven from Nishadha, neighed loudly as if Nala were beside them once again.

Damayanti also heard the approaching chariot, and her beating heart was like a cloud that thunders as the rain begins to fall. Her soul was thrilled by the familiar sound, and it seemed to her that Nala was getting closer.... Peacocks craned their necks and danced on the palace roofs, and elephants in their stalls trumpeted aloud as if rain were about to fall.

Damayanti said: "The sound of the chariot fills my soul with ecstasy. Surely my lord comes. Oh, if I do not soon see the moon-fair face of Nala I will surely die, for, thinking of his virtues, my heart is torn with sorrow. Unless he comes now I will no longer live, but will perish by fire."

THE HOMECOMING OF THE KING

Damayanti anxiously climbed to the roof terrace of the palace to gaze at the chariot as it entered the court. She saw Rituparna stepping down, and Varshneya, who followed him, while Vahuka began to tend to the horses.

King Bhima, who knew nothing of his daughter's plan, received the royal King of Ayodhya with courtesy, and said: "I bid you welcome, Oh king.... Why have you come here?"

Rituparna wondered why he saw no kings or princes, or even signs that a swayamvara was about to be held, but he kept his counsel and said: "I have come to salute you, Bhima."

The royal father of Damayanti smiled and said to himself: "He has not come so speedily through many cities for such a purpose. But we shall know before long why he has made this journey."

Rituparna was escorted to his chamber for rest and refreshment by a company of royal servants, and Varshneya went with them.

Meanwhile Vahuka led his horses to the stables, and Damayanti returned to her chamber, thinking again and again that the sound of the coming chariot was like to the sound of Nala coming near. So she called for Kesini, her fair handmaiden, and said to her: "Go and speak to the misshapen charioteer with short arms, because I think he is Nala.... Ask him who he is, and be mindful of his answer."

The handmaiden went and spoke to Váhuka, saying: "The Princess Damayanti would like to know where you have come from and for what reason."

Vahuka replied: "King Rituparna has heard that the swayamvara is to be held at dawn tomorrow, so he came here swifter than the wind from Ayodhya. I am his charioteer."

Kesini then asked him: "Who is the third man who has come?"

Vahuka responded: "Varshneya is his name. He went to Ayodhya when Nala fled away.... I am skilled in taming horses and in preparing food."

The handmaiden then asked: "And does this Varshneya know where Nala has gone and how he fares? Has he told you anything regarding him?"

Vahuka said: "Varshneya carried away Nala's children from Nishadha, but he knows nothing of the king. Indeed, no man knows. He has assumed a strange form, and wanders disguised around the world.... Nala alone knows, nor will he reveal himself."

Kesini then said: "When the holy Brahman went to the city of Ayodhya he uttered the words of Damayanti over and over again: 'Where are you, oh gambler, who tore my garment in half? You left your loved one as she lay sleeping in the savage wood. She is awaiting your return: by day and by night she sits alone, consumed by her grief. Oh hear her prayer and have compassion, you noble hero, because she forever weeps for you in the depths of her despair!'

Now say again the words which you uttered to the Brahman, for they gave healing to the stricken heart of Damayanti. Gladly would the princess hear that speech once more."

On hearing the message of Damayanti, Nala's soul was ripped with grief, and with tearful voice he repeated his former utterance: "In the excess of her sorrow a noble woman will compose herself and remain constant, and so win heaven by her

virtues. She is protected by the breastplate of her chastity, and
will suffer no harm. Nor will she give in to anger although she
was deserted by her lord, whose robe the birds have taken away,
leaving him in distress. She will not be moved to anger against
her husband, the sorrow-stricken and famine-wasted, who has
been deprived of his kingdom and robbed of happiness." Nala
could scarce restrain his emotion as he said these words.

Then the fair Kesini hurried to Damayanti and told all. In her
distress the princess said to her handmaiden: "Go and observe this
man closely, and return to inform me of all he does. When he prepares
food for his royal master let no fire be given to him nor any water."

Kesini went to watch the charioteer, and when she returned
she said: "Oh princess, this man is like a god. When he approaches
a low-built entrance he does not stoop; the portal rises in front
him. Much meat was given to him to prepare food for Rituparna.
He just gazed at the empty vessels and they were filled with
water. No fire was lit, and he took a handful of withered grass
and held it up to the sun, whereupon it blazed instantly, and his
fingers were unscorched by the flames. Water flows at his will,
and as quickly it vanishes. And I saw another marvel. When he
lifted up flowers that had faded they were immediately refreshed,
so that they had greater beauty and richer fragrance than before."

Damayanti was fully assured that Vahuka was none other
than her husband in altered form, and, weeping, she said softly:
"Ah, go once again to the kitchen, fair Kesini, and without
his knowledge take a small portion of the food which he
has prepared."

Before long the handmaiden returned with a morsel of well-
cooked meat, and when Damayanti tasted it, she cried: "That
charioteer is Nala!"

Then she sent her two children to the kitchen with Kesini. As soon as the charioteer saw Indrasena and her brother he embraced them tenderly: he gazed lovingly at the children, who were as beautiful as the children of the gods, and his soul was deeply moved, while tears ran down his cheeks. Seeing that the handmaiden was watching him closely, he said: "Ah, the little ones are so like my own children that I could not restrain my tears…. Let us part now, innocent maiden; we are in a land of strangers, and if you come so often men will speak ill of you."

When Damayanti was told how the charioteer had been so profoundly moved when he saw the royal children, she sent Kesini to her mother, the queen, for she was impatient to see her husband once again. The handmaiden said to the queen: "We have watched the charioteer closely, and believe that he is Nala, although in misshapen form. Damayanti wishes he would come before her, with or without the knowledge of her father, and quickly."

The queen immediately went to Bhima and told him all, and the king gave permission that the charioteer should be summoned. In an instant word was sent to Nala, and soon he stood before Damayanti and gazed at her, and was moved to anguish. The princess was dressed in a scarlet robe, and her hair was thrown into disarray: she wept and trembled with emotion.

Eventually Damayanti spoke, saying: "Oh Vahuka, have you ever heard of a noble and upright man who fled away, abandoning his sleeping wife in a forest? She was innocent, and worn out with grief. Who was he who so abandoned his wife but the lordly Nala?… What offence did I give to him that he should have deserted me while I slept? Was he not chosen by me as my husband even before the gods?… How could he abandon her who loved him – the mother of his children?... He pledged his faith in front of the celestial beings. How has he kept his vow?" She spoke with broken voice, and her dark eyes were filled with sadness.

Nala gazed at his beloved wife, and said: "I lost my kingdom by the dice, but I was innocent of evil, because Kali possessed my soul, and by that demon I was also swayed to desert you! But you struck him with your curse when you were in the forest mourning for me, yet he remained in my body until, in the end, he was conquered by my long-suffering and devotion. Now, beautiful one, our grief is near to its end. The evil one has gone, and through love of you I come here.... But how," he asked sternly, "may a high-born lady choose herself another husband, as you would gladly do, even now? The heralds have gone up and down the land saying: 'The daughter of Bhima will hold her second swayamvara because such is her fancy.' And for this reason Rituparna hurried to come here."

Damayanti shook with emotion at his harsh words, and she said to him: "Do not suspect me, noble one, of such shameful guilt. It was for you and you alone that the Brahmans repeated the message which I gave them. When I learned of the words you spoke to the wise Parnada, I conceived this plan to bring you here. I have remained faithful of heart, nor have I ever thought evil of you. I call upon the wind to slay me now if I have sinned: on the sun I call, too and on the moon, which enters into every thought of living beings. Let these three gods who govern the three worlds speak now to prove my words, or else turn against me."

Then the wind which the princess had urged said: "Oh Nala, Damayani has done no evil, nor has she thought of evil. For three long years she has treasured up her virtue in its fullness. She speaks the truth, even now. You have found the daughter of Bhima: the daughter of Bhima has found you."

Even as the wind was speaking, flowers fell from heaven all around them, and the soft music of the gods floated down the wind. Nala marvelled, and gazed with love at the innocent Damayanti. Then he put on the holy garment and thought of the king of serpents. Immediately he resumed his own form, and the daughter of Bhima saw her lost husband once again.

Damayanti shrieked and embraced Nala, and she hid her face in his chest. He was again travel-worn and dust-stained as he clasped her to his heart, and she sighed softly. They stood there for a long time in silent ecstasy, speaking no words.... The children were brought in and Nala embraced them once more.

Then the queen rejoiced and informed Bhima of Nala's return. Bhima declared: "Tomorrow he will be reunited with Damayanti."

The whole night long the happy couple sat together in the palace telling all that had happened to them during the years that they were parted one from another.

The following morning Nala was again married to Damayanti, and he paid homage to Bhima. The glad tidings of his return spread swiftly throughout the city, and there was great rejoicing. Soon all the houses were decorated with banners and garlands; the streets were watered and strewn with flowers. The altars of the gods were also adorned.

Rituparna was pleased when he learned that his charioteer, Vahuka, was the King of Nishadha, and he went to Nala and said: "May you have joy with your queen to whom you are reunited. Have I ever done anything unjustly to you whilst you were in my palace? If so, I now seek your forgiveness."

Nala replied: "I have never suffered any injustice from you, my old friend and kinsman…. I give you all I have – my skill in horses."

Rituparna was grateful to Nala for his gift. In return he gave fuller instruction in the science of dice before returning to his own city.

When a month had gone past Nala left King Bhima and went towards Nishadha with one great chariot, sixteen elephants, fifty armed horsemen, and six hundred foot soldiers. The whole force boldly entered the city and made the earth shake. Straightaway Nala went to Pushkara and said: "I would gladly throw dice with you once again. I have much wealth and will stake all my treasure and even Damayanti on the game. You, Pushkara, must stake your kingdom. Let us stake everything; let us play for our lives. And know, too, that, according to ancient law, he who wins a kingdom by gambling must accept the challenge to play the counter game…. If you will not play, then let us settle our difference in single combat."

Pushkara restrained from smiling because he was confident of success, and with haughty contempt he replied: "It is a joy to me that you once again possess great treasure to enable you to play. It is a joy also to me that I can win Damayanti. Soon Bhima's daughter will be decorated with the treasure which I shall win; she shall stand by my side as Apsaras, queen of heaven, stands beside Indra. I have waited a long time for you so that I might win Damayanti and be fully satisfied."

Nala would gladly have drawn his sword, but composed himself, and, with angry eyes and a scornful smile, he said: "Stop this idle chatter and let us play. Afterwards you will have no desire to speak."

Immediately the two brothers set to the game, and Nala won in a single play all that he had lost. Then he smiled and said: "Now the whole kingdom is mine once again. Fallen monarch! Never will you see the fair Damayanti.... Understand that you did not triumph the first time because of your own skill, but because Kali aided you, nor did you see this, Oh fool!... But do not fear that I will take vengeance.... I give you back your life. You will have an estate and revenues and my friendship, because I remember, Pushkara, that you are my brother.... May you live for a hundred years!"

Then Nala embraced his brother, who paid homage with folded hands, saying: "May your splendour endure forever! May you live for ten thousand years! You have given me my life and a city in which to live."

Pushkara remained with Nala for a month, and then went on his way.

All Nishadha rejoiced because their rightful king had returned. The counsellors of state paid homage to Nala, and said: "There is great joy now in city and country, and the people come to honour you even as Indra is honoured by all the gods."

When the rejoicings were over, and the city of Nishadha was tranquil once more, Damayanti returned home escorted by a great army, and she brought great treasures which her royal father had given her. With the long-eyed queen came her children, too.

Thereafter Nala lived in happiness, being restored to his kingdom, and once again the monarch among men. He achieved great renown as a ruler, and he performed every holy rite with generosity and devotion.

LEGENDS OF INDRA & YAMA

The ancient Eurasian 'hammer god', bearing the tribal name of Indra, was accompanied to India by the earliest invading bands of Aryans. He was the Thunderer who brought rain to quicken dried-up pasture lands; he was the god of fertility; he was 'the friend of man'; he was the artisan of the Universe which he shaped with his hammer; the dragon slayer, the giant killer, the slaughterer of enemies, the god of war. But although his name may belong to the early Iranian period, the Vedic King of the Gods assumed a distinctly Indian character after localization in the land of the 'Five Rivers'; he ultimately stepped from his chariot, drawn by the steeds of the Aryan horse tamers, and mounted an elephant.

Yama, King of the Dead, was the first man. He explored the hidden regions and discovered the road which became known as 'the path of the fathers'. In the Vedic 'land of the fathers', the shining Paradise, the two kings Varuna and Yama sit beneath a tree. Yama gathers his people to him like a shepherd gathers his flock. To the faithful he gives a drink of Soma; unbelievers were destroyed or committed to a hell called Put. In post-Vedic times he presided over a complicated system of Hells; he was Danda-dhara, 'the wielder of the rod or mace'. He carried out the decrees of the gods, taking possession of souls at their appointed time.

The Vedic character of Yama survives in Epic narrative and the two touching and beautiful stories, preserved in the *Mahabharata*, are probably very ancient Aryan folk tales which were cherished by the people and retold by the poets, who attached to them later religious beliefs and practices.

The final tale in this chapter tells of the beauties of Indra, Yama and Varuna's heaven.

TALES OF INDRA, KING OF THE GODS

Indra's combats are reflections of the natural phenomena of India. When the hot Indian summer draws to a close, the whole land is parched and thirsty for rain; rivers are low and many hill streams have dried up; man and beast are weary and wait release from the breathless atmosphere; they are even threatened by famine. Then dense masses of cloud gather in the sky; the tempest bellows, lightnings flash and thunder peals loudly; rain descends in a deluge; once again torrents pour down from the hills and rivers become swollen. Indra has waged his battle with the Drought Demons, broken down their fortress walls, and released the imprisoned cow-clouds which give nourishment to his human friends; the withered pastures become green with generous and rapid growth, and the rice harvest follows.

According to Vedic myth, Indra achieved his first great victory immediately after birth. Vritra, 'the encompasser', the Demon of Drought, was holding the cloud-cattle captive in his mountain fortress. Mankind begged for help from the gods, the shining ones, the world guardians.

Who will take pity? Who will bring refreshment?
Who will come nigh to help us in distress?
Counsels the thoughts within our hearts are counselling,
Wishes are wished and soar towards the highest –
O none but them, the shining ones, are merciful,
My longing wings itself towards the Eternals.

Indra heroically rose up to do battle for the sacrificers. Impulsively he seized the nectar of the gods, called Soma, and he drank that intoxicating juice. Then he snatched up his thunderstone which had been fashioned by the divine artisan Twashtri. His favourite horses, named the Bold and the Brown, were yoked in his golden chariot by his attendants and followers, the youthful Maruts.

Now, at the very beginning, Indra, the golden child, became the king of the three worlds. It was he who gave the air of life; he also gave strength. All the shining gods revered him and obeyed his commands. "His shadow is immortality; his shadow is death."

The Maruts, the sons of red Rudra, were the spirits of tempest and thunder. Their chariots were pulled by two spotted deer and one swift-footed, never-wearying red deer as leader. They were loyal and courageous youths; on their heads were golden helmets and they had golden breastplates, and wore bright skins on their shoulders; their ankles and arms were decked with golden bracelets. The Maruts were always strongly armed with bows and arrows and axes, and especially with gleaming spears. All beings feared those 'cloud shakers' when they charged forward with their lightning spears which 'shattered cattle like the thunderstone'; they were known to cleave cloud-rocks and drench the earth with quickening showers.

When Indra set off to attack the Drought Demon, the Maruts followed him, shouting with loud voices. They dashed towards the imprisoned cows of the clouds and chased them up into the air.

The dragon Vritra roared when Indra came near; at which heaven shook and the gods retreated. Mother Earth, the goddess Prithivi, was troubled regarding her golden son. But Indra advanced boldly with the roaring Maruts; he was inspired by the hymns of the priests; he had drank the Soma; he was strengthened by the sacrifices offered on earth's altars; and he wielded the thunderstone.

The Drought Demon deemed itself invulnerable, but Indra cast his weapon and soon discovered the vulnerable parts of its writhing body. He killed the monster and, as it lay face down in front of him, the torrents burst and carried it away to the sea of eternal darkness. Then Indra rejoiced and cried out:

> I have slain Vritra, O ye hastening Maruts;
> I have grown mighty through my own great vigour;
> I am the hurler of the bolt of Thunder –
> For man flow freely now the gleaming waters.

On earth the worshippers of the god were happy and the Rishi hymned his praises.

A post-Vedic version of the encounter between Indra and Vritra is found in the *Mahabharata*. Although it is coloured by the change which, in the process of time, passed over the religious beliefs of the Aryans, it retains some features of the original myth.

The story goes that in the first Age of the Universe a host of Danavas, or giants and demons, were so strongly armed that they were invincible in battle. They selected the dragon Vritra as their leader, and waged war against the gods, whom they scattered in all directions.

Realizing that they could not regain their power until they accomplished the death of Vritra, the celestials appeared before the Supreme Being, Brahma, the incarnation of the Soul of the Universe. Brahma instructed them to obtain the bones of a Rishi named Dadhicha, from which to construct a demon-slaying weapon. So the gods visited the Rishi and bowed down before him, and begged the request according to Brahma's advice.

Dadhicha agreed to renounce his body for the benefit of the gods. So the Rishi gave up his life, and from his bones Twashtri, the artisan god, shaped Indra's great weapon, which is called Vajra.

Twashtri spoke to Indra and said: "Oh chief of the celestials, with this, the best of weapons, reduce that fierce enemy of the gods to ashes! And, having slain him, happily rule the entire domain of heaven with those who follow you."

Then Indra led the gods against the mighty army. They found that Vritra was surrounded by dreaded Danavas, who resembled mountain peaks. A terrible battle was waged, but once again the gods were put to flight. Then Indra saw Vritra growing bolder, and he became dejected. But the Supreme Being protected him and the gods endowed him with their strength, so that he became mightier than before. Vritra was enraged, and roared loudly and fiercely, so that the heavens shook and the earth trembled with fear. Deeply agitated, Indra flung his divine weapon, which killed the leader of the Danavas. But Indra, thinking the demon was still alive, fled from the field in terror to seek shelter in a lake. The celestials, however, saw that Vritra had been slain, and they rejoiced and shouted the praises of Indra. Then, rallying once more, the gods attacked the panic-stricken Danavas, who turned and fled to the depths of ocean. There in the fathomless darkness they assembled together, and began to plot how they would accomplish the destruction of the three worlds.

Eventually the conspirators resolved to destroy all the Rishis who were possessed of knowledge and ascetic virtue, because the world was supported by them. So they made the ocean their home, raising waves high as hills for their protection, and they began to come out from their fortress to attack the mighty saints.

THE CALL OF YAMA, KING OF THE DEAD

Once upon a time Menaka, the beautiful Apsara (celestial fairy) left her newborn baby, the daughter of the King of Gandharvas (celestial elves) beside a hermitage. A Rishi, named Sthulakesha, found the child and raised her. She was called Pramadarva, and grew to be the most beautiful and most devout of all young women. Ruru, the great grandson of Bhrigu, looked at her with eyes of love, and at the request of his father, Pramati, the virgin was betrothed to the young Brahman.

Pramadarva was spending time with her friends a few days before the morning of the nuptials. As her time had come, she trod on a serpent, and the death-compelling reptile bit her. She then fell down and died, becoming more beautiful in death than she had been in life.

Brahmans assembled around the body of Pramadarva and sorrowed. Ruru crept away alone and went to a solitary place in the forest where he wept and cried out: "The fair one, whom I love more dearly than ever, lies dead on the bare ground. If I have performed penances and attained to great ascetic merit, let the power which I have achieved restore my beloved to life again."

Suddenly an emissary from the celestial regions appeared in front of Ruru, who said: "Your prayer is of no use, Ruru. One whose days have been numbered can never get back her own life again. Therefore you should not abandon your heart to grief. But the gods have decreed a means whereby you can receive back your beloved."

Ruru pleaded with him, and said: "Tell me how I can comply with the will of the celestials, so that I may be delivered from my grief."

The messenger replied: "If you will give up half of your own life to Pramadvara, she will rise up again."

Ruru happily consented, saying: "I will give up half of my own life so that my beloved may be restored to me."

Then the king of the Gandharvas and the celestial messenger stood before Dharma-rajah (Yama) and said: "If it be your will, Oh Mighty One, let Pramadarva rise up endowed with a part of Ruru's life."

The King of the Dead responded: "So be it."

After Dharma-rajah had spoken, the serpent-bitten young woman rose from the ground, and Ruru, whose life was curtailed for her sake, obtained the sweetest wife on earth. The happy pair spent their days deeply devoted to each other, awaiting the call of Yama at the appointed time.

YAMA AND SAVITRI

There was once a princess in the country of Madra, and her name was Savitri. She was the gift of the goddess Gayatri, wife of Brahma, the self-created, who had heard the prayers and received the offerings of Aswapati, the childless king of Madra, when he practised austere penances so that he might have children of his own. The young woman grew to be beautiful; her eyes had burning splendour, and were as fair as lotus leaves; she had exceeding sweetness and grace.

It came to pass that Savitri looked with eyes of love at a youth named Satyavan 'the Truthful'. Although Satyavan lived in a hermitage, he was of royal birth. His father was a virtuous king, named Dyumatsena, who became blind, and was then deprived of his kingdom by an old enemy living nearby. The dethroned monarch retired to the forest with his faithful wife and his only son, who in time grew up to be a handsome youth.

When Savitri confessed her love to her father, the great sage Narada, who sat beside him, spoke and said: "The princess has done wrong in choosing this royal youth Satyavan for her husband. He is attractive and courageous, he is truthful and magnanimous and forgiving, he is modest and patient and without malice; he possesses every virtue. But he has one defect, and no other. He is to have a short life; it has been decreed that within a year from this day he must die; within a year Yama, god of the dead, will come for him."

The king turned to his daughter: "Savitri, you have heard the words of Narada. Therefore go and choose another lord for yourself, for the days of Satyavan are numbered."

The beautiful young woman said to her father the king: "The die is cast; it can fall only once; only once can a daughter be given away by her father; only once can a woman say, 'I am yours'. I have chosen my lord. Let his life be brief or be long, I must marry Satyavan."

Narada said: "Oh king, the heart of your daughter will not waver; she will not be turned away from the path she has chosen. Therefore I approve of the marriage of Savitri and Satyavan."

The king replied: "As you advise, so I must do, Narada, because you are my teacher. I cannot disobey."

Then Narada said: "Peace be with Savitri! I must go now. My blessing to all of you!"

Aswapati went to visit Dyumatsena in the forest, and his daughter went with him. Dyumatsena asked his visitors: "Why have you come here?"

Aswapati replied: "Royal sage, this is my beautiful daughter Savitri. Take her for your daughter-in-law."

Dyumatsena responded by saying: "I have lost my kingdom, and live here in the woods with my wife and my son. We live as ascetics and perform great penances. How will your daughter endure the hardships of a forest life?"

Aswapati answered: "My daughter well knows that joy and sorrow come and go and that nowhere is bliss assured. Therefore accept her from me."

Dyumatsena consented that his son should marry Savitri. Satyavan was happy because he was given a wife who had every accomplishment. Savitri also rejoiced because she obtained a husband after her own heart, and she took off her royal garments and ornaments and dressed herself in bark and red cloth.

So Savitri became a hermit woman. She honoured Satyavan's father and mother, and she gave joy to her husband with her sweet speeches, her skill at work, her subdued and even temper, and especially her love. She lived the life of the ascetics and practised every austerity. But she never forgot the dreadful prophecy of Narada the sage; his sad words were always present in her secret heart, and she counted the days as they went past.

Soon the time came when Satyavan must cast off his mortal body. When he had just four days to live, Savitri took the Tritatra vow of three nights of sleepless penance and fast.

Dyumatsena warned her of how hard this would be, but Savitri was determined not to break her vow. So Savitri began to fast. She grew pale and became wasted by her rigid penance. Three days passed, and then, believing that her husband would die the following day, Savitri spent a night of bitter anguish through all the dark and lonely hours.

As the sun rose on the fateful morning, she said to herself, "Today is the day." Her face was bloodless but brave; she prayed in silence and made offerings at the morning fire;

then she stood before her father-in-law and her mother-in-law in reverent silence with joined hands, concentrating her senses. All the hermits of the forest blessed her and said: "May you never suffer widowhood."

Dyumatsena spoke to Savitri then, saying: "Now that your vow has been completed you may eat the morning meal."

But Savitri replied: "I will eat when the sun goes down."

Hearing her words Satyavan stood up, and taking his axe on his shoulder, turned towards the distant jungle to find fruits and herbs for his wife, whom he loved. He was strong and self-possessed.

Savitri spoke to him sweetly and said: "You must not go alone, my husband. It is my heart's desire to go with you. I cannot endure to be parted from you today."

Satyavan replied: "It is not for you to enter the dark jungle; the way is long and difficult, and you are weak on account of your severe penance. How can you walk so far on foot?"

Savitri laid her head on his chest and said: "I have not been made weary by my fast. Indeed I am now stronger than before. I will not feel tired when you are by my side. I have resolved to go with you: therefore do not seek to stand in the wat of my wish – the wish and the longing of a faithful wife to be with her lord."

Satyavan replied: "If it is your desire to accompany me I will allow it. But you must ask permission of my parents so that they do not find fault with me for taking you through the trackless jungle."

Then Savitri spoke to the blind sage and her husband's mother and said: "Satyavan is going towards the deep jungle to find fruits and herbs for me, and also fuel for the sacrificial fires. It is my heart's wish to go too, for today I cannot endure to be parted from him."

Dyumatsena said: "Since you have come to live with us in our hermitage you have not asked anything of us. So have your wish in this matter, but do not delay your husband in his duties."

Having received permission to leave the hermitage, Savitri turned towards the jungle with Satyavan, her beloved lord. Smiles covered her face, but her heart was torn with secret sadness.

Peacocks fluttered in the green woodland through which they walked together, and the sun shone in all its splendour in the blue heaven.

In a sweet voice Satyavan said: "How beautiful are the bright streams and the blossoming trees!"

The heart of Savitri was divided into two parts: with one she talked with her husband while she watched his face and followed his moods; with the other she awaited the dreaded coming of Yama, but she never uttered her fears. Birds sang sweetly in the forest, but sweeter to Savitri was the voice of her beloved. It was very dear to her to walk on in silence, listening to his words.

Satyavan gathered fruits and stored them in his basket. Then he began to cut down the branches of trees. The sun was hot and he perspired. Suddenly he felt weary and he said: "My head aches; my senses are confused and my limbs have grown weak. A sickness has seized me. My body seems to be pierced by a hundred darts. I would gladly lie down and rest, my beloved; I would gladly sleep even now."

Speechless and terror-stricken, the gentle Savitri wound her arms about her husband's body; she sat on the ground and she pillowed his head on her lap. Remembering the words of Narada, she knew that the dreaded hour had come; the very moment of death was at hand. Gently she held her husband's head with caressing hands; she kissed his panting lips; her heart was beating fast and loud. The forest grew dark and lonesome.

Suddenly an awful shape emerged from the shadows. He was of great stature; his clothing was blood-red; on his head he wore a gleaming crown; he had red eyes and was fearsome to look at; he carried a noose.... The shape was Yama, God of Death. He stood in silence, and gazed at the sleeping Satyavan.

Savitri looked up, and when she saw that a celestial had come near, her heart trembled with misery and with fear. She laid her husband's head on the green grass and stood up quickly: then she spoke, saying, "Who are you, divine one, and what is your mission to me?"

Yama replied: "You do love your husband; you are endued also with ascetic merit. I will therefore speak with you. I am the Monarch of Death. The days of this man, your husband, are now spent, and I have come to bind him and take him away."

Savitri responded by saying: "Wise sages have told me that your messengers carry mortals away. Why, then, mighty King, have you come here yourself?"

Yama replied: "This prince is of spotless heart; his virtues are without number; he is, indeed, an ocean of accomplishments. It would not be fitting to send messengers for him, so I have come here myself."

The face of Satyavan had grown ashen. Yama cast his noose and tore out from the prince's body the soul-form, which was no larger than a man's thumb; it was tightly bound and subdued.

So Satyavan lost his life; he stopped breathing; his body became unsightly; it was robbed of its lustre and deprived of its power to move.

Yama fettered the soul with tightness, and turned abruptly towards the south; silently and speedily he went on his way. Savitri followed him. Her heart was drowned in grief. She could not desert her beloved lord. She followed Yama, the Monarch of Death.

Yama said to her: "Turn back, Savitri. Do not follow me. Perform the funeral rites of your lord. Your allegiance to Satyavan has now come to an end: you are free from all wifely duties. Dare not to proceed further on this path."

But Savitri answered: "I must follow my husband whether he is carried or whether he goes of his own will. I have undergone great penance. I have observed my vow, and I cannot be turned back.... I have already walked with you seven paces, and the sages have declared that one who walks seven paces with another becomes a companion. I must converse with you, I must speak and you must listen.... I have attained the perfect life on earth by performing my vows and by reason of my devotion to my lord. It is not right that you should part me from my husband now, and prevent me from attaining bliss by saying that my allegiance to him has ended and another mode of life is opened to me."

Yama responded: "Turn back now.... Your words are wise and pleasing; therefore, before you go, you can ask a favour of me and I will grant it. Except the soul of Satyavan, I will give you whatever you desire."

Savitri said: "Because my husband's father became blind, he was deprived of his kingdom. Restore his eyesight, mighty One."

Yama agreed and said: "The wish is granted. I will restore the vision of your father-in-law…. But you have now grown faint on this difficult journey. Turn back, therefore, and your weariness will pass away."

Savitri responded: "How can I be weary when I am with my husband? The fate of my husband will be my fate also; I will follow him even to the place where you carry him…. Hear me, mighty One, whose friendship I cherish! It is a blessed thing to see a celestial; still more blessed is it to converse with one; the friendship of a god must bear great fruit."

Yama replied: "Your wisdom delights my heart. Therefore you can ask of me a second favour, except the life of your husband, and it will be granted to you."

So Savitri said: "May my wise and saintly father-in-law regain the kingdom he has lost. May he once again become the protector of his people."

Yama replied: "The wish is granted. The king will return to his people and be their wise protector…. Turn back now, princess; your desire is fulfilled."

To this Savitri said: "All people must obey your decrees; you take away life in accordance with divine ordinances and not of your own will. Therefore you are called Yama – he that rules by decrees. Hear my words, divine One. It is the duty of celestials to love all creatures and to award them according to their merit. The wicked are without holiness and devotion, but the saintly protect all creatures and show mercy even to their enemies."

Yama responded by saying: "Your wise words are like water to a thirsty soul. Therefore ask of me a third favour, except your husband's life, and it will be granted to you."

Savitri said: "My father, King Aswapati, has no son. Grant that a hundred sons may be born to him."

Yama replied: "A hundred sons will be born to your royal father. Your wish is granted.... Now turn back, princess; you cannot come any further. Long is the path you have already travelled."

But Savitri would not give up. She said: "I have followed my husband and the way has not seemed long. Indeed, my heart desires to go on much further. Hear my words, Yama, as you proceed on your journey. You are great and wise and powerful; you deal equally with all human creatures; you are the lord of justice.... One cannot trust oneself as one can trust a celestial; therefore, one seeks to win the friendship of a celestial. It is proper that one who seeks the friendship of a celestial should make answer to his words."

Yama responded: "No mortal has ever spoken to me as you have spoken. Indeed your words are pleasing, princess. I will grant you a fourth wish, except your husband's life, before you go."

Savitri said: "May a century of sons be born to my husband and me so that our race may endure. Grant me this, the fourth favour, Mighty One."

Then Yama said: "I grant to you a century of sons, princess; they will be wise and powerful and your race will endure.... Be without weariness now, and turn back; you have come too far already."

Savitri replied: "Those who are pious must practise eternal morality, Yama. The pious uphold the universe. The pious hold communion with the pious only, and are never weary; the pious do good to others without ever expecting any reward. A good deed done to the righteous is never thrown away; such an act does not entail loss of dignity nor is any interest impaired. Indeed, the doing of good is the chief office of the righteous, and the righteous therefore are the true protectors of all."

To this Yama said: "The more you speak, the more I respect you, princess. You, who are so deeply devoted to your husband, you can now ask of me some incomparable favour."

So Savitri said: "Mighty One, bestower of favours, you have already promised what cannot be fulfilled unless my husband is restored to me; you have promised me a century of sons. Therefore, I ask you, Yama, to give me back Satyavan, my beloved, my lord. Without him, I am like one who is dead; without him, I have no desire for happiness; without him I have no longing even for Heaven; I will have no desire to prosper if my lord is snatched away; I cannot live without Satyavan. You have promised me sons, Yama, yet you take away my husband from my arms. Hear me and grant this favour: Let Satyavan be restored to life so that your decree may be fulfilled."

Eventually Yama replied: "So be it. With cheerful heart I now unbind your husband. He is free.... Disease cannot afflict him again and he will prosper. Together you will both have a long life; you will live for four hundred years; you will have a century of sons and they will be kings, and their sons will be kings too."

Yama, the lord of death, then departed. And Savitri returned to the forest where her husband's body lay cold and pale; she sat on the ground and pillowed his head on her lap. Then Satyavan was given back his life…. He looked at Savitri with eyes of love; he was like one who had returned from a long journey in a strange land. He said: "My sleep was long; why did you not wake me, my beloved?… Where is that dark One who dragged me away?"

Savitri replied: "Yama has come and gone, and you have slept long, resting your head on my lap, and are now refreshed, blessed one. If you can rise up, let us now leave because the night is already dark…."

Satyavan rose up refreshed and strong. He looked round about and saw that he was in the middle of the forest.

Then he said: "Oh fair one, I came here to gather fruit for you, and while I cut down branches from the trees a pain afflicted me. I grew faint, I sank to the ground, I laid my head on your lap and fell into a deep sleep even whilst you embraced me. Then it seemed to me that I was enveloped in darkness, and that I saw someone…. Was this a vision or a reality?"

Savitri responded: "The darkness deepens…. I will tell you everything tomorrow…. Now let us find our parents. The beasts of the night are coming; I hear their awesome voices; they tread the forest in glee; the howl of the jackal makes my heart afraid."

Satyavan said: "Darkness has covered the forest with fear; we cannot find the path by which to return home."

So Savitri said: "I will gather sticks and make a fire and we will wait here until daylight comes."

Satyavan replied: "My sickness has gone and I would gladly see my parents again. I have never before spent a night away from the hermitage. My mother and father are old, and I am their crutch. They will be afflicted with sorrow because we have not returned."

Satyavan lifted up his arms and wept, but Savitri dried his tears and said: "I have performed penances, I have given away in charity, I have offered up sacrifices, I have never uttered a falsehood. May your parents be protected by virtue of the power which I have obtained, and may you, my husband, be protected too."

Satyavan replied: "Beautiful one, let us now return to the hermitage."

Savitri raised up her despairing husband. Then she placed his left arm on her left shoulder and wound her right arm around his body, and they walked on together…. After some time the moon came out and shone on their path.

Meanwhile Dyumatsena, the father of Satyavan, had regained his sight, and he went with his wife to search for his lost son, but had to return to the hermitage in despair. The sages comforted the weeping parents and said: "Savitri has practised great austerities, and there can be no doubt that Satyavan is still alive."

Finally Satyavan and Savitri reached the hermitage, and their own hearts and the hearts of their parents were freed from sorrow.

Then Savitri told of all that had taken place, and the sages said: "Oh chaste and illustrious lady, you have rescued the race of Dyumatsena, the foremost of kings, from the ocean of darkness."

The following morning messengers came to Dyumatsena and told him that the king who had deprived him of his kingdom was now dead, having fallen by the hand of his chief minister. All the people clamoured for their legitimate ruler. "Chariots are waiting for you, king. Therefore return to your kingdom," said the messengers.

So the king was restored to his kingdom, in accordance with the favour Savitri had obtained from Yama. And in time sons were born to her father. The gentle Savitri, because of her great devotion, had raised the family of her husband and her own father from misery to high fortune. She was the rescuer of all; the bringer of happiness and prosperity…. He who hears the story of Savitri will never endure misery again.

TALES OF HEAVEN

In that fair domain it is neither too hot nor too cold. Life there is devoid of sorrow; age does not bring frailties, and no one is ever hungry or thirsty; it is without wretchedness, or fatigue, or evil feelings. Everything, whether celestial or human, that the heart seeks after is found there. Sweet are the juicy fruits, delicious the fragrance of flowers and tree blossoms, and waters are there, both cold and hot, to give refreshment and comfort. Nymphs dance and sing to the piping of celestial elves, and merry laughter always blends with the strains of alluring music.

The Assembly House of Yama, which was made by Twashtri, has splendour equal to the sun; it shines like burnished gold. There the servants of the Lord of Justice measure out the allotted days of mortals. Great rishis and ancestors wait on Yama, King of the Pitris (fathers), and adore him. Sanctified by holiness, their shining bodies are dressed in swan-white garments, and decked with many-coloured bracelets and golden earrings. Sweet sounds, alluring perfumes, and brilliant flower garlands make that building eternally pleasant and supremely blessed. Hundreds of thousands of saintly beings worship the illustrious King of the Pitris.

The heaven of Indra was constructed by the great artisan-god himself. Like a chariot it can be moved anywhere at will. The Assembly House has many rooms and seats, and is adorned by celestial trees. Indra sits there with his beautiful queen, wearing his crown, with gleaming bracelets on his upper arms; he is decked with flowers, and dressed in white garments. He is waited on by brilliant Maruts, and all the gods and the rishis and saints, whose sins have been washed off their pure souls, which are as resplendent as fire. There is no sorrow, or fear, or suffering in Indra's home, which is inhabited by the spirits of wind and thunder, fire and water, plants and clouds, and planets and stars, and also the spirits of Prosperity, Religion, Joy, Faith, and Intelligence. Fairies and elves (Apsaras and Gandharvas) dance and sing to sweet music; feats of skill are performed by celestial battle heroes; auspicious rites are also practised. Divine messengers come and go in celestial chariots, looking as bright as Soma himself.

The heaven of Varuna was built by Vishwakarman (Twashtri) within the sea. Its walls and arches are pure white, and they are surrounded by celestial trees, made of sparkling jewels, which always blossom and always bear fruit. In the many-coloured bowers beautiful and variegated birds sing delightful melodies. In the Assembly House, which is also pure white, there are many rooms and many seats. Varuna, richly decked with jewels and golden ornaments and flowers, is throned there with his queen. Adityas wait on the lord of the waters, as also do hooded snakes (Nagas) with human heads and arms, and Daityas and Danavas (giants and demons) who have taken vows and have been rewarded with immortality. All the holy spirits of rivers and oceans are there, and the holy spirits of lakes and springs and pools, and the personified forms of the points of the heavens, the ends of the earth, and the great mountains. Music and dances provide entertainment, while sacred hymns are sung in praise of Varuna.

LEGENDS OF KRISHNA

Krishna was originally the hero of the *Mahabharata*, a destructive, evil and immoral warrior who was known for his cunning and martial skills.

Later, as Krishna became associated with Vishnu – his third human incarnation – his evil deeds were explained philosophically, and all manner of excuses were devised to explain his previous acts. The murders he had committed were to rid the earth of demons; his forays with women, and their subsequent search for him, have been explained in a metaphor of a worshipper seeking his god. Indeed, he came to represent the doctrine that devotion is a way to salvation.

Krishna is a popular god, and the late addition of the *Bhagavadgita* to the *Mahabharata* presents him, alongside work and knowledge, as the means by which believers can be saved. But it is his childhood pranks that have come to characterize Krishna, and it is some of these which follow.

KRISHNA'S BIRTH

There once was a king of Mathura, named Ugrasena, who had a beautiful wife. Now his wife was barren, a fact which dismayed them both and caused her to hold her head down in shame. One day, when walking in the wood, she lost her companions and found herself in the company of a demon who assumed her husband's form. Knowing not the difference between this man and the man who was her husband, she allowed him to lie with her and the product of this liaison was a long-awaited son, who they named Kansa.

When Kansa was a child he was cruel and a source of great sorrow to his family and his country. He shunned the religious teachings of the day and taunted his father for his devotion to Rama, the god of his race. His father could only reply, "Rama is my lord, and the dispeller of my grief. If I do not worship him, how shall I cross over the sea of the world?"

The ruthless Kansa laughed heartily at what he considered to be his father's foolishness and immediately usurped his place on the throne. Immediately a proclamation was issued throughout the kingdom, forbidding men to worship Rama and commanding them to pay their devotions to Siva instead.

This arrogance and tyranny went on for many years, and every man and woman throughout the kingdom prayed for relief from the rule of this truly evil man. Finally, the Earth, assuming the form of a cow, went to Indra and complained. And so it was that Brahma listened to the pleas of the Earth and led them to Siva, and then Vishnu. Vishnu had in the past taken on the incarnation of man and they reminded him of that now, begging him to do so in order to afford the destruction of the seemingly invincible Kansa. Each of the gods and goddesses cheered Vishnu in this mission and promised to leave their heavenly homes in order that they could accompany him on earth. Vishnu arranged that Lakshman, Bharata and Sutraghna would accompany him and

that Sita, who would take the name of Rukmini, would be
his wife.

One day Kansa was carrying the great Vasudeva and
his wife Devaki through the sky when a voice set out the
following prophecy:

"Kansa, fool that you are, the eighth child of the damsel
you are now driving shall take away your life!" And so Kansa
drew his sword and was about to take the life of Devaki when
Vasudeva intervened, and said:

"Spare her life and I will deliver to you every child she
brings forth." Kansa laid down his sword, but he placed a
guard with her who stayed by her side for her every living
hour. And as child after child was given up to him and slain,
he continued in his wretched mission.

But Devaki was a woman with a mind as quick as a tree
squirrel, and although Kansa had been advised that the
children he had destroyed were her own, this was not the
case. The children that had been handed over to him were
the children of Hiranyakasipu who had been lodged in the
womb of Devaki in order that the cruel Kansa might be
fooled. Vishnu said to the goddess Yoganindra, who brought
the children from the nether regions:

"Go Yoganindra, go and by my command conduct
successively six of their princes to be conceived by Devaki.
When these shall have been put to death by Kansa, the
seventh conception shall be formed of a portion of Sesha,
who is part of me; and you shall transfer before the time of
birth to Rohini, another wife of Vasudeva, who resides at
Gokula. The report shall run that Devaki miscarries and I
will myself become incarnate in her eighth conception; and

you shall take a similar character as the embryo offspring of Yasoda, the wife of a herdsman called Nanda. In the night of the eighth of the dark half of the month Nabhas I shall be born, and you will be born on the ninth. Aided by my power, Vasudeva shall bear me to the bed of Yasoda, and you to the bed of Devaki. Kansa shall take you and hold you up to dash you against a stone, but you shall escape into the sky, where Indra shall meet and do homage to you through reverence of me."

And so it was that when Devaki gave birth to her eighth son, Vasudeva took the child and hurried through the city. When he reached the River Yamuna, which he had to cross, the water rose only to his knees instead of seeking to drown him. And as he reached the house of Nanda, Yasoda had given birth to her child, which Vasudeva seized and, leaving Devaki's child in its place, returned to his wife's bed.

Soon after, the guard heard the cry of a newborn, and summoning himself from the depths of a good sleep, he called for Kansa, who immediately rushed into the home of Devaki and thrust the child against a stone. But as soon as this child touched the ground there was a cry as deep and angry as that of any rakshasa. It rose into the sky and grew into a huge figure with eight arms, each holding a great weapon. It laughed and said to Kansa, "What use is it to you to have hurled me to the ground? He is born that shall kill you, the mighty one amongst the gods."

Kansa collected his ministers and gathered them round. He insisted that every man who was generous in gifts and sacrifices and prayers to the gods must be put to death so that no god shall have subsistence. He said then, "I know now that the tool of my fate is still living. Let therefore active search be made for whatever young children there may be upon earth, and let every boy in whom there are signs of unusual vigour be slain without remorse."

Soon after this Vasudeva and Devaki were released from their confinement, and quickly sought out Nanda, who was still unaware of the change in their children. Vasudeva had brought with him another of his child, by Rohini, who was Balarama, and placed him under the care of Nanda to be brought up as his own child. By this means, as Rama and Lakshman were inseparable companions in previous incarnations, Krishna and Balarama were intimately connected.

Nanda and his family had not been settled long at Gokula before efforts were made to destroy the infant Krishna. A female fiend called Putana, whose breast caused instant death when sucked, had taken the child in her arms and offered him a drink. The infant Krishna seized it with such fervour and sucked with such violence that the horrible fiend roared with pain and met with an instant death.

The birth of Krishna had caused great happiness, despite the evil decrees of Kansa, and throughout the land trees blossomed, flowers bloomed and there was music in the souls of all who lived on earth.

THE YOUNG KRISHNA

The young Krishna was a very mischievous boy and his merry-making became legend throughout the land. One day, as a mere infant lying under the wagon of Nanda, he cried for his mother's breast, and impatient that she did not come to him at once, kicked the wagon over, to the great astonishment of all who witnessed this momentous occurrence.

When Krishna was but five months old, another fiend came in the form of a whirlwind to sweep him away, but at once he grew so heavy that his own surrogate mother could not hold him and had to lay him down. But when the storm became a cyclone, the infant allowed himself to be swept into the sky, and while all the people on the ground wept and bemoaned his sorry fate, he dashed the rakshasa down, killing him and ending the storm.

On another occasion, Krishna and Balarama played with the calves in the fields to such an extent that Yasoda became angry, and tied the errant Krishna to a heavy wooden mortar in which the corn from the farm was threshed. Krishna, trying to free himself, dragged it until it became wedged between two Arjuna trees and then, with a strong pull, uprooted the trees altogether. Again, the people of the surrounding farms were astonished because there had been no storm and yet the trees had fallen, and their roots were exposed. The land must be unlucky, they thought, and they moved away to Vrindavana.

Krishna's tricks were not only for the benefit of himself, for his companions were also defended by his fiery nature, trickery and quick thinking. One day, Brahma came and stole away the calves and the herd-boys, taking them to a cave among the mountains. Krishna quickly made another herd and another group of herd-boys in their likeness and placed them where he had found them. No one but Krishna knew their true identities and he waited impatiently for Brahma to come upon his trick. Now it was nearly a year later before Brahma remembered the herd and the children, and he found the boys and the calves asleep in the cave. But, when he went to Brindaban, he found the boys and the calves there too.

Brahma was puzzled, but he drew back in fear when Krishna, not content with his changelings, drew the herd-boys into the likeness of gods, with four arms and the shape of Brahma, Rudra and Indra. Krishna quickly returned the boys to their shape when he saw Brahma's fright, and Brahma restored them at once. When they awoke they knew nothing of the time that had passed, and Brahma was now in awe of the young Krishna, whose eager mind had caused such devilry.

There are many other tales related of Krishna's youth, for he liked nothing more than to stir a little trouble amongst the local gopis and cow-herds. There is a tale told of the day that Krishna stole the gopis' clothes. The girls had sought out a quiet place to bathe, and laying their clothes on the bank, they frolicked in the fresh water, their lotus eyes glowing with frivolity and the fervour of youth. They sang and played, and Krishna sat in the tree, watching his cows, but drawn to the happy songs of the gopis. Slipping down the bank, he snatched the clothes, and climbed up a kadamb tree which hugged the bank of the water hold.

When the gopis had completed their bath they returned to the banks to retrieve their clothes. They looked everywhere, raising their arms and brows in puzzlement at such a seemingly magical occurrence. Until one of the gopis looked up and saw Krishna sitting in the tree, gently laying out the clothes of each girl. He was wearing a crown and yellow robes and she called out, "There he is, Krishna, who steals our hearts and our clothes."

The girls squealed, as all girls across the ages would have done, and plunged into the water to hide themselves. They prayed silently for Krishna to return their clothes but he would not hand them over.

"You must come and fetch them," he said smartly, grinning from ear to ear.

"We shall tell on you," said the girls, "we shall tell your father and ours, and all our friends and you will be punished. Our husbands will protect our honour."

But Krishna only laughed and said to them then, "If you are bathing for me, then cast away your shame and come and take your clothes."

The girls said to each other, "We must respect him, for he knows our minds and our bodies. There is no shame with Krishna." And they strolled then from the water, their arms at their sides but their heads lowered in deference to Krishna. At Krishna's encouragement they joined hands and waited for their clothes, which were duly presented. And so the gopis returned home, wiser in some small way that was unknown to them, and more attracted to and confused by the mischievous Krishna than ever.

KRISHNA AND KALIYA

One day, the cow-herds set out early, wandering through the woods and along the banks of the river until they came to a place called Kaliya. There they drank of the river waters, and allowed their cows to drink as well. Suddenly there was blackness and each of the cow-herds and cows laid down, the rich and instant poison of the naga or water snake called Kaliya entering their veins and causing them to die a painful death. Kaliya had come there from Ramanaka Dwipa, where he had once made his home. Garuda, who was the enemy of all serpents, had gone to live at Ramanaka Dwipa and Kaliya had fled immediately, taking refuge in the only place that Garuda was unable to visit, due to an ancient curse. Kaliya was an evil, frothing snake, and for miles around his shimmering form, the river bubbled with the heat of his poison.

Now on this day, Krishna set out to seek the company of the cow-herds and their cows, and he came upon their lifeless forms by the banks of the Jamna with some surprise. Krishna's powers were such that it took only a glance to restore the life to their bodies once more, and this he did at once. But Krishna was unhappy about his friends being plagued and he leapt into the water. Now the great Kaliya rose with all one hundred and ten hoods spluttering his poison, and the cowherds wept and wrung their hands at his certain death in that water. But Balarama was calm.

"Krishna will not die," he said calmly. "He cannot be slain."

Now Kaliya had wrapped himself around the body of Krishna, and he tightened his grip with all of his force. But Krishna outwitted him, and making himself so large, he caused the serpent to set him free. Again, Kaliya squeezed his bulk around the youth, but once again Krishna cast him aside by growing in size.

Then, Krishna suddenly leapt onto Kaliya's heads, and taking on the weight of the entire universe, he danced on the serpent's heads until Kaliya began to splutter, and then die. But there was silence and weeping, and the serpent's many wives came forward and begged Krishna to set their husband free. They laid themselves at his feet, and pledged eternal worship.

"Please release him," they asked, "or slay us with him. Please, Krishna, know that a serpent is venomous through nature not through will. Please pardon him."

And so it was that Krishna stepped from Kaliya's head and set the serpent free. Kaliya gasped his gratefulness, and prayed forgiveness for failing to recognize the great Krishna, the Lord, earlier. Krishna commanded Kaliya to return to Ramanaka Dwipa, but Kaliya lowered his head and explained that he could not return there for Garuda would make a meal of him at first sight. Krishna laughed, and pointed to the mark on Kaliya's head.

"Show him my mark, my friend," he said to the serpent, "for when Garuda sees that he will not touch you."

From that day, the waters were cleared of poisons and the people rejoiced. Krishna was Lord.

KRISHNA AND THE MOUNTAIN

Krishna had long wished to annoy Indra – partly because he was mischievous by nature and partly because he envied the giver of rain for all the gifts he received from the people. And so it was on this day that Krishna spoke to the gopis who were preparing to worship Indra, and he urged them instead to worship the mountain that had supplied their cattle with food, and their cattle that yielded them with milk. And following the wise Krishna's advice, the gopis presented the mountain Govarddhana with curds and milk and flesh, the finest offerings they had.

The crafty Krishna at once transformed himself, appearing on the summit of the mountain saying "I am the mountain." There he ate greedily of the offerings while in his own form, as Krishna, he worshipped the mountains with the gopis. Little did they know that Krishna wished only to divert the worship of Indra to himself and that he could appear both as the mountain and in his own form at will.

Now Indra was not pleased that his offerings had all but dried up and pledging to punish the people, he sent down great floods and storms to destroy them and their cattle. An army of clouds swept across the skies and a rain like none had ever seen before was cast down.

"You told us to give up the worship of Indra," chanted the gopis angrily. "And now we will lose everything. You told us to worship the mountain and that we did. And so, great Krishna, bring that mountain to us now."

And so it was that Krishna filled Govarddhana with all of the burning energy that filled his celestial body and he lifted it easily on the tip of one finger. Laying it over the people of Braj and their cows, he sheltered them from the rains and the floods until Indra gave up. Not even a drop of rain had fallen in Braj and Indra knew he had met the Primal Male.

The following day, as Balarama and Krishna laid lazily in the meadows, enjoying the sun and good fortune, Indra arrived and laid himself at Krishna's feet. Krishna was Lord.

KRISHNA AND RADHA

One day, as the cool breeze wafted lazily at the ripples on the river, Krishna and Balarama lay in the grasses under the trees, playing on the flute and joking amongst themselves. As was usually the case they were soon joined by the lovely gopis, who had fallen under the spell of Krishna and who longed for his company. They came towards the music and took up his hands to dance. Now there were too many of these gopis to dance with Krishna and to hold his hands, but as they danced he multiplied himself into as many forms as there were woman so that each woman believed she held the hand of the true Krishna.

It was on this same day that Krishna watched the gopis bathe in the Yamuna river after their dance. He loved them all, of course, but his particular favourite was Radha, the wife of Ayanagosha. Radha's sister-in-law told her brother of his wife's misconduct with Krishna, and Radha was afraid that she would be murdered as she slept. But when she spoke her fears to Krishna he calmed her, and reassured her easily that when her husband came, he would transform himself into Kali, and instead of finding Radha with her lover, Ayanagosha would find her worshipping a goddess instead.

Krishna took Radha into his embrace, and as he did so, her husband passed. Looking up, he noticed his wife bowing down with Krishna, who appeared at once as the goddess Kali.

The love affair with Radha went on for many years. They walked together in the flowering woods, and she spent many hours worshipping his feet. When Radha made love to Krishna, they made the world, and their love-making was passionate and playful. After their love-making Krishna combed her hair and plaited and pinned it, a servant to his mistress, a servant to his great love. He helped her with her sari. Theirs was a true, divine love – personifying all that is good in the union of man and woman.

There are many more stories of Krishna, who continued his tricks and his love-making, eventually taking on some 16,000 wives, but that is the story of the *Mahabharata* and other tales.

LEGENDS OF SHIVA

Shiva is a Sanskrit word meaning 'auspicious one', and although he is worshipped as profoundly, he is a more remote god than Vishnu. Shiva is the Moon-god and lord of the mountains, with the moon in his hair from which flows Ganga, the sacred River Ganges. He is also god of the yogis, the father of Brahmans who know and recite the Vedas. Shiva has many other incarnations and as the centuries have passed he has taken on different roles and forms for each new generation of worshippers. Concepts of Shiva may have merged roles that were once assigned to various earlier gods, for his personifications seem so diverse. Shiva is considered to be both destroyer and restorer.

But the stories which surround Shiva are fascinating and full of allegorical messages. Shiva's dance is one of the most memorable representations in literature – a demon-like god who dances to show the source of all movement in the universe, and most of all his five acts: creation, preservation, destruction, embodiment and release. The stories that follow present a portrait of one of the two great gods of post-Vedic Hinduism, and the very real message they depict.

SHIVA

The third of the Hindu Triad, Shiva was first known as the destroyer, for his work would balance that of the triumvirate, the two other sides of which were Vishnu the preserver and Brahma the creator. In his early incarnations, he is said to be Rudra, who appears in the Vedas, and his story as Rudra of the *Mahabharata* and many of the other great Hindu works is this:

On the day that Rudra was born, the earth was lit from within. Into the world came a boy, but he entered crying, and Prajapati said to him, "Why do you weep when you have been born after toil?"

The boy said then, "My evil has not been cleansed from me and I have not been given a name. Give one to me now," he begged. And so Prajapati pronounced: "You are Rudra."

Now Rudra, or Shiva as he came to be known, was created by Brahma in order to create the world, and in order for him to do so, he required a wife. A goddess is a god's other half, and both of these halves must work together to create the energy necessary for divine acts. Brahma realized that Shiva would need a partner, and so it was arranged that he would have one.

SHIVA AND SATI

There once was a chief of gods by the name of Daksha. He was married to Prasuti, the daughter of Manu, and she conceived and bore him sixteen daughters. The youngest of these daughters was Sati, and it was she who would become the wife of the supreme Shiva.

Now Daksha was not happy about marrying his youngest daughter to Shiva, for it had come to his notice, once before at a festival, that he had not offered homage to Daksha. Being a man of small mind, Daksha had held this against him as a grudge, and had pronounced a curse upon Shiva that he would receive none of the offerings made to the gods. A wandering Brahman, however, had been witness to the curse, and had laid down a contrary curse in order that Daksha should have nothing in his life but the wastage of material goods and pleasures.

As Sati grew, she knew her future was with Shiva, and she quietly worshipped him. When she reached an age at which it was suitable to marry, Sati was given a swayamvara, or 'own-choice', to which Daksha invited gods, princes and men of all great ranks from around the country. Sati was handed a wreath and with great excitement, she entered the assembly of men, eagerly searching the crowds for Shiva.

Now Shiva had not been invited to the swayamvara, for Daksha wanted nothing more to do with him, but he had not counted on the deep feelings of his youngest daughter. Her despair crumpled her young face and as she stared out into the crowd she felt nothing but love for Shiva. Calling out his name, she threw her wreath, and made to retreat. But there, in the middle of the court, her prayer had been answered. Summoned by her heart-felt cry, Shiva had responded and he stood there now, her wreath around his noble neck.

Daksha was bound by honour to marry his daughter to Shiva, and it was with great bitterness that he said, "Though unwilling I will give my daughter to this impure and proud abolisher of rites and demolisher of barriers, like the word of a Veda to a Sudra."

The happy couple travelled at once to Shiva's home in Kailas. His palace was exquisite, with every luxury and catered for by all manner of servants and women.

But Shiva was not content with the good things alone, and he spent many hours wandering the hills surrounding Kailas, dressed in the robes of a beggar, his bedraggled wife Sati at his side. But Sati and Shiva were, one day, dressed well, and out to seek some air in their chariot when Sati received Daksha's invitation to take part in a great sacrifice that he was about to make.

Because of the enmity between the two men, Shiva had not been invited. Sati was broken hearted when Shiva explained to her, "The former practice of the gods has been that in all sacrifices no portion should be divided to me. By custom, established by the earliest arrangement, the gods lawfully allot me no share in the sacrifice."

But Sati was determined to attend the sacrifice, and although Shiva tried to dissuade her, she set off for her father's home. She was received there without honour, for she rode on the back of Shiva's bull and she wore the dress of a beggar. Daksha immediately became the victim of her tongue, for she gave him a sharp redressing for his treatment of Shiva the good. But in the middle of her speech, her father broke in, calling Shiva nothing more than a 'goblin', a 'beggar' and an 'ashman'. Sati, who had found great peace with her husband, announced, "Shiva is friend to all, Father. No one but you speaks ill of him. All that you are saying his people know, and yet they love those qualities in him for he is a man of·peace and goodness."

Sati paused now, and thought for a moment. Then, with a fire that glinted from her eyes she made a decision and spoke once more: "A wife, when her lord is reviled, if she cannot slay the evil speakers, must leave the place and close her ears until she hears no more. Or if she has the power, she must take her own life, and this I will do, for I am deeply shamed to have a body that was once a part of your own."

And so it was that Sati released the fire within her and fell at the feet of her father. Sati was dead.

The news of his dear wife's death reached Shiva within moments, and he tore at his hair with a frenzy of despair and fury. His eyes glowed red and then gold, and with all the energy he could summon he called forth a demon as terrible as there ever was. This demon kissed the feet of Shiva and pledged to undertake any request he might have.

Shiva spat out the words, hardly able to control his great anger, "Lead my army against Daksha and take care that his sacrifice is destroyed."

And so the demon flew at once to the assembly, and with Shiva's ganas, he broke the vessels, polluted the offerings, insulted the holy men and then, with one fell swoop, cut off the head of Daksha and tainted the guests with smears of his fresh blood. Then the demon returned to Shiva at Kailas but he was deep in meditation and could not be reached. Brahma prayed to him to pardon Daksha, and to ease the suffering of the injured gods and rishis who had been in attendance at the sacrifice.

So Shiva lifted himself from his deep dreams and proceeded to Daksha's home, where he permitted his dead wife's father the head of a goat which would allow him to live. Shiva was invited then to the sacrifice, and allowed to partake of the offerings. Daksha looked upon him with reverence, and as he did so, Vishnu appeared on the back of Garuda. He spoke then to Daksha with a gentleness that touched the hearts of all who saw him:

"Only the unlearned deem myself and Shiva indistinct. He and I and Brahma are as one. We have different names for we are creation, preservation and destruction, but we three make up one as a whole. We are the tribune self. We pervade all creatures. The wise therefore regard all others as themselves."

And then, as the crowds cheered and saluted these most wise and noble gods, the three parts of the universe left and went their separate ways – Shiva to his garden, where he fell once more into the solace of his dreams.

SHIVA'S DANCE

Shiva dances to mark change, to show the transition from one stage to another. When the body of his wife Sati was burned, he took her ashes and began to dance, whirling in a flurry of movement that tore at the air around him and sent up a torrid flash of colour. He held a drum as he danced, turning and circling until the entire world began to shake. He moved swiftly, and whirled and turned around the world seven times before he was caught and stopped.

The gods were frightened by the violence of his sorrow and they promised then to restore Sati to him. She was returned to him several days later as Uma, or mother. Shiva himself had become Nataraja, or the king of the dance.

There are many other legends of Shiva's dance, and another is recounted here. Shiva heard word that there were, in the forests of Taragam, ten thousand rishis who had become heretics who taught a false religion.

Shiva was determined that they should know the truth, and he summoned his brother Vishnu to take the form of a beautiful woman and to accompany him to the forest. Shiva himself dressed as a yogi, and he wore his customary rags and ashes. As they entered the forests, they were immediately set upon by the wild wives of the rishis, women whose lust for men caused them to throw themselves at Shiva in his yogi disguise. The rishis themselves were attracted to Vishnu as well, and so there was pandemonium, as the unholy men and women crowded round the two visitors, clawing at them.

And then there was silence. For all at once it had occurred to the people of Taragam forest that things were not quite right, and gathering together they threw curses at the visitors.

A sacrificial fire was built, and then from it was called a mighty tiger, who flung himself upon Shiva in order to eat him whole. Shiva plucked at the tiger and set him to one side, removing his skin whole and causing the heretics to gasp. He wrapped the skin around himself like a shawl, and then, as the rishis produced a serpent more terrible than even Kaliya, he wound it round his neck and began to move.

A malevolent dwarf goblin took the centre of the room, swinging his great club with one purpose alone. Shiva dealt with him easily, and with one foot pressed upon its back he began to twirl, and to execute an angry dance.

The heavens opened and the gods lined the walls, anxious to witness the splendid fervour of Shiva in action.

The rishis watched in an amazement that fed their diminished belief so that they threw themselves down before Shiva and proclaimed him their most glorious god.

Shiva's dance lived on in their memories and Shiva and his dance were invoked on more than one occasion by everyone who had borne witness. Some believe that when devotion is fading, Shiva will appear and dance. For when the faithless see this dance there can be nothing but conviction in their hearts.

LEGENDS OF BUDDHA

Buddha means 'Awakened One', or one who has found insight and enlightenment. There are many Buddhas, for he has had many incarnations, but the Buddha to which we refer today is the last incarnation of the great teacher Gautama Buddha, who was born in 563 BCE as the son of Suddhodana, the king of Shakya. He is also called Siddhartha and Tathagata, or the one who walks the same path as his predecessors, his earlier incarnations.

The myths of Buddha surround the privations and austerity he underwent to attain his enlightenment, and then, the miracles he was able to perform thereafter. When he had attained his awakening, Buddha passed away peacefully, surrounded by his disciples.

There are many stories of Buddha's birth, and it became an accepted belief that others could follow in his path – becoming Buddhist deities and being worshipped themselves. The following tales are some of the richest examples of Buddhist mythology, which has, over the years, become embroidered to encompass philosophy from both Hindu and Buddhist religion.

THE LIFE OF BUDDHA

It was in the fifth century, when Prince Gautama was born in Kapiavastu, the capital of Shakya. The Raja at this time was Suddhodana and he was married to the two daughters of the Raja of the neighbouring tribe, the Koiyans. There are many myths which set out the birth of Buddha, each subsequent version more splendid and divine. Queen Maya, wife of Suddhodana, recounts a dream in which she saw a white elephant lowered from heaven, and how the moon itself fell into her lap, a ball of pure, white light. And when the birth occurred, Buddha was thrust from her side, like the opening of the letter 'B'.

Now the young prince was born into great luxury, and he was cosseted and adored by the household on all sides. When he learned to walk there were arms outstretched in every direction, but the young prince shunned them all and took seven steps to the north, seven steps to the east, seven steps to the south and seven steps to the west, which signalled to all his spiritual conquest of the earth.

The prince was trained in every sport, becoming an expert in all kinds of martial skills. He was well versed in the arts, and he married, at a very early age, Yasodhara, who he won in a contest at the age of only sixteen. It was not long after this marriage that Yasodhara bore him a son, who he named Rahula.

Gautama lived the life of a normal Indian ruler, eating and drinking plenty, and finding great pleasure in the women the place offered. He had concubines and a chariot that took him far and wide. Although he was a wise man, he thought little about the world around him for it had been his oyster for as long as he could remember and he polished his own little pearl daily, enjoying what he saw in his reflection.

One day, as Gautama was out in his chariot with his respected confidante and charioteer Channa, he spied an old man shuffling along the earth and mumbling to himself. He leant heavily on his stick and clearly had some difficulty moving at all. Channa said wisely, "Ah, that shall be the fate of all of us one day."

Several days later Gautama was out once again with Channa, and he saw a man lying poor and ill in the gutter. He expressed some surprise that a man could be in such a state and asked Channa how this had happened.

Channa spoke wisely, "Ah, this shall be the fate of all of us. Suffering comes to us all."

It was on their third such trip that Gautama saw the body of a man who had recently died. He looked puzzled for such occurrences were not the common sight of princes. Any ugliness like illness and death had been swept from his sight until now.

Channa spoke wisely, "Ah, this shall be the fate of us all."

Now Gautama was deeply affected by his three experiences and it caused him to spend many long hours pondering his condition, and the fate that would eventually befall him – and them all. He found no pleasure in his food or drink. He left his women in peace and he decided that there was nothing lasting or true in his life. And so it was decided that he would leave his palaces and all the trappings of his life to live a life of meditation and solitude.

Later that night, by the glow of the silver moon, he ordered Channa to saddle his favourite horse Kanthaka, and they rode away from the palace, silently escaping from a life that Gautama now knew he could not live. The gods had smiled on him and his enlightenment, and they helped quiet the hooves of his horse so that the sound of their clatter on the flagstones would not waken his family. Without a whisper, the men left, Channa accompanying Gautama until they reached the edge of the forest. And there, stripping himself of his finery, the prince said good-bye to his dear companion and to his life. At the age of just twenty-nine, Gautama had left it all.

In the wilds of the Indian countryside, the prince lost himself to the world. For many years he sat in meditation. The gods sent him many temptations, including the daughters of Mara, the goddess of seduction, whose wiry bodies writhed and danced, offering him pleasures for which he had at one time hungered. But he resisted them all, for within Gautama was a new calm. He was on the verge of enlightenment.

Gautama fasted for long periods, until he realized the need for food. Reaching out, he plucked the fruit of the fig tree and in its leafy shade he achieved complete bodhi, or enlightenment.

His philosophy had been worked out in his meditations, and all had become clear. He knew now that desire was the root of evil, of anger and violence. He realized that desire made fools of man, chasing money and women and an afterlife. He realized that a person who cannot control desire goes through chains of existences – birth and then death and then birth again, over and over. This was a wheel which could be stopped; this was a chain which could be broken. By suppressing desire, links of the chain can be removed, and instead of there being rebirth after death, there would be the state of nirvana, where there could be no suffering, no more death, no more births.

And so the supreme Buddha took it upon himself to go back into the world, to preach his new wisdom. He could, then, have given himself over to nirvana but his calling drew him to spread the message, to reach out as a teacher to the people who needed deliverance from the unholy waste that their lives had become.

Buddha walked to Varanasi, where he dressed himself in yellow robes – a personification of the sunlight which flowed through his veins and fed his wisdom. He returned to Kapiavastu, and there he appeared to his own people, joined by his son Rahula. For the next forty-five years, Buddha wandered and preached. Animosity and anger were quietened by his gentle words – even the most ferocious of animals bowed to his touch.

SUMEDHA

To cease from all sin,
To get virtue,
To cleanse one's own heart –
This is the religion of the Buddhas.
Henry S. Olcott, A Buddhist Catechism

t is possible for any man to take the form of a Buddha, provided he can find enlightenment. There was, however, one case of a man becoming a Buddha-elect while the great Buddha lived. He was called Sumedha, and he lived in the great city of Amara.

Sumedha was a good man who was both wise and wealthy. He had been widely educated and his studies brought to his attention the unhappy lot that was the world around him. He was a Brahman and well-respected, and Sumedha knew he could count on the support of his peers and family in whatever he did. And so it was one day that Sumedha sat down and reflected on the misery that surrounded him. He too saw the unhappy chain of events that followed events – birth, death, rebirth and then death. And in between that unhappy chain fell the links of old age, disease, and for many, the poverty of the elderly.

So Sumedha took himself away then, far away to the Himalayas where he lived as a hermit in a house of leaves. He meditated and strove to attain enlightenment. A day came when the great Buddha would be passing near to Sumedha's hut, and the people of the mountain had come together to prepare a path for his feet. Sumedha joined eagerly in his work, and when the Buddha approached, he laid himself in the muddy rocks and leaves and sought a higher consciousness. And as he laid there, he realized that he could, at that moment, cast all his evil aside and enter into nirvana.

But the good Sumedha paused. How, he said to himself, how can I do this for myself. It would be better for all that I someday achieve complete omniscience and bring with me many people with the doctrines of Buddha.

There appeared at his side Dipankara, the Buddha who was known as One-who-overcame. Dipankara knelt beside

Sumedha and rejoiced in his choice. The trees around them blossomed, and their leaves at once became lush. The earth became rich under his body, more fecund and fertile. From the clouds, the gods threw cascades of perfumed flowers.

"You have made the right choice," said Dipankara. "Go on and advance. Surely a Buddha you shall be, and give many others the chance to do the same."

Sumedha returned then to the forest, where he practised carefully the conditions of a Buddha. They were perfection in alms, in keeping the precepts in renunciation, in good will and in indifference, and Sumedha learned them all. Beginning to fulfil the conditions of the quest he entered his hut and he stayed there. And then, one day, Sumedha died.

The forms by which he was reborn are countless, and in every one he stayed by his chosen path. Indeed, it has been said that there is not a particle of earth where the Buddha has not sacrificed his life for the sake of the creatures.

THE SIX-TUSKED ELEPHANT

The *Jataka book* outlines the 550 rebirths of the Buddha-elect Sumedha, and this is just one. Once upon a time he was born as the son of an elephant chief, high in the Himalayas on the banks of a great lake. He was born into a royal herd, and they lived happily by the clear waters, enjoying the rich foods that grew on its shores, and finding shelter in the warm caves when the rains came each year. There was a great banyan tree, and the elephants lolled in its cool shade when the heat of the summer burned at their tender hides.

One steamy day, the Buddha-elect took shelter under the tree with his two wives, Chullasubhadda and Mahasubhadda. As the Buddha-elect reached up with his trunk to root out an insect, he accidentally sent down a shower of green leaves and flowers on his wife Mahasubhadda. On the other side, he had dislodged a spray of dry leaves and ants, and these struck Chullasubhadda smartly on the head causing her some pain, and even more jealousy. Later that day, another of the elephants presented the Buddha-elect with a lovely, fresh seven-sprayed lotus, and this he gave to Mahasubhadda. Chullasubhadda watched from behind the tree, her anger clouding what goodness remained within her.

That night Chullasubhadda laid under the tree and prayed that she might be reborn as the daughter of the king so that she could return as the queen of the king of Benares. She fell into a deep slumber, and her wicked wishes were granted. Chullasubhadda did not awake, and she returned as the favoured wife of the king of Benares. She remembered her wish to come back in this form and she remembered even more clearly the jealousy she had for the Buddha-elect's relationship with Mahasubhadda. She had returned for one reason alone – to destroy him – and that it what she set out to do.

The king of Benares returned to his chamber one evening to find his lovely wife in tears. He begged her to allow him to serve her in some way, and she spoke then of a wish that had been hers since she had been a child. With false innocence lighting her eyes, Chullasubhadda told the king that she had dreamed of a magnificent white elephant with six tusks. She longed for those tusks, she said, and if she could not have them she would surely die.

A hunter was chosen from the palace, and the queen explained to him where he would find the elephant. She promised him great riches and the hunter grudgingly agreed to go. He travelled deep into the Himalayas, far beyond the reaches of ordinary men, and he finally came upon the sweet waters of the lake, by which the herd of royal elephants rested. It was seven years since he had left the palace and he was weary from his travels. The great elephant was beautiful, and the hunter was suddenly saddened by the task ahead of him. Dressing himself in the yellow robes of a hermit who he had met on his travels, he slept for several hours in a hole he had dug near the herd.

When he awoke, he summoned up his courage. Preparing his poisoned arrow, he waited until the great elephant passed, and he shot him straight through the head. Now the Buddha-elect would most certainly have sent this hunter to a sorry death if he had not seen his yellow robes. Intrigued by such poor behaviour on the part of a man of god, he knelt over the hunter and asked why he had performed an act of such violence.

The hunter, frightened by the presence of the elephant, confessed all. The Buddha-elect remembered his wife and he decided then that he would give in to her wishes. He allowed the hunter to saw at his tusks, an act which the poor tired traveller seemed unable to commit. He sawed at the tusks but with such ineffectual action that he caused the great elephant enormous pain and suffering, and filled his mouth with blood. And so it was that the great white elephant took the hunter's saw in his own hands and cut off his tusks himself. He presented them to the hunter, along with magic which would return him to the palace in seven days and seven hours.

As the hunter left, the great elephant laid down and died. That evening he was burned on the pyre by the others in his herd.

When the hunter returned to the queen, she leapt up and down with happiness at her conquest. She clutched the tusks to her breast and took to her bed in order to gloat. But as she looked at them there, saddled in her lap, she felt empty. And then, creeping into the empty hollow that had been her emotions, she felt despair and inconsolable grief. She remembered her life and her husband, and little by little the despair cracked her heart. The queen died.

When she was reborn, it was as Savatthi, a nun. One day she travelled to hear the doctrines of Buddha, and as she sat there, she realized that she had been married to him, and that he had once been the great white elephant. She swooned then, and burst into tears. But the great Buddha only smiled down on her, and when she told her story he only smiled again. Savatthi went on, it is said, to attain the sainthood, and it is her story that was responsible for many men following the great one's path.

PARINIRVANA

The great Buddha spread the word for forty-five years, and in the final year of his ministry, he suffered a grave illness.

He knew then that his nirvana was approaching, and he prepared for the final release, called parinirvana for the great one. Buddha's illness came as he ate with a good smith called Chunda, who had prepared for him the most succulent pork.

It was this meat which brought on the final sickness, for it was tainted and it caused the great one to fall into a fever and a wretched faintness to which his whole body succumbed.

But Buddha felt no anger towards the Chunda, and indeed, as soon as he realized that his illness would, this time, be fatal, he called Chunda to his side.

"Chunda, your offering will bring a great reward. It is your doing which has brought on the attainment of nirvana, and for that I am thankful."

Buddha made his pleasure clear to all his friends for he feared that Chunda would be blamed for his death when it was a time for rejoicing. Buddha lay himself down on a couch in a grove of sal-trees near Kushinagara.

He sent a message to the princes of Malwa to come at once to his side, for he knew they would have a deep regret if they did not witness his final release, if they did not bid him farewell in person. Buddha's couch was soon surrounded by men of the highest order. There were kings and princes, priests and nobles, devas and brahmas of the ten thousand worlds, and they all gathered by his bed to see him pass. There was deep desolation and much weeping, which Buddha was unable to control.

Just before he was to take his last breath, Buddha was approached by a hostile Brahman of Kushinagara, who had not yet reached an understanding or acceptance of Buddha's teachings.

Despite the cries of those around his bed to suppress the arrogant Brahman, Buddha was able to raise himself once more, in order to answer the young man's questions, and to argue the points to which he objected. In the end, there was a supreme silence, for the Brahman became a disciple and Buddha had the satisfaction of carrying his work, his teachings to his final rest.

He said to those around him, "Now my friends I depart to nirvana, leaving you with my ordinances. Do not weep – seek the path to release and you may all reach nirvana. Work on your salvation," he said quietly, and then he slipped into an unconsciousness which took from him his life.

The body of Buddha was wrapped in the finest cloths and laid in state for six days. And then it was burnt on a pyre in the coronation hall of the princes. The pyre ignited without match, for Buddha's body was ready for the final release, for parinirvana, and it was consumed at once. He left behind his teachings, and the goodness with which he had filled the world.

TALES OF THE HITOPADESHA

The Sanskrit name *'Hitopadesha'* is a combination of 'Hita', meaning welfare or benefit and 'Upadesha', meaning counsel, and as its name suggests it is a collection of fables intended to give good counsel.

The story is narrated by Vishnu, who is depicted as a sage offering wise counsel to the sons of Sudarsana, the King of Pataliputra, through stories within stories involving talking animals. Each short tale embedded in the overall narrative of the story contains a nugget of good advice with an underlying moral intended to promote wise behaviour.

Many consider the *Hitopadesha* to be a revised version of an ancient classic Sanskrit text called *Panchatantra* from the third century BCE. It was presumably written by Narayan Pandit, but as no other work by this author has ever been unearthed, little is known about the origin of this text. Scholars believe it may have been written in East India during the Pala Empire (sometime from the eighth to twelfth centuries), although the earliest known manuscript was discovered in Nepal and has been dated to 1373.

THE VULTURE, THE CAT, AND THE BIRDS

On the banks of the Ganges there is a cliff called Vulture-Crag, and there grew a great fig-tree. It was hollow, and within its shelter lived an old Vulture, named Grey-pate, whose hard fortune it was to have lost both his eyes and his talons. The birds that roosted in the tree fed him from their own store, out of sheer pity, and by that means he managed to live. One day, when the old birds were gone, Long-ear, the Cat, came there to get a meal of the nestlings; alarmed at seeing him, they set up a chirruping that roused Grey-pate.

"Who goes there?" croaked Grey-pate.

Now Long-ear, on catching sight of the Vulture, thought himself undone; but as flight was impossible, he resolved to trust his destiny and approach. "My lord," he said, "I have the honour to salute you."

"Who is it?" said the Vulture.

Long-ear replied: "I am a Cat."

"Be off with you, Cat, or I shall kill you," said the Vulture.

"I am ready to die if I deserve death," answered the Cat. "But let what I have to say be heard."

"For what reason have you come then?" asked the Vulture.

"I live," began Long-ear, "on the Ganges, bathing, and eating no flesh, practising the moon-penance, like a Bramacharya. The birds that visit there constantly praise your worship to me as one wholly given to the study of morality, and worthy of all trust; and so I came here to learn law from you, Sir, who are so deep in learning and in years. Do you so read the law of strangers as to be ready to slay a guest? What do the books say about the householder?:

"*Bar your door not to the stranger,*
be he friend or be he foe,
For the tree will shade the woodman
while his axe does lay it low,
And if means fail, what there is should
be given with kind words, as –
Greeting fair, and room to rest in; fire,
and water from the well –
Simple gifts – are given freely in the
house where good men dwell.

"And without respect of person:

"*Young, or bent with many winters; rich,*
or poor, whatever your guest,
Honour him for your own honour – better is he than the best.

"Or else comes the rebuke:

"*Pity them that ask your pity: who are you to stint your hoard,*
When the holy moon shines equal on the leper and the lord!

"And that other, too:

"*When your gate is roughly fastened,*
and the asker turns away,
He bears your good deeds with him,
and his sins on you do lay.

"For truly:

> *"In the house the husband rules, men*
> *the Brahmans 'master' call;*
> *Agni is the Twice-born Master — but*
> *the guest is lord of all."*

To these weighty words Grey-pate answered: "Yes! But cats like meat, and there are young birds here, and therefore I said, go."

"Sir," said the Cat, and as he spoke he touched the ground, and then his two ears, and called on Krishna to witness to his words, "I that have overcome passion, and practised the moon-penance, know the Scriptures; and however they assert, in this primal duty of abstaining from injury they are unanimous. Which of them says not:

> *"He who does and thinks no wrong —*
> *He who suffers, being strong —*
> *He whose harmlessness men know —*
> *To Swerga such do go."*

And so, winning the old Vulture's confidence, Long-ear, the Cat, entered the hollow tree and lived there. And day after day he stole away some of the nestlings, and brought them down to the hollow to devour. Meanwhile the parent birds, whose little ones were being eaten, made an inquiry after them in all quarters; and the Cat, discovering this fact, slipped out from the hollow, and made his escape. Afterwards, when the birds came to look closely, they found the bones of their young ones in the hollow of the tree where Grey-pate lived; and the birds at once concluded that their nestlings had been killed and eaten by the old Vulture, whom they accordingly executed.

The advice of this story is to be wary of unknown acquaintances.

THE DEAD GAME AND THE JACKAL

In a town called **Well-to-Dwell** there lived a mighty hunter, whose name was Grim-face. Feeling a desire one day for a little venison, he took his bow, and went into the woods; where he soon killed a deer. As he was carrying the deer home, he came across a wild boar of enormous proportions. Laying the deer on the earth, he fixed and discharged an arrow and struck the boar, which instantly rushed at him with a roar louder than thunder, and ripped the hunter up. He fell like a tree cut by the axe, and lay dead along with the boar, and a snake also, which had been crushed by the feet of the combatants.

Not long afterwards, a Jackal named Howl o'Nights came that way in his prowl for food. He laid eyes on the hunter, the deer, the boar and the snake lying dead together. "Aha!" he said, "What luck! Here's a grand dinner got ready for me! Good fortune can come, I see, as well as ill fortune. Let me think: the man will be fine pickings for a month; the deer with the boar will last two more; the snake will do for tomorrow; and, as I am particularly hungry, I will treat myself now to this bit of meat on the bow-horn." So he began to gnaw it apart, and the bow-string slipped, the bow sprang back, and resolved Howl o'Nights into the five elements by death.

The advice of this story is that the secret of success is a free, contented, and yet enterprising mind.

THE OLD JACKAL AND THE ELEPHANT

In the forest of Brahma lived an Elephant, whose name was White-front. The Jackals knew him, and said amongst themselves, "If this great brute would just die, there would be four months' food for us, and plenty out of his carcase." With that an old Jackal stood up, and pledged himself to accomplish the death of the Elephant by his own wit. Accordingly, he searched for White-front, and, going up to him, he made the reverential prostration of the eight members, gravely saluting him.

"Divine creature," he said, "grant me the courtesy of one look."

"Who are you?" grunted the Elephant, "and where do you come from?"

"I am only a Jackal," said the other, "but the beasts of the forest are convinced that it is not expedient to live without a king, and they have met in full council, and sent me to tell you your Royal Highness, endowed with so many lordly qualities, that their choice has fallen on you to be the sovereign of the forest here; for:

> *"Who is just, and strong, and wise?*
> *Who is true to social ties?*
> *He is formed for Emperies.*

"Let your Majesty, therefore, go there at once, so that the moment may not escape us."

So the Jackal led the way, followed at a great pace by White-front, who was eager to begin his reign. Soon the Jackal brought him to a deep swamp, into which he plunged heavily before he could stop himself.

"Good master Jackal," cried the Elephant, "what's to do now? I am up to my belly in this quagmire."

"Perhaps your Majesty," said the Jackal, with an insolent laugh, "will deign take hold of the tip of my brush with your trunk, and so get out."

Then White-front, the Elephant, knew that he had been deceived; and he sank in the slime, and was devoured by the Jackals.

The advice of this story is that fraud may achieve what force would never try.

THE MONKEY AND THE WEDGE

In South Behar, close to the retreat of Dhurmma, there was an open plot of ground on which a temple was being built under the management of a man named Subhadatta.

A carpenter working on the construction had partly sawed through a long beam of wood, and had wedged it open. He had since gone away, leaving the wedge fixed.

Shortly afterwards a large herd of monkeys came frolicking that way, and one of their number, no doubt directed by the Angel of death, got astride the beam, and grasped the wedge, with his tail and lower parts dangling down between the pieces of wood. Not content with this, in the mischief natural to monkeys, he began to tug at the wedge until at last it gave way to the great effort and came out. Then the wood closed on him, and jammed him fast. So perished the monkey, miserably crushed.

The advice of this story is that matters that do not concern us are best left alone. Indeed, let meddlers mark it, and be edified.

THE WASHERMAN'S JACKASS

There was a certain Washerman at Benares, whose name was Carpurapataka, and he had an Ass and a Dog in his courtyard; the first tethered, and the last roaming loose. Once day he had been spending his morning in the company of his wife, whom he had just married, and had fallen asleep in her arms, when a robber entered the house, and began to carry off his goods. The Ass observed the activities of the thief, and was very concerned.

"Good Dog," he said, "this is your matter: why do you not bark aloud, and rouse the master?"

"Gossip Ass," replied the Dog, "leave me alone to guard the premises. I can do it, if I choose; but the truth is, this master of ours thinks he is so safe lately that he clean forgets me, and I don't find my allowance of food nearly regular enough. Masters will do so; and a little fright will put him in mind of his defenders again."

"You worthless mongrel!" exclaimed the Ass. "At the work-time, asking wages – is that like a faithful herd?"

"You extreme Ass!" replied the Dog. "When the work's done, grudging wages – is that acting like a lord?"

"Mean-spirited beast," retorted the Ass, "who neglects your master's business! Well, then, I at least will try to wake him; it is no less than religion:

> "Serve the Sun with sweat of body;
> starve your mouth to feed the flame;
> Stead your lord with all your service;
> to your death go, rid of blame."

So saying, he put forward his very best braying. The Washerman sprang up at the noise, and missing the thief, turned in a rage towards the Ass for disturbing him, and beat it with a club to such an extent that the blows resolved the poor animal into the five elements of death. The advice of this story is that subordinates should not interfere in the department of their chief.

THE CAT WHO SERVED THE LION

Far away in the North, on a mountain named Thousand-Crags, there lived a Lion called Mighty-heart; and he was much annoyed by a certain mouse, who made a habit of nibbling his mane while he lay asleep in his den. The Lion would wake in a great rage at finding the ends of his magnificent mane made ragged, but the little mouse ran into his hole, and he could never catch it.

After much consideration he went down to a village, and persuaded a Cat named Curd-ear to come to his cave. He kept the Cat royally on all kinds of dainties, and slept comfortably without having his mane nibbled, as the mouse would now never venture out. Whenever the Lion heard the mouse scratching about, that was always a signal for regaling the Cat in a most distinguished style. But one day, the wretched mouse being nearly starved, he took the courage to creep timidly from his hole, and was directly pounced on by Curd-ear and killed. After that the Lion heard no more of the mouse, and promptly forgot his regular entertainments of the cat.

The advice of this story is not to set your lord at ease, for doing that might starve you.

THE TERRIBLE BELL

Once, in Brahmapoora, a thief had stolen a bell from the city, and was making off with that prize, and more, into the Sri-parvata hills, when he was killed by a tiger. The bell lay in the jungle until one day some monkeys picked it up, and began amused themselves by constantly ringing it. The townspeople found the bones of the man, and heard the noise of the bell all across the hills; so they began to believe that there was a terrible devil there, whose ears rang like bells as he swung them about, and whose delight was to devour men. Everyone, accordingly, was leaving the town, when a peasant woman named Karala, who liked belief the better for a little proof, came to the king.

"Highness!" she said, "for a reward I could settle the secret of Swing-ear the spirit."

"You could!" exclaimed the king.

"I think so!" replied the woman.

"Pay her at once," said the king.

Karala, who had her own ideas on the matter, took the present and set out. After coming to the hills, she made a circle, and paid homage to Gunputtee, without whom nothing prospers. Then, taking some fruit she had brought, the kind that monkey's adore, she scattered it up and down in the wood, and withdrew to watch. Very soon the monkeys finding the fruit, put down the bell, to do justice to it, and the woman picking it up, took it back to the town, where she became an object of great respect.

The advice of this story is that it does not do to be alarmed by a noise. It is the cause that has to be found out.

THE PRINCE AND THE PROCURESS

In the city of Golden-Streets there reigned a King, named Viravikrama, whose officer of justice was one day taking a certain Barber away for punishment, when he was stopped by a strolling beggar, who held him by the skirts, and cried out, "Punish not this man – punish them that do wrong of their own knowledge." Being asked his meaning, he recited the following verses:

> *"I that could not leave alone*
> *Streak-o'-Gold', must therefore moan.*
> *She that took the Housewife's place*
> *Lost the nose from off her face.*
> *Take this lesson to your heart –*
> *Fools for folly suffer smart."*

Still further questioned, he told this story:

"I am Prince Kandarpaketu, son of the King of Ceylon. Walking one day in my summer-garden, I heard a merchant-captain telling of how that out at sea, deep under water, he had seen what was like nothing but the famous tree of Paradise, and sitting under it a lady of most radiant beauty, bedecked with strings of pearls like Lakshmi herself, reclining, with a lute in her hands, on what appeared to be a golden couch encrusted with precious stones.

"At once I engaged the captain and his ship, and steered to the spot of which he told me. On reaching it I saw the beautiful apparition as he had described it, and, transported with the exquisite beauty of the lady, I leapt after her into the sea. In a moment I found myself in a city of gold; and in an apartment of a golden palace, surrounded by young and beautiful girls, I found the Sea-queen.

"She saw my approach, and sent an attendant with a courteous message to meet me. In reply to my questions, I learned that the lady was the Princess Ratnamanjari, daughter of the King of All the Spirits – and how she had made a vow that whoever should first come to see her golden city, with his own eyes, should marry her. So I married her and spent many happy days in her delightful society.

"One day she took me aside, and said, 'Dear Prince! All these delights, and I myself, are yours to enjoy; only that picture over there, of the Fairy Streak-o'-Gold, that you must never touch!' For a long time I observed this command until at last, impelled by resistless curiosity, I laid my hand on the picture of Streak-o'-Gold. In an instant her little foot, lovely as the lotus-blossom, advanced from out of the painting, and launched me through sea and air into my own country.

"Since then I have been a miserable wanderer; and passing through this city, I happened to lodge at a Cowkeeper's hut, and saw the truth of this Barber's affair. The herdsman returned at night with his cattle, and found his wife talking with the wife of the Barber, who is no better than a madam. Enraged at this, the man beat his wife, tied her to the milking-post, and fell asleep.

"In the dead of the night the Barber's wife came back, and said to the woman, 'He, whom you know, is burnt with the cruel fire of your absence, and lies near to death; therefore go and console him, and I will tie myself to the post until you return.'

"This was done, and the Cowkeeper soon awoke. 'Ah, you light thing!' he said jeeringly, 'why do you not keep your promise, and meet your gallant man?'

"The Barber's wife could not reply; so becoming incensed, the man cried out, 'What! Do you scorn to speak to me? I will cut your nose off!' And so he did, and then he lay down to sleep again.

"Very soon the Cowkeeper's wife came back and asked if all was well. 'Look at my face!' said the Barber's wife, 'and you will see if all is well.' The woman could do nothing but take her place again, while the Barber's wife, picking up the severed nose, and at a sad loss of how to account for it, went to her house.

"In the morning, before it was light, the Barber called to her to bring his box of razors. She brought one only, and he flung it away in a passion. 'Oh, the knave!' she shouted out, 'Neighbours, neighbours, he has cut my nose off!' and so she took him before the officers.

"In the meantime, the Cowkeeper, wondering at his wife's patience, made some inquiry about her nose; to which she replied, 'Cruel wretch! You cannot harm a virtuous woman. If Yama and the seven guardians of the world know me chaste, then be my face unmaimed!'

"The herdsman hurried to fetch a light, and finding her features unaltered, he flung himself at her feet, and begged forgiveness. For:

> "Never tires the fire of burning, never
> wearies death of slaying,
> Nor the sea of drinking rivers, nor the
> bright-eyed of betraying.''

The king's officer immediately dismissed Kandarpaketu, and did justice by setting the Barber free, shaving the head of the Barber's wife, and punishing the Cowkeeper's.

The advice of this story is that people must suffer for their own mistakes.

THE LION AND THE OLD HARE

On the Mandara mountain there lived a Lion named Fierce-of-heart, and he was perpetually massacring of all the wild animals. Things grew so bad that the beasts held a public meeting, and drew up a respectful protest to the Lion in these words:

"Why should your Majesty so make carnage of us all? If it may please you, we ourselves will daily provide a beast for your Majesty's meal."

The Lion responded, "If that arrangement is more agreeable to you, so be it."

From then on a beast was allotted to him daily, and daily devoured. One day came the turn of an old hare to supply the royal table, who reflected to himself as he walked along, "I can but die, and I will go to my death leisurely."

Now Fierce-of-heart, the lion, was strained with hunger, and seeing the Hare so approaching he roared, "How dare you so delay in coming?"

"Your Highness," replied the Hare, "I am not to blame. I was detained on the road by another lion, who demanded an oath from me to return when I should have informed your Majesty."

"Go," exclaimed King Fierce-of-heart in a rage, "show me, instantly, where this insolent villain of a lion lives."

So the Hare led the way until he came to a deep well, at which he stopped, and said, "Let my lord the King come here and behold him." The Lion approached, and saw his own reflection in the water of the well, on which, in his passion, he directly flung himself, and so perished.

The advice of this story is that he that has sense has strength; the fool is weak.

THE WAGTAIL AND THE SEA

On the shore of the Southern Sea there lived a pair of Wagtails. The Hen-bird was about to lay, and so said her mate, "Husband, we must look around for a suitable place to lay my eggs."

"My dear," replied the Cock-bird, "will this spot not do?"

"This spot!" exclaimed the Hen, "why, the tide overflows it."

"Good woman," said the Cock, "am I so pitiful a fellow that the Sea will venture out to wash the eggs out of my nest?"

"You are my very good Lord," replied the Hen, with a laugh," but still there is a great difference between you and the Sea."

Afterwards, however, at the desire of her mate, she agreed to lay her eggs on the beach. Now the Ocean had overheard all this, and, bent on displaying its strength, it rose up and washed away the nest and eggs. Overwhelmed with grief, the Hen-bird flew to her mate, and cried, "Husband, the terrible disaster has occurred! My eggs are gone!"

"Be of good heart! My Life," he replied.

And soon after that he called a meeting of fowls, and went with them into the presence of Gurud, the Lord of the birds. When the Master of the Mighty Wing had listened to their complaint, he conveyed it to the God Narayen, who keeps, and kills, and makes the world alive. The almighty mandate given, Gurud bound it on his forehead, and carried it to the Ocean, which, as soon as it heard the will of Narayen, at once gave back the eggs.

The advice of this story is that before you scorn your enemy, you should ask who his friends are.

MISCELLANEOUS MYTHS

There are a huge number of fascinating fables, fairy tales, myths and legends which form the backbone of Indian philosophy explaining ideologies that are often complex. Some of these stories have their root in the Epics and in religious works. And later Hindu religious literature calls upon a host of characters and creatures introduced in the Vedas, the Brahamanas, the *Puranas* and some of the lesser-known Epics to draw attention to their message, and to exemplify the points they wish to put forth.

Many of these stories, plucked from a larger original, and bejewelled with the words of generations, can now stand alone as individual tales and lessons. It is often these shorter parables that provide the guidelines for living, which allow new gods to force their way into the pantheon, and which represent some of the most compelling literature of any country in the world. There are thousands of variations of each of these tales, for most of them were not put down in writing for many centuries after their composition – the oral tradition keeping them burning in the consciousness, memories and perceptions of the culture.

THE BIRTH OF GANGA

There once was a king of Ayodhya named Sagara who was anxious to have a son. He provided the saint Bhrigu many penances over the years and finally, the saint was happy to announce that Sagara's worship would be rewarded.

"You shall have a glorious name, and one of your queens shall bear a son to maintain your race and to become your heir. And of the other, there shall be some sixty thousand born to you," said the saint.

Now the wives of Sagara were most anxious to know which of them would have one son and which would have the vast number predicted. Kesini wished for one child, while Sumati was happy to have sixty thousand. Time passed and Kesini gave birth to a son called Ansuman, who became the heir. And Sumati, the younger of the two wives, gave birth to a gourd whose rind broke to reveal sixty thousand babies.

About this time King Sagara decided to make a horse sacrifice in order to become the reigning Indra, or king of the gods. As the preparations were being made, Ansuman was given the task of following the horse set apart for the sacrifice for according to ritual it was to be set free and allowed to wander for a whole year wherever it would.

Now the present Indra began to fear that such a sacrifice would rid him of his crown, and veiling himself as a demon, he arrived on the appointed day and drove the horse away. King Sagara called at once for his sons to search for the stolen horse, begging them to pursue the demon that had caused it to escape.

And so the sons of Sagara began their search, each digging one league in depth towards the centre of the earth. But still they could not see the horse. The gods were alarmed by the digging of the earth, and they went to Brahma to advise him of the destruction. Brahma was calm, for the earth was protected by Vishnu, and the sons of Sagara would be turned to ashes for their handiwork. The gods returned home to wait for retribution, and as they did so, the sons dug on.

Sixty thousand leagues were dug into the earth without any sight of the horse, and the princes returned to their father requesting guidance. Sagara bid them to dig on, and to continue their search until the horse was found. The sons began to dig once again until there before them stood Vishnu. Thinking that the glitter in his eyes was one of welcome, the sons rushed forward to greet him. Moments later they were but ashes.

King Sagara waited disconsolately for news of his sons, but none arrived. Soon he sent his grandson Ansuman to look for them, but he learned nothing of their fate. Ansuman travelled widely, searching for news but he remained unrewarded, until the day when he reached the very spot of their deaths. Ansuman fell to the ground with dismay when he realized the significance of the ashes. As his tears hit the ashes, his uncle Garuda appeared and offered him consolation, holding carefully the harness of the horse that had been lost so long ago.

Prince Ansuman returned to the kingdom. Garuda had given him some advice and he thought carefully about it before he approached his grandfather.

"Garuda has said," whispered Ansuman, "that if Ganga would turn her stream below, her waves would wash the ashes of the two princes pure again, and the sixty thousand leagues would be restored while you took Indra's place in the heavens."

The king thought carefully, thoughts which carried over thirty thousand long years. He had no idea how to induce Ganga to come down from the heavens, and at last he went there himself. After his death, the task became his grandson's and then that grandson's son's. And so it was finally given to Bhagirath to accomplish the work, for he had no son. After many years of austerity, Brahma came to Bhagirath and said to him then:

"You have been blessed, for your austerities have won my grace. What can I do to help you?"

Bhagirath replied, "I would like Ganga to be let loose with her holy wave, so that the ashes of the heroes shall be washed pure and my kinsmen, Sagara's sons, shall ascend to heavenly bliss for the rest of their days. And please," he added, "I wish for a son so that my house shall not end here with me."

And Brahma said to him then, "If you pray for this, so it shall be." Bhagirath stayed in his position of prayer for one year, even as Brahma returned to heaven. Shiva, pleased with the devotion, promised to sustain the shock of the waters. Ganga, however, was not pleased with the command that she descend to earth.

Ganga threatened to wash Bhagirath into hell with her waters and as she made for the earth she was caught by the wily Shiva, who held on to the coils of her hair until her anger abated. Then she fell into the Vindu lake, from which came the seven sacred streams of India. One branch of the stream followed Bhagirath wherever he went. At last Bhagirath reached the ocean and ascended to the depths where Sagara's sons were lying. Ganga followed until her waters touched the ashes. Suddenly their spirits rose and like glittering birds they entered heaven in a burst of light.

The faith in this legend has not died. Indeed, one of the most common places of pilgrimage in India is Sagara Island, where the river Ganges and the ocean meet. Sagara's sons and his son's sons rank high in heaven and will forever more.

THE ELEPHANT AND THE CROCODILE

There once was a royal elephant who made his home with a royal herd on the banks of Triple Peak. They were happy here, for there was plentiful food and drink, and he had many wives who held him dear to their hearts. The day arrived when the royal elephant felt hot and fevered by the oppressive weather, and struggling towards an unknown lake, he plunged in and drank thirstily, stopping to cool his brow with a rush of water from his trunk.

As he reached into the water again to draw water for his wives and his children, he was attacked by a wrathful crocodile whose weight and size made him a very fearful opponent.

Crocodile and elephant fought together in the lake until the old elephant, weakened by the struggle and by his earlier fever, began to fade. His wives and children watched helplessly from the banks, calling out in terror and crying for help. And then, all at once, the elephant closed his eyes and began to pray. He prayed with such devotion to Vishnu, the supreme being, that his ardour was at once rewarded and Vishnu himself appeared on the back of Garuda. With ease he lifted the crocodile from the lake and cut its throat, throwing it back so that its blood stained the waters.

The royal elephant was saved. Now this was not just devotion that had caused Vishnu to come to the elephant's rescue. Every event has another meaning and it soon transpired that this was the culmination of an old curse. The elephant was a gandharva who had, in another life, cursed a rishi who had disturbed him. That rishi was reborn as the crocodile, and by another curse that gandharva had become an elephant.

Vishnu says that the elephant of the story represents the human soul of our age, excited by desires, given over to sensual pleasures which are too great to control. There was no salvation for him until he expressed his devotion to Vishnu, who was the only hope for wicked man.

THE KING, THE PIGEON AND THE HAWK

There once was a story told by Bhishma to Yudhishthira, and it is a story that, once told, will cleanse the teller and the listener of all sin. This is that tale:

There once was a lovely blue pigeon, hotly pursued by a hawk. The pigeon landed, breathless and terrified on the balcony of the home of King Vrishadarbha of Benares.

The gentle king looked with concern at the bird, and taking it into his care, he asked the cause of his distress.

"I am being chased," said the pigeon, casting down his eyes.

The king spoke quietly and soothed the bird with his kind words. "Ah, you are a beautiful bird, blue as the sky on a summer's evening, blue as the lotus that has freshly bloomed. Ah, you have eyes like flowers, like the blossoms of an ashoka tree. I will give you protection here. You have come to a place of safety. Rest, dear bird and take comfort."

Suddenly there was a rush of wings and there, on his balcony, appeared the hawk, irate and breathing as heavily with indignation as the poor pigeon had with fear.

"That," he said sternly to the king, "that is my appointed food and you have no right to interfere."

"Ah," said the king, "leave the poor bird. I'll have a boar and some deer dressed for you at once."

The hawk sniffed. "Perhaps, my lord," he said haughtily, "perhaps you have control over those who call themselves men, but here in the sky you cannot intervene. This is the law of nature. I am hungry. Without the food that this pigeon offers me, I will starve. Boar and deer are the food of men. I want pigeon. Release him at once."

The king thought for a moment, and then he shook his head. "I cannot do that," he said sadly.

The hawk sniffed again. "Well, King Vrishadarbha, if you are so intent on saving the life of this pigeon, perhaps you will exchange some of your own flesh for his. Give me flesh from your body equal to the pigeon's weight and I will allow him to go free."

Vrishadarbha agreed at once, and taking a blade, he began to cut away at the flesh on his arms and legs, weighing it carefully on a scale against the pigeon. He cut away at his body, and piled the flesh on the scales but they refused to budge. All across the kingdom there rose a great wail as Vrishadarbha cut his way to certain death. At last he was no more than a skeleton, and he threw his whole body on the scale against the pigeon.

There was at once a flash of light, and from the sky appeared a convoy of gods, headed by Indra. The sound of celestial music filled the air and lotus blossoms tumbled down from the heavens. King Vrishadarbha was borne away in a magnificent chariot to take his place in heaven.

It can only be true that whosoever protects another shall receive a good end.

THE ASHVIN TWINS

There once were two brothers, divine twins who were the sons of the sky-god Surya. Their names were Dasra and Nasatya and they were the most exquisitely beautiful boys, looks with which they were blessed into adulthood. The Ashvins were bright and friendly, and they attracted only the best attention wherever they flew. They rode in a gilded carriage – gold which appeared tarnished next to the burnished good looks of the Ashvin twins. They flew quickly and travelled widely, for they sought a place among the pantheon of Hindu gods, an honour which had not yet been accorded.

One day, Dasra and Nasatya were stopped in their travels by the sight of the most delicate and elegant woman, who was taking her bath in a stream near her home. This was

Sukanya, or 'Fair-Maid', and she was the wife of the aged rishi Chyavana, who had held her hand in marriage for many years and to whom she had pledged her heart and eternal devotion.

The twins were stunned by the sight of her beauty, and they flew to her side, their pearly smiles flashing as they moved forward to greet her.

"You are the most beauteous of all creatures, fair-limbed girl. Who is your father? And how is it that you have been allowed to bathe alone here in these woods?" asked the twins.

"Why I am the wife of Chyavana," said Sukanya, "and I bathe here each day."

The twins shook with laughter. "How could your father bear for you to give your hand to someone so old and near death. You are the very essence of beauty, fair maiden, and yours should have been the choice of every man."

"I love Chyavana," said Sukanya with dignity, preparing to dress.

"Leave your husband," suggested the Ashvins. "Come away with us and have a taste of youth. You'll have a life with us and our beauty will be the perfect complement to one another."

But Sukanya refused their offer and turned to leave her toilet.

But the Ashvins stopped her once again, praying that she should listen to their new request. "We are medicine men," they announced, "and we will make your husband young again, and fair of face. If we do so, fair maiden, will you agree to choose between us a husband for life?"

Sukanya consulted with her husband, who agreed to the plan, and the Ashvins did as they had promised. Within a few moments, Chyavana was at their sides and all three men entered the pool and sank into its depths. There was a pause and then they emerged, all three equal. All three identical.

The three men said in unison, "Choose among us Sukanya."

The fair maiden searched carefully for traces of her husband, and when she found them she chose him to be her lord and husband for the remainder of her life.

Chyavana had suffered no indignities, and from this fateful interlude he had had his youth returned to him. He smiled widely, and in gratitude to the Ashvin twins, he promised to win for them the right to sit with the gods, and share in their offerings.

The twins went on their way again, fleet of foot and then high in their gilded chariot. The happy couple lived together in great joy, gods in their own home.

A GLOSSARY OF MYTH & FOLKLORE

Aaru Heavenly paradise where the blessed go after death.

Ab Heart or mind.

Abiku (Yoruba) Person predestined to die. Also known as ogbanje.

Absál Nurse to Salámán, who died after their brief love affair.

Achilles The son of Peleus and the sea-nymph Thetis, who distinguished himself in the Trojan War. He was made almost immortal by his mother, who dipped him in the River Styx, and he was invincible except for a portion of his heel which remained out of the water.

Acropolis Citadel in a Greek city.

Adad-Ea Ferryman to Ut-Napishtim, who carried Gilgamesh to visit his ancestor.

Adapa Son of Ea and a wise sage.

Adar God of the sun, who is worshipped primarily in Nippur.

Aditi Sky goddess and mother of the gods.

Adityas Vishnu, children of Aditi, including Indra, Mitra, Rudra, Tvashtar, Varuna and Vishnu.

Aeneas The son of Anchises and the goddess Aphrodite, reared by a nymph. He led the Dardanian troops in the Trojan War According to legend, he became the founder of Rome.

Aengus Óg Son of Dagda and Boann (a woman said to have given the Boyne river its name), Aengus is the Irish god of love whose stronghold is reputed to have been at New Grange. The famous tale 'Dream of Aengus' tells of how he fell in love with a maiden he had dreamt of. He eventually discovered that she was to be found at the Lake of the Dragon's Mouth in Co. Tipperary, but that she lived every alternate year in the form of a swan. Aengus thus plunged into the lake transforming himself also into the shape of a swan. Then the two flew back together to his palace on the Boyne where they lived out their days as guardians of would-be lovers.

Aesir Northern gods who made their home in Asgard; there are twelve in number.

Afrásiyáb Son of Poshang, king of Túrán, who led an army against the ruling shah Nauder. Afrásiyáb became ruler of Persia on defeating Nauder.

Afterlife Life after death or paradise, reached only by the process of preserving the body from decay through embalming and preparing it for reincarnation.

Agamemnon A famous King of Mycenae. He married Helen of Sparta's sister Clytemnestra. When Paris abducted Helen, beginning the Trojan War, Menelaus called on Agamemnon to raise the Greek troops. He had to sacrifice his daughter Iphigenia in order to get a fair wind to travel to Troy.

Agastya A rishi (sage). Leads hermits to Rama.

Agemo (Yoruba) A chameleon who aided Olorun in outwitting Olokun, who was angry at him for letting Obatala create life on her lands without her permission. Agemo outwitted Olokun by changing colour, letting her think that he and Olorun were better cloth dyers than she was. She admitted defeat and there was peace between the gods once again.

Aghasur A dragon sent by Kans to destroy Krishna.

Aghríras Son of Poshang and brother of Afrásiyáb, who was killed by his brother.

Agni The god of fire.

Agora Greek marketplace.

Ahura-Mazda Supreme god of the Persians, god of the sky. Similar to the Hindu god Varuna.

Ajax Ajax the Greater was the bravest, after Achilles, of all warriors at Troy, fighting Hector in single combat and distinguishing himself in the Battle of the Ships. He was not chosen as the bravest warrior and eventually went mad.

Ajax of Locris Another warrior at Troy. When Troy was captured, he committed the ultimate sacrilege by seizing Cassandra from her sanctuary with the Palladium.

Aje (Igbo) Goddess of the earth and the underworld.

Aje (Yoruba) Goddess of the River Niger, daughter of Yemoja.

Akhet Season of the year when the River Nile traditionally flooded.

Akkadian Person of the first Mesopotamian empire, centred in Akkad.

Akwán Diw An evil spirit who appeared as a wild ass in the court of Kai-khosráu. Rustem fought and defeated the demon, presenting its head to Kai-khosráu.

Alba Irish and Scottish Gaelic word for Scotland.

Alberich King of the dwarfs.

Alcinous King of the Phaeacians.

Alf-heim Home of the elves, ruled by Frey.

All Hallowmass All Saints' Day.

Allfather Another name for Odin; Yggdrasill was created by Allfather.

Alsvider Steed of the moon (Mani) chariot.

Alsvin Steed of the sun (Sol) chariot.

Amado Outer panelling of a dwelling, usually made of wood.

Ama-no-uzume Goddess of the dawn, meditation and the arts, who showed courage when faced with a giant who scared the other deities, including Ninigi. Also known as Uzume.

Amaterasu Goddess of the sun and daughter of Izanagi after Izanami's death; she became ruler of the High Plains of Heaven on her father's withdrawal from the world. Sister of Tsuki-yomi and Susanoo.

Ambalika Daughter of the king of Benares.

Ambika Daughter of the king of Benares.

Ambrosia Food of the gods.

Amemet Eater of the dead, monster who devoured the souls of the unworthy.

Amen Original creator deity.

Amen-Ra A being created from the fusion of Ra and Osiris. He champions the poor and those in trouble. Similar to the Greek god Zeus.

Ananda Disciple of Buddha.

Anansi One of the most popular African animal myths, Anansi the spider is a clever and shrewd character who outwits his fellow animals to get his own way. He is an entertaining but morally dubious character. Many African countries tell Anansi stories.

Ananta Thousand-headed snake that sprang from Balarama's mouth, Vishnu's attendant, serpent of infinite time.

Andhrímnir Cook at Valhalla.

Andvaranaut Ring of Andvari, the King of the dwarfs.

Angada Son of Vali, one of the monkey host.

Anger-Chamber Room designated for an angry queen.

Angurboda Loki's first wife, and the mother of Hel, Fenris and Jormungander.

Aniruddha Son of Pradyumna.

Anjana Mother of Hanuman.

Anunnaki Great spirits or gods of Earth.

Ansar God of the sky and father of Ea and Anu. Brother-husband to Kishar. Also known as Anshar or Asshur.

Anshumat A mighty chariot fighter.

Anu God of the sky and lord of heaven, son of Ansar and Kishar.

Anubis Guider of souls and ruler of the underworld before Osiris; he was one of the divinities who brought Osiris back to life. He is portrayed as a canid, African wolf or jackal.

Apep Serpent and emblem of chaos.

Apollo One of the twelve Olympian gods, son of Zeus and Leto. He is attributed with being the god of plague, music, song and prophecy.

Apsaras Dancing girls of Indra's court and heavenly nymphs.

Apsu Primeval domain of fresh water, originally part of Tiawath with whom he mated to have Mummu. The term is also used for the abyss from which creation came.

Aquila The divine eagle.

Arachne A Lydian woman with great skill in weaving. She was challenged in a competition by the jealous Athene who destroyed her work and when she killed herself, turned her into a spider destined to weave for eternity.

Aralu Goddess of the underworld, also known as Eres-ki-Gal. Married to Nergal.

Ares God of War, 'gold-changer of corpses', and the son of Zeus and Hera.

Argonauts Heroes who sailed with Jason on the ship Argo to fetch the golden fleece from Colchis.

Ariki A high chief, a leader, a master, a lord.

Arjuna The third of the Pandavas.

Aroha Affection, love.

Artemis The virgin goddess of the chase, attributed with being the moon goddess and the primitive mother-goddess. She was daughter of Zeus and Leto.

Arundhati The Northern Crown.

Asamanja Son of Sagara.

Asclepius God of healing who often took the form of a snake. He is the son of Apollo by Coronis.

Asgard Home of the gods, at one root of Yggdrasill.

Ashvatthaman Son of Drona.

Ashvins Twin horsemen, sons of the sun, benevolent gods and related to the divine.

Ashwapati Uncle of Bharata and Satrughna.

Asipû Wizard.

Asopus The god of the River Asopus.

Assagai Spear, usually made from hardwood tipped with iron and used in battle.

Astrolabe Instrument for making astronomical measurements.

Asuras Titans, demons, and enemies of the gods with magical powers.

Atef crown White crown made up of the Hedjet, the white crown of Upper Egypt, and red feathers.

Atem The first creator-deity, he is also thought to be the finisher of the world. Also known as Tem.

Athene Virgin warrior-goddess, born from the forehead of Zeus when he swallowed his wife Metis. Plays a key role in the travels of Odysseus, and Perseus.

Atlatl Spear-thrower.

Atua A supernatural being, a god.

Atua-toko A small carved stick, the symbol of the god whom it represents. It was stuck in the ground whilst holding incantations to its presiding god.

Augeas King of Elis, one of the Argonauts.

Augsburg Tyr's city.

Avalon Legendary island where Excalibur was created and where Arthur went to recover from his wounds. It is said he will return from Avalon one day to reclaim his kingdom.

Ba Dead person or soul. Also known as ka.

Bairn Little child, also called bairnie.

Balarama Brother of Krishna.

Balder Son of Frigga; his murder causes Ragnarok. Also spelled as Baldur.

Bali Brother of Sugriva and one of the five great monkeys in the *Ramayana*.

Balor The evil, one-eyed King of the Fomorians and also grandfather of Lugh of the Long Arm. It was prophesied that Balor would one day be slain by his own grandson so he locked his daughter away on a remote island where he intended that she would never fall pregnant. But Cian, father of Lugh, managed to reach the island disguised as a woman, and Balor's daughter eventually bore him a child. During the second battle of Mag Tured (or Moytura), Balor was killed by Lugh who slung a stone into his giant eye.

Ban King of Benwick, father of Lancelot and brother of King Bors.

Bannock Flat loaf of bread, typically of oat or barley, usually cooked on a griddle.

Banshee Mythical spirit, usually female, who bears tales of imminent death. They often deliver the news by wailing or keening outside homes. Spelled *bean sí* in Gaelic.

Bard Traditionally a storyteller, poet or music composer whose work often focused on legends.

Barû Seer.

Basswood Any of several North American linden trees with a soft light-coloured wood.

Bastet Goddess of love, fertility and sex and a solar deity. She is often portrayed with the head of a cat.

Bateta (Yoruba) The first human, created alongside Hanna by the Toad and reshaped into human form by the Moon.

Bau Goddess of humankind and the sick, and known as the 'divine physician'. Daughter of Anu.

Bawn Fortified enclosure surrounding a castle.

Beaver Largest rodent in the United States of America, held in high esteem by Native American people. Although a land mammal, it spends a great deal of time in water and has a dense waterproof fur coat to protect it from harsh weather conditions.

Behula Daughter of Saha.

Bel Name for the god En-lil, the word is also used as a title meaning 'lord'.

Belus Deity who helped form the heavens and earth and created animals and celestial beings. Similar to Zeus in Greek mythology.

Benten Goddess of the sea and one of the Seven Divinities of Luck. Also referred to as the goddess of love, beauty and eloquence and as being the personification of wisdom.

Bere Barley.

Berossus Priest of Bel who wrote a history of Babylon.

Berserker Norse warrior who fights with a frenzied rage.

Bestla Giant mother of Aesir's mortal element.

Bhadra A mighty elephant.

Bhagavati Shiva's wife, also known as Parvati.

Bhagiratha Son of Dilipa.

Bharadhwaja Father of Drona and a hermit.

Bharata One of Dasharatha's four sons.

Bhaumasur A demon, slain by Krishna.

Bhima The second of the Pandavas.

Bhimasha King of Rajagriha and disciple of Buddha.

Bier Frame on which a coffin or dead body is placed before being carried to the grave.

Bifrost Rainbow bridge presided over by Heimdall.

Big-Belly One of Ravana's monsters.

Bilskirnir Thor's palace.

Bodach The term means 'old man'. The Highlanders believed that the Bodach crept down chimneys in order to steal naughty children. In other territories, he was a spirit who warned of death.

Bodkin Large, blunt needle used for threading strips of cloth or tape through cloth; short pointed dagger or blade.

Boer Person of Dutch origin who settled in southern Africa in the late seventeenth century. The term means 'farmer'. Boer people are often called Afrikaners.

Bogle Ghost or phantom; goblin-like creature.

Boliaun Ragwort, a weed with ragged leaves.

Book of the Dead Book for the dead, thought to be written by Thoth, texts from which were written on papyrus and buried with the dead, or carved on the walls of tombs, pyramids or sarcophagi.

Bors King of Gaul and brother of King Ban.

Bothy Small cottage or hut.

Brahma Creator of the world, mythical origin of colour (caste).

Brahmadatta King of Benares.

Brahman Member of the highest Hindu caste, traditionally a priest.

Bran In Scottish legend, Bran is the great hunting hound of Fionn Mac Chumail. In Irish mythology, he is a great hero.

Branstock Giant oak tree in the Volsung's hall; Odin placed a sword in it and challenged the guests of a wedding to withdraw it.

Brave Young warrior of Native American descent, sometimes also referred to as a 'buck'.

Bree Thin broth or soup.

Breidablik Balder's palace.

Brigit Scottish saint or spirit associated with the coming of spring.

Brisingamen Freyia's necklace.

Britomartis A Cretan goddess, also known as Dictynna.

Brocéliande Legendary enchanted forest and the supposed burial place of Merlin.

Brokki Dwarf who makes a deal with Loki, and who makes Miolnir, Draupnir and Gulinbursti.

Brollachan A shapeless spirit of unknown origin. One of the most frightening in Scottish mythology, it spoke only two words, 'Myself' and 'Thyself', taking the shape of whatever it sat upon.

Brownie A household spirit or creature which took the form of a small man (usually hideously ugly) who undertakes household chores, and mill or farm work, in exchange for a bowl of milk.

Brugh Borough or town.

Brunhilde A Valkyrie found by Sigurd.

Buddha Founder of buddhism, Gautama, avatar of Vishnu in Hinduism.

Buddhism Buddhism arrived in China in the first century BCE via the silk trading route from India and Central Asia. Its founder was Guatama Siddhartha (the Buddha), a religious teacher in northern India. Buddhist doctrine declared that by destroying the causes of all suffering, mankind could attain perfect enlightenment. The religion encouraged a new respect for all living things and brought with it the idea of reincarnation; i.e. that the soul returns to the earth after death in another form, dictated by the individual's behaviour in his previous life. By the fourth century, Buddhism was the dominant religion in China, retaining its powerful influence over the nation until the mid-ninth century.

Buffalo A type of wild ox, once widely scattered over the Great Plains of North America. Also known as a 'bison', the buffalo was an important food source for Native American tribes and its hide was also used in the construction of tepees and to make clothing. The buffalo was also sometimes revered as a totem animal, i.e. venerated as a direct ancestor of the tribesmen, and its skull used in ceremonial fashion.

Bull of Apis Sacred bull, thought to be the son of Hathor.

Bulu Sacrificial rite.

Bundles, sacred These bundles contained various venerated objects of the tribe, believed to have supernatural powers. Custody or ownership of the bundle was never lightly entered upon, but involved the learning of endless songs and ritual dances.

Bushel Unit of measurement, usually used for agricultural products or food.

Bushi Warrior.

Byre Barn for keeping cattle.

Byrny Coat of mail.

Cacique King or prince.

Cailleach Bheur A witch with a blue face who represents winter. When she is reborn each autumn, snow falls. She is mother of the god of youth (Angus mac Og).

Calabash Gourd from the calabash tree, commonly used as a bottle.

Calchas The seer of Mycenae who accompanied the Greek fleet to Troy. It was his prophecy which stated that Troy would never be taken without the aid of Achilles.

Calpulli Village house, or group or clan of families.

Calumet Ceremonial pipe used by Native Americans.

Calypso A nymph who lived on the island of Ogygia.

Camaxtli Tlascalan god of war and the chase, similar to Huitzilopochtli.

Camelot King Arthur's castle and centre of his realm.

Caoineag A banshee.

Caravanserai Traveller's inn, traditionally found in Asia or North Africa.

Carle Term for a man, often old; peasant.

Cat A black cat has great mythological significance, is often the bearer of bad luck, a symbol of black magic, and the familiar of a witch. Cats were also the totem for many tribes.

Cath Sith A fairy cat who was believed to be a witch transformed.

Cazi Magical person or influence.

Ceasg A Scottish mermaid with the body of a maiden and the tail of a salmon.

Ceilidh Party.

Cerberus The three-headed dog who guarded the entrance to the Underworld.

Chalchiuhtlicue Goddess of water and the sick or newborn, and wife of Tlaloc. She is often symbolized as a small frog.

Changeling A fairy substitute-child left by fairies in place of a human child they have stolen.

Channa Guatama's charioteer.

Chaos A state from which the universe was created – caused by fire and ice meeting.

Charon The ferryman of the dead who carries souls across the River Styx to Hades.

Charybdis *See* Scylla and Charybdis.

Chicomecohuatl Chief goddess of maize and one of a group of deities called Centeotl, who care for all aspects of agriculture.

Chicomoztoc Legendary mountain and place of origin of the Aztecs. The name means 'seven caves'.

Chinawezi Primordial serpent.

Chinvat Bridge Bridge of the Gatherer, which the souls of the righteous cross to reach Mount Alborz or the world of the dead. Unworthy beings who try to cross Chinvat Bridge fall or are dragged into a place of eternal punishment.

Chitambaram Sacred city of Shiva's dance.

Chrysaor Son of Poseidon and Medusa, born from the severed neck of Medusa when Perseus beheaded her.

Chryseis Daughter of Chryses who was taken by Agamemnon in the battle of Troy.

Chullasubhadda Wife of Buddha-elect (Sumedha).

Chunda A good smith who entertains Buddha.

Churl Mean or unkind person.

Circe An enchantress and the daughter of Helius. She lived on the island of Aeaea with the power to change men to beasts.

Citlalpol The Mexican name for Venus, or the Great Star, and one of the only stars they worshipped. Also known as Tlauizcalpantecutli, or Lord of the Dawn.

Cleobis and Biton Two men of Argos who dragged the wagon carrying their mother, priestess of Hera, from Argos to the sanctuary.

Clio Muse of history and prophecy.

Clytemnestra Daughter of Tyndareus, sister of Helen, who married Agamemnon but deserted him when he sacrificed Iphigenia, their daughter, at the beginning of the Trojan War.

Coatepetl Mythical mountain, known as the 'serpent mountain'.

Coatl Serpent.

Coatlicue Earth mother and celestial goddess, she gave birth to Huitzilopochtli and his sister, Coyolxauhqui, and the moon and stars.

Codex Ancient book, often a list with pages folded into a zigzag pattern.

Confucius (Kong Fuzi) Regarded as China's greatest sage and ethical teacher, Confucius (551–479 BCE) was not especially revered during his lifetime and had a small following of some three thousand people. After the Burning of the Books in 213 BCE, interest in his philosophies became widespread. Confucius believed that mankind was essentially good, but argued for a highly structured society, presided over by a strong central government which would set the highest moral standards. The individual's sense of duty and obligation, he argued, would play a vital role in maintaining a well-run state.

Coracle Small, round boat, similar to a canoe. Also known as curragh or currach.

Coyolxauhqui Goddess of the moon and sister to Huitzilopochtli, she was decapitated by her brother after trying to kill their mother.

Creel Large basket made of wicker, usually used for fish.

Crodhmara Fairy cattle.

Cronan Musical humming, thought to resemble a cat purring or the drone of bagpipes.

Crow Usually associated with battle and death, but many mythological figures take this form.

Cu Sith A great fairy dog, usually green and oversized.

Cubit Ancient measurement, equal to the approximate length of a forearm.

Cuculain Irish warrior and hero. Also known as Cuchulainn.

Cutty Girl.

Cyclopes One-eyed giants who were imprisoned in Tartarus by Uranus and Cronus, but released by Zeus, for whom they made thunderbolts. Also a tribe of pastoralists who live without laws, and on, whenever possible, human flesh.

Daedalus Descendant of the Athenian King Erechtheus and son of Eupalamus. He killed his nephew and apprentice. Famed for constructing the labyrinth to house the Minotaur, in which he was later imprisoned. He constructed wings for himself and his son to make their escape.

Dagda One of the principal gods of the Tuatha De Danann, the father and chief, the Celtic equivalent of Zeus. He was the god reputed to have led the People of Dana in their successful conquest of the Fir Bolg.

Dagon God of fish and fertility; he is sometimes described as a sea-monster or chthonic god.

Daikoku God of wealth and one of the gods of luck.

Daimyō Powerful lord or magnate.

Daksha The chief Prajapati.

Dana Also known as Danu, a goddess worshipped from antiquity by the Celts and considered to be the ancestor of the Tuatha De Danann.

Danae Daughter of Acrisius, King of Argos. Acrisius trapped her in a cave when he was warned that his grandson would be the cause of his ultimate death. Zeus came to her and Perseus was born.

Danaids The fifty daughters of Danaus of Argos, by ten mothers.

Daoine Sidhe The people of the Hollow Hills, or Otherworld.

Dardanus Son of Zeus and Electra, daughter of Atlas.

Dasharatha A Manu amongst men, King of Koshala, father of Santa.

Deianeira Daughter of Oeneus, who married Heracles after he won her in a battle with the River Achelous.

Deirdre A beautiful woman doomed to cause the deaths of three Irish heroes and bring war to the whole country. After a soothsayer prophesied her fate, Deidre's father hid her away from the world to prevent it. However, fate finds its way and the events come to pass before Deidre eventually commits suicide to remain with her love.

Demeter Goddess of agriculture and nutrition, whose name means earth mother. She is the mother of Persephone.

Demophoon Son of King Celeus of Eleusis, who was nursed by Demeter and then dropped in the fire when she tried to make him immortal.

Dervish Member of a religious order, often Sufi, known for their wild dancing and whirling.

Desire The god of love.

Deva A god other than the supreme God.

Devadatta Buddha's cousin, plots evil against Buddha.

Dhrishtadyumna Twin brother of Draupadi, slays Drona.

Dibarra God of plague. Also a demonic character or evil spirit.

Dik-dik Dwarf antelope native to eastern and southern Africa.

Dilipa Son of Anshumat, father of Bhagiratha.

Dionysus The god of wine, vegetation and the life force, and of ecstasy. He was considered to be outside the Greek pantheon, and generally thought to have begun life as a mortal.

Dioscuri Castor and Polydeuces, the twin sons of Zeus and Leda, who are important deities.

Distaff Tool used when spinning which holds the wool or flax and keeps the fibres from tangling.

Divan Privy council.

Divots Turfs.

Dog The dog is a symbol of humanity, and usually has a role helping the hero of the myth or legend. Fionn's Bran and Grey Dog are two examples of wild beasts transformed to become invaluable servants.

Dōshin Government official.

Dossal Ornamental altar cloth.

Doughty Persistent and brave person.

Dragon Important animal in Japanese culture, symbolizing power, wealth, luck and success.

Draiglin' Hogney Ogre.

Draupadi Daughter of Drupada.

Draupnir Odin's famous ring, fashioned by Brokki.

Drona A Brahma, son of the great sage Bharadwaja.

Druid An ancient order of Celtic priests held in high esteem who flourished in the pre-Christian era. The word 'druid' is derived from an ancient Celtic one meaning 'very knowledgeable'. These individuals were believed to have mystical powers and in ancient Irish literature possess the ability to conjure up magical charms, to create tempests, to curse and debilitate their enemies and to perform as soothsayers to the royal courts.

Drupada King of the Panchalas.

Dryads Nymphs of the trees.

Dun A stronghold or royal abode surrounded by an earthen wall.

Durga Goddess, wife of Shiva.

Durk Knife. Also spelled as dirk.

Duryodhana One of Drona's pupils.

Dvalin Dwarf visited by Loki; also the name for the stag on Yggdrasill.

Dwarfie Stone Prehistoric tomb or boulder.

Dwarfs Fairies and black elves are called dwarfs.

Dwarkanath The Lord of Dwaraka; Krishna.

Dyumatsena King of the Shalwas and father of Satyavan.

Ea God of water, light and wisdom, and one of the creator deities. He brought arts and civilization to humankind. Also known as Oannes and Nudimmud.

Eabani Hero originally created by Aruru to defeat Gilgamesh, the two became friends and destroyed Khumbaba together. He personifies the natural world.

Each Uisge The mythical water-horse which haunts lochs and appears in various forms.

Ebisu One of the gods of luck. He is also the god of labour and fishermen.

Echo A nymph who was punished by Hera for her endless stories told to distract Hera from Zeus's infidelity.

Ector King Arthur's foster father, who raised Arthur to protect him.

Edda Collection of prose and poetic myths and stories from the Norsemen.

Eight Immortals Three of these are reputed to be historical: Han Chung-li, born in Shaanxi, who rose to become a Marshal of the Empire in 21 BCE. Chang Kuo-Lao, who lived in the seventh to eighth century CE, and Lü Tung-pin, who was born in 755 CE.

Einheriear Odin's guests at Valhalla.

Eisa Loki's daughter.

Ekake (Ibani) Person of great intelligence, which means 'tortoise'. Also known as Mbai (Igbo).

Ekalavya Son of the king of the Nishadas.

Electra Daughter of Agamemnon and Clytemnestra.

Eleusis A town in which the cult of Demeter is centred.

Elf Sigmund is buried by an elf; there are light and dark elves (the latter called dwarfs).

Elokos (Central African) Imps of dwarf-demons who eat human flesh.

Elpenor The youngest of Odysseus's crew who fell from the roof of Circe's house on Aeaea and visited with Odysseus at Hades.

Elysium The home of the blessed dead.

Emain Macha The capital of ancient Ulster.

Emma Dai-o King of hell and judge of the dead.

En-lil God of the lower world, storms and mist, who held sway over the ghostly animistic spirits, which at his bidding might pose as the friends or enemies of men. Also known as Bel.

Eos Goddess of the dawn and sister of the sun and moon.

Erichthonius A child born of the semen spilled when Hephaestus tried to rape Athene on the Acropolis.

Eridu The home of Ea and one of the two major cities of Babylonian civilization.

Erin Term for Ireland, originally spelled Éirinn.

Erirogho Magical mixture made from the ashes of the dead.

Eros God of Love, the son of Aphrodite.

Erpa Hereditary chief.

Erysichthon A Thessalian who cut down a grove sacred to Demeter, who punished him with eternal hunger.

Eshu (Yoruba) God of mischief. He also tests people's characters and controls law enforcement.

Eteocles Son of Oedipus.

Eumaeus Swineherd of Odysseus's family at Ithaca.

Euphemus A son of Poseidon who could walk on water. He sailed with the Argonauts.

Europa Daughter of King Agenor of Tyre, who was taken by Zeus to Crete.

Eurydice A Thracian nymph married to Orpheus.

Excalibur The magical sword given to Arthur by the Lady of the Lake. In some versions of the myths, Excalibur is also the sword that the young Arthur pulls from the stone to become king.

Fabulist Person who composes or tells fables.

Fafnir Shape-changer who kills his father and becomes a dragon to guard the family jewels. Slain by Sigurd.

Fairy The word is derived from 'Fays' which means Fates. They are immortal, with the gift of prophecy and of music, and their role changes according to the origin of the myth. They were often considered to be little people, with enormous propensity for mischief, but they are central to many myths and legends, with important powers.

Faro (Mali, Guinea) God of the sky.

Fates In Greek mythology, daughters of Zeus and Themis, who spin the thread of a mortal's life and cut it when his time is due. Called Norns in Viking mythology.

Fenris A wild wolf, who is the son of Loki. He roams the earth after Ragnarok.

Ferhad Sculptor who fell in love with Shireen, the wife of Khosru, and undertook a seemingly impossible task to clear a passage through the mountain of Beysitoun and join the rivers in return for winning Shireen's hand.

Fialar Red cock of Valhalla.

Fianna/Fenians The word 'fianna' was used in early times to describe young warrior-hunters. These youths evolved under the leadership of Finn Mac Cumaill as a highly skilled band of military men who took up service with various kings throughout Ireland.

Filheim Land of mist, at the end of one of Yggdrasill's roots.

Fingal Another name for Fionn Mac Chumail, used after MacPherson's Ossian in the eighteenth century.

Fionn Mac Chumail Irish and Scottish warrior, with great powers of fairness and wisdom. He is known not for physical strength but for knowledge, sense of justice, generosity and canny instinct. He had two hounds, which were later discovered to be his nephews transformed. He became head of the Fianna, or Féinn, fighting the enemies of Ireland and Scotland. He was the father of Oisin (also called Ossian, or other derivatives), and father or grandfather of Osgar.

Fir Bolg One of the ancient, pre-Gaelic peoples of Ireland who were reputed to have worshipped the god Bulga, meaning god of lighting. They are thought to have colonized Ireland around 1970 BCE, after the death of Nemed and to have reigned for a short period of thirty-seven years before their defeat by the Tuatha De Danann.

Fir Chlis Nimble men or merry dancers, who are the souls of fallen angels.

Flitch Side of salted and cured bacon.

Folkvang Freyia's palace.

Fomorians A race of monstrous beings, popularly conceived as sea-pirates with some supernatural characteristics who opposed the earliest settlers in Ireland, including the Nemedians and the Tuatha De Danann.

Frey Comes to Asgard with Freyia as a hostage following the war between the Aesir and the Vanir.

Freyia Comes to Asgard with Frey as a hostage following the war between the Aesir and the Vanir. Goddess of beauty and love.

Frigga Odin's wife and mother of gods; she is goddess of the earth.

Fuath Evil spirits which lived in or near the water.

Fulla Frigga's maidservant.

Furies Creatures born from the blood of Cronus, guarding the greatest sinners of the Underworld. Their power lay in their ability to drive mortals mad. Snakes writhed in their hair and around their waists.

Furoshiki Cloths used to wrap things.

Gae Bolg Cuchulainn alone learned the use of this weapon from the woman-warrior, Scathach and with it he slew his own son Connla and his closest friend, Ferdia. Gae Bolg translates as 'harpoon-like javelin' and the deadly weapon was reported to have been created by Bulga, the god of lighting.

Gaea Goddess of Earth, born from Chaos, and the mother of Uranus and Pontus. Also spelled as Gaia.

Gage Object of value presented to a challenger to symbolize good faith.

Galahad Knight of the Round Table, who took up the search for the Holy Grail. Son of Lancelot, Galahad is considered the purest and most perfect knight.

Galatea Daughter of Nereus and Doris, a sea-nymph loved by Polyphemus, the Cyclops.

Gandhari Mother of Duryodhana.

Gandharvas Demi-gods and musicians.

Gandjharva Musical ministrants of the upper air.

Ganesha Elephant-headed god of scribes and son of Shiva.

Ganges Sacred river personified by the goddess Ganga, wife of Shiva and daughter of the mount Himalaya.

Gareth of Orkney King Arthur's nephew and knight of the Round Table.

Garm Hel's hound.

Garuda King of the birds and mount Vishnu, the divine bird, attendant of Narayana.

Gautama Son of Suddhodana and also known as Siddhartha.

Gawain Nephew of King Arthur and knight of the Round Table, he is best known for his adventure with the Green Knight, who challenges one of Arthur's knights to cut off his head, but only if he agrees to be beheaded in turn in a year and a day, if the Green Knight survives. Gawain beheads the Green Knight, who simply replaces his head. At the appointed time, they meet, and the Green Knight swings his axe but merely nicks Gawain's skin instead of beheading him.

Geisha Performance artist or entertainer, usually female.

Geri Odin's wolf.

Ghommid (Yoruba) Term for mythological creatures such as goblins or ogres.

Giallar Bridge in Filheim.

Giallarhorn Heimdall's trumpet – the final call signifies Ragnarok.

Giants In Greek mythology, a race of beings born from Gaea, grown from the blood that dropped from the castrated Uranus. Usually represent evil in Viking mythology.

Gilgamesh King of Erech known as a half-human, half-god hero similar to the Greek Heracles, and often listed with the gods. He is the personification of the sun and is protected by the god Shamash, who in some texts is described as his father. He is also portrayed as an evil tyrant at times.

Gillie Someone who works for a Scottish chief, usually as an attendant or servant; guide for fishing or hunting parties.

Gladheim Where the twelve deities of Asgard hold their thrones. Also called Gladsheim.

Gled Bird of prey.

Golden Fleece Fleece of the ram sent by Poseidon to substitute for Phrixus when his father was going to sacrifice him. The Argonauts went in search of the fleece.

Goodman Man of the house.

Goodwife Woman of the house.

Gopis Lovers of the young Krishna and milkmaids.

Gorgon One of the three sisters, including Medusa, whose frightening looks could turn mortals to stone.

Graces Daughters of Aphrodite by Zeus.

Gramercy Expression of surprise or strong feeling.

Great Head The Iroquois believed in the existence of a curious being known as Great Head, a creature with an enormous head poised on slender legs.

Great Spirit The name given to the Creator of all life, as well as the term used to describe the omnipotent force of the Creator existing in every living thing.

Great-Flank One of Ravana's monsters.

Green Knight A knight dressed all in green and with green hair and skin who challenged one of Arthur's knights to strike him a blow with an axe and that, if he survived, he would return to behead the knight in a year and a day. He turned out to be Lord Bertilak and was under an enchantment cast by Morgan le Fay to test Arthur's knights.

Gruagach Mythical creature, often a giant or ogre similar to a wild man of the woods. The term can also refer to other mythical creatures such as brownies or fairies. As a brownie, he is usually dressed in red or green as opposed to the traditional brown. He has great power to enchant the hapless, or to help mortals who are worthy (usually heroes). He often appears to challenge a boy-hero, during his period of education.

Gudea High priest of Lagash, known to be a patron of the arts and a writer himself.

Guebre Religion founded by Zoroaster, the Persian prophet.

Gugumatz Creator god who, with Huracan, formed the sky, earth and everything on it.

Guha King of Nishadha.

Guidewife Woman.

Guinevere Wife of King Arthur; she is often portrayed as a virtuous lady and wife, but is perhaps best known for having a love affair with Lancelot, one of Arthur's friends and knights of the Round Table. Her name is also spelled Guenever.

Gulistan *Rose Garden*, written by the poet Sa'di

Gungnir Odin's spear, made of Yggdrasill wood, and the tip fashioned by Dvalin.

Gylfi A wandering king to whom the Eddas are narrated.

Haab Mayan solar calendar that consisted of eighteen twenty-day months.

Hades One of the three sons of Cronus; brother of Poseidon and Zeus. Hades is King of the Underworld, which is also known as the House of Hades.

Haere-mai Maori phrase meaning 'come here, welcome.'

Haere-mai-ra, me o tatou mate Maori phrase meaning 'come here, that I may sorrow with you.'

Haere-ra Maori phrase meaning 'goodbye, go, farewell.'

Haji Muslim pilgrim who has been to Mecca.

Hakama Traditional Japanese clothing, worn on the bottom half of the body.

Hanuman General of the monkey people.

Harakiri Suicide, usually by cutting or stabbing the abdomen. Also known as seppuku.

Hari-Hara Shiva and Vishnu as one god.

Harmonia Daughter of Ares and Aphrodite, wife of Cadmus.

Hatamoto High-ranking samurai.

Hathor Great cosmic mother and patroness of lovers. She is portrayed as a cow.

Hati The wolf who pursues the sun and moon.

Hatshepsut Second female pharaoh.

Hauberk Armour to protect the neck and shoulders, sometimes a full-length coat of mail.

Hector Eldest son of King Priam who defended Troy from the Greeks. He was killed by Achilles.

Hecuba The second wife of Priam, King of Troy. She was turned into a dog after Troy was lost.

Heimdall White god who guards the Bifrost bridge.

Hel Goddess of death and Loki's daughter. Also known as Hela.

Helen Daughter of Leda and Tyndareus, King of Sparta, and the most beautiful woman in the world. She was responsible for starting the Trojan War.

Heliopolis City in modern-day Cairo, known as the City of the Sun and the central place of worship of Ra. Also known as Anu.

Helius The sun, son of Hyperion and Theia.

Henwife Witch.

Hephaestus or **Hephaistos** The Smith of Heaven.

Hera A Mycenaean palace goddess, married to Zeus.

Heracles An important Greek hero, the son of Zeus and Alcmena. His name means 'Glory of Hera'. He performed twelve labours for King Eurystheus, and later became a god.

Hermes The conductor of souls of the dead to Hades, and god of trickery and of trade. He acts as messenger to the gods.

Hermod Son of Frigga and Odin who travelled to see Hel in order to reclaim Balder for Asgard.

Hero and Leander Hero was a priestess of Aphrodite, loved by Leander, a young man of Abydos. He drowned trying to see her.

Hestia Goddess of the hearth, daughter of Cronus and Rhea.

Hieroglyphs Type of writing that combines symbols and pictures, usually cut into tombs or rocks, or written on papyrus.

Himalaya Great mountain and range, father of Parvati.

Hiordis Wife of Sigmund and mother of Sigurd.

Hoderi A fisher and son of Okuninushi.

Hodur Balder's blind twin; known as the personification of darkness.

Hoenir Also called Vili; produced the first humans with Odin and Loki, and was one of the triad responsible for the creation of the world.

Hōichi the Earless A biwa hōshi, a blind storyteller who played the biwa or lute. Also a priest.

Holger Danske Legendary Viking warrior who is thought to never die. He sleeps until he is needed by his people and then he will rise to protect them.

Homayi Phoenix.

Hoodie Mythical creature which often appears as a crow.

Hoori A hunter and son of Okuninushi.

Horus God of the sky and kinship, son of Isis and Osiris. He captained the boat that carried Ra across the sky. He is depicted with the head of a falcon.

Hotei One of the gods of luck. He also personifies humour and contentment.

Houlet Owl.

Houri Beautiful virgin from paradise.

Hrim-faxi Steed of the night.

Hubris Presumptuous behaviour which causes the wrath of the gods to be brought on to mortals.

Hueytozoztli Festival dedicated to Tlaloc and, at times, Chicomecohuatl or other deities. Also the fourth month of the Aztec calendar.

Hugin Odin's raven.

Huitzilopochtli God of war and the sun, also connected with the summer and crops; one of the principal Aztec deities. He was born a full-grown adult to save his mother, Coatlicue, from the jealousy of his sister, Coyolxauhqui, who tried to kill Coatlicue. The Mars of the Aztec gods. In some origin stories he is one of four offspring of Ometeotl and Omecihuatl.

Hurley A traditional Irish game played with sticks and balls, quite similar to hockey.

Hurons A tribe of Iroquois stock, originally one people with the Iroquois.

Huveane (Pedi, Venda) Creator of humankind, who made a baby from clay into which he breathed life. He is known as the High God or Great God. He is also known as a trickster god.

Hymir Giant who fishes with Thor and is drowned by him.

Iambe Daughter of Pan and Echo, servant to King Celeus of Eleusis and Metaeira.

Icarus Son of Daedalus, who plunged to his death after escaping from the labyrinth.

Ichneumon Mongoose.

Idunn Guardian of the youth-giving apples.

Ifa (Yoruba) God of wisdom and divination. Also the term for a Yoruban religion.

Ife (Yoruba) The place Obatala first arrived on Earth and took for his home.

Igigi Great spirits or gods of Heaven and the sky.

Igraine Wife of the duke of Tintagel, enemy of Uther Pendragon, who marries Uther when her first husband dies. She is King Arthur's mother.

Ile (Yoruba) Goddess of the earth.

Imhetep High priest and wise sage. He is sometimes thought to be the son of Ptah.

Imam Person who leads prayers in a mosque.

Imana (Banyarwanda) Creator or sky god.

In The male principle who, joined with Yo, the female side, brought about creation and the first gods. In and Yo correspond to the Chinese Yang and Yin.

Inari God of rice, fertility, agriculture and, later, the fox god. Inari has both good and evil attributes but is often presented as an evil trickster.

Indra The King of Heaven.

Indrajit Son of Ravana.

Indrasen Daughter of Nala and Damayanti.

Indrasena Son of Nala and Damayanti.

Inundation Annual flooding of the River Nile.

Iphigenia The eldest daughter of Agamemnon and Clytemnestra who was sacrificed to appease Artemis and obtain a fair wind for Troy.

Iris Messenger of the gods who took the form of a rainbow.

Iseult Princess of Ireland and niece of the Morholt. She falls in love with Tristan after consuming a love potion but is forced to marry King Mark of Cornwall.

Ishtar Goddess of love, beauty, justice and war, especially in Ninevah, and earth mother who symbolizes fertility. Married to Tammuz, she is similar to the Greek goddess Aphrodite. Ishtar is sometimes known as Innana or Irnina.

Isis Goddess of the Nile and the moon, sister-wife of Osiris. She and her son, Horus, are sometimes thought of in a similar way to Mary and Jesus. She was one of the most worshipped female

Egyptian deities and was instrumental in returning Osiris to life after he was killed by his brother, Set.

Istakbál Deputation of warriors.

Izanagi Deity and brother-husband to Izanami, who together created the Japanese islands from the Floating Bridge of Heaven. Their offspring populated Japan.

Izanami Deity and sister-wife of Izanagi, creator of Japan. Their children include Amaterasu, Tsuki-yomi and Susanoo.

Jade It was believed that jade emerged from the mountains as a liquid which then solidified after ten thousand years to become a precious hard stone, green in colour. If the correct herbs were added to it, it could return to its liquid state and when swallowed increase the individual's chances of immortality.

Jambavan A noble monkey.

Jason Son of Aeson, King of Iolcus and leader of the voyage of the Argonauts.

Jatayu King of all the eagle-tribes.

Jesseraunt Flexible coat of armour or mail.

Jimmo Legendary first emperor of Japan. He is thought to be descended from Hoori, while other tales claim him to be descended from Amaterasu through her grandson, Ninigi.

Jizo God of little children and the god who calms the troubled sea.

Jord Daughter of Nott; wife of Odin.

Jormungander The world serpent; son of Loki. Legends tell that when his tail is removed from his mouth, Ragnarok has arrived.

Jorō Geisha who also worked as a prostitute.

Jotunheim Home of the giants.

Ju Ju tree Deciduous tree that produces edible fruit.

Jurasindhu A rakshasa, father-in-law of Kans.

Jyeshtha Goddess of bad luck.

Ka Life power or soul. Also known as ba.

Kai-káús Son of Kai-kobád. He led an army to invade Mázinderán, home of the demon-sorcerers, after being persuaded by a demon. Known for his ambitious schemes, he later tried to reach Heaven by trapping eagles to fly him there on his throne.

Kaikeyi Mother of Bharata, one of Dasharatha's three wives.

Kai-khosrau Son of Saiawúsh, who killed Afrásiyáb in revenge for the death of his father.

Kai-kobád Descendant of Feridún, he was selected by Zál to lead an army against Afrásiyáb. Their powerful army, led by Zál and Rustem, drove back Afrásiyáb's army, who then agreed to peace.

Kailyard Kitchen garden or small plot, usually used for growing vegetables.

Kali The Black, wife of Shiva.

Kalindi Daughter of the sun, wife of Krishna.

Kaliya A poisonous hydra that lived in the jamna.

Kalki Incarnation of Vishnu yet to come.

Kalnagini Serpent who kills Lakshmindara.

Kal-Purush The Time-man, Bengali name for Orion.

Kaluda A disciple of Buddha.

Kalunga-ngombe (Mbundu) Death, also depicted as the king of the netherworld.

Kama God of desire.

Kamadeva Desire, the god of love.

Kami Spirits, deities or forces of nature.

Kamund Lasso.

Kans King of Mathura, son of Ugrasena and Pavandrekha.

Kanva Father of Shakuntala.

Kappa River goblin with the body of a tortoise and the head of an ape. Kappa love to challenge human beings to single combat.

Karakia Invocation, ceremony, prayer.

Karna Pupil of Drona.

Kaross Blanket or rug, also worn as a traditional garment. It is often made from the skins of animals which have been sewn together.

Kasbu A period of twenty-four hours.

Kashyapa One of Dasharatha's counsellors.

Kauravas or Kurus Sons of Dhritarashtra, pupils of Drona.

Kaushalya Mother of Rama, one of Dasharatha's three wives.

Kay Son of Ector and adopted brother to King Arthur, he becomes one of Arthur's knights of the Round Table.

Keb God of the earth and father of Osiris and Isis, married to Nut. Keb is identified with Kronos, the Greek god of time.

Kehua Spirit, ghost.

Kelpie Another word for each uisge, the water-horse.

Ken Know.

Keres Black-winged demons or daughters of the night.

Keshini Wife of Sagara.

Khalif Leader.

Khara Younger brother of Ravana.

Khepera God who represents the rising sun. He is portrayed as a scarab. Also known as Nebertcher.

Kher-heb Priest and magician who officiated over rituals and ceremonies.

Khnemu God of the source of the Nile and one of the original Egyptian deities. He is thought to be the creator of children and of other gods. He is portrayed as a ram.

Khosru King and husband to Shireen, daughter of Maurice, the Greek Emperor. He was murdered by his own son, who wanted his kingdom and his wife.

Khumbaba Monster and guardian of the goddess Irnina, a form of the goddess Ishtar. Khumbaba is likened to the Greek gorgon.

Kia-ora Welcome, good luck. A greeting.

Kiboko Hippopotamus.

Kikinu Soul.

Kimbanda (Mbundu) Doctor.

Kimono Traditional Japanese clothing, similar to a robe.

King Arthur Legendary king of Britain who plucked the magical sword from the stone, marking him as the heir of Uther Pendragon and 'true king' of Britain. He and his knights of the Round Table defended Britain from the Saxons and had many adventures, including searching for the Holy Grail. Finally wounded in battle, he left Britain for the mythical Avalon, vowing to one day return to reclaim his kingdom.

Kingu Tiawath's husband, a god and warrior who she promised would rule Heaven once he helped her defeat the 'gods of light'. He was killed by Merodach who used his blood to make clay, from which he formed the first humans. In some tales, Kingu is Tiawath's son as well as her consort.

Kinnaras Human birds with musical instruments under their wings.

Kinyamkela (Zaramo) Ghost of a child.

Kirk Church, usually a term for Church of Scotland churches.

Kirtle One-piece garment, similar to a tunic, which was worn by men or women.

Kis Solar deity, usually depicted as an eagle.

Kishar Earth mother and sister-wife to Anshar.

Kist Trunk or large chest.

Kitamba (Mbundu) Chief who made his whole village go into mourning when his head-wife, Queen Muhongo, died. He also pledged that no one should speak or eat until she was returned to him.

Knowe Knoll or hillock.

Kojiki One of two myth-histories of Japan, along with the *Nihon Shoki*.

Ko-no-Hana Goddess of Mount Fuji, princess and wife of Ninigi.

Kore 'Maiden', another name for Persephone.

Kraal Traditional rural African village, usually consisting of huts surrounded by a fence or wall. Also an animal enclosure.

Krishna The Dark one, worshipped as an incarnation of Vishnu.

Kui-see Edible root.

Kumara Son of Shiva and Paravati, slays demon Taraka.

Kumbha-karna Ravana's brother.

Kunti Mother of the Pandavas.

Kura Red. The sacred colour of the Maori.

Kusha or Kusi One of Sita's two sons.

Kvasir Clever warrior and colleague of Odin. He was responsible for finally outwitting Loki.

Kwannon Goddess of mercy.

Labyrinth A prison built at Knossos for the Minotaur by Daedalus.

Lady of the Lake Enchantress who presents Arthur with Excalibur.

Laertes King of Ithaca and father of Odysseus.

Laestrygonians Savage giants encountered by Odysseus on his travels.

Laili In love with Majnun but unable to marry him, she was given to the prince, Ibn Salam, to marry. When he died, she escaped and found Majnun, but they could not be legally married. The couple died of grief and were buried together. Also known as Laila.

Laird Person who owns a significant estate in Scotland.

Lakshmana Brother of Rama and his companion in exile.

Lakshmi Consort of Vishnu and a goddess of beauty and good fortune.

Lakshmindara Son of Chand resurrected by Manasa Devi.

Lancelot Knight of the Round Table. Lancelot was raised by the Lady of the Lake. While he went on many quests, he is perhaps best known for his affair with Guinevere, King Arthur's wife.

Land of Light One of the names for the realm of the fairies. If a piece of metal welded by human hands is put in the doorway to their land, the door cannot close. The door to this realm is only open at night, and usually at a full moon.

Lang syne The days of old.

Lao Tzu (Laozi) The ancient Taoist philosopher thought to have been born in 571 BCE a contemporary of Confucius with whom, it is said, he discussed the tenets of Tao. Lao Tzu was an advocate of simple rural existence and looked to the Yellow Emperor and Shun as models of efficient government. His philosophies were recorded in the Tao Te Ching. Legends surrounding his birth suggest that he emerged from the left-hand side of his mother's body, with white hair and a long white beard, after a confinement lasting eighty years.

Laocoon A Trojan wiseman who predicted that the wooden horse contained Greek soldiers.

Laomedon The King of Troy who hired Apollo and Poseidon to build the impregnable walls of Troy.

Lava Son of Sita.

Leda Daughter of the King of Aetolia, who married Tyndareus. Helen and Clytemnestra were her daughters.

Legba (Dahomey) Youngest offspring of Mawu-Lisa. He was given the gift of all languages. It was through him that humans could converse with the gods.

Leman Lover.

Leprechaun Mythical creature from Irish folk tales who often appears as a mischievous and sometimes drunken old man.

Lethe One of the four rivers of the Underworld, also called the River of Forgetfulness.

Lif The female survivor of Ragnarok.

Lifthrasir The male survivor of Ragnarok.

Lil Demon.

Liongo (Swahili) Warrior and hero.

Lofty mountain Home of Ahura-Mazda.

Logi Utgard-loki's cook.

Loki God of fire and mischief-maker of Asgard; he eventually brings about Ragnarok. Also spelled as Loptur.

Lotus-Eaters A race of people who live a dazed, drugged existence, the result of eating the lotus flower.

Ma'at State of order meaning truth, order or justice. Personified by the goddess Ma'at, who was Thoth's consort.

Macha There are thought to be several different Machas who appear in quite a number of ancient Irish stories. For the purposes of this book, however, the Macha referred to is the wife of Crunnchu. The story unfolds that after her husband had boasted of her great athletic ability to the King, she was subsequently forced to run against his horses in spite of the fact that she was heavily pregnant. Macha died giving birth to her twin babies and with her dying breath she cursed Ulster for nine generations, proclaiming that it would suffer the weakness of a woman in childbirth in times of great stress. This curse had its most disastrous effect when Medb of Connacht invaded Ulster with her great army.

Machi-bugyō Senior official or magistrate, usually samurai.

Macuilxochitl God of art, dance and games, and the patron of luck in gaming. His name means 'source of flowers' or 'prince of flowers'. Also known as Xochipilli, meaning 'five-flower'.

Madake Weapon used for whipping, made of bamboo.

Maduma Taro tuber.

Mag Muirthemne Cuchulainn's inheritance. A plain extending from River Boyne to the mountain range of Cualgne, close to Emain Macha in Ulster.

Magni Thor's son.

Mahaparshwa One of Ravana's generals.

Maharaksha Son of Khara, slain at Lanka.

Mahasubhadda Wife of Buddha-select (Sumedha).

Majnun Son of a chief, who fell in love with Laili and followed her tribe through the desert, becoming mad with love until they were briefly reunited before dying.

Makaras Mythical fish-reptiles of the sea.

Makoma (Senna) Folk hero who defeated five mighty giants.

Mana Power, authority, prestige, influence, sanctity, luck.

Manasa Devi Goddess of snakes, daughter of Shiva by a mortal woman.

Manasha Goddess of snakes.

Mandavya Daughter of Kushadhwaja.

Man-Devourer One of Ravana's monsters.

Mandodari Wife of Ravana.

Mandrake Poisonous plant from the nightshade family which has hallucinogenic and hypnotic qualities if ingested. Its roots resemble the human form and it has supposedly magical qualities.

Mani The moon.

Manitto Broad term used to describe the supernatural or a potent spirit among the Algonquins, the Iroquois and the Sioux.

Man-Slayer One of Ravana's counsellors.

Manthara Kaikeyi's evil nurse, who plots Rama's ruin.

Mantle Cloak or shawl.

Manu Lawgiver.

Manu Mythical mountain on which the sun sets.

Mara The evil one, tempts Gautama.

Markandeya One of Dasharatha's counsellors.

Mashu Mountain of the Sunset, which lies between Earth and the underworld. Guarded by scorpion-men.

Matali Sakra's charioteer.

Mawu-Lisa (Dahomey) Twin offspring of Nana Baluka. Mawu (female) and Lisa (male) are often joined to form one being. Their own offspring populated the world.

Mbai (Igbo) Person of great intelligence, also known as Ekake (Ibani), which means 'tortoise'.

Medea Witch and priestess of Hecate, daughter of Aeetes and sister of Circe. She helped Jason in his quest for the Golden Fleece.

Medusa One of the three Gorgons whose head had the power to turn onlookers to stone.

Melpomene One of the muses, and mother of the Sirens.

Menaka One of the most beautiful dancers in Heaven.

Menat Amulet, usually worn for protection.

Mendicant Beggar.

Menelaus King of Sparta, brother of Agamemnon. Married Helen and called war against Troy when she eloped with Paris.

Menthu Lord of Thebes and god of war. He is portrayed as a hawk or falcon.

Mere-pounamu A native weapon made of a rare green stone.

Merlin Wizard and advisor to King Arthur. He is thought to be the son of a human female and an incubus (male demon). He brought about Arthur's birth and ascension to king, then acted as his mentor.

Merodach God who battled Tiawath and defeated her by cutting out her heart and dividing her corpse into two pieces. He used these pieces to divide the upper and lower waters once controlled by Tiawath, making a dwelling for the gods of light. He also created humankind. Also known as Marduk.

Merrow Mythical mermaid-like creature, often depicted with an enchanted cap called a cohuleen driuth which allows it to travel between land and the depths of the sea. Also known as murúch.

Metaneira Wife of Celeus, King of Eleusis, who hired Demeter in disguise as her nurse.

Metztli Goddess of the moon, her name means 'lady of the night'. Also known as Yohualtictl.

Michabo Also known as Manobozho, or the Great Hare, the principal deity of the Algonquins, maker and preserver of the earth, sun and moon.

Mictlan God of the dead and ruler of the underworld. He was married to Mictecaciuatl and is often represented as a bat. He is also the Aztec lord of Hades. Also known as Mictlantecutli. Mictlan is also the name for the underworld.

Midgard Dwelling place of humans (Earth).

Midsummer A time when fairies dance and claim human victims.

Mihrab Father of Rúdábeh and descendant of Zohák, the serpent-king.

Milesians A group of iron-age invaders led by the sons of Mil, who arrived in Ireland from Spain around 500 BCE and overcame the Tuatha De Danann.

Mimir God of the ocean. His head guards a well; reincarnated after Ragnarok.

Minos King of Crete, son of Zeus and Europa. He was considered to have been the ruler of a sea empire.

Minotaur A creature born of the union between Pasiphae and a Cretan Bull.

Minúchihr King who lives to be one hundred and twenty years old. Father of Nauder.

Miolnir *See* Mjolnir.

Mithra God of the sun and light in Iran, protector of truth and guardian of pastures and cattle. Alo known as Mitra in Hindu mythology and Mithras in Roman mythology.

Mixcoatl God of the chase or the hunt. Sometimes depicted as the god of air and thunder, he introduced fire to humankind. His name means 'cloud serpent'.

Mjolnir Hammer belonging to the Norse god of thunder, which is used as a fearsome weapon which always returns to Thor's hand, and as an instrument of consecration.

Mnoatia Forest spirits.

Moccasins One-piece shoes made of soft leather, especially deerskin.

Modi Thor's son.

Moly A magical plant given to Odysseus by Hermes as protection against Circe's powers.

Montezuma Great emperor who consolidated the Aztec Empire.

Mordred Bastard son of King Arthur and Morgawse, Queen of Orkney, who, unknown to Arthur, was his half-sister. Mordred becomes one of King Arthur's knights of the Round Table before betraying and fatally wounding Arthur, causing him to leave Britain for Avalon.

Morgan le Fay Enchantress and half-sister to King Arthur, Morgan was an apprentice of Merlin's. She is generally depicted as benevolent, yet did pit herself against Arthur and his knights on occasion. She escorts Arthur on his final journey to Avalon. Also known as Morgain le Fay.

Morholt The knight sent to Cornwall to force King Mark to pay tribute to Ireland. He is killed by Tristan.

Morongoe the brave (Lesotho) Man who was turned into a snake by evil spirits because Tau was jealous that he had married the beautiful Mokete, the chief's daughter. Morongoe was returned to human form after his son, Tsietse, returned him to their family.

Mosima (Bapedi) The underworld or abyss.

Mount Fuji Highest mountain in Japan, on the island of Honshū.

Mount Kunlun This mountain features in many Chinese legends as the home of the great emperors on Earth. It is written in the *Shanghaijing* (*The Classic of Mountains and Seas*) that this towering structure measured no less than 3300 miles in circumference and 4000 miles in height. It acted both as a central pillar to support the heavens, and as a gateway between Heaven and Earth.

Moving Finger Expression for taking responsibility for one's life and actions, which cannot be undone.

Moytura Translated as the 'Plain of Weeping', Mag Tured, or Moytura, was where the Tuatha De Danann fought two of their most significant battles.

Mua An old-time Polynesian god.

Muezzin Person who performs the Muslim call to prayer.

Mugalana A disciple of Buddha.

Muilearteach The Cailleach Bheur of the water, who appears as a witch or a sea-serpent. On land she grew larger and stronger by fire.

Mul-lil God of Nippur, who took the form of a gazelle.

Muloyi Sorcerer, also called mulaki, murozi, ndozi or ndoki.

Mummu Son of Tiawath and Apsu. He formed a trinity with them to battle the gods. Also known as Moumis. In some tales, Mummu is also Merodach, who eventually destroyed Tiawath.

Munin Odin's raven.

Murile (Chaga) Man who dug up a taro tuber that resembled his baby brother, which turned into a living boy. His mother killed the baby when she saw Murile was starving himself to feed it.

Murtough Mac Erca King who ruled Ireland when many of its people – including his wife and family – were converting to Christianity. He remained a pagan.

Muses Goddesses of poetry and song, daughters of Zeus and Mnemosyne.

Musha Expression, often of surprise.

Muskrat North American beaver-like, amphibious rodent.

Muspell Home of fire, and the fire-giants.

Mwidzilo Taboo which, if broken, can cause death.

Nabu God of writing and wisdom. Also known as Nebo. Thought to be the son of Merodach.

Nahua Ancient Mexicans.

Nakula Pandava twin skilled in horsemanship.

Nala One of the monkey host, son of Vishvakarma.

Nana Baluka (Dahomey) Mother of all creation. She gave birth to an androgynous being with two faces. The female face was Mawu, who controlled the night and lands to the west. The male face was Lisa and he controlled the day and the east.

Nanahuatl Also known as Nanauatzin. Presided over skin diseases and known as Leprous, which in Nahua meant 'divine'.

Nandi Shiva's bull.

Nanna Balder's wife.

Nannar God of the moon and patron of the city of Ur.

Naram-Sin Son or ancestor of Sargon and king of the Four Zones or Quarters of Babylon.

Narcissus Son of the River Cephisus. He fell in love with himself and died as a result.

Narve Son of Loki.

Nataraja Manifestation of Shiva, Lord of the Dance.

Natron Preservative used in embalming, mined from the Natron Valley in Egypt.

Nauder Son of Minúchihr, who became king on his death and was tyrannical and hated until Sám begged him to follow in the footsteps of his ancestors.

Nausicaa Daughter of Alcinous, King of Phaeacia, who fell in love with Odysseus.

Nebuchadnezzar Famous king of Babylon. Also known as Nebuchadrezzar.

Necromancy Communicating with the dead.

Nectar Drink of the gods.

Neith Goddess of hunting, fate and war. Neith is sometimes known as the creator of the universe.

Nemesis Goddess of retribution and daughter of night.

Neoptolemus Son of Achilles and Deidameia, he came to Troy at the end of the war to wear his father's armour. He sacrificed Polyxena at the tomb of Achilles.

Nephthys Goddess of the air, night and the dead. Sister of Isis and sister-wife to Seth, she is also the mother of Anubis.

Nereids Sea-nymphs who are the daughters of Nereus and Doris. Thetis, mother of Achilles, was a Nereid.

Nergal God of death and patron god of Cuthah, which was often known as a burial place. He is also known as the god of fire. Married to Aralu, the goddess of the underworld.

Nestor Wise King of Pylus, who led the ships to Troy with Agamemnon and Menelaus.

Neta Daughter of Shiva, friend of Manasa.

Ngai (Gikuyu) Creator god.

Ngaka (Lesotho) Witch doctor.

Niflheim The underworld In Norse mythology, ruled over by Hel.

Night Daughter of Norvi.

Nikumbha One of Ravana's generals.

Nila One of the monkey host, son of Agni.

Nin-Girsu God of fertility and war, patron god of Girsu. Also known as Shul-gur.

Ninigi Grandson of Amaterasu, Ninigi came to Earth bringing rice and order to found the Imperial family. He is known as the August Grandchild.

Niord God of the sea; marries Skadi.

Nippur The home of En-lil and one of the two major cities of Babylonian civilization.

Nirig God of war and storms, and son of Bel. Also known as Enu-Restu.

Nirvana Transcendent state and the final goal of Buddhism.

Nis Mythological creature, similar to a brownie or goblin, usually harmless or even friendly, but can be easily offended. They are often associated with Christmas or the winter solstice.

Noatun Niord's home.

Noisy-Throat One of Ravana's counsellors.

Noondah (Zanzibar) Cannibalistic cat which attacked and killed animals and humans.

Norns The fates and protectors of Yggdrasill. Many believe them to be the same as the Valkyries.

Norvi Father of the night.

Nott Goddess of night.

Nsasak bird Small bird who became chief of all small birds after winning a competition to go without food for seven days. The

Nsasak bird beat the Odudu bird by sneaking out of his home to feed.

Nü Wa The Goddess Nü Wa, who in some versions of the Creation myths is the sole creator of mankind, and in other tales is associated with the God Fu Xi, also a great benefactor of the human race. Some accounts represent Fu Xi as the brother of Nü Wa, but others describe the pair as lovers who lie together to create the very first human beings. Fu Xi is also considered to be the first of the Chinese emperors of mythical times who reigned from 2953 to 2838 BCE.

Nuada The first king of the Tuatha De Danann in Ireland, who lost an arm in the first battle of Moytura against the Fomorians. He became known as 'Nuada of the Silver Hand' when Diancecht, the great physician of the Tuatha De Danann, replaced his hand with a silver one after the battle.

Nunda (Swahili, East Africa) Slayer that took the form of a cat and grew so big that it consumed everyone in the town except the sultan's wife, who locked herself away. Her son, Mohammed, killed Nunda and cut open its leg, setting free everyone Nunda had eaten.

Nut Goddess of the sky, stars and astronomy. Sister-wife of Keb and mother of Osiris, Isis, Set and Nephthys. She often appears in the form of a cow.

Nyame (Ashanti) God of the sky, who sees and knows everything.

Nymphs Minor female deities associated with particular parts of the land and sea.

Obassi Osaw (Ekoi) Creator god with his twin, Obassi Nsi. Originally, Obassi Osaw ruled the skies while Obassi Nsi ruled the Earth.

Obatala (Yoruba) Creator of humankind. He climbed down a golden chain from the sky to the earth, then a watery abyss, and formed land and humankind. When Olorun heard of his success, he created the sun for Obatala and his creations.

Oberon Fairy king.

Odin Allfather and king of all gods, he is known for travelling the nine worlds in disguise and recognized only by his single eye; dies at Ragnarok.

Oduduwa (Yoruba) Divine king of Ile-Ife, the holy city of Yoruba.

Odur Freyia's husband.

Odysseus Greek hero, son of Laertes and Anticleia, who was renowned for his cunning, the master behind the victory at Troy, and known for his long voyage home.

Oedipus Son of Leius, King of Thebes and Jocasta. Became King of Thebes and married his mother.

Ogdoad Group of eight deities who were formed into four male-female couples who joined to create the gods and the world.

Ogham One of the earliest known forms of Irish writing, originally used to inscribe upright pillar stones.

Oiran Courtesan.

Oisin Also called Ossian (particularly by James Macpherson who wrote a set of Gaelic Romances about this character, supposedly garnered from oral tradition). Ossian was the son of Fionn and Sadbh, and had various brothers, according to different legends. He was a man of great wisdom, became immortal for many centuries, but in the end he became mad.

Ojibwe Another name for the Chippewa, a tribe of Algonquin stock.

Okuninushi Deity and descendant of Susanoo, who married Suseri-hime, Susanoo's daughter, without his consent. Susanoo tried to kill him many times but did not succeed and eventually forgave Okuninushi. He is sometimes thought to be the son or grandson of Susanoo.

Olokun (Yoruba) Most powerful goddess who ruled the seas and marshes. When Obatala created Earth in her domain, other gods began to divide it up between them. Angered at their presumption, she caused a great flood to destroy the land.

Olorun (Yoruba) Supreme god and ruler of the sky. He sees and controls everything, but others, such as Obatala, carry out the work for him. Also known as Olodumare.

Olympia Zeus's home in Elis.

Olympus The highest mountain in Greece and the ancient home of the gods.

Omecihuatl Female half of the first being, combined with Ometeotl. Together they are the lords of duality or lords of the two sexes. Also known as Ometecutli and Omeciuatl or Tonacatecutli and Tonacaciuatl. Their offspring were Xipe Totec, Huitzilopochtli, Quetzalcoatl and Tezcatlipoca.

Ometeotl Male half of the first being, combined with Omecihuatl.

Ometochtli Collective name for the pulque-gods or drink-gods. These gods were often associated with rabbits as they were thought to be senseless creatures.

Onygate Anyway.

Opening of the Mouth Ceremony in which mummies or statues were prayed over and anointed with incense before their mouths were opened, allowing them to eat and drink in the afterlife.

Oracle The response of a god or priest to a request for advice – also a prophecy; the place where such advice was sought; the person or thing from whom such advice was sought.

Oranyan (Yoruba) Youngest grandson of King Oduduwa, who later became king himself.

Orestes Son of Agamemnon and Clytemnestra who escaped following Agamemnon's murder to King Strophius. He later returned to Argos to murder his mother and avenge the death of his father.

Orpheus Thracian singer and poet, son of Oeagrus and a Muse. Married Eurydice and when she died tried to retrieve her from the Underworld.

Orunmila (Yoruba) Eldest son of Olorun, he helped Obatala create land and humanity, which he then rescued after Olokun flooded the lands. He has the power to see the future.

Osiris God of fertility, the afterlife and death. Thought to be the first of the pharaohs. He was murdered by his brother, Set, after which he was conjured back to life by Isis, Anubis and others before becoming lord of the afterworld. Married to Isis, who was also his sister.

Otherworld The world of deities and spirits, also known as the Land of Promise, or the Land of Eternal Youth, a place of everlasting life where all earthly dreams come to be fulfilled.

Owuo (Krachi, West Africa) Giant who personifies death. He causes a person to die every time he blinks his eye.

Palamedes Hero of Nauplia, believed to have created part of the ancient Greek alphabet. He tricked Odysseus into joining the fleet setting out for Troy by placing the infant Telemachus in the path of his plough.

Palermo Stone Stone carved with hieroglyphs, which came from the Royal Annals of ancient Egypt and contains a list of the kings of Egypt from the first to the early fifth dynasties.

Palfrey Docile and light horse, often used by women.

Palladium Wooden image of Athene, created by her as a monument to her friend Pallas who she accidentally killed. While in Troy it protected the city from invaders.

Pallas Athene's best friend, whom she killed.

Pan God of Arcadia, half-goat and half-man. Son of Hermes. He is connected with fertility, masturbation and sexual drive. He is also associated with music, particularly his pipes, and with laughter.

Pan Gu Some ancient writers suggest that this God is the offspring of the opposing forces of nature, the yin and the yang. The yin (female) is associated with the cold and darkness of the earth, while the yang (male) is associated with the sun and the warmth of the heavens. 'Pan' means 'shell of an egg' and 'Gu' means 'to secure' or 'to achieve'. Pan Gu came into existence so that he might create order from chaos.

Pandareus Cretan King killed by the gods for stealing the shrine of Zeus.

Pandavas Alternative name for sons of Pandu, pupils of Drona.

Pandora The first woman, created by the gods, to punish man for Prometheus's theft of fire. Her dowry was a box full of powerful evil.

Papyrus Paper-like material made from the pith of the papyrus plant, first manufactured in Egypt. Used as a type of paper as well as for making mats, rope and sandals.

Paramahamsa The supreme swan.

Parashurama Human incarnation of Vishnu, 'Rama with an axe'.

Paris Handsome son of Priam and Hecuba of Troy, who was left for dead on Mount Ida but raised by shepherds. Was reclaimed by his family, then brought them shame and caused the Trojan War by eloping with Helen.

Parsa Holy man. Also known as a zahid.

Parvati Consort of Shiva and daughter of Himalaya.

Passion Wife of desire.

Pavanarekha Wife of Ugrasena, mother of Kans.

Peerie Folk Fairy or little folk.

Pegasus The winged horse born from the severed neck of Medusa.

Peggin Wooden vessel with a handle, often shaped like a tub and used for drinking.

Peleus Father of Achilles. He married Antigone, caused her death, and then became King of Phthia. Saved from death himself by Jason and the Argonauts. Married Thetis, a sea nymph.

Penelope The long-suffering but equally clever wife of Odysseus who managed to keep at bay suitors who longed for Ithaca while Odysseus was at the Trojan War and on his ten-year voyage home.

Pentangle Pentagram or five-pointed star.

Pentecost Christian festival held on the seventh Sunday after Easter. It celebrates the holy spirit descending on the disciples after Jesus's ascension.

Percivale Knight of the Round Table and original seeker of the Holy Grail.

Persephone Daughter of Zeus and Demeter who was raped by Hades and forced to live in the Underworld as his queen for three months of every year.

Perseus Son of Danae, who was made pregnant by Zeus. He fought the Gorgons and brought home the head of Medusa. He eventually founded the city of Mycenae and married Andromeda.

Pesh Kef Spooned blade used in the Opening the Mouth ceremony.

Phaeacia The Kingdom of Alcinous on which Odysseus landed after a shipwreck which claimed the last of his men as he left Calypso's island.

Pharaoh King or ruler of Egypt.

Philoctetes Malian hero, son of Poeas, received Heracles's bow and arrows as a gift when he lit the great hero's pyre on Mount Oeta. He was involved in the last part of the Trojan War, killing Paris.

Philtre Magic potion, usually a love potion.

Pibroch Bagpipe music.

Pintura Native manuscript or painting.

Pipiltin Noble class of the Aztecs.

Pismire Ant.

Piu-piu Short mat made from flax leaves and neatly decorated.

Po Gloom, darkness, the lower world.

Polyphemus A Cyclops, but a son of Poseidon. He fell in love with Galatea, but she spurned him. He was blinded by Odysseus.

Polyxena Daughter of Priam and Hecuba of Troy. She was sacrificed on the grave of Achilles by Neoptolemus.

Pooka Mythical creature with the ability to shapeshift. Often appears as a horse, but also as a bull, dog or in human form, and has the ability to talk. Also known as púca.

Popol Vuh Sacred 'book of counsel' of the Quiché or K'iche' Maya people.

Poseidon God of the sea, and of sweet waters. Also the god of earthquakes. His is brother to Zeus and Hades, who divided the earth between them.

Pradyumna Son of Krishna and Rukmini.

Prahasta (Long-Hand) One of Ravana's generals.

Prajapati Creator of the universe, father of the gods, demons and all creatures, later known as Brahma.

Priam King of Troy, married to Hecuba, who bore him Hector, Paris, Helenus, Cassandra, Polyxena, Deiphobus and Troilus. He was murdered by Neoptolemus.

Pritha Mother of Karna and of the Pandavas.

Prithivi Consort of Dyaus and goddess of the earth.

Proetus King of Argos, son of Abas.

Prometheus A Titan, son of Iapetus and Themus. He was champion of mortal men, which he created from clay. He stole fire from the gods and was universally hated by them.

Prose Edda Collection of Norse myths and poems, thought to have been compiled in the 1200s by Icelandic historian Snorri Sturluson.

Proteus The old man of the sea who watched Poseidon's seals.

Psyche A beautiful nymph who was the secret wife of Eros, against the wishes of his mother Aphrodite, who sent Psyche to perform many tasks in hope of causing her death. She eventually married Eros and was allowed to become partly immortal.

Ptah Creator god and deity of Memphis who was married to Sekhmet. Ptah built the boats to carry the souls of the dead to the afterlife.

Puddock Frog.

Pulque Alcoholic drink made from fermented agave.

Purusha The cosmic man, he was sacrificed and his dismembered body became all the parts of the cosmos, including the four classes of society.

Purvey To provide or supply.

Pushkara Nala's brother.

Pushpaka Rama's chariot.

Putana A rakshasi.

Pygmalion A sculptor who was so lonely he carved a statue of a beautiful woman, and eventually fell in love with it. Aphrodite brought the image to life.

Quauhtli Eagle.

Quern Hand mill used for grinding corn.

Quetzalcoatl Deity and god of wind. He is represented as a feathered or plumed serpent and is usually a wise and benevolent god. Offspring of Ometeotl and Omecihuatl, he is also known as Kukulkan.

Ra God of the sun, ruling male deity of Egypt whose name means 'sole creator'.

Radha The principal mistress of Krishna.

Ragnarok The end of the world.

Rahula Son of Siddhartha and Yashodhara.

Raiden God of thunder. He traditionally has a fierce and demonic appearance.

Rakshasas Demons and devils.

Ram of Mendes Sacred symbol of fatherhood and fertility.

Rama or **Ramachandra** A prince and hero of the *Ramayana*, worshipped as an incarnation of Vishnu.

Ra-Molo (Lesotho) Father of fire, a chief who ruled by fear. When trying to kill his brother, Tau the lion, he was turned into a monster with the head of a sheep and the body of a snake.

Rangatira Chief, warrior, gentleman.

Regin A blacksmith who educated Sigurd.

Reinga The spirit land, the home of the dead.

Reservations Tracts of land allocated to the Native American people by the United States Government with the purpose of bringing the many separate tribes under state control.

Rewati Daughter of Raja, marries Balarama.

Rhadha Wife of Adiratha, a gopi of Brindaban and lover of Krishna.

Rhea Mother of the Olympian gods. Cronus ate each of her children, but she concealed Zeus and gave Cronus a swaddled rock in his place.

Rill Small stream.

Rimu (Chaga) Monster known to feed off human flesh, which sometimes takes the form of a werewolf.

Rishis Sacrificial priests associated with the devas in Swarga.

Rituparna King of Ayodhya.

Rohini The wife of Vasudeva, mother of Balarama and Subhadra, and carer of the young Krishna. Another Rohini is a goddess and consort of Chandra.

Rōnin Samurai whose master had died or fallen out of favour.

Rubáiyát Collection of poems written by Omar Khayyám.

Rúdábeh Wife of Zál and mother of Rustem.

Rudra Lord of Beasts and disease, later evolved into Shiva.

Rukma Rukmini's eldest brother.

Rustem Son of Zál and Rúdábeh, he was a brave and mighty warrior who undertook seven labours to travel to Mázinderán to rescue Kai-káús. Once there, he defeated the White Demon and rescued Kai-káús. He rode the fabled stallion Rakhsh and is also known as Rustam.

Ryō Traditional gold currency.

Sabdh Mother of Ossian, or Oisin.

Sabitu Goddess of the sea.

Sagara King of Ayodhya.

Sahadeva Pandava twin skilled in swordsmanship.

Sahib diwan Lord high treasurer or chief royal executive.

Saiawúsh Son of Kai-káús, who was put through trial by fire when Sudaveh, Kai-káús's wife, told him that Saiawúsh had taken advantage of her. His innocence was proven when the fire did not harm him. He was eventually killed by Afrásiyáb.

Saithe Blessed.

Sajara (Mali) God of rainbows. He takes the form of a multi-coloured serpent.

Sake Japanese rice wine.

Sakuni Cousin of Duryodhana.

Salam Greeting or salutation.

Saláman Son of the Shah of Yunan, who fell in love with Absál, his nurse. She died after they had a brief love affair and he returned to his father.

Salmali tree Cotton tree.

Salmon A symbol of great wisdom, around which many Scottish legends revolve.

Sám Mighty warrior who fought and won many battles. Father of Zál and grandfather to Rustem.

Sambu Son of Krishna.

Sampati Elder brother of Jatayu.

Samurai Noblemen who were part of the military in medieval Japan.

Sanehat Member of the royal bodyguard.

Sango (Yoruba) God of war and thunder.

Sangu (Mozambique) Goddess who protects pregnant women, depicted as a hippopotamus.

Santa Daughter of Dasharatha.

Sarapis Composite deity of Apis and Osiris, sometimes known as Serapis. Thought to be created to unify Greek and Egyptian citizens under the Greek pharaoh Ptolemy.

Sarasvati The tongue of Rama.

Sarcophagus Stone coffin.

Sargon of Akkad Raised by Akki, a husbandman, after being hidden at birth. Sargon became King of Assyria and a great hero. He founded the first library in Babylon. Similar to King Arthur or Perseus.

Sarsar Harsh, whistling wind.

Sasabonsam (Ashanti) Forest ogre.

Sassun Scottish word for England.

Sati Daughter of Daksha and Prasuti, first wife of Shiva.

Satrughna One of Dasharatha's four sons.

Satyavan Truth speaker, husband of Savitri.

Satyavati A fisher-maid, wife of Bhishma's father, Shamtanu.

Satyrs Elemental spirits which took great pleasure in chasing nymphs. They had horns, a hairy body and cloven hooves.

Saumanasa A mighty elephant.

Scamander River running across the Trojan plain, and father of Teucer.

Scarab Dung beetle, often used as a symbol of the immortal human soul and regeneration.

Scylla and Charybdis Scylla was a monster who lived on a rock of the same name in the Straits of Messina, devouring sailors. Charybdis was a whirlpool in the Straits which was supposedly inhabited by the hateful daughter of Poseidon.

Seal Often believed that seals were fallen angels. Many families are descended from seals, some of which had webbed hands or feet. Some seals were the children of sea-kings who had become enchanted (selkies).

Seelie-Court The court of the Fairies, who travelled around their realm. They were usually fair to humans, doling out punishment that was morally sound, but they were quick to avenge insults to fairies.

Segu (Swahili, East Africa) Guide who informs humans where honey can be found.

Sekhmet Solar deity who led the pharaohs in war. She is goddess of healing and was sent by Ra to destroy humanity when people turned against the sun god. She is portrayed with the head of a lion.

Selene Moon-goddess, daughter of Hyperion and Theia. She was seduced by Pan, but loved Endymion.

Selkie Mythical creature which is seal-like when in water but can shed its skin to take on human form when on land.

Seneschal Steward of a royal or noble household.

Sensei Teacher.

Seriyut A disciple of Buddha.

Sessrymnir Freyia's home.

Set God of chaos and evil, brother of Osiris, who killed him by tricking him into getting into a chest, which he then threw in the Nile, before cutting Osiris's body into fourteen separate pieces. Also known as Seth.

Sgeulachd Stories.

Sháhnámeh *The Book of Kings* written by Ferdowsi, one of the world's longest epic poems, which describes the mythology and history of the Persian Empire.

Shaikh Respected religious man.

Shaivas or Shaivites Worshippers of Shiva.

Shakti Power or wife of a god and Shiva's consort as his feminine aspect.

Shaman Also known as the 'Medicine Men' of Native American tribes, it is the shaman's role to cultivate communication with the spirit world. They are endowed with knowledge of all healing herbs, and learn to diagnose and cure disease. They are believed to foretell the future, find lost property and have power over animals, plants and stones.

Shamash God of the sun and protector of Gilgamesh, the great Babylonian hero. Known as the son of Sin, the moon god, he is also portrayed as a judge of good and evil.

Shamtanu Father of Bhishma.

Shankara A great magician, friend of Chand Sadagar.

Shashti The Sixth, goddess who protects children and women in childbirth.

Sheen Beautiful and enchanted woman who casts a spell on Murtough, King of Ireland, causing him to fall in love with her and cast out his family. He dies at her hands, half burned and half drowned, but she then dies of grief as she returns his love. Sheen is known by many names, including Storm, Sigh and Rough Wind.

Shesh A serpent that takes human birth through Devaki.

Shi-en Fairy dwelling.

Shinto Indigenous religion of Japan, from the pre-sixth century to the present day.

Shireen Married to Khosru. Her beauty meant that she was desired by many, including Khosru's own son by his previous marriage. She killed herself rather than give in to her stepson.

Shitala The Cool One and goddess of smallpox.

Shiva One of the two great gods of post-Vedic Hinduism with Vishnu.

Shogun Military ruler or overlord.

Shoji Sliding door, usually a lattice screen of paper.

Shu God of the air and half of the first divine couple created by Atem. Brother and husband to Tefnut, father to Keb and Nut.

Shubistán Household.

Shudra One of the four fundamental colours (caste).

Shuttle Part of a machine used for spinning cloth, used for passing weft threads between warp threads.

Siddhas Musical ministrants of the upper air.

Sif Thor's wife; known for her beautiful hair.

Sigi Son of Odin.

Sigmund Warrior able to pull the sword from Branstock in the Volsung's hall.

Signy Volsung's daughter.

Sigurd Son of Sigmund, and bearer of his sword. Slays Fafnir the dragon.

Sigyn Loki's faithful wife.

Símúrgh Griffin, an animal with the body of a lion and the head and wings of an eagle. Known to hold great wisdom. Also called a symurgh.

Sin God of the moon, worshipped primarily in Ur.

Sindri Dwarf who worked with Brokki to fashion gifts for the gods; commissioned by Loki.

Sirens Sea nymphs who are half-bird, half-woman, whose song lures hapless sailors to their death.

Sisyphus King of Ephrya and a trickster who outwitted Autolycus. He was one of the greatest sinners in Hades.

Sita Daughter of the earth, adopted by Janaka, wife of Rama.

Skadi Goddess of winter and the wife of Niord for a short time.

Skanda Six-headed son of Shiva and a warrior god.

Skraeling Person native to Canada and Greenland. The name was given to them by Viking settlers and can be translated as 'barbarian'.

Skrymir Giant who battled against Thor.

Sleipnir Odin's steed.

Sluagh The host of the dead, seen fighting in the sky and heard by mortals.

Smote Struck with a heavy blow.

Sohráb Son of Rustem and Tahmineh, Sohráb was slain in battle by his own father, who killed him by mistake.

Sol The sun-maiden.

Soma A god and a drug, the elixir of life.

Somerled Lord of the Isles, and legendary ancestor of the Clan MacDonald.

Soothsayer Someone with the ability to predict or see the future, by the use of magic, special knowledge or intuition. Known as seanagal in Scottish myths.

Squaw A Native American woman or wife (now offensive).

Squint-Eye One of Ramana's monsters.

Squire Shield- or armour-bearer of a knight.

Srutakirti Daughter of Kushadhwaja.

Stirabout Porridge made by stirring oatmeal into boiling milk or water.

Stone Giants A malignant race of stone beings whom the Iroquois believed invaded their territory, threatening the Confederation of the Five Nations. These fierce and hostile creatures lived off human flesh and were intent on exterminating the human race.

Stoorworm A great water monster which frequented lochs. When it thrust its great body from the sea, it could engulf islands and whole ships. Its appearance prophesied devastation.

Stot Bullock.

Styx River in Arcadia and one of the four rivers in the Underworld. Charon ferried dead souls across it into Hades, and Achilles was dipped into it to make him immortal.

Subrahmanian Son of Shiva, a mountain deity.

Sugriva The chief of the five great monkeys in the *Ramayana*.

Sukanya The wife of Chyavana.

Suman Son of Asamanja.

Sumantra A noble Brahman.

Sumati Wife of Sagara.

Sumedha A righteous Brahman who dwelt in the city of Amara.

Sumitra One of Dasharatha's three wives, mother of Lakshmana and Satrughna.

Suniti Mother of Dhruva.

Suparshwa One of Ravana's counsellors.

Supranakha A rakshasi, sister of Ravana.

Surabhi The wish-bestowing cow.

Surcoat Loose robe, traditionally worn over armour.

Surtr Fire-giant who eventually destroys the world at Ragnarok.

Surya God of the sun.

Susanoo God of the storm. He is depicted as a contradictory character with both good and bad characteristics. He was banished from Heaven after trying to kill his sister, Amaterasu.

Sushena A monkey chief.

Svasud Father of summer.

Swarga An Olympian paradise, where all wishes and desires are gratified.

Sweating A ritual customarily associated with spiritual purification and prayer practised by most tribes throughout North America prior to sacred ceremonies or vision quests. Steam was produced within a 'sweat lodge', a low, dome-shaped hut, by sprinkling water on heated stones.

Syrinx An Arcadian nymph who was the object of Pan's love.

Tablet of Destinies Cuneiform clay tablet on which the fates were written. Tiawath had given this to Kingu, but it was taken by Merodach when he defeated them. The storm god Zu later stole it for himself.

Taiaha A weapon made of wood.

Tailtiu One of the most famous royal residences of ancient Ireland. Possibly also a goddess linked to this site.

Tall One of Ravana's counsellors.

Tammuz Solar deity of Eridu who, with Gishzida, guards the gates of Heaven. Protector of Anu.

Tamsil Example or guidance.

Tangi Funeral, dirge. Assembly to cry over the dead.

Taniwha Sea monster, water spirit.

Tantalus Son of Zeus who told the secrets of the gods to mortals and stole their nectar and ambrosia. He was condemned to eternal torture in Hades, where he was tempted by food and water but allowed to partake of neither.

Taoism Taoism (or Daoism) came into being at roughly the same time as Confucianism, although its tenets were radically different and were largely founded on the philosophies of Lao Tzu (Laozi). While Confucius argued for a system of state discipline, Taoism strongly favoured self-discipline and looked upon nature as the architect of essential laws. A newer form of Taoism evolved after the Burning of the Books, placing great emphasis on spirit worship and pacification of the gods.

Tapu Sacred, supernatural possession of power. Involves spiritual rules and restrictions.

Tara Also known as Temair, the Hill of Tara was the popular seat of the ancient High-Kings of Ireland from the earliest times to the sixth century. Located in Co. Meath, it was also the place where great noblemen and chieftains congregated during wartime, or for significant events.

Tara Sugriva's wife.

Tartarus Dark region, below Hades.

Tau (Lesotho) Brother to Ra-Molo, depicted as a lion.

Taua War party.

Tefnut Goddess of water and rain. Married to Shu, who was also her brother. She, like Sekhmet, is portrayed with the head of a lion. Also known as Tefenet.

Telegonus Son of Odysseus and Circe. He was allegedly responsible for his father's death.

Telemachus Son of Odysseus and Penelope who was aided by Athene in helping his mother to keep away the suitors in Odysseus's absence.

Temu The evening form of Ra, the Sun god.

Tengu Goblin or gnome, often depicted as bird-like. A powerful fighter with weapons.

Tenochtitlán Capital city of the Aztecs, founded around 1350 CE and the site of the 'Great Temple'. Now Mexico City.

Teo-Amoxtli Divine book.

Teocalli Great temple built in Tenochtitlán, now Mexico City.

Teotleco Festival of the Coming of the Gods; also the twelfth month of the Aztec calendar.

Tepee A conical-shaped dwelling constructed of buffalo hide stretched over lodge-poles. Mostly used by Native American tribes living on the plains.

Tepeyollotl God of caves, desert places and earthquakes, whose name means 'heart of the mountain'. He is depicted as a jaguar, often leaping at the sun. Also known as Tepeolotlec.

Tepitoton Household gods.

Tereus King of Daulis who married Procne, daughter of Pandion King of Athens. He fell in love with Philomela, raped her and cut out her tongue.

Tezcatlipoca Supreme deity and Lord of the Smoking Mirror. He was also patron of royalty and warriors. Invented human sacrifice to the gods. Offspring of Ometeotl and Omecihuatl, he is known as the Jupiter of the Aztec gods.

Thalia Muse of pastoral poetry and comedy.

Theia Goddess of many names, and mother of the sun.

Theseus Son of King Aegeus of Athens. A cycle of legends has been woven around his travels and life.

Thetis Chief of the Nereids loved by both Zeus and Poseidon. They married her to a mortal, Peleus, and their child was Achilles. She tried to make him immortal by dipping him in the River Styx.

Thialfi Thor's servant, taken when his peasant father unwittingly harms Thor's goat.

Thiassi Giant and father of Skadi, he tricked Loki into bringing Idunn to him. Thrymheim is his kingdom.

Thomas the Rhymer Also called 'True Thomas', he was Thomas of Ercledoune, who lived in the thirteenth century. He met with the Queen of Elfland, and visited her country, was given clothes and a tongue that could tell no lie. He was also given the gift of prophecy, and many of his predictions were proven true.

Thor God of thunder and of war (with Tyr). Known for his huge size, and red hair and beard. Carries the hammer Miolnir. Slays Jormungander at Ragnarok.

Thoth God of the moon. Invented the arts and sciences and regulated the seasons. He is portrayed with the head of an ibis or a baboon.

Three-Heads One of Ravana's monsters.

Thrud Thor's daughter.

Thrudheim Thor's realm. Also called Thrudvang.

Thunder-Tooth Leader of the rakshasas at the siege of Lanka.

Tiawath Primeval dark ocean or abyss, Tiawath is also a monster and evil deity of the deep. She took the form of a dragon or sea serpent and battled the gods of light for supremacy over all living beings. She was eventually defeated by Merodach, who used her body to create Heaven and Earth.

Tiglath-Pileser I King of Assyria, who made it a leading power for centuries.

Tiki First man created, a figure carved of wood, or other representation of man.

Tirawa The name given to the Great Creator (see Great Spirit) by the Pawnee tribe who believed that four direct paths led from his house in the sky to the four semi-cardinal points: north-east, north-west, south-east and south-west.

Tiresias A Theban who was given the gift of prophecy by Zeus. He was blinded for seeing Athene bathing. He continued to use his prophetic talents after his death, advising Odysseus.

Tirfing Sword made by dwarves which was cursed to kill every time it was drawn, be the cause of three great atrocities, and kill Suaforlami (Odin's grandson), for whom it was made.

Tisamenus Son of Orestes, who inherited the Kingdom of Argos and Sparta.

Titania Queen of the fairies.

Tlaloc God of rain and fertility, so important to the people, because he ensured a good harvest, that the Aztec heaven or paradise was named Tlalocan in his honour.

Tlazolteotl Goddess of ordure, filth and vice. Also known as the earth-goddess or Tlaelquani, meaning 'filth-eater'. She acted as a confessor of sins or wrongdoings.

Tohu-mate Omen of death.

Tohunga A priest; a possessor of supernatural powers.

Toltec Civilization that preceded the Aztecs.

Tomahawk Hatchet with a stone or iron head used in war or hunting.

Tonalamatl Record of the Aztec calendar, which was recorded in books made from bark paper.

Tonalpohualli Aztec calendar composed of twenty thirteen-day weeks called trecenas.

Totec Solar deity known as Our Great Chief.

Totemism System of belief in which people share a relationship with a spirit animal or natural being with whom they interact. Examples include Ea, who is represented by a fish.

Toxilmolpilia The binding up of the years.

Tristan Nephew of King Mark of Cornwall, who travels to Ireland to bring Iseult back to marry his uncle. On the way, he and Iseult consume a love potion and fall madly in love before their story ends tragically.

Triton A sea-god, and son of Poseidon and Amphitrite. He led the Argonauts to the sea from Lake Tritonis.

Trojan War War waged by the Greeks against Troy, in order to reclaim Menelaus's wife Helen, who had eloped with the Trojan prince Paris. Many important heroes took part, and form the basis of many legends and myths.

Troll Unfriendly mythological creature of varying size and strength. Usually dwells in mountainous areas, among rocks or caves.

Truage Tribute or pledge of peace or truth, usually made on payment of a tax.

Tsuki-yomi God of the moon, brother of Amaterasu and Susanoo.

Tuat The other world or land of the dead.

Tupuna Ancestor.

Tvashtar Craftsman of the gods.

Tyndareus King of Sparta, perhaps the son of Perseus's daughter Grogphone. Expelled from Sparta but restored by Heracles. Married Leda and fathered Helen and Clytemnestra, among others.

Tyr Son of Frigga and the god of war (with Thor). Eventually kills Garm at Ragnarok.

Tzompantli Pyramid of Skulls.

Uayeb The five unlucky days of the Mayan calendar, which were believed to be when demons from the underworld could reach Earth. People would often avoid leaving their houses on uayeb days.

Ubaaner Magician, whose name meant 'splitter of stones', who created a wax crocodile that came to life to swallow up the man who was trying to seduce his wife.

Uile Bheist Mythical creature, usually some form of wild beast.

Uisneach A hill formation between Mullingar and Athlone said to mark the centre of Ireland.

uKqili (Zulu) Creator god.

Uller God of winter, whom Skadi eventually marries.

Ulster Cycle Compilation of folk tales and legends telling of the Ulaids, people from the northeast of Ireland, now named Ulster. Also known as the *Uliad Cycle*, it is one of four Irish cycles of mythology.

Unseelie Court An unholy court comprising a kind of fairies, antagonistic to humans. They took the form of a kind of Sluagh, and shot humans and animals with elf-shots.

Urd One of the Norns.

Urien King of Gore, husband of Morgan le Fey and father to Yvain.

Urmila Second daughter of Janaka.

Usha Wife of Aniruddha, daughter of Vanasur.

Ushas Goddess of the dawn.

Utgard-loki King of the giants. Tricked Thor.

Uther Pendragon King of England in sub-Roman Britain; father of King Arthur.

Utixo (Hottentot) Creator god.

Ut-Napishtim Ancestor of Gilgamesh, whom Gilgamesh sought out to discover how to prevent death. Similar to Noah in that he was sent a vision warning him of a great deluge. He built an ark in seven days, filling it with his family, possessions and all kinds of animals.

Uz Deity symbolized by a goat.

Vach Goddess of speech.

Vajrahanu One of Ravana's generals.

Vala Another name for Norns.

Valfreya Another name for Freyia.

Valhalla Odin's hall for the celebrated dead warriors chosen by the Valkyries.

Vali The cruel brother of Sugriva, dethroned by Rama.

Valkyries Odin's attendants, led by Freyia. Chose dead warriors to live at Valhalla. Also spelled as Valkyrs.

Vamadeva One of Dasharatha's priests.

Vanaheim Home of the Vanir.

Vanir Race of gods in conflict with the Aesir; they are gods of the sea and wind.

Varuna Ancient god of the sky and cosmos, later, god of the waters.

Vasishtha One of Dasharatha's priests.

Vassal Person under the protection of a feudal lord.

Vasudev Descendant of Yadu, husband of Rohini and Devaki, father of Krishna.

Vasudeva A name of Narayana or Vishnu.

Vavasor Vassal or tenant of a baron or lord who himself has vassals.

Vedic Mantras, hymns.

Vernandi One of the Norns.

Vichitravirya Bhishma's half-brother.

Vidar Slays Fenris.

Vidura Friend of the Pandavas.

Vigrid The plain where the final battle is held.

Vijaya Karna's bow.

Vikramaditya A king identified with Chandragupta II.

Vintail Moveable front of a helmet.

Virabhadra A demon that sprang from Shiva's lock of hair.

Viradha A fierce rakshasa, seizes Sita, slain by Rama.

Virupaksha The elephant who bears the whole world.

Vishnu The Preserver, Vedic sun god and one of the two great gods of post-Vedic Hinduism.

Vision Quest A sacred ceremony undergone by Native Americans to establish communication with the spirit set to direct them in life. The quest lasted up to four days and nights and was preceded by a period of solitary fasting and prayer.

Vivasvat The sun.

Vizier High-ranking official or adviser. Also known as vizir or vazir.

Volsung Family of great warriors about whom a great saga was spun.

Vrishadarbha King of Benares.

Vrishasena Son of Karna, slain by Arjuna.

Vyasa Chief of the royal chaplains.

Wairua Spirit, soul.

Wanjiru (Kikuyu) Maiden who was sacrificed by her village to appease the gods and make it rain after years of drought.

Weighing of the Heart Procedure carried out after death to assess whether the deceased was free from sin. If the deceased's heart weighed less than the feather of Ma'at, they would join Osiris in the Fields of Peace.

Whare Hut made of fern stems tied together with flax and vines, and roofed in with raupo (reeds).

White Demon Protector of Mázinderán. He prevented Kai-káús and his army from invading.

Withy Thin twig or branch which is very flexible and strong.

Wolverine Large mammal of the musteline family with dark, very thick, water-resistant fur, inhabiting the forests of North America and Eurasia.

Wroth Angry.

Wyrd One of the Norns.

Xanthus & Balius Horses of Achilles, immortal offspring of Zephyrus the west wind. A gift to Achilles's father Peleus.

Xipe Totec High priest and son of Ometeotl and Omecihuatl. Also known as the god of the seasons.

Xiupohualli Solar year, composed of eighteen twenty-day months. Also spelt Xiuhpōhualli.

Yadu A prince of the Lunar dynasty.

Yakshas Same as rakshasas.

Yakunin Government official.

Yama God of Death, king of the dead and son of the sun.

Yamato Take Legendary warrior and prince. Also known as Yamato Takeru.

Yashiki Residence or estate, usually of a daimyō.

Yasoda Wife of Nand.

Yemaya (Yoruba) Wife of Obatala.

Yemoja (Yoruba) Goddess of water and protector of women.

Yggdrasill The World Ash, holding up the Nine Worlds. Does not fall at Ragnarok.

Ymir Giant created from fire and ice; his body created the world.

Yo The female principle who, joined with In, the male side, brought about creation and the first gods. In and Yo correspond to the Chinese Yang and Yin.

Yomi The underworld.

Yudhishthira The eldest of the Pandavas, a great soldier.

Yuki-Onna The Snow-Bride or Lady of the Snow, who represents death.

Yvain Son of Morgan le Fay and knight of the Round Table, who goes on chivalric quests with a lion he rescued from a dragon.

Zahid Holy man.

Zál Son of Sám, who was born with pure white hair. Sám abandoned Zál, who was raised by the Símúrgh, or griffins. Zal became a great warrior, second only to his son, Rustem. Also known as Ním-rúz and Dustán.

Zephyr Gentle breeze.

Zeus King of gods, god of sky, weather, thunder, lightning, home, hearth and hospitality. He plays an important role as the voice of justice, arbitrator between man and gods, and among them. Married to Hera, but lover of dozens of others.

Zohák Serpent-king and figure of evil. Father of Mihrab.

Zu God of the storm, who took the form of a huge bird. Similar to the Persian símúrgh.

Zukin Head covering.